Also by Sam Barone

Dawn of Empire

Empire Rising

Quest For Honour
(Published outside the United States as
Conflict of Empires)

Eskkar & Trella – The Beginning

Battle For Empire

Clash of Empires

Eskkar & Bracca – Rogue Warriors 1
(Kindle singlet)

ISBN: 0985162678
ISBN 13: 9780985162672

Esskar Enterprises

Please feel free to contact the
author with suggestions and comments

www.sambarone.com

SAM BARONE

CLASH
OF
EMPIRES

A Alur Meriki Passage from Elam
B Battle at the Stream
C Alur Meriki Camp
D Ur Nammu Camp
E Jkarian Pass
F Dellen Pass
G Orodes Passage

H Chaiyanar's Supply Beach
I Zanbil Resupply Depot
J Sushan (Susa) - War Palace
K Elam's main Palace at Anshan
L Sargon's Ride to Zanbil
M Arattta Camp

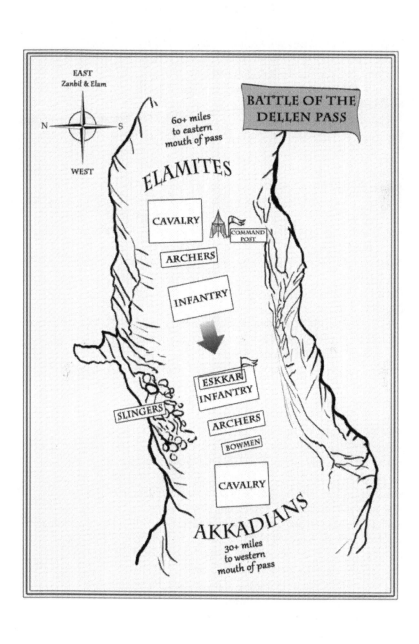

Cast of Characters

Eskkar Family:

    Eskkar – born a barbarian, became King of the City of Akkad

    Trella – noble born, but enslaved as a young girl, now Queen of Akkad

    Sargon – Eskkar and Trella's son and heir

    Zakita – Eskkar and Trella's daughter (second born)

    Melkorak – Eskkar and Trella's son (third born)

    Tashanella – daughter of Ur Nammu clan leader Subutai and wife of Sargon

    Escander – son of Sargon, grandson of Eskkar and Trella

Akkadians:

    Alexar – originally an archer, now in command of Akkad's infantry

    Alcinor – son of Corio, Master Builder of Akkad. Alcinor is Akkad's first Engineer

    Annok-sur – wife of Bantor and friend to Trella, commands all of Akkad's agents & spies

    Bantor – former soldier, now senior commander of the city of Akkad's defenses

    Daro – a senior commander of Akkad's riverboat archers

    Draelin – a sub-commander in Akkad's army

    Drakis – originally an archer, now a senior commander of Akkad's infantry

    En-hedu – wife of Tammuz, a spy in Akkad's service

    Harnos – a Master Riverboat archer

    Hathor – Egyptian outcast, once fought against Akkad, now commander of Akkad's cavalry

    Ismenne – Akkad's Master Map Maker, wife of Daro

    Jahiri – Master Apprentice to Alcinor

    Markesh – A sub-commander of Shappa's slingers

    Mitrac – Master Bowman, senior commander of Akkad's archers

    Muta – once a slave, now a senior commander, second in command of Akkad's cavalry

    Orodes – richest man in Akkad, Master of the Nuzi Gold Mine

    Rue-el – one of Wakannh's subcommanders

    Sabatu - nobleman and former commander in the Elamite army, sentenced to death by torture. Rescued by Dar

    Shappa – a senior commander of Akkad's slingers

    Steratakis – a spy in the service of Akkad

    Tammuz – husband of En-hedu, a spy in Akkad's service

    Tooraj – commander of the mine at Nuzi

    Wakannh – Captain of the City of Akkad's Guards

    Uvela – one of Annok-sur's senior spies

    Yavtar – wealthy merchant and river trader, advisor to King Eskkar

    Zahara – an Akkadian spying for the Elamites

    Luka – second in command of Akkad's slingers

City of Sumer:
    King Gemama – ruler of the City of Sumer
    Jarud – Commander of Sumer's Guard and soldiers

City of Isin:
    King Naxos – ruler of the City of Isin
    Kuara – chief advisor to King Naxos
    Barbarian Clans – Alur Meriki and Ur Nammu
    Chief Bekka – Sarum (Leader) of Alur Meriki
    Suijan – an Alur Meriki clan leader
    Den'rack – an Alur Meriki clan leader, friend to Sargon
    Virani – an Alur Meriki clan leader
    Unegen – an Alur Meriki clan leader
    Chief Subutai – Sarum of the Ur Nammu clan, father of Tashanella
    Fashod – an Ur Nammu clan leader
    Chinua – an Ur Nammu clan leader, mentor to Sargon
    Garal – an Ur Nammu warrior, tutor and friend to Sargon
    Jennat – an Ur Nammu warrior, friend to Sargon

Elamites:
    King Shirudukh – ruler of the Elamite Empire
    Lord Modran – the favorite general of King Shirudukh
    Grand Commander Chaiyanar – another general of King Shirudukh
    General Jedidia – another general of King Shirudukh
    General Martiya – second in command of Lord Modran's army
    General Zathras – second in command of General Jedidia's cavalry force
    Shesh-kala – an advisor to King Shirudukh
    Meweldi – one of King Shirudukh's military advisors
    Kedor – a seagoing trader from the city of Sushan (Susa)
    Simaski – Grand Commander Chaiyanar's cavalry commander
    Bracca / Aram-Kitchu – former Sumerian thief and companion of Eskkar, now
        a wealthy trader and master spy for the Elamite Empire and advisor to the
        King Shirudukh

Prologue

3129 BC, the harbor of Sushan, in the Land of Elam . . .

Daro leaned against the single mast of the *Star of Sumer*, his eyes scanning the dockside crowd and the broad pathway that led from the wharf to Sushan's river gate, a few hundred paces away. He had finished stowing the last of the trade goods and supplies at first light, and since then, the ship stood ready to begin its passage home. Now Daro struggled to conceal his impatience while Yavtar, the *Star's* owner, finished his dealings with the Dock Master.

The lazy official should have arrived at dawn, so the departing ships could get an early start on their journeys. Instead the sun had nearly cleared the horizon before the yawning Dock Master waddled to his station, unconcerned by the impatient mutterings of the three ship masters awaiting him, and all chaffing to be on their way. Well before daybreak, Yavtar had claimed the head of the line, determined to get his ship out of the harbor as early as possible.

Daro ignored the cloudless blue sky overhead, the gentle rubbing of the boat against the roped stanchion, and the pleasant gurgle of the river. He kept his eyes on Master Trader Yavtar, who had almost concluded the seemingly endless and probably unnecessary haggling with the official. A sudden movement drew Daro's gaze back toward the city's walls. Six harbor guards jogged through the gate, heading straight for the dock.

Daro never hesitated. His single shout alerted Yavtar, who needed only one look to comprehend the danger. Leaving the confused Dock Master stammering in surprise, Yavtar darted across the dock, and leapt onto the *Star*. Not as agile as in his youth, Yavtar's sandal snagged on the gunwale and he nearly fell into the harbor. But Daro caught the man's arm and pulled Yavtar into the boat.

"Cast off! Get the boat moving!" Yavtar's booming voice left no doubt about the urgency of the moment.

The eight crew members, already alerted to the possibility of a hurried departure, rushed into motion. Two men sprang onto the dock, cast off the fore and aft ropes that secured the *Star*, and then jumped nimbly back aboard. Daro and the others snatched up oars and pushed the ship away from the wharf. With Yavtar urging them on, the crew plunged their oars into the water, grunting under the effort to get the *Star* underway and into the Karum River.

They managed to get ten paces of water between the ship and the wharf before the harbor guards arrived. Daro, one of the few crew members fluent in the language of Elam, heard the guard's commander bellow an order to stop and return the ship to the dock. Neither Daro nor Yavtar had any intention of complying. Both knew what fate awaited them onshore.

Fortunately, these guards had carried no bows, so they waved their swords and filled the air with curses and demands that the boat come back. Looking back toward the city's walls, Daro saw the first of the city's professional soldiers race into view. Six archers, alerted by the commotion, rushed toward the wharf.

By the time the bowmen reached the water's edge and strung their weapons, the *Star* had caught the river's current and dragged itself almost out of range. A few arrows sliced into the river, but only one lucky or well-aimed shaft managed to strike the side of the boat. A moment later the ship pulled out of reach.

As Daro watched the guards and dockside idlers milling about, he saw another troop of at least thirty soldiers pouring through the gate, all of them armed with swords and carrying bows in their hands. This latest contingent rushed onto the dock, knocking aside anyone in their path. In moments, they seized possession of the nearest ship.

The *Star of Sumer* rowed out to the center of the river, where the most favorable current flowed. Meanwhile, the Elamites climbed on board their commandeered vessel, a larger craft that displayed Sushan's pennant at its mast head. With thirty or more men on board, they slipped loose the ropes holding the vessel to the dock.

In his twenty-eighth season, Daro had grown up around boats and sailed many a craft on the Tigris. He needed only a quick glance to know that the heavily laden ship could not catch the *Star of Sumer,* no matter how many oarsmen she carried. But almost as soon as the

Elamite ship cleared the dock, the soldiers aboard started tossing whatever cargo the vessel carried over the side. Even before they finished heaving the trade goods overboard, Daro noticed the ship picked up speed. The chase had begun.

What should have been an easy run downstream for the *Star of Sumer* to the mouth of the Karum River had turned into a desperate race. Daro observed that the ship chasing them lacked the *Star's* fast lines, but the leader of the soldiers who assumed command of the vessel had shown both quickness and skill in getting his boat moving. Nor had he evinced any compunction about dumping its goods into the river, even as the ship's owner danced along the edge of the wharf, waving his arms in a rage.

Yavtar, at the tiller of his ship, also watched the bales and bundles splash into the river. He, too, understood what it meant. In moments the much lighter Elamite vessel, manned by a crew of well-armed men, straightened its course and now churned through the water in pursuit.

While the *Star's* narrow hull and tight construction made it the swifter vessel, the far greater number of enemy oarsmen would likely compensate for the pursuing boat's larger size and heavier weight.

"Damn every Elamite god!" Yavtar's curse echoed over the water. "Daro, take three men and toss our cargo over the side. Make sure you don't swamp the boat while you're doing it. The rest of you bastards, row for your life!"

While aboard the *Star*, Daro functioned as First Mate, and he jumped to do Yavtar's bidding. As soon as the last of their cargo splashed into the river, Daro returned to the stern of the boat, and stared at the vessel hunting them. "Can we keep ahead of them?"

Tight-lipped, Yavtar glanced over his shoulder. The *Star*, much lighter now, rode easily in the river's current, and had opened the gap between ships to almost half a mile. "The *Apikin* handles like a pig. We'll stay ahead of her for now. But they can rest half their rowers at a time. They may wear us out before we can reach the sea."

Once they left the Karum River and entered the Great Sea, Daro knew the *Star of Sumer* would show her heels to the lumbering Elamite ship. He could also see that whoever commanded her knew his business and would reach the same conclusion. With the *Apikin's* cargo gone, there was plenty of room for oarsmen, and Daro counted eight men on each side. Sixteen rowers against the eight men the *Star* possessed, and the *Apikin* probably contained another full bank of oarsmen ready to relieve the first batch.

"We can't be taken alive." Daro glanced down at the near-lifeless body at Yavtar's feet, the man responsible for the vigorous pursuit by the soldiers on board the *Apikin*. The *Star's* single passenger remained sprawled on the bottom of the craft, unconscious, asleep, or maybe dying. Last night, Daro had saved Sabatu's life, rescuing him from the Elamite prison the night before Sabatu's scheduled execution.

Dark bruises covered Sabatu's battered body, interspersed with the bright red marks from the lash. Blood still oozed from some of the open sores. His torturers had broken both his thumbs, and the man's right eye could scarcely be seen, a small slit in a swollen and inflamed face.

Sabatu's ordeal extended far beyond his battered body. The six days of public torment in Sushan's marketplace had included forcing him to watch as the members of his family were brutalized before his eyes, one each day, before being put to death. Wife, sister, brother, and his three young children, all had suffered greatly before dying.

Daro had seen men whipped to death before. Vicious criminals, murderers, and even bandits might face such a punishment for a heinous crime. But Daro had never seen anyone's family persecuted and tortured to death for the crimes of another. By the time the last of Sabatu's kin had succumbed, his weakened body and mind had endured so much that Daro worried Sabatu might not survive a rescue followed by a long journey.

Nevertheless, the potential benefit to King Eskkar and Lady Trella had convinced Daro to attempt the rescue. Yavtar's trading voyage, the goods he'd sold in Sushan, even the *Star of Sumer* mattered little. He and Daro had undertaken the difficult and dangerous passage primarily to gather information about the Elamite Empire and their plans to invade the Land Between the Rivers.

Passing through Sushan's crowded market, Daro had paused to watch the public torture. But as soon as he learned the identity of the victim, he realized the opportunity. What better way, Daro reasoned, to learn about the Elamite army than by spiriting out one of its high-ranking commanders. Such a man would undoubtedly know everything about Elam's generals, their weapons and tactics, even their personal strengths and weaknesses.

And so Daro had risked his own life to slip into the prison barracks in the middle of the night and carry Sabatu from Sushan's torture room. The Elamite ruler would be furious at Sabatu's escape, not to mention the two guards Daro had killed in the process. Grand Commander Chaiyanar, the satrap of Sushan, might not have figured out exactly what had happened, but he'd ordered the harbor sealed, lest his missing prisoner attempt to escape by ship.

Yavtar frowned at the helpless man. "I hope he's worth it. I warned you this might happen."

Daro shrugged. A soldier first and last, he seldom worried about the cause of any dilemma. What was done was done. "Anything you want me to do?"

"Just row, damn you."

Daro nodded, and picked up an oar. The race had indeed started. He added his strength to those of the crew. For this voyage, Yavtar had selected his best men from his crews of rowers in Sumer, the home port of the *Star*, and now those choices would prove their worth. Every man straining at his oar knew what was at stake. If the Elamites captured the *Star*, Yavtar and Daro would be tortured to death, but the fate of the crew would be little better. They would be turned into slaves, then lashed and worked until they dropped dead.

With no choice except to flee, the men needed little urging to do their utmost. Reach, pull, withdraw, and reach again. The oars dipped rhythmically into the river, propelling the graceful ship through the water.

The long chase continued. By midmorning, a favorable wind blew down the river, and allowed Yavtar to rest his men. The ship hunting them had a sail as well, but whatever boatmen remained onboard lacked Yavtar's skill. The Elamite ship yawed from time to time, wasting both the wind and its rowers' best efforts.

Even so, the Elamites' greater number of oarsmen nearly made up for the squat lines and clumsy attributes of the *Apikin*. The brute strength of her rowers kept the race close. Now only Yavtar's proficiency with his ship prevented the Elamites from closing the distance and getting near enough to launch their arrows. One or two wounded men, and the *Star* would be overtaken.

Not that they hadn't tried. Twice they had loosed volleys at the *Star of Sumer*, but each time the enemy shafts had plunged into the *Star's* wake, and no shaft reached within fifty paces.

The wind held steady for most of the day, but whenever it slackened or died down, every man went back to the oars, driving the boat downriver as fast as they could. Despite the *Star's* utmost travail, the pursuing ship clung stubbornly to their stern, sometimes closing to within a quarter of a mile. What the trailing ship lacked in speed and grace, it more than made up with the extra number of its soldiers, determined to drive the *Apikin* through the water until they could catch the *Star*.

The long day dragged on, as Yavtar's exhausted men sweated and rowed, too tired even to swear at their situation.

The sun finally neared the western horizon. "Pull, damn you, pull!" Yavtar, standing at the tiller shouted. "We're almost at the sea. We'll be safe in deep water."

This late in the afternoon, the swift passage down the river had extracted a high price from every man. Daro ignored the pain in his arms, across his chest and shoulders, and down his back. The hands that wielded the oar ran with blood, and the raw scrapes on his knees added to his misery.

A sharp wind blew across Daro's face as he dragged his oar through the choppy water, but even the cool breeze off the Great Sea failed to dry the sweat from his brow. All the men rowing the *Star of Sumer* had labored to exhaustion, fighting wind and water that sought to roll over the lightly-laden ship. Despite the danger, Daro didn't worry about drowning, nor did his crewmates. The ship pursuing them promised far greater pain than a quick death beneath the waves. The *Star's* oarsmen would row until they collapsed.

Daro glanced around at the other members of the crew. Each man endured, working as hard as he could. Still, Daro knew the ship's crew couldn't keep up this pace much longer. But Yavtar knew his trade, so he must have some plan ready to shake the Elamites.

Now, just before dusk, the *Star* approached the end of the Karum River, where its waters emptied and dissipated into the Great Sea. After leaving the river's mouth, the vessel needed to turn its bow to the west, toward its home port of Sumer. However the stubborn wind and the sea's current had a different plan, as they combined to force the ship to the east.

By now even Daro's powerful arms, strengthen by years of archery practice and countless voyages up and down the Tigris, protested the grueling demands. He struggled to keep his rhythm – reach, pull, withdraw, and reach – but the rocking and pitching of the vessel fought his efforts. His hands burned from the oar's roughness, and pain grated against his knees with every stroke.

More than any man in the crew, Daro knew exactly what awaited them if they were captured. He'd seen Sushan's prison and its torturers.

"Pull, you bastards! Pull, unless you want to sail to the Indus!" Ship Master Yavtar bellowed above the grunts and heavy breathing of his crew.

"Pull yourself, damn you," one of the rowers called out. "I'll steer the boat."

Daro and a few of the crew found enough breath for a brief laugh. Yavtar, one of the wealthiest men in Akkad, probably hadn't touched an oar in years.

"When you own the boat," Yavtar shouted in reply, "you can steer. Until then, you lazy excuses for sailors had better earn your pay, and row!"

Daro glanced over his shoulder at their passenger. Sabatu hadn't moved, and might not even be aware of the frenetic activity taking place around him. Before his arrest and condemnation, Sabatu had climbed high in the Elamite army's hierarchy, attaining the position of High Commander. That rank meant he'd led at least five hundred men, which made him far more valuable than Yavtar's lost cargo. What Sabatu could reveal about Elam's armies, strategies, and tactics might save hundreds of Akkadian lives in the coming war.

Daro had hoped the Elamite garrison would suspect some of Sabatu's loyal soldiers or close relatives had carried off the rescue. But either someone had noticed Daro's midnight swim to the military compound's dock, or the city's soldiers were just being thorough when they rushed to search the boats in Sushan's harbor. Of course, the Star's flight told the Elamites all they needed to know.

Now, however, no one gave a thought to Sabatu. Yavtar's next bellow ordered Daro to drop the sail. It also warned the crew that the moment of danger approached – against wind and tides, the boat needed to turn to the west. Every rower strained at the grueling labor, aware of what was at stake. If the Great Sea didn't roll the ship over and drown all of them, the *Star of Sumer* would be driven far to the east, wasting who knew how many days of hard rowing to get back to this very location. And if that happened, they might find the *Apikin* and even more Elamite ships waiting for them.

Ignoring the sweat dripping from his brow, the pain in his knees, and the strain on his arms, Daro pulled at his oar with all the remaining strength in his body. To his surprise, Yavtar continued to guide the *Star* directly toward the heart of the Great Sea.

The roiling water smacked the *Star's* broadside, and threatened to swamp the vessel. Daro heard the crew muttering. *Turn the boat, head into the wind. Turn now.* Daro's mind echoed the same thoughts, but he trusted in Yavtar's seamanship. The Ship Master knew more about boats and water than any man in the Land Between the Rivers.

Yavtar ignored the grumbling and kept the craft moving into deeper water for almost a mile, until Daro could just make out the thin line of sand that marked the shore behind him. At last, as Daro's muscles weakened, Yavtar shouted the order to turn, even as he leaned all his weight on the tiller.

The crew of the *Star of Sumer* responded, summoning what little remained of their strength. For a moment, the vessel hung up in its turn, and a wave splashed over the bow, splattering the rowers with water and threatening to capsize the ship. A few men cried out, and Daro, too, thought their watery demise had come.

But Yavtar knew both his crew and his boat. Suddenly the *Star* leveled out and lunged ahead, as the vessel slipped past the worst of the shoreline current. The crew's day-long unrelenting labor had nearly ended, as the *Star of Sumer* at last reached the open sea. The craft had traveled far enough from the river's mouth and the wind-tossed breakers. Now the boat rode gracefully in its motion, rising and falling with the water instead of struggling against it.

"Make headway!" Even Yavtar's voice revealed a trace of relief.

With a chorus of sighs and groans, the oarsmen slacked their efforts, rowing just hard enough to keep the *Star* moving. Once again, a skilled Ship Master and an experienced crew had thwarted the powerful waves, driven by the wind from the west.

After gulping a long breath, Daro glanced behind him. The Elamite ship, powering its way through the choppy waters, had turned far sooner than the *Star*, clearly attempting to cut off the Sumerian ship. But the bigger boat could not handle the cross-currents that Yavtar had so carefully avoided. Before the *Apikin* could get its bow pointed westward, a wave spilled over the vessel's side.

Daro watched, fascinated by the spectacle playing out before his eyes, only a few hundred paces away. He could hear the men shouting, the fear in their voices carrying over the water. Another wave splashed onto the *Apikin's* pitching deck, and he saw three men tumble over the side and into the water. Despite the crew's desperate efforts, the boat slowed its pace, and sealed its own doom. Two more waves pushed it broadside, and the next one swamped the boat.

Scrambling back to the stern, Daro watched the *Apikin's* death struggles. "Can they make it?

Yavtar shook his head. "Too much water, and too much weight. There's not enough time."

And then it was over. The boat's stern dipped beneath the sea. Men clung to the hull, as its bow lifted into the air for a moment, before sliding backward into the sea, pulled beneath the waves by the weight of water in its stern. Daro heard the sound of snapping beams. In moments, the ship, the crew, all had disappeared beneath the fast moving water.

"Will any of them get to shore?"

"Not here. The current's too strong. Even if a few survive, they'll be carried far to the east. It will be days before anyone gets back to Sushan."

Daro hoped every single man aboard the *Apikin* drowned, but knew he would risk the sea gods' anger to say something like that aloud. "Thank you, Yavtar. You saved all of us."

"Let's just hope your precious prisoner was worth risking our lives, and my lost cargo." He swore again at the thought, then lifted his voice. "Up sail!"

The crew's collective sigh of relief was loud enough to make Daro smile. He moved to the slender mast, ignoring the pain in his knees and the ache in his back. With the help of two crewmen, he dragged the heavy cloth up to its highest position. His hands, still stiff from holding the oar, fumbled with the fastenings. At last Daro secured the sail, taller than two men, and watched with satisfaction as it filled with air. The mast creaked under the strain and the boat heeled a little, while the crew cheered.

"In oars, men," Yavtar shouted.

The groaning crew pulled in their oars, and slumped against the gunwales, too exhausted even to crawl to the water skins stored in the bow.

"Daro! Your friend is tossing about." Yavtar's voice resumed its usual rough growl now that the danger had passed.

No one on board, save Yavtar and Daro, knew Sabatu's name. The crew remained unaware of their passenger's identity or how the bloody and unconscious man had inexplicably appeared onboard the *Star* in the middle of the night. After today's terrifying chase, they might guess at what had happened. Even so, the less they understood the better.

Daro moved to Sabatu's side. A square of linen covered the sick man's face, protecting him from the sun rays. Daro moved it aside.

"Where are we?" Sabatu had drifted in and out of consciousness since his rescue, and even when he appeared aware, his eyes looked vacant and unfocused. For this moment, however, his mind once again controlled his tongue.

"Out of the Karum River at last, thank the gods, and onto the Great Sea, heading west for Sumer." Daro smiled encouragingly at his patient, even as he searched Sabatu's face for any hint of madness. Men tortured to such an extreme often lost their wits, never to regain them. "With luck and a favorable wind, we'll reach the mouth of the Tigris by midmorning the day after tomorrow."

"Sumer." Sabatu took a ragged breath, as he struggled with the knowledge of their destination. "I've heard of the city in the Land Between the Rivers."

Daro nodded reassuringly at Sabatu's words. But before Daro could reply, Sabatu's head lolled back. Asleep or unconscious, Daro couldn't be sure. He replaced the cloth over the man's face.

"Will he make it?" Yavtar had disapproved of Daro's rescue efforts. Whether Sabatu lived or died, Yavtar could never dare voyage to Sushan again.

"He's strong," Daro said. "And he's a soldier. He'll fight to live."

"Well, if he's going to die, let's hope he dies before we get to Sumer. That way we can just dump his body and avoid all those prying eyes on the dock."

Sumer would indeed be Yavtar's first stop, but Daro knew the boat would be in port just long enough to pick up cargo and take on a new ship master. Then it would continue on to the Euphrates and its final destination port, the City of Lagash. Yavtar would ensure that the *Star* and this crew did not get back to Sumer for at least a month or more. By then, the memory of the injured and unnamed passenger would be well in the past and hopefully forgotten.

Yavtar, Daro, and Sabatu would disembark at Sumer, where another of Yavtar's river ships waited to take them up the Tigris to the City of Akkad.

Daro had served Eskkar, the King of Akkad, and Lady Trella, his queen, for many years. Despite his youth, he'd commanded the three fighting boats at the Battle of Isin ten years ago. Last year he'd fought again, against the barbarian horde of the Alur Meriki in the battle at the northern stream. Though trained as an archer, Daro's early experiences as a boy on the river brought him to Yavtar's attention. Before long, Daro had become a leader of one hundred, and in command of Yavtar's fleet of fighting boats.

Three years ago, Daro had married Ismenne, Akkad's most skilled Map Maker, and another of King Eskkar and Trella's close confidants. When Daro asked her father Corio for permission to marry Ismenne, Corio had turned to his young daughter. "Is this the man you want to marry?" Ismenne answered yes. "Well, you're more than old enough. If Lady Trella gives her blessing, then you can marry Daro."

For all practical purposes, Corio had relinquished his authority over his daughter years ago, knowing that opportunities to work with Trella seldom came. Even before Ismenne passed through the women's rites, she had assisted Lady Trella in the secret Map Room. For many years the Queen of Akkad had functioned as the girl's mentor and a second mother. Since their marriage, Ismenne had already given Daro two sons.

Yavtar, another of King Eskkar's close advisors, had used his wealth and influence in the last fifteen years to expand his river trading ventures. He, too, had fought at the Battle of Isin, working the tiller in the same boat as Daro. The two had grown close over the years, and Yavtar looked upon Daro as one of his sons.

Sabatu moaned in his sleep, and Daro glanced down at their passenger. The man could still die. After so many beatings, Sabatu might have serious injuries within his body. Not to mention that a man's mind might also be destroyed as a result of prolonged torture and repeated whippings. Daro shuddered at the thought of undergoing the same fate, and wondered, as every man did, how well and how long he would last under the same punishment.

Pushing that gloomy thought aside, he muttered a prayer to the sea gods, asking for a fast trip back to Akkad. In the city, Lady Trella's healers might be able to save Sabatu's life and mend his wounds. Whether the man would regain his wits was another question. The sooner they reached the City on the Tigris, the better.

Seven days later, Sabatu awoke. Opening his eyes, he gazed at the narrow walls and ceiling of what must be a private chamber. A small window high in the wall glowed with the powerful noonday sun, illuminating the room. The bed felt soft, and a light blanket covered his body, as much to discourage the flies as to keep him warm. His head rested on a second blanket, folded over to form a pillow.

Sabatu tried to sit up, and for the first time, realized that bandages covered both his hands. He tried to speak, but only a hoarse croak emerged from his mouth. Nevertheless, the sound brought the patter of running feet, and a small boy peered at Sabatu from the doorway. Before Sabatu could speak, the boy disappeared.

A few moments later an old man, moving with care, stepped into the room. The grinning boy followed behind, carrying with both hands the heavy wooden box that held what must be the healer's instruments, potions, and herbs.

The healer drew up a stool and sat beside the bed. He smiled and spoke, but Sabatu didn't understand. For a moment he thought his mind had lost its ability to comprehend, but then he realized the healer was speaking in a strange tongue. By the time Sabatu understood what was happening, another man entered the room.

"It is good to see you awake. For a time, I thought we were going to lose you."

The man's voice and face seemed familiar, but Sabatu couldn't recollect where or when.

"Where am I? Who . . . what is this place?"

"You are in the City of Akkad, on the River Tigris, in the Land Between the Rivers," Daro explained. "This is the home of the King of Akkad. We rescued you from the prison barracks in Sushan eight, no, nine days ago. My name is Daro, and this is the healer, Ventor. Since your arrival, he's spent most of his days at your side, trying to mend your injuries."

Sabatu, his mouth open, stared at the man who called himself Daro. Then Sabatu's mind recalled the past, the disgrace, his attempted flight, his capture and the sentence of death by torture for his whole family. His head sagged back on the pillow. Sabatu's hands fumbled at the blanket. The memory of the days of suffering and pain washed over him, and he screamed. But whether the sound ever left the prison of his mind, he couldn't be certain. His head spinning, Sabatu slumped back against the pillow, almost welcoming the blackness that ended his thoughts.

When he awoke the second time, Sabatu knew his senses had returned. His body ached and his hands hurt, but agony had assaulted his body for so long that he seemed incomplete without it. Only when Sabatu thought of his torture did he realize that, for once, the pain seemed to have lessened, faded to little more than a dull ache. He realized there were no fresh injuries to sear his body and mind.

Soft voices penetrated his thoughts, first a man's, then a woman's. Sabatu opened his eyes. A clean, whitewashed ceiling overhead. He recognized the same small chamber, with its single high window and plastered over walls. He looked up from a large bed which took up most of the room. In one corner he saw two odd-sized chests, stacked one atop the other. Facing the bed stood a narrow bench, with two people seated on it.

"They said you were coming around," Daro said. "How do you feel?"

Sabatu recognized the voice, but couldn't recall the man's name. Vaguely he remembered speaking to the man on a boat, a small craft that pitched and tossed on the Great Sea. He tried to lift his head. Immediately the woman moved to his side and placed another folded blanket under his head.

Sabatu kept his gaze on the man. "Your name. Can't remember your name." The words sounded harsh in his ears.

"Daro. My name is Daro. Do you remember your rescue from the barrack's prison?"

The woman held a cup to Sabatu's lips. "Drink some water. Then we'll give you some soup."

With the woman's help, Sabatu emptied the cup. "More."

She shook her head. "In a few moments. Too much might make you sick."

"Where am I . . . did we sail all the way to Akkad?" Sabatu vaguely remembered hearing the name of that city. He returned his eyes to Daro.

"Yes, we're in Akkad, in the King's Compound. We sailed from Sushan ten days ago. You were delirious most of the voyage. We made a very fast passage and got you here two days ago."

The woman took his bandaged hand and held it lightly. "You are safe now. No one will harm you."

In his weakness, Sabatu did not pull his hand away. Her voice seemed oddly reassuring, comforting. Thick dark tresses, held away from her brow by a simple silver fillet, framed the woman's face. He returned his gaze to the man called Daro.

"Why? Why did you bring me here?"

"We know a war with Elam is coming." Daro leaned closer. "We hope that you can help us. In the boat, you said you wanted to take your revenge for the deaths of your family. If you help us, help Akkad, you may avenge those deaths."

For the first time, Sabatu realized that Daro and the woman were both speaking the language of Elam's southern lands. He looked at the servant. It seemed odd that a woman servant would know how to speak his language.

"I am not a traitor." His voice held a hint of anger mixed with the pain.

The woman shook her head. "There is nothing you need to do. All we seek is information about Elam's armies, its leaders, its strengths and weaknesses."

"And if I do not tell you these things?"

She smiled, a warm gesture that nearly made Sabatu smile in return.

"Then when you are well, you may leave Akkad, go wherever you wish. You'll be given a horse, some coins, enough to establish yourself."

"And why would you give me anything, in exchange for nothing?" Sabatu couldn't keep the anger from his voice. His life, his world, had ended, and now a servant offered to bribe him to betray his country.

The servant laughed, a melodious sound that filled the chamber. "You have already helped us more than you know. Now we understand how ruthless Elam's rulers are, to torture for no reason one of their most important military commanders, just as we understand how efficient their soldiers are. So we are in your debt."

She stood. "Stay with him, Daro. I think he needs your company more than mine. I'll have food sent in for our patient."

With another smile, she left the room.

For a moment, Sabatu stared at the empty doorway. "For a servant, she speaks boldly. In Elam, she would be whipped."

Daro laughed. "Well, if you think you'll be more comfortable back in Elam, you can return there. Perhaps Grand Commander Chaiyanar will restore your rank."

The name struck Sabatu like another blow from the lash. He remembered being dragged, hands bound behind him, into Chaiyanar's presence. The always affable Grand Commander had informed Sabatu that King Shirudukh had condemned Sabatu and his family to death.

Sabatu had tried to protest, but one of the guards had punched him in the stomach so hard that his breath fled his body. By the time he recovered, Chaiyanar had dismissed the guards with a wave of his hand, and they dragged Sabatu out of the Palace. When they reached the barracks, the beatings began.

As the horrific memories overwhelmed Sabatu, he felt hot tears on his cheeks. His wife, his children, tortured and murdered before his eyes, his life destroyed at the whim of the brutal King, who let nothing stand in the way of his desires.

"In Akkad," Daro kept his voice soft, but a hard edge crept into his words, "we do not torture the women and children of those sentenced to death. Such a punishment as you've suffered has never been witnessed in Akkad."

He reached down and gently clasped Sabatu's shoulder. "I risked my life to rescue you, but if you are unwilling to help us resist the armies of those who tortured you, then so be it. As Lady Trella said, you will be free to go as soon as you are able."

Sabatu frowned. "Who's Lady Trella?"

Daro's voice resumed its usual cheerful tone. "The woman who gave you the water with her own hand. Lady Trella. She's the only reason you're alive. The Queen of Akkad."

1

Fifteen days later . . .

When Eskkar entered the Workroom, he found Trella and Daro already there. The King of Akkad took his seat behind the long table with an unusual sigh of satisfaction. The oversized and comfortable chair, made especially for him, provided a welcome relief from the back of his horse. A tall man with a frame still covered in hard muscle, Eskkar seldom enjoyed a comfortable place to sit and take his ease.

The Workroom, on the upper level of Eskkar's house, had provided a secure and quiet place for many an important conversation. The chamber held two tables and eight chairs, as well as a large chest. On its top rested all the cups, candles, platters for fruits and cakes, and several red clay pitchers that contained two varieties of wine and fresh water from the Compound's private well.

The wall behind the table where Eskkar had taken his seat displayed various weapons. Three swords, two knives, a well-polished copper helmet, and a slim throwing lance hung from various hooks. A long Akkadian bow also rested on pegs, with a quiver of arrows beneath. In the center of the display, a leather sling dangled in the place of honor. Over the years, Eskkar had mastered all of them, and he maintained his proficiency by training part of each day.

For almost a month, Eskkar had ridden the foothills and passes through the Zagros Mountains, studying the land and searching for favorable terrain. He'd also met with his allies, the Ur Nammu, as well as the Alur Meriki. A weary Eskkar had come back to Akkad well after sunset last night, and for once he freely admitted to his wife that it felt good to be home.

He'd slept soundly, and an early morning bout of lovemaking improved his good mood. But now Eskkar had duties to resume. And the first order of the day involved his wife Trella and Daro.

"It's good to have you back, Captain." Daro used the title Eskkar preferred, at least from his friends and closest companions. More than fifteen years ago, as Captain of Akkad's Guard, Eskkar had saved the city from annihilation by invading barbarians. "Did you find what you sought?"

Eskkar laughed. "That's the first question Trella asked me last night. I may have, though we'll need more work before we can be sure. But I understand that you and Trella have managed to find a well-placed commander in Elam's army."

"Daro is the one who rescued Sabatu and brought him to Akkad," Trella said. She sat at her usual place, at the end of the table, while her husband faced Daro across the long side. "He risked his life, so he should tell you how it all came about. He observed many details that you may find important."

With the occasional prompting from Eskkar and Trella, Daro related the entire story of his expedition with Yavtar to the land of Elam. The scene in the marketplace in Sushan, the stealthy midnight swim up the river, the search and rescue of Sabatu, the sea chase, and the difficult passage along the edge of the Great Sea until ship and crew reached the Tigris and Sumer.

Eskkar asked many questions about the journey. Daro added more details about the voyage, and explained how Yavtar had raced the boat back to Sumer, and then up river to Akkad. Doubts about whether their passenger would live or die had worried both men.

When Eskkar had heard the whole tale, he turned to Trella. "And how helpful has Sabatu been? Has he told you anything we can use?"

"No, Husband, not yet. He was close to death when he arrived here, and I thought it best to let him recover as much as he could. It's only been in the last few days that he and Daro have ventured out of the Compound and into the City."

"But he will help us?" Eskkar glanced at Daro. "You've been with him for all these days. He must have said something."

Daro hesitated. "He has not yet decided to assist us. Naturally he wants revenge against Grand Commander Chaiyanar, but his heart seems to think it would be traitorous to aid us. I thought it best not to push him."

Eskkar frowned, and he looked toward Trella. "You couldn't convince him to give us information?"

Trella's sincerity and power of persuasion had opened many hearts and minds to gain their support. Eskkar had complete faith in her uncanny ability to win people to her side, and if she couldn't convince this Sabatu, then a problem existed.

"I've spoken to Sabatu nearly every day," Trella said, "but I don't think he's dealt with many women before. He's polite to me, and nothing more. And even though Daro saved his life, Sabatu will not open up to him."

"I've also talked with him several times each day," Daro said, "and he's learned our language well enough to converse, but something holds him back."

"I told him he could leave Akkad whenever he wished," Trella said. "He's nearly able to travel now."

"And you want me to speak to him." Over the years, Eskkar had learned that whenever Trella didn't propose some course of action, she wanted him to deal with the situation.

"From what we've learned about Elam and its people," Trella said, "it appears that their leaders and rulers all have their defined place in society. The people are little better than slaves, and everyone does what they're told. Otherwise they're publicly beaten, or condemned into slavery. Soldiers strut about the marketplace, abusing the common people."

"Yet they have a vast military," Eskkar said, "and have used it to conquer all the lands east of the Zagros Mountain and all the way to the Indus. Whatever the lot of its people, Elam's government is efficient enough."

Daro nodded. "Yes, it's true. But it is not a land I would like to live in."

"Perhaps that is why Sabatu doesn't feel comfortable with Akkad's more relaxed way of doing things," Trella said. "He was taken aback when he learned that this is our only house, and that we rule the city from here, not some vast palace filled with riches, slaves and servants. Somehow we must convince him that our way of doing things is at least equal or better than Elam's."

"Then I think I should see him," Eskkar said, "and at once. I don't want anyone, let alone a soldier with Sabatu's experience and training, wandering throughout Akkad. Think what he could tell his former masters. The knowledge that we're aware of the coming war would be harmful enough. He might even be able to trade such information for the return of his old privileges."

"Yes, Husband, I agree." Trella turned to Daro. "It's time for Sabatu to choose his future."

Noon approached when Sabatu climbed the stairs to the upper level of the Compound's main house, the wooden treads creaking beneath his feet. His fear – he knew it was fear, even though a soldier should never admit to such a feeling – rose up from his belly to his throat. Daro had delivered the summons. King Eskkar of Akkad wanted to speak with Sabatu.

"You will translate for me?"

Daro had shaken his head. "I won't be with you, so you'll have to communicate as best you can in Akkadian. King Eskkar doesn't speak the language of Elam, and Lady Trella has business in another part of the City."

Sabatu knew the King had returned only last night from some training mission in the north, and it had surprised Sabatu to be sent for so soon. But he understood what it meant. The time for Daro and the Queen's gentle persuasions had passed.

When Sabatu entered the main house, a vigilant Hawk Clan guard at the foot of the stairs had briefly studied the visitor, but Sabatu's simple tunic fit too well to conceal a weapon. Another guard, equally formidable, at the top of the stairs repeated the examination, but both soldiers appeared to trust more to Daro's nod of approval.

At the upper landing, the second guard opened the door, and gestured Sabatu to pass inside. The door closed behind him, and Sabatu was alone with the Akkadian ruler.

"Come in. Sit down."

The King spoke slowly and clearly, no doubt aware of Sabatu's recent learning of the language of the Land Between the Rivers.

No one sat in the presence of King Shirudukh of Elam. Sabatu glanced around the plainly furnished chamber, but the only chairs stood beside the table where the King sat, his back to the wall. No fancy tapestries, no jeweled swords displayed, no statues of gold, nothing to overawe a visitor and remind him of the haughty power of the King. Merchants in Sushan displayed more wealth, the better to impress their clients and customers.

The ruler of Akkad seemed as ordinary as the room. A large man, Sabatu guessed Eskkar would stand a head taller and considerably broader. The King's tunic, much the same as the one Daro wore, left his arms bare, and powerful muscles rippled under the skin. Dark brown hair, with only a hint of gray at the temples, was fastened with a simple strip of leather. Brown eyes set in a wide forehead examined the visitor. A scar on his cheek lent a grim look to Akkad's leader. Sabatu knew the King was an old man, in his middle forties, but the years sat lightly on his shoulders.

Even in his brief stay, Sabatu had heard many stories of King Eskkar's prowess and fighting skills, and dismissed them as the usual tales circulated about every ruler. But now, seeing the man face to face, Sabatu decided that the narratives might be true.

The King gestured to the chair opposite his own. Sabatu crossed the room, and bowed low. Unsure of what to do, he held the position, awaiting the King's permission to straighten up.

"Just sit, Sabatu." King Eskkar smiled. "No need to bow like that to anyone in Akkad, or anywhere in the Land Between the Rivers. The leaders of Sumer and Isin and the other cities prefer to look at a man's face, not stare down at the back of his head."

Suddenly nervous, Sabatu eased himself into the seat, aware that the King's eyes were studying Sabatu closely. He sensed the power behind those eyes. The King was a leader of fighting men as well as ruler of the wealthiest city in the Land Between the Rivers, and as such no doubt knew much about what went on inside a soldier's mind. Leaders who could not size up a soldier's strengths and weaknesses seldom rose to command an army.

"Let me see your hands."

Sabatu's eyes widened at the strange request, but the simple command carried the force of the King's presence stronger than any words from any ruler in Elam. Sabatu lifted his hands onto the table, ashamed of their condition. The broken thumbs, injured for so many days without being set, had healed awkwardly, the bones twisted from their usual position. He could scarcely use them. Sabatu had also lost almost all feeling in the fourth and fifth finger of each hand, the result of the tough ropes that had bound his hands throughout his confinement.

The King took only a moment to examine Sabatu's hands. "Have you tried to hold a sword?"

"King Eskkar, Daro let me try his sword, but I could not grasp it properly." Embarrassed, he lowered his gaze. When he lifted his eyes, Sabatu saw the King deep in thought, his gaze focused only on the table.

The silence lingered for more than a few moments, and Sabatu started to think the King had forgotten his visitor, when the King abruptly rose. "Wait here a moment." Eskkar went to the door and called out to the guard.

The King spoke too fast for Sabatu to follow the words, and the conversation went on for some time, with the guard asking several questions. At last Eskkar returned to his seat across the table.

"It is difficult thing when a fighting man can no longer fight," the King said, as he settled back into his chair. "I've seen many men who had to face that bitter truth. A crushed leg, a lost arm, even a hard fall can end a soldier's trade. Some lose all hope, others take to drinking too much ale, and a few even kill themselves, unwilling to face their friends and companions."

The words were spoken without emotion, just a simple statement. But Sabatu felt them burn into his heart. Night and day, he had cursed the shameful fate that had taken the sword from his hands, and turned him into something less than a man. It came as a shock that a king could know such things.

"What did the healer say?"

Sabatu lifted his eyes, and found the King watching him. "The healer, Ventor, says that there is some hope, that over the years, I may regain some use of my hands."

Eskkar grunted. "Ventor is a good healer, but a bad liar."

"Yes, King Eskkar. But I believe he meant well."

"He saved my life when I first came to Akkad, and he healed Trella after she was struck by an assassin's knife. But giving false hope to a fighting man . . . better to tell a soldier the truth."

The admission that the King had once been near death surprised Sabatu. "Yes, King Eskkar."

Sabatu wondered what all this meant. He expected the King to order him to divulge information about Elam, with the threat of more torture or death accompanying the command. Instead, the King spoke about his life.

"Like you, Sabatu, my family was killed. As a boy, I watched my mother and brother die, and my sister . . . I hope that she died quickly. I fled my clan, and had to grow to manhood among my enemies. I was alone, and each day I struggled to survive, always prepared for death."

A knock sounded on the door, and without waiting for a reply, a tall soldier with a dark complexion entered the chamber. He crossed the room in three long strides and took a seat at the table. Sabatu noted that the man did not seek permission to sit.

"This is Hathor, the commander of Akkad's cavalry," King Eskkar said. "We just returned from the north, and Hathor rode with me. I thought you should meet him."

Hathor nodded at Sabatu, but said nothing.

"Hathor comes from the distant land of Egypt, far to the west. Nearly fifteen years ago, he was once the enemy of Akkad. In the battle for the city, Hathor was wounded and captured during the fighting, before he could kill himself. But he had shown mercy to Trella when she was captured. To repay that kindness, and because she knew Hathor was more than a mere soldier, she wanted to spare him. From that day, he, too, was alone among strangers, but he has become my friend. Like many in Akkad, he has found a home and a new family here. The soldiers under his command fight willingly and bravely."

Sabatu stared at the Egyptian.

"It's true." Hathor's voice held just a faint trace of an accent. "I can still remember what it felt like to be completely alone and facing death. But King Eskkar and Lady Trella gave me not only my life, but a new purpose. Now my family is not just my wife and children, but my soldiers, and the people of Akkad. In time, they not only forgave me, but also befriended me."

Another knock sounded, a different pattern, and once again the door opened. The guard stepped into chamber. "They're here. Should I bring them in?"

"Yes. Thank you for getting them so quickly."

This time Sabatu knew his surprise showed on his face. The King of Akkad thanking a guard for obeying orders, and no one thought it odd or unusual.

A sturdy young man strode in, and a moment later, two more men, both older, slowly paced their way into the room. One man had a patch covering an eye, and the other appeared lame. They held onto each other, the lame guiding the half-blind.

To Sabatu's shock, both Eskkar and Hathor rose to their feet, and the tall Egyptian moved quickly to arrange the chairs so that the two older men could sit comfortably.

"Captain, it is good to see you again." These words came from the young man, who apparently felt free to speak before the King gave permission. Suddenly Sabatu noticed that the man was a cripple, with his left arm hanging awkwardly.

"This is Tammuz," King Eskkar said, nodding to the young man. "And it is good to see my other companions, Dragan and Ibi-sin. They are brothers, and both of them had suffered torture and injury by the hand of the King of Larsa. At the risk of their lives, they helped me defeat his forces and capture his city, and they have been honored in Akkad ever since."

The King resumed his seat. "And Tammuz, he fought beside me in my very first fight, when the people of Akkad battled against the invading barbarians. Only a horse boy at the time, he disobeyed orders, took up a bow, and managed to kill a warrior before his arm was crushed. He has been a member of the Hawk Clan since that day. In our war against Sumer, he once again fought for Akkad and helped bring about our victory."

Sabatu bowed slightly. He'd heard about the Hawk Clan and its status. Daro had spoken of it with obvious pride. But these others? Three cripples, not only allowed into the presence of the King, but welcomed as companions and fellow fighting men. In all of Sabatu's visits to King Shirudukh's palace, he had never seen a cripple. Sabatu didn't know what to say.

King Eskkar paused a moment, to let his words sink in. "Sabatu was tortured in a distant land, but found his way to Akkad. He has only been here a short time, and is yet unfamiliar with our ways. His hands are injured, and he will likely not ever use a weapon again. But I thought it might be good for him to see that there are other ways a soldier can fight. A sword is not always needed to make a man a warrior. Dragan and Ibi-sin proved that. They risked even worse torture and death, but saved hundreds of Akkadian soldiers."

"King Eskkar is too kind," Dragan said. "It was little enough that we did. But even if we had died, it would have been worth it to see those who tortured and killed our family destroyed. For that, we will always be thankful to King Eskkar and Lady Trella."

"The Hawk Clan will always be in your debt," King Eskkar said.

Dragan glanced at his brother. "If there is anything that we can do to assist Sabatu, we will be glad to help. We understand the pain he suffers." He turned to Sabatu. "It is said that torture weakens a man, but I say it makes him stronger, even though it may leave him maimed and mangled. As many of us have learned, even a man with a crooked leg or one eye can fight."

Tammuz leaned forward. "I was only fifteen when my arm was crushed. I thought my life had ended, and I prayed for death. Instead, Lady Trella and King Eskkar took me into their family. Lady Trella arranged a wise wife for me, one who shares my life. For that, she and I willingly went into battle against their enemies."

Unsure of what to say, Sabatu bowed his head.

"I am glad Sabatu had the chance to meet all of you," King Eskkar said. "A man needs to know that he is not alone, that others have suffered as he did and survived, even thrived. In the next few days, he may want to spend time with you, and hear your stories." The King stood. "Hathor, will you see that Dragan and Ibi-sin are escorted home? And my thanks to you, Tammuz."

"Yes, Captain." Hathor rose, and with Tammuz helping, they assisted the two brothers out of the chamber.

Sabatu could scarcely keep his thoughts under control. He still wasn't sure what it all meant. But as soon as the door closed, the conversation took a different tone.

"Sabatu, I asked them here to meet with you, so that you could see that a new life can be made, even when it seems impossible. You have been given that chance, and Trella and Daro say more than enough time has passed for you to choose. Now you must decide what it is you will do, and in the morning you will give us your decision. If you choose not to help us, then you will be given some coins and a horse, and you will be banished from Akkad. You may go wherever you like, but you cannot remain here. I cannot have anyone who is not completely loyal within the City."

"I . . . I know I am in your debt, King Eskkar. Daro and Yavtar saved my life at the risk of their own. But what you ask is not something that comes easy to me."

The King nodded. "A soldier's life is indeed a hard one, with death always at hand. Every man must make his own path, and uphold his honor in his own way. And while we would welcome your assistance, such a choice must be freely made. Otherwise, we could not put our trust in you. But sometimes a man needs to choose who his people will be. I was born in the steppes clan, and I fought against my own kind again and again. But many years ago, I chose Akkad and its people to be my kin and family."

Sabatu sensed the understanding behind the King's words.

"But Sabatu, I want you to think on this. If you saw the man who put your family to death walking in the lane, what would you do? Would you attack him, even if it meant the loss of your own life? Or would you let him pass by, unaware of your presence? That may be the choice that you face."

"King Eskkar, I don't . . ."

"There is no need to say anything now, Sabatu. Go. Decide what you want to do. In the morning, tell Daro of your decision."

Surprised at the abrupt dismissal, Sabatu stood. He'd expected more entreaties or threats or promises of gold for his service. But this King offered nothing, merely a chance to serve and become one of his people.

Once again Sabatu bowed low, and then turned and left the chamber. On the landing, he looked down and saw Daro lounging in a chair with his legs sprawled, waiting for him.

The King of Akkad had spoken the truth. The time for a decision had indeed arrived. Sabatu knew he would sleep little tonight.

Sabatu and Daro strolled through Akkad's lanes, moving at a slow pace as almost everyone they encountered seemed to know Daro and wanted to have a few words with him. They visited the marketplace and the docks, stopped by the site of the new temple being built for the goddess Ishtar, and even paused at the soldiers' barracks.

While there Daro led the way behind the rambling structures, to an open space where the soldiers trained or practiced with their weapons. A small area served as a narrow archery range, and even this late in the day, Sabatu saw ten or twelve men using the targets.

"The barracks grew too large and crowded, so they moved the regular archery range across the river. This one is used mainly by the instructors to test new bows and shafts, or for any soldiers needing extra work."

One master bowman functioned as range master, offering guidance or help to anyone who needed it. He made sure that everyone put aside their bows before walking down to examine their targets. The man nodded to Daro, but kept his eyes on the archers.

Sabatu understood. Accidents happened often enough, and a moment's carelessness might mean someone's misfortune.

Daro insisted on launching a few arrows at the small archery range. "It's been days since I pulled a bow." He selected a new bow from the testing table, strung the weapon, and collected a handful of target arrows. Taking his stance, Daro launched the first arrow toward the target.

Sabatu stood beside Daro, and found himself impressed despite his own experiences with the bow. Daro proved himself a fine bowman, and the heavy Akkadian arrows struck with a powerful force. The typical Akkadian bow stood a hand's length longer than the bows used by Elam's archers, and appeared thicker as well.

"Most of the wood comes from the far north," Daro explained. "Mitrac, he commands all of Akkad's archers, told King Eskkar about the famous trees of the northern forest. Mitrac's kin returned home after they settled their blood feud with the barbarians. But since we fought together, Mitrac's family established a steady trade with Akkad for the select wood. Very rare and expensive, of course, but the bows constructed from the heartwood of the steppes last far longer, and keep their power."

By now Sabatu had heard most of the tales of the mighty Akkadian archers, and those, too, he had discounted. But after seeing Daro bend a bow, not to mention the obvious pleasure the man took in his craft, Sabatu revised his ideas. When the range master proclaimed a halt, Daro reluctantly lowered the weapon.

"Can I try your bow?" The words slipped from Sabatu's mouth almost without thought.

Daro's eyes widened. "If you think you can draw it . . ." He extended the weapon toward Sabatu, then pulled it back. "Wait here a moment. I have an idea."

He turned and trotted over to the archer's shed, a flimsy wooden structure that held extra bows, strings, target shafts, wrist guards, and the rest of the items needed for any bowman. After a quick discussion with the boy tending the weapons, Daro strode back to his companion.

"Here, try this one." Daro handed Sabatu a smaller, sharply curved bow. "This is a little smaller than those that Hathor's cavalry use, but at close range, it's just as deadly."

Sabatu accepted the weapon. Holding it up, he examined its length, and found it similar to those used by some of Elam's soldiers. With difficulty, he managed to grasp the bow with his left hand. His stiff fingers resisted, but he ignored the pain in his thumb. Daro handed him a target shaft.

However without full use of his thumb, fitting the arrow to the bowstring proved a challenge. Sabatu felt his frustration rise, but before he could react, Daro moved to his side.

"Let me do that." He nocked the shaft to the string.

Once again, Sabatu struggled, trying to draw the weapon without losing his grip on the arrow or bowstring. Once, twice, his fingers slipped from the shaft. He grit his teeth, and tried again, this time using all of his fingers behind the string. The bow bent, and Sabatu realized how weak his arm had become.

The other bowmen on the range had stopped their practice and their talking. Every man watched Sabatu's struggle. Aware of their eyes, Sabatu ignored the ache in his hands. Using all his strength, he drew the arrow back until his fingers brushed his cheek, aiming at the butt. Then he loosed the missile.

The shaft flew through the air. At the barrack's small range, the targets were only thirty paces away from the shooting line. Sabatu's shaft struck the bale of straw well below the target, the flight just high enough to avoid landing in the dirt.

Nevertheless, a cheer went up, and every man on the line gave a shout of approval or offered a word of encouragement. Each archer understood the pain that Sabatu must feel, what he must endure, and so they rejoiced in his success. After all, the power of the gods flowed through bow and string to the shaft. How else to explain the magical power of the weapon that could slay a man at a hundred paces?

Daro, a big grin on his face, smacked Sabatu on the back so hard that he nearly dropped the bow. "Well done! A fine shot!"

Sabatu had to pry the fingers of his left hand from the grip of the bow, but he managed a smile. "Not much of a bowman." He handed the weapon back to Daro.

"Not today," Daro agreed. "Not today, but tomorrow and the day after, who knows?" He handed the cavalry bow to the range master, and swept his long arm around Sabatu's shoulders. "I think it's time we get something to eat." They resumed their walk, leaving the barracks area and heading back toward the center of the city.

The sun had turned to dusk, and Sabatu felt the stirrings of his appetite, as if launching a single arrow had taxed his strength.

"Tonight I've something special planned for you," Daro said, as he guided Sabatu down the lane. "Since this may be your last night in Akkad, I thought you should at least enjoy yourself."

"As long as the food is good, I'll be more than satisfied."

Daro led the way into the more exclusive part of Akkad, where the houses stood taller and the outer walls higher.

"This is Zenobia's," Daro said, as they approached one particularly impressive home. "Here you can sample the finest food in Akkad, along with its most beautiful and skilled women. Only the well-off can afford to visit her house. Fortunately, as a commander in the Hawk Clan, I am allowed an occasional visit." He grinned at his companion. "They say Zenobia came from the Indus all the way to Akkad, just to favor us with her gifts."

Sabatu tried to protest, but Daro ignored him. They passed through the guarded red gate, and found themselves in a lush and carefully cultivated garden. Far nicer than the few plants that the King's Compound boasted, the carefully tended flowers yielded a pleasant perfume that scented the air. The structure's outer walls shone in the setting sun, no doubt from a fresh coat of whitewash.

A tall woman with blond hair that reached below her waist waited at the door, and welcomed Daro by name, though her smile for Sabatu was just as warm. She escorted them into the main house, where the enticing smells of roasting meat permeated the air, overpowering the more delicate scents worn by their guide.

Sabatu saw the main room held five good sized tables, and though the evening had scarcely begun, four of them were occupied. Women dressed in light brown dresses cut low across the bosom served the seated men, often kneeling on the floor as they offered tidbits of food to their guests.

But Daro headed straight for the wide stairs that led to the upper chamber. "Upstairs are the most expensive rooms and the most skilled girls. I sent a messenger this morning, telling Zenobia that we would be coming."

Another guard stood at the base of the steps, but he nodded respectfully to Daro as they went up. At the top, another woman, this one will thick dark hair and ochre stain around her eyes, held out her arms and clasped Daro around the neck.

"Daro! It's been years since you've visited Zenobia's," she said. "I thought you had forgotten all about your favorites."

"What man could forget a night of pleasure with you, Te-ara. Even Zenobia says you are the most skilled courtesan in Akkad."

Te-ara laughed, a long musical sound that brought a smile even to Sabatu's lips. "She says that about all her girls." She favored Sabatu with another smile. "And who is this handsome man who I have never seen before? Is this a special occasion for him?"

"Yes, one that requires the finest your House can offer. My friend Sabatu is a stranger to Akkad, and is recovering from his wounds. He may be leaving Akkad soon, and I wanted to give him one last night of pleasure. So don't tempt me with your charms, save them all for my friend. Just ignore his protests."

Sabatu did protest, but to no avail. Te-ara put her arm around his waist and rubbed her breast against his arm. "Then we will do everything in our power to entertain the honorable Sabatu." She moved her lips to his cheek, and let them brush his ear.

Te-ara guided Sabatu down the hall and into a room. It contained a massive bed, one big enough for four people to sleep comfortably. A copper-colored blanket covered its surface, and three bright red pillows rested at the head.

"Take your ease, Sabatu," Te-ara said. "I'll be back with food and wine."

She favored him with another smile and slipped from the room.

Daro lay down on the bed with a long sigh of relaxation, and clasped his hands behind his head. "Zenobia's cooks are the best in Akkad. And the wine . . . ah! Even Lady Trella's table can't match their quality. Some people claim that Zenobia adds a few drops of a secret love potion."

Sabatu remained standing. "Daro, this is not something I want to do. I feel no urge for a woman. Even if I did, my body is too weak. . . the scars."

"Just lie down for a moment. You don't have to do anything. But let us share one last meal together, as friends. Is that so much to ask?"

Before Sabatu could reply, two girls rushed into the room. One struggled with a large tray that held three pitchers and two cups. The second girl carried a platter that displayed bread, oil, dates, and Akkad's famous sweet cakes. She climbed onto the bed beside Daro, set the platter down, and pulled off her dress, revealing firm breasts that glistened in the light of the room's two candles.

"My name is Ducina, and I am for you, Sabatu." She reached out and clasped his hand, and tugged him toward the bed.

"You'd better give in, Sabatu," Daro said. "The girls get nothing to eat and earn no pay unless their customers are completely satisfied."

"Yes, and I don't want to have to whip their bottoms again," Te-ara said, sweeping back into the chamber. "They enjoy it too much." She guided a suddenly helpless Sabatu closer to the bed, pulled off her own garment, and jumped onto the mattress. She pulled Sabatu down onto a pillow, and popped a sweet cake into his mouth.

"Let's start with these," Te-ara said. "Then Ducina has other delicacies to tempt your lips."

Daro laughed, a contented sound that filled the room. He reached for a wine cup. "Yes, there are always many delights to taste at Zenobia's."

The bright morning sun streaming through the tiny window woke Sabatu. His head hurt from too much wine and not enough sleep, and when he lifted it from the pillow, he found himself still at Zenobia's. Ducina lay curled up along his right side, like a kitten, sleeping soundly. On his left, Te-ara lay clinging to his arm, her long hair scattered across his chest.

Trapped between them, Sabatu struggled to remember all the events of the evening. Despite his protests, the women had soon removed his garment, even as they kept offering food and wine. Unable to resist, he had drained one cup of wine, then another. Before long, Ducina was kneeling between his legs, sucking on his manhood with an energy that overwhelmed Sabatu.

But it was Te-ara who first mounted his rod, and she rode him with more skill than anything Sabatu had experienced in Elam. With Ducina's breast in his mouth, he soon burst inside Te-ara. When she finally let him go, he lay there, as exhausted as if he'd mounted her and ridden her for half a night.

The girls scarcely noticed. They kept feeding him and refilling his wine cup even as they worked on his manhood without ceasing. This morning Sabatu could not even remember how many times he spent his seed.

Glancing around, Sabatu saw no sign of Daro, and didn't even remember the man leaving. The two women, with the help from a few others who stopped in Sabatu's chamber, had drained him completely even as they erased, at least for a brief time, the pain that burned in his heart.

Now the memories returned. His wife, his children, his family, all dead, their broken and bloody bodies dumped into the river. Nothing of Sabatu's life remained. His very existence, his place in Elam's society, had been ripped out by the roots.

The intense feelings of sorrow, humiliation, and defeat that had swept over him when Chaiyanar's soldiers first tied him to the stake in the marketplace still remained. In fact, they burned as brightly as before, but the gloom and despair had transformed into an urge to take revenge on Chaiyanar.

Perhaps Daro was right. Perhaps something could be done, some way that Sabatu could strike a real blow against the man who tortured and murdered his wife and children. Any blow, even the slightest, would bring some relief to the spirits of his family, and to Sabatu's own sense of honor.

With as much care as he could manage, Sabatu sat up in the bed, slipping from the embrace of the women. Neither one woke, despite his clumsy efforts to climb down off the bed. No doubt the women at Zenobia's slept long in the morning, to make up for their hard work at night.

At last he got to his feet. Sabatu found his tunic and sandals piled neatly on a stool in the corner of the room. When he lifted the garment, he saw that someone had attached a sheathed knife to his belt. A parting gift from Daro no doubt, who understood the importance of a weapon to any soldier, even one who could not yet use it properly.

It took extra moments to dress, his maimed hands still refusing to work properly. But at last he finished. He stared down at the two naked women, both sleeping soundly. Even in repose, their beauty made him catch his breath. Sabatu had no coins, nothing to leave them for his long night of pleasure. They had asked for no payment. Te-ara had lavished her finest efforts on him at Daro's simple suggestion. He hoped they would not think less of him.

Sabatu sighed. Perhaps one day he would return to this place, and enjoy again the company of Te-ara and Ducina.

He left the chamber, went down the steps, and out into the courtyard. Sabatu saw a few yawning servants moving about, before he passed by the guard still at the door. The bright sun, reflected off the spotless wall, made it difficult to see. Sabatu moved into the shade of the portico, until his eyes adjusted.

His thoughts returned to King Eskkar. He and Daro had both delivered the same message, without once speaking the words. A man could lose everything in his life, and still be a man as long as he kept his honor. And honor demanded that Sabatu avenge his family's destruction, by any means, and no matter what the cost. Otherwise his whole life was wasted, his name deservedly forgotten.

In the end, the only thing that really counted was how a man lived, and how he died. Life was, after all, only a prelude to death, and no warrior should fear to die. Death is only one of the possible consequences of a man's actions, neither valued nor feared above any other. Death is merely a release from a man's obligations.

Last night, Te-ara and Ducina had shown Sabatu that life still went on, and that he was yet a man. Suddenly he remembered how Daro's bow had felt in his hand yesterday, the power that had flowed from his arm to the shaft. Perhaps in time, Sabatu would be able to once again harness that power. And if he could guide an arrow to its mark, he could still fight. For the first time since he arrived in Akkad, Sabatu straightened his shoulders and lifted his head high.

His thoughts turned to his meeting with King Eskkar yesterday. A plain man, without pretensions. Perhaps there was more to being a king than a gilded throne or golden statues.

In that moment, Sabatu made his decision. He would fight against those who had destroyed his life, killed his family, and sentenced him to death. Perhaps with Akkad's help, he could strike some small blow against his enemies. Perhaps someday, maybe he, too, would find and embrace a new family.

Most of all, Grand Commander Chaiyanar, ruler of the city of Sushan, and loyal servant of the King of Elam, needed to be reminded that Sabatu still lived, still fought, and would one day take his revenge. That would be the price Sabatu would require from King Eskkar – the chance to destroy the man who murdered his family.

2

3128 BC, eleven months later . . .

The midday sun shone down on the grove of trees, awash in a blaze of spring colors. Eskkar, who had not left Akkad's mud brick walls in the last ten days, couldn't help but contrast the farm's cheerful surroundings with the dull and dirty lanes that separated the crowded structures of the city. Nestled against fields of golden wheat and barley, the white sycamores supported a tall and leafy awning. On the other side of the grove, a stretch of pale green and purple alfalfa waved in the afternoon breeze. Further on, Eskkar glimpsed the soft blue flowers of the hardy flax plant.

The farm sounded a melody of life. Brightly feathered chickens clucked as they hunted through the grass. Birds sang overhead, bees hummed as they hovered over yellow and red tulips, and a light wind from the nearby Tigris River rustled the leaves overhead and wafted the soothing scent of living and growing things. The occasional lowing of cattle from the nearby pasture added to the peaceful sounds and smells so familiar to anyone raised on a farm.

Eskkar, however, had not grown up tilling the soil or herding livestock, but rather, so his barbarian ancestors claimed, on the back of a horse. Years later, and with Trella's help, he had learned the value of planting and harvesting the earth's gifts, and how these pleasant fields created the wealth that flowed throughout the Land Between the Rivers. But today Eskkar scarcely noticed these signs of serenity as he paced back and forth, striding from one end of the small grove to the other.

From habit, his eyes took in the terrain around him. To the south, well separated from the main farm house, stood crooked fences and pens that enclosed small herds of sheep and pigs. To the north and east, the crops stretched out over the fertile ground for more than a quarter mile, until they merged with those of the neighboring holding. On the west side, a wider than usual irrigation ditch connected this farmstead to the Tigris, which flowed peacefully along about three hundred paces away. The summer breeze waved the grain back and forth, in a soft, undulating motion.

In a few months, the gleaning and harrowing would begin, and this fall every tiller of the soil expected a bountiful crop yield. As usual, Akkad's farmers kept their eyes and their thoughts on the coming harvest. Most had forgotten the other activity of men that often followed the end of the annual gathering – preparations for war.

Eskkar and Trella had not forgotten. Her agents in Akkad had already promised a generous price for each basket of grain gleaned from the soil, and much of this would be stored in the granaries that Trella had ordered constructed in the past year. Food, Eskkar knew, was as much a weapon of war as the sword. When the Elamite invasion came, the City would be well prepared to feed the influx of people clamoring to take shelter behind its walls.

In the last two and a half years, the King and Queen of Akkad had taken many other small steps to prepare the City for war, most of them in secret. Now the day had arrived to reveal not only what precautions they had put in place, but to set in motion the plans that they hoped would save their City.

Today, that need had brought them to Yavtar's extensive farm holding a few miles south of Akkad. Important guests were arriving, and their decisions would determine not only Akkad's future, but the destiny of all the people and all the cities in the Land Between the Rivers.

Eskkar, his hands clasped behind his back, halted at the edge of the sycamores, and stared at the offshoot of the Tigris. One aspect of this homestead made it different from all the others that dotted the countryside south of Akkad – the weathered quay, long enough to dock three good sized boats, that ran alongside the canal.

Many farms possessed a few warped planks or a rocky stone jetty projecting out into the rivers and streams, big enough for one or two of the small and often precarious boats that carried men, crops, and the occasional animal to nearby markets. But this solidly built docking place could handle river craft capable of plying the Tigris from its headwaters to the Great Southern Sea.

The connection to the river had taken months of backbreaking labor to dig out and line with stones to prevent its collapse. That effort had cost the farm's owner a goodly sum of gold, but that had presented no problem to Yavtar. Over the last ten years, the Boat Master had become one of the richest men in Akkad. His river trading ventures paid handsomely, and his fleet of ships traveled up and down both the Tigris and Euphrates, as well as many of their smaller tributaries that crossed the land from west to east.

Yavtar also fulfilled another role – advisor to the King and Queen of Akkad. His connections to traders throughout the land provided a steady stream of valuable information. In addition, Yavtar's wide-ranging boats moved supplies needed for Akkad's army. And when Trella had sought a quiet place away from the city, Yavtar had volunteered both his services and his farm as a place for today's meeting.

Even that offer fretted on Eskkar's nerves. He hated relying on others for anything. Now he had to plot and plan in secret, away from his city, lest anyone guess what he and Trella might be doing.

Nevertheless, he had no choice. Akkad, its people still unaware of the looming danger from the east, could not be saved by their rulers' efforts alone. The efficient military force he had developed, even the city's thick and high walls, would not be enough. Eskkar required the help of others, and despite his misgivings and reluctance, the time had come to ask for it.

Today's meeting, carefully arranged and kept secret from all but a handful of the most trustworthy, would soon begin. Not that Eskkar concerned himself with the beginning. He worried more about how the gathering would end.

"Come and sit with me, Eskkar." Trella's voice, soft yet persuasive, sounded appropriate in the grove. She had, after all, grown up surrounded by farms.

Eskkar, far too tense to just sit around and wait, ignored his wife's suggestion. "This seems a strange place to prepare for a war."

He rapped his fist on the surface of the large table, sheltered from the warm sun by the trees' canopy, and big enough to accommodate ten or twelve people. Servants had removed the usual benches that flanked the table, and replaced them with seven mismatched chairs, more appropriate to the expected guests. Trella sat there, alone, going over the maps needed for the meeting one last time.

"This war would come to us whether we prepared or not, Husband. Best not to dwell on what brought us here."

Trella wore a simple brown dress, and her only jewelry was the silver head band that held her hair away from her eyes. Neither she nor Eskkar had wanted to attract any undue attention today by dressing in more formal clothes. As far as the people of Akkad knew, the King and Queen had gone out riding.

Eskkar returned his gaze to the dock. Only one craft lay tied up there – the ship from Sumer that had arrived not long ago. For a moment, he frowned at the gaudy vessel, decorated with a wide stripe of deep red along its hull, and with the yellow sun of Sumer carved and painted on its prow. To his eyes, a boat should be plain and sturdy, whether built for war or trade. Eskkar disliked men who called attention to themselves.

He took one last look around to make sure everything was in place. The four mud brick houses that sheltered the owner and his servants were a hundred and fifty paces from where Eskkar stood. The servants and laborers had all been sent off to another farm for the day.

Only the sixty Hawk Clan soldiers remained, scarcely noticeable as they patrolled the grove in a wide ring that brought them no closer than two hundred paces, well out of earshot. Rousted from their barracks before dawn, not even Eskkar's most loyal soldiers knew what today's meeting portended.

He turned his thoughts back to the grove, and glanced toward the table. His wife showed not the least hint of anxiety, though she had planned and worked for almost two years to prepare for this meeting.

A dog barked, a deep sound powerful enough to frighten a wolf. Eskkar swung around to face the main farmhouse. Yavtar had emerged from the house, accompanied by two men. Each man carried a large platter, covered with a cloth to keep away the flies. The dog, black as a night demon, trotted over and rubbed against his master's thigh for a moment before it settled down to match Yavtar's pace.

Eskkar eyed the brute as they approached. Yavtar swore the animal was tame, but Eskkar had some bad experiences in his younger days with farm dogs, and he still distrusted anything that could rip the flesh from a man's leg with a single bite. The two men accompanying Yavtar appeared to have similar doubts about the dog. They gave the creature plenty of space.

"Lord Eskkar," Yavtar said when he drew near, "this is King Gemama of Sumer, and the leader of his soldiers, Lord Jarud."

Gemama, bald, stout, and with a straggly white beard, looked exactly what he was, a rich merchant trader. Perspiration gleamed on his forehead, though he'd done little but walk to the grove. His stomach pressed hard against his spotless tunic stitched with a red and black design.

Once merely one of Sumer's leading merchants, Gemama had been acclaimed ruler of Sumer by its people nine years ago, albeit encouraged in their choice by Trella's agents. Yavtar had been one of those agents, and he and Gemama had already been trading partners and friends for many years. Without Akkad's help, Gemama would have died, murdered by the Queen of Sumer. Instead he became Sumer's ruler.

His companion, Jarud, had about fifty seasons, and he also looked as expected. A soldier first and last, he'd obviously grown up with a sword in his hand. In the same wave that swept Gemama to the kingship, Jarud rose from a newly assigned Captain of the Guard to commander of Sumer's soldiers.

To everyone's surprise, probably including their own, the trader-turned-king and the soldier-turned-leader had grown close over time, and for the last nine years had ruled the city of Sumer together. They had also restored prosperity to the inhabitants, who had suffered long under the harsh rule of their previous despotic and war-hungry leaders.

Eskkar had met neither man before, but numerous messages had passed between the two cities in those nine years. Trella's agents, of course, had provided many details about Sumer's leaders.

He forced a smile to his face and bowed to the visitors. "I thank you both for coming. Our other guest should be here soon." Eskkar reached out and took the platter from King Gemama's hands. No doubt it had been years since Gemama had lifted anything heavier than a leg of mutton or a slave girl's breast. "Join us at the table."

As Eskkar set the platter down, Trella stood. She bowed to the Sumerians, then helped arrange the platters.

"You should not have put our guests to work, Yavtar," she chided him gently. "I could have carried the platters."

"My wife just finished preparing them." Yavtar took a seat at the table, the dog settling at his feet. "And none of us are too proud to carry our own food."

Trella turned to her husband. "Yavtar has done well with the arrangements. We must find a way to thank him."

Eskkar gazed at his wife. "I'm sure that asking him to risk his life a few more times will be more than enough thanks."

She didn't bother to reply to that. Trella recognized the small signs that indicated Eskkar's anxiety, though he hid them well. She knew that he would be impassive enough in front of the others.

"It's good to finally meet you, Lord Eskkar, Lady Trella." King Gemama eased his bulk onto the largest chair he could find. He tossed the cloth off the nearest platter and inspected its contents – dark dates from the south, a bowl of apples, another of sweet cakes. "Ah, the famous Akkadian sweet cakes. There are none better in the land."

Trella reached out and removed the other two cloths. The smell of fresh bread rose into the air. There were also bowls of honey for dipping. Two pitchers of water and two of wine completed the preparations.

"It is we who are in your debt, King Gemama." Trella gave him a warm smile. "Though I am sorry that your visit to our lands comes at this time."

"Yavtar has told us little, except that grave danger threatens all of us. We decided to accept your invitation, and find out for ourselves."

"Sumer is peaceful enough." Jarud broke off a hunk of bread and tested the honey. "No bandits, not even the usual pirate raid or two from the sea."

A distant horn sounded, a low growl that floated over the water. Everyone glanced toward the canal.

"Naxos must be on his way in." Yavtar pushed himself to his feet. "I'll meet him at the jetty. He and Kuara can carry the rest of the food. The two of them will eat most of it anyway." Yavtar headed back toward his house, to greet and fetch the remainder of their guests. He couldn't quite manage to keep the smile off his face. The rest of the day promised to be very, very interesting, and he intended to enjoy every moment of it.

On the canal, a boat hove into sight and glided toward the shore, slipping gracefully through the water. The craft flew a pennant from its mast, the emblem of the City of Isin. A second boat appeared in its wake. One of Akkad's fighting boats escorted the ship from Isin, and the two boats touched the dock at almost the same moment.

Following their orders, the Akkadian crew remained on board. From the other craft, two men jumped to the dock, one tall and powerfully built. He glanced around, left hand on the hilt of his sword, as if expecting trouble. Though Eskkar had not seen him in several years, he recognized King Naxos of Isin, ruler of the second most powerful city in the Land Between the Rivers.

Yavtar greeted the two men at the end of the jetty. But instead of escorting them to the grove, he led them past the house, where Yavtar's plump wife met them at the door. She handed over two more platters and another pitcher. It took only a moment before the three men were again on their way to the grove.

Jarud chuckled. "That's a sight I'll never see again. King Naxos carrying a pitcher of wine."

Eskkar had to smile as well. "I'm glad I didn't go to the dock. Yavtar would have me carrying a platter, too."

Everyone rose to greet the new arrivals. King Naxos, as tall and well-muscled as Eskkar and about the same age, thumped his pitcher down on the table, as if daring anyone to say something. His companion, however, had a broad smile on his face. For many years, Kuara acted as Chief Advisor to Naxos and the City of Isin.

Kuara had about the same number of seasons as Gemama and Yavtar, all in their late fifties. Unlike them, however, he also had fought in several battles. His right hand possessed only a thumb and forefinger, the other fingers sliced off by an enemy sword. As the story went, Kuara had still managed to kill his attacker. A long shock of gray hair reached to his shoulders, and a thick mustache half-covered his mouth.

"We thank you both for coming, King Naxos, Noble Kuara," Lady Trella said. "Please, sit down. There is water and wine to refresh you."

Naxos remembered his manners enough to bow. "It is good to see you again, Lady Trella. And you, Eskkar." His gruff voice sounded out of place in the pleasant glade.

Eskkar bowed as well. Both were rulers of a city, and supposedly of equal rank. But Naxos also knew who held the real power. Akkad, with its ability to call on all the other cities, far outnumbered Isin in numbers and industry. And so Isin had journeyed to Akkad, and not Akkad to Isin.

"Yes, Lord Naxos. Our thanks to you for coming to see us in secret." Trella's words would have soothed an angry lion.

She, like Eskkar, understood how touchy Naxos was. Even after nine years, he still resented the fact that Eskkar had once threatened to destroy his city.

As Naxos tried to sit, his sword caught on the seat. Glancing around, he noticed that Eskkar's sword rested a few paces away, leaning against the white trunk of a nearby sycamore tree. Naxos realized that he was the only one armed. For a moment he struggled with the urge to keep his sword, but he yielded to his better instincts. Unbuckling the scabbard, he shoved the weapon under the table and took his seat, facing Eskkar across the table.

Kuara took the chair to the left of his King. Gemama faced Trella, with Jarud to his right. Yavtar sat at the end of the table, separating himself from the rulers of the three cities.

None of the men questioned Trella's presence at a gathering of leaders. However valuable her husband's fighting skills and leadership might be, the rulers of Isin and Sumer knew Trella's keen wits had guided the City of Akkad for the last fifteen years. Only a fool would reject such a talent, and these men were no fools.

Eskkar waited until everyone had a cup of water or wine at hand. "I asked both Sumer and Isin here to warn you of a danger that threatens us all. An invasion is coming from the east, from the land of the Elamites." A glance around the table showed that he had their attention. "I'll let Trella tell you the story. She has gathered most of the information, and knows more about the Elamite threat than anyone." He smiled. "Besides, that way I won't forget anything."

They had agreed before the meeting that Trella should bring the others up to date. Her reputation for reasonableness and honesty would make them more likely to swallow the bitter news. And the leaders of Isin and Sumer were well aware of the role she played in ruling the city of Akkad.

Eskkar would lead the discussion later, which would give Trella a better opportunity to study their guests' faces and reactions.

"You all know of the land of the Elamites to the east," Trella began. "Almost two years ago, we learned they were planning to invade the Land Between the Rivers, conquer our cities, and reduce us all to slaves."

She told them everything, except how they had first learned of the approaching threat from Eskkar's old companion, Bracca. Step by step Trella explained what her agents had learned, and told them of the preparations that Akkad had already begun. No one spoke, and the only other sound besides her voice was the sighing of the leaves in the trees.

The sun moved a hand's breadth across the sky before Trella finished. While she delivered the news, Eskkar eyed his visitors. Neither Naxos nor Kuara let anything show on their faces. Jarud looked grave, and Gemama paled as the story unfolded. He broke the silence that followed the last of Trella's words.

"Are you certain that they are coming against Sumer?"

"They are coming against all of us," Eskkar said. "It would make no sense for them to invade these lands to attack and capture a single city. The Elamites want all the Land Between the Rivers. Sumer and Akkad will be their first targets, Sumer because of its position on the coast. The Elamites will use it to supply their forces. Then Isin and the others."

"How sure are you of their numbers?" Kuara's good hand had tightened on his cup, and he set it down carefully. "Forty to fifty thousand soldiers?"

"The Elamites have more than that number spread out across their empire, possibly another four or five thousand. But they dare not leave their lands unguarded. Most of their cities and villages have been brutally subjugated by King Shirudukh, and their people are ripe for a revolt against their masters."

"How can they march such a large number of men from Elam to here?" Naxos shook his head. "There's not enough food to feed them on the way."

"That's true. Trella and I have studied their forces as best we can. We believe that they will come at us in three separate armies. One army, probably ten to fifteen thousand, will journey along the coast, supplied by boats along the route, until it reaches Sumer. Once Sumer is taken, their ships will continue bringing supplies and men in, and start taking gold and important prisoners back to Elam."

As Eskkar spoke, Trella unfolded one of the maps, and spread it out before her. Every head leaned forward. "A second force, and likely the bulk of their army, will come through the Zagros Mountains, through the Dellen pass, straight toward Akkad. Probably about twenty-five thousand men."

Eskkar traced the path on the map with his finger. "The third force will also come through the mountains, but farther north, through the Jkarian pass. That army will be used to collect supplies along the way, and help resupply the main force, which will be attacking Akkad. The northern force will also prevent any of our own forces escaping in that direction. Probably they will continue west and cross the Tigris and come down the Euphrates, to seal off and capture the cities of Uruk, Lagash, and Nippur. Assuming, of course, that Akkad and Isin have fallen by then."

"How do you know all this?" Naxos voice held a trace of anger. "When is this all happening?"

Eskkar shrugged. "I can't be certain of these facts. But during the last two years, we have sent many spies into the Elamite lands. Also, our agents brought back an Elamite commander a year ago, a leader of five hundred accused of treason and sentenced to death. He was forced to watch the torture and murder of his wife and children. In return for a chance to strike a blow against those who killed his kin, he's told us much about their tactics. With his help, and the latest reports from our spies, we think we've worked out Elam's plan of attack. As for the rest," Eskkar tapped the map, "it's what I'd do if I had that many men, and wanted to invade and conquer this land in a single campaign."

"If I may speak," Trella said, "this effort is by far the largest the Elamites have undertaken. If it fails, their entire empire may collapse. They know this, which is why they have prepared for so many years. They need to ensure that the invasion succeeds. To accomplish that, they will bring as many soldiers as they can spare. Once they conquer our land, the gold and resources here will support their rule in Elam for many years."

"And what else did your traitor tell you?" Naxos refilled his cup with wine, and only added a splash of water to it.

If Trella were offended by Naxos's surly tone, she didn't show it. "He advised us that his former masters are skilled in the capturing of walled cities. They will bring or construct ramps, ladders, and scaling tools. They also know how to dig beneath a city's walls, until they collapse. He claimed they had taken over fifteen well defended cities in the Indus alone."

"But there is no way to defeat such a vast army." Gemama couldn't keep the fear out of his voice. "Even if we collected every fighter from all our cities, we could only gather less than half their number."

"That's true, Lord Gemama," Trella said. "And the forces we could raise would not be as well trained as these invaders. I fear that only Akkad and Isin can put soldiers as disciplined into the field."

"When are they coming?" Kuara's resigned voice did not reflect the anger of Naxos, his king.

"In the fall, after the harvest. They want the crops from our fields to live on while they conquer our cities." Trella kept her voice calm. "And their three armies will march at the same time, so that we will have to face them all at once. In less than five months from now, they will be on their way through the Zagros Mountains."

"Why have you waited so long to tell us?" Gemama's voice quavered in anger. "You should have warned us as soon as you learned of the danger!"

Eskkar kept his voice calm. "First, we could not be certain they were really coming. We only recently confirmed that the invasion preparations had begun. Second, we needed to learn as much as possible. Otherwise you might not have believed us. And last, we needed to find a way to defeat them."

"So you do have a plan to stop them?" Jarud spoke for the first time. Like Kuara, he kept whatever he might be feeling out of his voice.

Eskkar glanced from face to face. "I do not plan to defeat them. One city alone cannot resist such numbers. But there may be a way, if the three of us work together, to drive them back across the mountains."

"And what is this way?" King Naxos's voice still sounded harsh.

"With my most trusted commanders," Eskkar began, "I've ridden and studied the lands between here and the Zagros Mountains for almost two years, from the far north all the way to the Great Sea. We've prepared maps to identify watering places, supply routes, and even likely camp grounds. We have also considered many ways to stop or defeat them."

Eskkar leaned forward. "But the key to defeating these Elamites is Sumer. If we can drive them away from Sumer's walls and keep control of the Tigris, we can destroy their main supply route. Without that, they cannot sustain themselves for long in these lands"

"How do you propose to do that," Naxos repeated his question, his hand a tight fist rapping on the table.

"I don't propose to do that." Eskkar leaned back with a smile. "I propose that you do it, King Naxos."

Naxos's mouth fell open. For a moment, he remained speechless.

"A daring plan indeed." Jarud laughed. "Why doesn't that surprise me?"

"Akkad always has a plan to protect itself." Naxos regained his composure. "They care nothing about the rest of us."

"If I may?" Trella gazed at Naxos for a moment. "I was born and raised in Sumeria. Do you think I wish my people to live as slaves under the Elamites?"

"Let me finish," Eskkar went on. "The enemy will capture and occupy Sumer. They must do that to establish and protect their supply line. It is far easier for them to move men and supplies along the coast. They will offer treaties and guarantees to all the other cities that do not resist them. Once their armies are in place, they will ignore their promises. Remember, they do not come here to live in peace with us. They intend to rule over us as masters. They also want gold, food, horses, everything that a conquering army demands, and in vast quantities. All our people will be reduced to slaves, working for their new masters."

He turned from Naxos to Gemama. "So even if you surrender, if you offer peace to the Elamites, they will remove you from power. At best, you may be permitted to live, or even to rule as their figurehead for a time, until they no longer need you. But the power of Sumer will be forever crushed and its people enslaved. Thousands of Elamites and their followers will soon occupy the city and its surrounding farms. Alone, your choice is simple – to fight, or surrender."

Eskkar shifted his gaze back to Naxos. "So it is up to you, King Naxos. If you do not choose to fight the Elamites, the Land Between the Rivers is lost. Akkad will fight to the end, but there can be no victory unless the three of us work together."

"And if I chose to make peace with them, instead of fighting your battles?"

Even Esskar understood Naxos's clenched jaw. The man could scarcely keep his anger in check.

"You must do what is best for yourself and your city, King Naxos." Trella spoke quickly, before Esskar could reply to the taunt. "But if you submit to them, consider what role you would play in their plans. For a time, you and Isin's soldiers would be used to attack the other cities, your men always in the forefront. When your numbers were reduced, they would simply absorb your remaining soldiers into their armies, scattering them among many units and places. That is the way the Elamite army continues to grow. At that time, you would no longer be needed. At best, you might find a place in their army, commanding other soldiers recruited from places they have conquered. But you would never command men from Isin again, and there would be no future for you in their rule, except as a simple soldier. If that is acceptable to you, then you should consider making contact with the Elamites."

"I believe we already have." Kuara's words turned every head, including Naxos's. "I did not tell you before this, Naxos, but I met with a trader claiming to speak for the Elamites only two days ago. He declared that he wished to increase Isin's trade with the cities of the Indus. The terms he mentioned were most favorable, exceedingly so. Even as we spoke, two hundred gold coins were delivered to my steward."

A huge sum, Esskar knew, and far more than necessary for any mutual trading venture.

"And you did not see fit to tell me of this?" Naxos's face reddened at this unexpected news from his chief advisor.

"The trader suggested that it might be best for me to keep this between the two of us, for now. Of course, once I had taken his gold, he would assume I was in his debt. Not long after, the demands would have begun. Since I already knew we were to visit Akkad, and I suspected we would hear something like this, I decided to wait. Until now."

"Do not let your anger cloud your thoughts, King Naxos." Trella's soothing voice reduced the tension at the table. "This is indeed how the Elamites work, sowing confusion and distrust among their enemies long before they arrive with their armies."

The table grew silent. Eskkar followed Trella's lead, and resisted the urge to speak. These men needed time to digest what they'd heard. To try and rush them into a decision would only fail.

Jarud broke the silence. "I have wives and children in Sumer, as well as many kin. I would not see them live as slaves, nor would I take them and flee to safety without a fight."

Trella nodded agreement. "There is, after all, no place in the Land Between the Rivers to go. To escape, at least for a time, would mean trusting your lives to strangers and in distant lands. Meanwhile, the Elamites will believe you have fled with all your fortune, so they will offer a bounty to track you down."

"If there is a way to resist," Jarud thumped his fist on the table, "then I say fight."

Eskkar caught the slight movement of Trella's finger that meant she wanted him to answer. "There is a way to defeat them. The risk will be great. But we will need King Naxos to help us."

Everyone's eyes went to the King of Isin. But before Naxos could speak, Kuara cleared his throat. "Like Jarud, I would not flee my home, nor leave my family and friends behind to face a conquering army. And I have fought too many fights against Isin's enemies to hand her over to a strange overlord." He glanced at Naxos. "But I too, must see a way to victory."

This time no one looked toward Naxos. His Chief Advisor had said his piece. Now the final decision belonged to Naxos.

"I will not yield my city to anyone. But I will not fight the battles of others, not unless I see a way to win."

"You would not be alone," Trella said. "The men of Akkad and Sumer, and all the other cities, will stand beside you. That is Akkad's promise." She glanced at Eskkar.

"I give you my word, Naxos" Eskkar said, "as one warrior to another. I give it to all of you, to fight to defend your cities as fiercely as my own. I cannot promise that we will be victorious, but I believe we have a chance to win. Remember, we do not need to destroy the armies of Elam, just drive them off with such fierceness that they never dare invade our lands again."

Before Naxos could reply, Jarud spoke. "Akkad has kept its promises to Sumer for more than nine years. Not only that, but they have helped us when we needed it. So if Eskkar and Lady Trella now say it is time to fight, then that is good enough for me." Jarud turned to his friend. "Are we agreed, Gemama?"

The King of Sumer also glanced around the table, but his gaze came to rest on Yavtar, still sitting away from the others, almost by himself. "You are in favor of this, old friend? That we put our trust in Akkad?"

Yavtar picked up his empty cup and twirled it between his fingers. "Much of the information on the Elamites has come through my agents and traders. We have sent many boats and caravans into the eastern lands. Eskkar speaks the truth about the Elamites' plans. They come to conquer and enslave." He set the cup down. "So I make the same promise as King Eskkar. I will stand by you, old friend, to the end."

Gemama turned toward Naxos for the first time. "Then Jarud and I will fight with Akkad."

Eskkar understood how hard that decision must have been for the soft merchant turned king. Soldiers, even after they became kings or advisors, understood that there always came a time when you had to fight to keep what you had built. Those who did not grow up with a sword in their hand had to be even braver to go to war.

"Then we will be at your side, King Gemama." Trella's voice held an intensity that turned every eye back to her. "Now it is up to you, King Naxos."

Naxos met her gaze. "I will not bend my knee to any foreign ruler, not as long as I can fight. If there is a way to drive them off, if Sumer and Akkad are united, then Isin will stand with you."

Eskkar realized that Naxos had at last grasped the full situation. The last nine years of peace had changed the power structure in the Land Between the Rivers. Prosperity, at least for a time, had dimmed the glory of war and conquest. If Naxos did not join them, sooner or later, Akkad and Sumer would deal with him. And Naxos understood that, if it came to a choice, the other cities would choose Akkad, whose intentions had proved peaceful, over Isin.

"Then we are agreed." Eskkar leaned back in his chair. He felt as if a vast weight had lifted from his shoulders. "Now, let me show you how we can defeat these invaders and drive them back across the mountains."

3

Later that evening, well after the moon had risen, Annok-sur set in motion the last step of her plan to confound and confuse the Elamites. She had waited at the Compound until King Eskkar and Trella rode back from their meeting at Yavtar's farm. As soon as Eskkar helped his wife dismount from her spirited horse, Annok-sur needed only a few whispered words from Trella to confirm the success of the day's meeting at the farmhouse.

"Is everything ready?" After the long day of tense negotiations, Trella's weariness sounded in her voice, though only Annok-sur knew her well enough to notice.

"Yes, Trella. Everything is in place."

They hugged for a brief moment, then Annok-sur crossed the courtyard and stepped out into the lane. Two Hawk Clan guards waited to escort her. She set out for her destination, with one guard walking ahead and the other behind.

At the time when the hard-working men and women of the city prepared for sleep, Annok-sur and her guards passed through the city's narrow lanes. The few people who glimpsed the shadowy figures shrank aside, more apprehensive of Annok-sur's presence than that of the formidable looking guards. The sentinels at Akkad's northern gate passed them through without a word, and the trio headed for the farm almost two miles away.

The half-moon made the night walk pleasant enough, illuminating the few places where the ground might prove difficult. Annok-sur had traversed the path many more times than her escorts. Her sturdy legs had no trouble keeping pace with the longer strides of the soldiers.

They arrived at the small farmhold close to midnight, but more than enough night remained for her purpose. Some things were best done while the city slept, and far from the eyes and ears of others.

Three mud-brick huts comprised the homestead. All the dwellings needed repair, and daylight would reveal the extent of the neglect. Only one showed a glimmer of light through a narrow doorway as they approached. Annok-sur knew the others would be waiting for her inside. She spoke to her guards. They halted fifty paces from the farmhouse, and Annok-sur finished her journey alone.

She eased her lean body through the narrow doorway and sat down on an old stool with its shaky legs, behind a wobbly plank table. Annok-sur barely noticed the odor that permeated the room, though newcomers had a tendency to gag the first time they entered the chamber. Over the years, she had grown accustomed to the rank smell of dried blood, sweat, piss, and excrement that had seeped into and now lingered in the mud walls and dirt floor, despite an occasional sweeping or bucket of water.

A glowing fire pot on the opposite side of the table gave off its own vapors that ascended to the roof's sagging wooden scantlings, covered with mud. A jagged hole overhead provided the room's only ventilation, aside from the door, but plenty of smoke from the fire never seemed to find its way out.

Two candles also burned, an unknown luxury for most households, but somehow provided little light, as if the flickering flames themselves recoiled from the dank room and its foul air. A solitary but stout pole in the center of the room helped support the weight of the roof. It also had other, darker purposes.

In the light of day, the single room hut didn't appear so sinister. But once the sun went down, the chamber became a place of pain and terror, a secret place where Annok-sur questioned Akkad's most dangerous enemies. And learned, in time, their secrets.

Tonight the half-moon had risen late, and only now touched the highest point in the sky. It was time to begin.

Annok-sur stared at the man sitting less than three paces away, a dirty grain sack covering his head. "Is he conscious yet?"

Years ago, the torturers had nailed a small bench to the center pole. Zahara sat on its blood encrusted surface, his hands bound behind the pole and his spread ankles fastened to the wide legs of the bench. Aside from the hood, Zahara was naked.

"He's coming around." Wakannh's booming voice filled the chamber. The hood jerked and twitched, reacting to Wakannh's words. He reached over and yanked off the covering, then tossed it on the table.

Zahara's eyes stared blankly for a moment, then widened in horror as he took in his surroundings. First he stared at Wakannh, Akkad's Captain of the Guard. When his gaze rested on Annok-sur, his mouth fell open and he gasped, seemingly unable to catch his breath.

The door behind her opened and a man named Rue-el, Wakannh's second in command, entered. Using a rag to protect his hand, he carried a dented copper bowl brimming with glowing embers, and proceeded to dump them into the fire pot. The flames crackled, welcoming the additional fuel, and another burst of smoke rushed upwards, to swirl around over their heads.

Annok-sur waited until the prisoner grasped the extent of his situation. "It's good that you understand your position, Zahara. You're going to talk to me. And if you don't tell me the truth, if you don't tell me everything I want to know, you're going to die, slowly and painfully. I can see to it that you linger in agony for several days. But if you speak truthfully," she hesitated for several moments, to stretch out the suspense, "you may yet be allowed to live. The choice is yours, so make it carefully."

"But I've done nothing! Nothing!" Zahara glanced down, as if seeing his widespread legs for the first time. The ropes held him fast, his genitals completely exposed. "My grandfather is Noble Rebba. He will tell you. Whatever you think I did, it's not true!"

Annok-sur sighed, and shifted to a more comfortable position on the stool. She kept her voice low and pleasant. "Do you think we don't know that you've spied on Akkad for the Elamites for over a year? That you've made two trips through the mountains, to report to your masters in Elam? And that you've sent messengers to them on nearly every caravan that departs to the east? Did you think we didn't know what you were doing? Are you going to say that you are not a spy?"

Zahara gaped at the revelations, no doubt wondering exactly what and how much Annok-sur knew. "I . . . I don't know what to say. I would never spy on Akkad. I'm loyal to the king. Ask my grandfather. I'm a member of the Noble Families. Ask anyone . . ."

"The last two men who sat on that bench swore that they took your orders, that you gave them information for a man named Sacarra, who lives in the village of Zanbil, just beyond the Zagros Mountains.

One of them died, unfortunately. But not before he revealed your name. The other spoke to you only two days ago, didn't he? But I haven't all night to waste on you, Zahara. You can start by giving me the names of those who have carried messages for you. Now."

"I . . . I don't know what it . . . what you want. Please believe me. I'm loyal to King Eskkar."

Annok-sur glanced toward the Captain of the Guard.

"I think our guest needs encouragement," Wakannh said. "Rue-el, warm him up a little."

"Yes, Captain." From the wall behind him, Rue-el selected a long bronze rod and thrust it into the fire pot. Wood strips bound with cord formed a crude handle, to protect the holder's hand from the heat the bronze absorbed from the fire. He stood there, twisting the rod around and stirring the embers, but always keeping the tip in the hottest part of the fire. The smell of heated metal joined the other vapors that wafted through the chamber. Zahara's chest rose and fell.

Annok-sur noted the prisoner's agitation. By now fear, and the room's vapors, would be making it hard for him to breathe.

Zahara's eyes darted from one to the other, then back to the fire. "You must believe me! You're making a mistake. Talk to Noble Rebba! He'll tell you who I am."

"It's warm enough." Wakannh's impatience sounded in his voice. "Give him a taste."

Rue-el snorted at his commander's eagerness. But he withdrew the rod. He only had to turn and take a single step to slap the heated tip against the inside of the Zahara's left thigh.

Zahara had no time to protest or prepare. His scream filled the room, as he jerked and tried to shrink his leg away from the heated metal, his back arching up and away from the pole. Rue-el held the rod fast, for as long as a man might count to three.

When he removed it, an angry welt about the length of a man's small finger had already blossomed on the prisoner's leg. Zahara's cry of agony slowly eased into a drawn out and gasping moan, as he slumped back onto the bench. Wide-eyed, he stared at the source of pain exuding from his leg.

The smell of burning flesh mixed with Zahara's urine wafted through the room.

"It'll be better when it's hotter." Rue-el shoved the rod back into the fire, and wiped his hand on his tunic.

"That pain, what you just felt, is only a start." Annok-sur leaned forward. "The bronze was scarcely warm. We have all night, if necessary, and the rod grows hotter the longer it lingers in the flames. When the rod is held against your prick, you'll learn the real meaning of pain."

Breathing hard, Zahara managed to catch his breath. Sweat covered his face and dripped down onto his chest.

"So, what are the names of your men?" Annok-sur waited for a response. When none came, she nodded to Rue-el.

"No! By the gods, no!"

Rue-el gave the rod one last poke in the flames, then rapped the bronze against the edge of the bowl, to shake off the ashes. With a grin, he turned back to the prisoner. This time Rue-el chose the right leg.

Zahara's screams filled the room, as his body contorted, trying to shrink itself away from the glowing bronze. But the ropes around his ankles held firm, and all he could manage was to twitch his legs. When Rue-el lifted the tip away, Zahara slumped against his bonds, tears already merging with the sweat from his brow. The odor of burning flesh grew stronger, even as it joined the other vapors within the closed and dank room.

Zahara's eyes fixed on Rue-el, as he returned the rod to the coals, moving it around to keep it heating evenly.

"Almost hot enough." Rue-el's cheerful voice sounded out of place in the torture chamber. "A few more moments should do it."

"What are their names . . . look at me, Zahara!" Annok-sur's voice demanded obedience. "Tell me their names!"

"Please, don't burn me again!" His hoarse voice struggled with the words, and his legs twitched from the pain. "I'll tell you whatever you want to know." Gasping, Zahara gave up the men's names. Even those few words exhausted him, and he gulped air into his chest.

"That's good, Zahara, that's good." Annok-sur used her most soothing voice. "So, Zahara, I want you to tell me everything you've told the Elamites. You've been their most important and reliable source of information, someone very close to Akkad's Council of advisors. Now you will tell me all you know about them, everything you've revealed. Everything. Since the first day they approached you. If you do that, you may keep your life. But you must not lie to me. We already know much more than you think. If you leave anything out, if I think you're holding back anything." She gave the signal to Rue-el.

"Where should I place it this time?" He held the rod close to the prisoner's cheek, forcing him to lean back against the pole to escape the heat. "On his face, or on his balls?" With a quick movement, he waved the glowing bronze just above Zahara's shrunken member.

"NO!" Zahara thrashed against his bonds, his ankles already bloody from the friction of the ropes. "Please, I'll tell you what you want to know! Anything. Anything."

"Good. Very good. Would you like some water? You must be thirsty by now."

A pitcher of fresh water from the farm's well rested on the table, next to a pair of battered cups. These interrogations often lasted long into the night, and Annok-sur saw no reason for being thirsty.

"Yes, please! Water, by the gods! Please."

Annok-sur filled a cup to the brim with water, then rose and carried it to Zahara. She touched his cheek gently, almost intimately, before she held the cup to his lips. After three swallows, she took the cup away. "Not too much, Zahara, not until you've told us what we want to know. You have much to reveal, don't you? And remember, the rod is still in the fire, and now it is red hot. Its next touch will give you more pain than you've ever known."

"Please . . . no more . . .please!"

"We'll see." Annok-sur returned to her stool. She doubted she would need Rue-el's touch again, certainly not more than once. In the last fifteen years, Annok-sur had questioned many of Akkad's enemies in this room, as well as the usual lot of murderers and thieves. She had learned how to gauge a person's tolerance to pain, and how much pain a man, and the occasional woman, could take. Only a few had the good fortune to escape into an early death before revealing what their inquisitor wanted to know.

She'd watched many a man squirm and shrink under the torture. Some men were strong, others weak. Zahara's noble upbringing and easy wealth made him weaker than most. He lacked not only the strength of character to resist, but also the physical stamina. Annok-sur had no doubts about his coming conversion, no matter how reluctant.

He had two wives and several children. They, too, had much to lose if Zahara's betrayal was revealed. His family would be stripped of all their goods and banished from the City. That threat had worked equally well against those Akkadians who'd traded information for Elam's gold. Their families very way of life would depend on their remaining loyal. Long before dawn arrived, Zahara would turn to her side and become one of her most loyal spies.

Zahara would soon say and do exactly as she wanted. Starting tomorrow, he would be a spy for Akkad, telling the Elamites only what the rulers of the City wanted them to learn.

To make sure of his complete conversion, she would remind Zahara that Elam had no further use for failed spies, and that Elam's torturers were considered even more brutal than Akkad's.

"Now, let's talk. Shall we begin with the first time you were approached and asked to provide information for Elam?" She smiled pleasantly at her guest.

Question followed question, and only once more did Rue-el need to prompt his victim's memory.

At last Annok-sur leaned back, satisfied. Over the last two years, she and her agents had uncovered all of the Elamite spies working for Zahara. One by one, she already had twisted all of them to her side. Fortunately, an offer of even more gold to reveal what they knew often sufficed to make them collaborate.

The threat of returning to this chamber helped keep them loyal, of course. They knew that Annok-sur could find them anywhere within the Land Between the Rivers. And should they attempt to flee to Elam, they could expect nothing more than a quick death. Faced with those choices, they had cooperated readily enough.

Those who resisted, or she deemed untrustworthy, had died screaming on the same bench now occupied by Zahara. But only after they revealed every secret and gave up every name they wished to hide.

Today, the final stage of the campaign of misdirection and lies against the Elamites had begun. And so Wakannh and his men had swept up Zahara, as he left his favorite ale house. A member of one of Akkad's Noble Families, he knew much about what was discussed in the ruling council chamber. His occupation as a trader gave him access to many of Akkad's training camps and made him the perfect, well-placed spy for the Elamites. But now he would be forced to work for Akkad.

'With the threat of war only months away, the Elamite King and his war leaders had come to trust what information his spies had collected. After all, everything they learned had proven true. From today, however, all that would change. Those planning the invasion would receive only that information Trella wished them to know.

In a few days, Zahara would dispatch another courier to Elam, detailing the open distrust and suspicion between Akkad, Sumer and Isin, along with the latest preparations for the anticipated siege. Even more intriguing would be the description of Eskkar's plan to abandon Akkad in the event of an invasion and flee to the north, taking all his gold and most trusted retainers and soldiers with him.

By the time King Shirudukh of Elam learned he'd been duped, he would have committed his forces, his armies would be in the field, and it would be too late.

4

The morning after Trella and Eskkar met with the kings of Isin and Sumer, another meeting took place, this one in the upper room of the Compound. There private matters could be discussed without worrying about anyone overhearing.

"Welcome, Alcinor." Trella motioned their visitor to a seat across the table. "We didn't expect you back so soon."

Tall and thin, with hunched shoulders that emphasized a narrow face beneath a serious brow, Alcinor did not resemble someone raised in a wealthy family. He looked more like some over-worked apprentice, one who rarely received enough to eat. Nevertheless, in his twenty-eight seasons, the oldest son of Noble Corio had already faced danger once before, when he had traveled with Eskkar's army and participated in the Battle of Isin.

"Always good to see you." Eskkar smiled as he took his seat, facing their visitor.

Trella noted the warmth of Eskkar's greeting. Her husband had not smiled much in the last few days, but a special bond existed between Eskkar and Alcinor. The two men had fought together, after a fashion, during the conflict.

Not that Alcinor had ever swung a sword at anyone in anger. His weapon at the Battle of Isin had been a shovel, or rather, hundreds of them. Alcinor's threat to flood the city of Isin had forced King Naxos out of the battle, and out of the war.

And Eskkar, Trella knew, placed great value on such bonds. Any man, he'd often said, who fought at your side deserves to be treated as a friend.

Alcinor bowed as he sat. "Lady Trella, Lord Eskkar, it is good to be back in Akkad."

"You must be weary after your long journey," Trella said. "You could have waited until tomorrow to see us."

Alcinor's face turned somber. "No, I dared not waste a moment."
He took a deep breath. "I must report what I discovered in the
Jkarian Pass."

Two months ago, Trella had dispatched the young man to the
Jkarian Pass, the northern passage to the lands of the Indus.
According to her spies, the Elamites planned to send a major cavalry
force through the old trade route, to harry Akkad's northern borders
and cut supply lines to the besieged city. Such havoc would be
devastating to the farms and small villages in that region, not to
mention Eskkar's plan to defend the city.

She had tasked Alcinor with finding a defensible place where a
few men might hold back the coming invaders, at least until Eskkar
could free up enough soldiers to deal with them. From the signs of
unease on his face, Trella knew he had failed.

Eskkar, too, recognized Alcinor's expression, and his smile faded.
"You did not find a suitable site?"

"No, my Lord." Alcinor took a deep breath. "I traveled the length
of the pass, nearly all the way through the mountains, almost to the
lands of the Indus. I mapped the route, and identified several places
where the Pass might be defended. I even retraced my steps several
times, just to be certain. But each defensible position I found would
require a large force of men. I calculated it would take at least two or
three thousand soldiers."

Trella watched her husband's shoulders slump. For almost a year,
a key component of Eskkar's plan to stop the Elamite invasion
depended on holding the Jkarian Pass with a small force. Now
Alcinor was saying it couldn't be done.

She knew her husband did not have an extra two thousand men, let
alone three thousand. Not to mention the vast amount of supplies
needed to support such an army at that distance from the City, or the
fact that the Elamites would be sending at least five or six thousand
men through the Pass. Every man Akkad could raise and outfit
would be needed elsewhere to repel the main invasion.

Eskkar broke the silence. "I suppose we'll have to find the men
somewhere."

Trella, however, had detected something else in Alcinor's
demeanor. She leaned forward, her gaze fixed on her visitor. "What
else did you find, Alcinor?"

Alcinor hesitated. "There is one place . . . I found one place where it might be possible to close the pass. Permanently."

Aware of the young man's nervousness, Trella leaned closer even as she allowed herself a glimmer of hope. "And how would you do that, Master Engineer?"

She used the formal and recently invented title for their guest. In the almost ten years that had passed since the Battle of Isin, Alcinor had become the most famous and skilled of all the builders in Akkad. He'd even surpassed his father, Corio, who had built the great wall that saved the City – it was still a village back then – from the first barbarian invasion by the Alur Meriki.

Both father and his apprentice son had learned much about the construction of large and complicated structures from that enterprise. Afterwards, Alcinor helped design and build Akkad's newest walls, gates, towers, and fortifications. In so doing, he showed such skill that he soon earned an even greater accolade than any his father ever received.

In the ensuing years, Akkad's other builders and master craftsmen used a new title to describe him – Engineer. The word came to mean someone who understood not only how to build structures, but who also delved into the study of all materials, and understood how they worked together.

Over the years, Trella had observed with interest as Alcinor developed more efficient ways to utilize wood, stone, and even the omnipresent mud bricks. He had already discovered several new techniques that permitted the building of higher and stronger structures, and had created standards of measurements now used by almost all the builders in the land. Even more important, Alcinor possessed a special skill that allowed him to imagine something new, and transform that mental picture into a physical reality.

Alcinor lifted his eyes, and put aside any misgivings. "Rather than waste men trying to defend the Jkarian Pass, I think we should close it."

Eskkar's mouth opened in surprise, and even Trella seemed at a loss for words.

After Alcinor's words were spoken, his voice grew more confident. "There is a particular place, just short of the highest point on the western slope, where I believe I can bring down enough of the surrounding cliffs, part of the mountain, really, to close the Pass once and for all."

Eskkar leaned forward with interest. "What do you mean by close it? A rock slide won't stop an army for long. With so many men and horses, they could soon clear any blockage."

"If I can bring down the cliff, it will be much more than a mere landslide. The Jkarian Pass will be choked with large chunks of the mountain itself. No horse, cart, or wagon could climb over such an obstacle. Men with the proper tools and supply animals might be able to clear the debris, but it would take months, perhaps half a year. An army on the move would have none of those things. Of course I will need to return, to study the site more closely, confirm my estimates, and make sure there is not any way to get around the obstacle."

"And you believe you can seal the Pass long enough to halt the Elamites?" Trella asked the question, but her husband surprised her by answering it.

"When young Master Builder Alcinor claimed he could destroy an entire city, I didn't really think it could be done, not until I saw the channel dug and the river's water poised to flow. So now, if he says he can move a mountain to close the Pass, I believe him."

"Then Akkad's finest Engineer," Trella said, "needs only to tell us what he requires to accomplish this feat, and we will supply it."

Alcinor took a deep breath. "It won't be easy. I'll need plenty of men, skilled stone workers. The work will be dangerous, and it is likely that some will be injured or die. Also, I will need a large number of the great logs from the northern steppes. I would have to dispatch Jahiri, my senior apprentice, at once, to purchase exactly what we require, then float the logs down the Tigris. And I must have a large force of laborers and pack animals to transport everything back to the Pass."

"And soldiers to guard you and your equipment," Eskkar said. "Well, they can help carry your supplies."

"All this will cost a great deal," Alcinor said.

"Whatever it costs," Trella answered, "will be far less than what it takes to feed and equip three thousand men in the field. You will have whatever is necessary."

"Then I'll dispatch Jahiri to the north as soon as possible. He will need several boats, plenty of gold, and an escort to protect both him and the logs."

"I can have soldiers ready for you within a few days." Eskkar's voice now sounded confident, the way it always did at the prospect of action. "Commander Draelin is eager for a new assignment, and he has dealt with the northern tribesmen before. Yavtar can provide however many fighting boats and transport vessels you need."

"How much gold will you require?" Trella knew the practical details of the operation would fall on her and her clerks.

Alcinor hesitated. "I'm not sure. The usual time of year to purchase the great logs has passed. The tribesmen may want more than their customary demands."

None of the trees, mostly date palm and willows, that grew in the Land Between the Rivers, possessed the size and strength of timber taken from the northern lands. Nor did the local trees grow as straight and tall as the northern oaks. Akkad's gates were constructed from such timber floated down the Tigris, as were the beams that supported the upper chamber of Eskkar's house where the three now sat.

"You will have more than enough." Trella turned to her husband. "One of my clerks can carry the gold and go with Jahiri. He will need to be protected and guarded as well."

"Draelin will see to it," Eskkar said.

"Then as soon as you can provide an escort," Alcinor said, "I must return to the Jkarian Pass. I'll stay five or six days at the site, to study the cliffs. As soon as I am certain, one way or the other, I'll come back."

Trella reached out and touched Alcinor's arm. "This is important, Alcinor, even more than you know. Make sure you have everything you require. The Elamites must not be allowed through the Jkarian Pass. We will be stretched thin here at Akkad, and need every soldier we can find."

Eskkar laughed. "When he built the ditch at Isin, I complained about all the tools and men he demanded. Now, if Alcinor says he can move a mountain to block our enemies, then I believe he will do it. Trella and I will ensure you have everything you demand."

"I'll use all my skills to make certain the mountain comes down."

"And no one must know what you intend," Trella cautioned. "Your plan must remain a secret for as long as possible."

"Only Jahiri knows, and Corio, my father."

Trella nodded in satisfaction. "No man has ever moved a mountain before," she said. "But if anyone can do it, it will be Akkad's first and foremost Engineer."

5

The Palace of Grand Commander Chaiyanar, in the city of Sushan . . .

General Jedidia paced back and forth in the narrow confines of the Palace's anteroom. Only a single window provided an occasional breeze, which did little to dispel the stifling heat. He felt the sweat dripping from his face and armpits, adding to the odor of men in close quarters. Not a pitcher of water, no platter of dates, not even cloths to wipe away the perspiration. Nevertheless, neither Jedidia nor the chamber's other four occupants dared to complain, as they awaited the summons from King Shirudukh to attend his presence.

Jedidia had arrived at well before the requested time of midday, but as usual, King Shirudukh preferred to keep his visitors waiting. Noon had come and gone, and now, according to the sun, the middle of the afternoon would soon be upon them.

Jedidia recognized the deliberate insult. King Shirudukh knew the interminable waiting would grate upon the nerves of his generals, and increase any tendency they might have to say something foolish. Though General Jedidia understood the tactic, he still hated its effectiveness.

King Shirudukh, ruler of the Land of Elam and all its subjects, had arrived in Sushan ten days ago. Naturally he had taken over the quarters of Grand Commander Chaiyanar, who ruled the city as Shirudukh's satrap. Chaiyanar's waiting room, such as it was, contained no chairs, not even an un-cushioned bench or two.

Grand Commander Chaiyanar had no concern for either the comfort or patience of his guests, no matter who they might be or how long they had to wait. Now visitors to the King had to suffer in the same fashion as any of Sushan's merchants appealing for some favor, no matter how distinguished they might be.

General Jedidia, tall and dark, resembled many of his battle hardened soldiers, most of whom came from Elam's northern lands. A hook nose jutted arrogantly from beneath deep set brown eyes, and black hair tinged with gray half-concealed a wide brow. A thick beard covered his chin and reached well onto his muscular chest.

A fighting man, Jedidia had earned the respect of the men he commanded even as he rose to the rank of general. About to enter his thirty-eighth season, he cared little for the soft luxuries both King Shirudukh and Grand Commander Chaiyanar favored. Jedidia had known more than his share of pain and discomfort over the years.

Today, however, Jedidia felt his temper rising. Four years ago, in a battle near the Indus River, his horse had taken a wound. Mad with pain, the animal had thrown its rider. Jedidia's left knee had struck a rock when he tumbled to the earth. Since that day, the knee often gave him trouble, especially when he had to remain on his feet for long periods. His prolonged standing had aggravated the injury, and soon Jedidia would face the humiliating need to ask for a chair.

One of the other occupants, Lord Modran, had no such difficulty. Lean and wiry, the commanding general of the largest contingent of Elamite's forces appeared unaffected by King Shirudukh's decision to keep two of his senior generals waiting. As if to annoy Jedidia even more, Modran had scarcely moved since they first entered the chamber.

Jedidia hated Modran with a fierce intensity that probably matched Modran's feelings toward Jedidia. Both men sought the prestige and power that came with leading the majority of soldiers under the King. Jedidia knew that he was far more capable than Modran, but for years Modran had remained Shirudukh's favorite, and he commanded nearly twenty thousand soldiers spread across the heart of Elam.

Grand Commander Chaiyanar, the least experienced of King Shirudukh's three generals, already attended on the King. Since this palace in Sushan belonged, of course under the King's authority, to Chaiyanar, Shirudukh had graciously permitted the Grand Commander to join him ahead of the others. No doubt Chaiyanar and the King had dined well, lounging on their respective couches, and enjoying the ministrations of the countless young slave girls who accompanied King Shirudukh wherever he traveled.

Jedidia gave scarcely a thought to the three other men also summoned to today's audience. Soft city dwellers, they, too, showed signs of discomfort. Traders and merchants, they formed part of the Council that helped advise the King on matters of trade and policy. Though men of wealth, Jedidia considered them insignificant minions with no power or authority. Likely neither Shirudukh nor Chaiyanar ever bothered to heed their words. Jedidia doubted if any of them knew how to hold a sword.

The oldest, Shesh-kala, had well over fifty seasons. He owned most of the large tracts of fertile land that surrounded the city of Sushan. Though he might be a man of enormous wealth, he clearly suffered from a bad back. He clutched the arm of the youngest advisor, a trader named Aram-Kitchu, still a man in the prime of life.

The third man, Dajii, also traded up and down the River Karum, but he specialized in slaves, not goods. In fact, Dajii and his agents would be accompanying the invasion armies into the Land Between the Rivers, to begin the process of breaking and transporting vast numbers of new slaves into the lands of Elam.

The door to the chamber opened, and a messenger bowed to those waiting. "King Shirudukh regrets keeping you waiting. He is ready to receive you now. Please follow me."

Jedidia forced a smile to his lips, clenching his teeth against the growing pain in his knee and refusing to show the slightest sign of weakness or discomfort. Any such display would soon have Modran and Chaiyanar whispering in the King's ear that General Jedidia was unwell, perhaps not fit for the coming campaign.

Everyone in the room had straightened up when the door opened. Lord Modran moved first, falling in behind the messenger, and Jedidia followed. The three advisors, as befitting their lack of station, trailed the two generals.

The little procession didn't have far to travel. Down a long corridor, around a corner, then through a doorway guarded by two soldiers and into the Palace's main chamber. A raised dais at the far end normally held the throne-like chair that Chaiyanar preferred. Today that platform stood empty. Just in front, however, three couches of different sizes rested, all occupied. The largest held King

Shirudukh. Grand Commander Chaiyanar reclined on the second, and another man sat upright on the third.

Jedidia needed a moment to recall the third man's name – Meweldi – one of Shirudukh's High Commanders. Jedidia glance took in the King's personal guards, who lined the walls. Two stood behind Shirudukh's couch, their hard eyes examining the latest arrivals. Jedidia knew they would kill anyone, even a general, who showed the slightest sign of hostility. And the soldiers lining the walls would be only a step behind them.

Jedidia counted twelve guards, and every one a member of the Immortals. An elite force of battle-tested veterans who fought only for King Shirudukh, the Immortals performed the dual role of personal household guards to the King, and the primary instrument of his power. They numbered exactly five thousand, and were the best and most loyal fighters in Elam.

By firm custom, whenever one Immortal was killed, seriously wounded or fell ill, he was immediately replaced with a new recruit, thus maintaining the number and cohesion of the Five Thousand. Every soldier considered it an honor to enter the Immortal's ranks.

"Ah, Lord Modran, General Jedidia! The time for our final preparations has come, and your presence is most welcome." Shirudukh didn't waste his breath on greeting his advisors.

Jedidia bowed low, and held himself in that position until Lord Modran straightened up. Both men uttered the usual flattering words that kept the King in a pleasant mood. But Jedidia had already noticed the hint of a smile on Grand Commander Chaiyanar's face. Something was in the wind, something that greatly pleased Chaiyanar. With a sinking feeling in his chest, Jedidia guessed that bad news was coming.

"My three favorite and loyal generals," Shirudukh went on, "the last decisions on troops and dispositions have been made. Commander Meweldi will provide the information."

Meweldi stood and waved his hand toward the guards. Two of them picked up a table and carried it to the center of the room. A large map rested atop its surface.

"The invasion of the Land Between the Rivers will begin in a few months," Meweldi began. "Grand Commander Chaiyanar will take fifteen thousand men and advance along the coast of the Great Sea, to invest and capture the city of Sumer from the south. He will be supported by every ship that can transport a cargo."

"It will be a great honor to capture the city of Sumer, and present it as a gift to My King." Chaiyanar's oily words garnered a smile from Shirudukh.

Jedidia noted that Meweldi showed no irritation at the interruption. Chaiyanar clearly remained in good standing with the King.

"At the same time, Lord Modran will lead a mixed force of thirty thousand men through the Dellen Pass, to capture the city of Akkad, where we expect the most resistance. And so we will hurl our largest army and finest troops at its walls. Two thousand Immortals will be among that force."

"A great honor, my King." Modran's words sounded even more simpering that Chaiyanar's.

"Meanwhile, General Jedidia will take a large cavalry force, at least six thousand men, through the Jkarian Pass, to cut Akkad's food supply. Once that is accomplished, General Jedidia will swing to the south and provide whatever support is needed to Lord Modran and his siege of Akkad."

The words came like a blow, and Jedidia struggled to keep his astonishment and anger under control. "My King, if I may speak, I have raised, equipped, and trained nearly fifteen thousand men. The lands north of Akkad are mostly barren and . . ."

"Most of your infantry and siege workers will be transferred to Lord Modran, General Jedidia," Meweldi cut in. "Some will be assigned to Grand Commander Chaiyanar. You will not need them once you leave the Jkarian Pass, since there are no cities or villages there capable of serious resistance. Our plan," Meweldi turned slightly and bowed to King Shirudukh, "the King's plan, is to overwhelm Sumer and Akkad with irresistible force, and so force them to collapse as quickly as possible. Once they fall, the remaining cities of Ur, Lagash, and Isin will be only too eager to throw open their gates and welcome our armies."

Jedidia stood there, speechless. Not only were his best fighters being taken from his command, but he would have no chance to capture a jewel worthy of the campaign. The riches of Sumer and Akkad would guarantee enormous wealth to Chaiyanar and Modran, while he, Jedidia, Elam's most capable general, would have to search for any crumbs remaining.

"My King, if I may protest, my soldiers are some of the best in Elam. I would . . ."

"There is no need for concern, General Jedidia," Shirudukh said. "Once Sumer and Akkad fall, there will be plenty of opportunity to demonstrate your leadership. And there are many other cities in the Land Between the Rivers that will challenge your skills. You will have many chances to win glory and wealth."

Clenching his jaw, Jedidia fought to retain his composure. The King had made his decision, and would certainly not change his mind. Anything else that Jedidia said now would only undermine his position even more. Modran and Chaiyanar would get the two richest cities to capture and plunder, and Jedidia would get nothing. If he argued or protested, Jedidia might lose more than his soldiers. He took a deep breath.

"My King, it is an honor to serve. I will sweep the northern lands clean of every Akkadian dog."

"Excellent, General Jedidia. You are a great leader, and your men will help speed the fall of our enemies."

Jedidia didn't dare let himself look at Modran or Chaiyanar. Their smug expressions would only infuriate him.

Meweldi glanced at the King, who nodded. "There is still much work required to plan and make the final provisions for our invasion. Our three great generals will need to remain here in Sushan until those plans are complete. Meanwhile, orders will be sent to General Jedidia's northern camp, to begin the movement of his troops to the locations where Lord Modran is assembling his forces."

Meweldi lied, of course. Those orders, signed by the King and delivered by a few hundred Immortals, would have gone north the day Jedidia entered Sushan. Even if he slipped out of the city and tried to return to his army, by the time he arrived, Lord Modran's men would be firmly in command. And, of course, that would be the same as committing suicide. Even with his entire army, he would be no match for the forces of Modran and Chaiyanar, and the King's Immortals.

Jedidia would have to wait his turn. In time, sooner or later, Modran or Chaiyanar would grow too strong, so powerful that either man might present a threat to King Shirudukh. Then the wheel would turn, roles would be reversed, and Jedidia would be used to counterbalance their forces.

The King did indeed know how to manipulate and control his generals.

King Shirudukh smiled pleasantly. "And our mighty armies will be well served by our loyal subjects. My Council of Advisors have their role to play in the invasion as well." He waved his hand toward Meweldi.

"Master Trader Dajii," Meweldi said, "will provide slave masters and guards to accompany Lord Modran and Grand Commander Chaiyanar. His men will ensure that, as captures are made, only the fittest are transported back to Elam. Much of the wealth we take from Sumer and Akkad will consist of slaves, and we will need that wealth brought to Elam as soon as possible."

Jedidia had forgotten about the three advisors, hanging back silently several paces behind he and Modran. Their presence insured that the entire city of Sushan would soon know of Jedidia's loss of status. Many of the friends and supporters Jedidia had worked so hard to cultivate in the last two years would disappear, transferring their efforts to the others.

"And Master Trader Shesh-kala will be responsible for providing all the food the invasion armies will need, enough to get them through the mountains and ensure the capture of Sumer and Akkad. Once our soldiers capture the enemy cities, they will be able to fend for themselves."

Shesh-kala's voice quavered. "It is my pleasure to serve, My King."

"Master Trader Aram-Kitchu," Meweldi went on, "will see that our men have all the supplies and weapons they will need to capture the enemy's cities."

"I am pleased to help our great generals defeat the King's enemies," Aram-Kitchu said. He, too, bowed low.

"Aram-Kitchu has also learned much about our enemy's strengths and weakness. And he has established a network of spies through Sumer, Akkad, and Isin. Most of our information regarding the Akkadians and Sumerians has come through his efforts."

For the first time, Jedidia glanced with interest at the three advisors. He had heard of Aram-Kitchu, but had never met the man.

So this was the man who provided so much detailed information about the enemy.

"Is there anything new that you have learned, Aram-Kitchu?" King Shirudukh showed his respect for the man by addressing him directly. "Is the enemy preparing to resist?"

"My King, the latest reports are somewhat confusing," Aram-Kitchu had a deep voice that seemed out of place in his small stature. "It is almost certain that Akkad has learned of the coming invasion. With so many trade caravans, there are more than enough people who will talk too much. I believe that Akkad most likely will attempt to resist. They are training more soldiers and reinforcing their walls even now."

"You failed to have Eskkar assassinated?" Meweldi made his question sound like a rebuke.

"Yes, Commander, I have been unable to strike him down." Aram-Kitchu's voice admitted his failure. "Twice we have made attempts on his life, and both times they have failed. Nor have we been able to get rid of King Eskkar's wife, the real ruler of Akkad. She spends most of her time within their guarded compound, which we have not been able to enter. But it may not matter. Lately my spies have heard rumors that the barbarian Eskkar may take his gold and flee to the north. He is aware of Elam's might, and knows his city cannot withstand an invasion."

Jedidia had let his attention wander, but he picked up on Aram-Kitchu's statement that the Akkadian King might flee to the north with his personal retainers and wealth. Perhaps there might be an opportunity to seize that treasure.

"But only recently," Aram-Kitchu said, "we've learned that King Naxos of Isin is secretly readying his soldiers to attack Akkad. Naxos has hated Eskkar for many years. Naxos is also trying to secure Sumer's support, but so far they have not committed themselves despite his entreaties. If the barbarian Eskkar abandons his city, King Naxos will assume his rule. I believe he will be much more amenable to our offers of cooperation."

Meweldi frowned at that lack of progress as well. "And the Sumerians? Will they resist?"

"They have not yet decided what course of action they will take. But even if they choose to fight," Aram-Kitchu answered, "their numbers are far too small to withstand Grand Commander Chaiyanar's forces."

"That is so," Chaiyanar spoke for the first time. "Some of my soldiers, skilled in siege craft, accompanied one of Aram-Kitchu's caravans. They verified his assessment and studied Sumer's weak defenses. They declare that the city will fall within a month at most."

Jedidia clenched his jaw again. With fifteen thousand men, that fat fool Chaiyanar would capture Sumer and its wealth with ease, while Jedidia would be chasing after cows and collecting sacks of grain in the north.

"And what do your men say of Akkad's defenses?" Lord Modran's voice held a slight hint of jealousy at Chaiyanar's good fortune.

"Akkad's defenses are far stronger, and they have already withstood one siege," Aram-Kitchu said. "If the barbarian decides to fight, the siege will be a difficult one. But with so many soldiers, Lord Modran, the city can be cut off and starved into submission within a few months. They will have many more mouths to feed than Sumer. But while Akkad is the largest city, it can raise and equip at best five or six thousand men."

Meweldi nodded his agreement. "And what can you tell us . . ."

But King Shirudukh had endured enough talk for the day. "We can speak more of this tomorrow. Tonight, we will celebrate with a fine meal that Commander Chaiyanar has arranged for our generals. And now, I am sure that they have important matters that need their attention."

King Shirudukh rose to his feet, indicating the end of the audience. Everyone bowed low, but the King hadn't quite finished. "Each of you will be expected to crush your enemies quickly and ruthlessly. This campaign must be a short one, and any general or advisor who does not do his utmost to ensure our victory will be punished."

With those chilling words hanging in the air, Shirudukh, accompanied by six of his guards, swept out of the room, while everyone bowed low. Jedidia understood the warning. Even victory might not be enough to assuage the King's judgment. All of them, including Modran and Chaiyanar, would be appraised not only on what they accomplished, but how efficiently they managed their armies in the process. And as Jedidia had just learned, the King's favorite today might be at the greatest risk tomorrow.

6

25 five days later, the City of Sumer . . .

Steratakis strolled through Sumer's lanes, enjoying the cool of evening after a warm day completed by an excellent repast. As he wandered through the marketplace, he nodded to several acquaintances, and even paused to exchange greetings and pleasantries with many he encountered, especially those with whom he did business.

A very popular man, Steratakis enjoyed the good will of almost everyone he saw. From midmorning to dusk, Steratakis had his own stall, where he offered the famous Akkadian sweet cakes, prepared, baked, and covered with honey only two days earlier. They were a luxury good that only the well-off could afford, and to offer them to friends and visitors increased the prestige of any host.

Even the ruler of Sumer, King Gemama, favored the sweets. Each day, a buyer from the Palace purchased ten of the cakes, supposedly for the city's Council of Advisors. However a single glance at King Gemama's portly figure had convinced Steratakis that most of those cakes went directly into the royal stomach.

A fast trading boat carried the precious cakes down river, delivering the sought-after delight that so far none in Sumer had managed to duplicate. The bakers in Akkad claimed it was something in the well water, something unique to the city. Their frustrated counterparts in Sumer and elsewhere grumbled that the secret ingredient was dog piss. People ate them anyway.

Steratakis met the trading boat around midday, and escorted three or four baskets of the delicacy to the marketplace. Since his first day in Sumer, Steratakis had never carried the cakes himself. For the promise of a free cake, any of those laboring at the docks eagerly offered their services for the chance to transport his goods.

Sumer's marketplace, however, changed dramatically after the sun went down. During the day merchants, traders, craftsmen, laborers, and farmers thronged the large area near the docks. At night, a different class of people frequented the stalls and tables. More women offered themselves, either on their own or at the urgings of their always frowning masters.

Wine and ale sellers, loudly praising the quality of their inferior goods, took over the tables reserved for craftsmen. As it grew later in the evening, the prices went down. When the full darkness of night arrived, shadowy figures appeared, blanket-wrapped bundles under their arms, to deal goods likely stolen during the day.

Steratakis seldom kept his stall open past sundown. By then, the eighty or so sweet cakes had vanished, and he'd collected a respectable amount of copper coins. When he first started selling the cakes, he tended to eat the last two or three cakes himself. But after nearly two years, he'd weaned himself of the habit, and now limited himself to only one per day. A necessity, he declared, to maintain the high quality of his goods for his customers.

The trading venture provided a comfortable profit, but the small house Steratakis had purchased cost far more than any trade in sweet cakes could provide. Fortunately, Annok-sur had supplied those coins. In exchange, she had made only a few demands. The dwelling must be in a good neighborhood frequented by other merchants and traders, have a private entrance, and a back door. Other than that, she'd left the choice up to him.

"You may never be contacted," Annok-sur had said. "In any case, you'll stay no longer than two and a half years. Then you will be free to remain in Sumer if that is your choice, or to come home."

Home to a substantial amount of gold, Steratakis reminded himself. Once he returned, his family would be well established, and under the protection of Annok-sur. Meanwhile, his mother and sister prospered as bakers of bread and sweet cakes. The future looked bright indeed. Not that long ago, Steratakis and his family had nearly starved to death.

His father had been killed by soldiers from Larsa in the last war, and only Steratakis, his younger brother and sister, and their mother had managed to escape to Akkad. In their flight, his mother had fallen ill, and her children could do nothing to help her. Hungry, destitute, and with a dying mother, Steratakis had faced the grim choice of selling his little sister to buy food for the rest of his family.

On the very morning that Steratakis planned to bring his sister to the slave market, Annok-sur had arrived with both a healer and a handful of silver coins. Under the ministrations of the healer, Steratakis's mother had recovered, and they soon established a small bakery where she could make her mouth-watering desserts. In exchange, all Annok-sur asked was that Steratakis work for her. For years, that had involved little more than carrying messages from one place to another.

Almost two years ago, she had approached Steratakis with a new assignment. He would move to Sumer under the guise of selling his mother's cakes. In reality, he would wait for a special courier who would bring an important message. But since Steratakis's arrival, no courier had made an appearance, and by now Steratakis doubted if anyone ever would.

Tonight, he had enjoyed a good meal at one of Sumer's better taverns, then took some pleasure with one of the establishment's girls. She'd crouched between his knees, working his rod until he burst inside her mouth, a most relaxing ending to another pleasant day.

His housekeeper waited for his return, guarding the residence and its contents until her master came home. Then she rushed off to her own family.

Yawning, Steratakis barred the door behind her, and settled down for a good night's rest. A most agreeable day, indeed.

Steratakis awoke with a weight crushing his chest, and a hand pressed firmly against his mouth. Terrified, he struggled to reach the knife he kept on the stool beside the bed, but when his frantically grasping hand brushed its surface, the blade was gone.

"Don't struggle, and you won't be harmed."

The voice could scarcely be heard over the beating of Steratakis's heart.

"What is your name?" The rough hand lessened its pressure on his mouth, allowing Steratakis to speak.

"Please don't hurt me. You can have . . ."

"I'll not ask you again." This time the chilling whisper was reinforced by the pressure of a sharp point against his throat.

For a moment, panic seized him, and he almost answered with his true name. But he remembered in time. "Steratakis! My name is Steratakis!"

"Then I have a message for you to take to Akkad. Can you remember what I tell you?"

A feeling of relief washed over Steratakis. He would survive the night. "Yes, yes, I've been trained to repeat any message word for word."

"Good. Then memorize this. In less than four months time, Chaiyanar to Sumer, fifteen thousand by the sea. Modran to Akkad, thirty-thousand through the Dellen Pass. And Jedidia with six thousand, all horse, through the Jkarian Pass. Now you repeat it."

Gulping air, Steratakis managed to stammer out the message, stumbling only once. The hooded figure, the knife still at Steratakis's throat, made him say it four more times.

"Good, very good. Make sure you don't forget a single word. In three days, you will leave Sumer and never return. Move out quietly, and without fanfare. If anyone asks, tell them you are ill, that you have the Bad Blood."

The terrible punishment sent by the gods that formed pustules on a man's penis, growing larger and more painful. In time, the disease ravaged body and mind, and reduced its victim to a gibbering idiot.

"In any case, you will leave on the third day, not a day longer, not a day shorter. Do you understand?"

"Yes, yes, I understand." Steratakis's breathing had finally slowed. "And what is your name?"

"Give my name only to your master. I'm called Tarrata. Now don't get out of your bed until I'm well away."

With a quick movement, Tarrata backed away from the bed, unbarred the door, and opening it no more than needed, slipped out into the night.

Steratakis lay there until he could get his thoughts under control. He had never been so frightened in his life. Sweat had soaked the blanket beneath him. Instinctively, he touched his neck where the tip of the knife had rested. How in the name of the gods had the man gotten into the house? He'd secured the front door after his servant left, and the blocked and barred rear door hadn't opened in a year.

The only other way into the chamber was the ladder to the roof. But that had been sealed, too, with knotted ropes and cross branches bound together. Anyone trying to enter that way would make plenty of noise.

Sitting up, he stared at the ceiling. The ropes had been cut, though the slender branches remained. A small man, Steratakis decided, one who could move like a cat and make just as little noise. This Tarrata must have cut through the ropes, then dropped through the beams, all without making a sound loud enough to awaken anyone.

Steratakis shuddered. Never had he imaged that he would be contacted this way, in the dead of night by brute force and at the point of a blade. He'd expected someone to come up to him in the market, perhaps buy a sweet cake or two, deliver the message, and be off.

He shivered. Suddenly he realized that if he had forgotten the name Steratakis, the knife would have cut his throat and he'd be dead. He'd come that close. Yes, time to return to Akkad. He didn't think he could survive the delivery of a second message.

2

Eskkar stared across the table at Trella and Annok-sur, as they delivered the grim tidings. For a moment anger showed on his face. Until now, despite all their preparations for the Elamite invasion, there had always remained a glimmer of hope that it might not happen. After all, any unforeseen event could change Elam's plans. King Shirudukh might have died, disease or plague might have broken out among his soldiers or cities, or even a crop failure might have upset the Elamite schedule. But the news could not be denied. The enemy was coming.

"You're sure of the information?" Eskkar kept his voice calm. "And the numbers?"

"Yes, it came from Bracca himself," Annok-sur said. "Five nights ago, Bracca – he gave the name Tarrata to Steratakis – woke him in the middle of the night. Steratakis was ordered not to leave Sumer before the third day, which is why he just arrived this morning. Likely Bracca wanted to get out of Sumer before anyone noticed a merchant suddenly shutting down his stall and rushing back to Akkad."

The numbers confirmed Bracca's first estimate, as well as the routes into the Land Between the Rivers.

"At least we now know who will lead each army," Eskkar said. "I would have thought that General Jedidia would lead the force to Sumer or Akkad. Everything we've learned from Sabatu and the others claimed he was Shirudukh's ablest general."

In the last year, Annok-sur had paid deserters from Elam's armies for information about their leaders, but none had provided as much intelligence as Sabatu.

"Perhaps that is the very reason he was given the fewest soldiers," Trella said. "King Shirudukh likely does not want his strongest general commanding such a large force, especially one so far from home. With that many soldiers, Jedidia might decide to rule Akkad in his own name, or even return to Elam at the head of an invading army of his own. Better to keep him down, dependent on Shirudukh's decisions."

"It seems there are plots everywhere," Eskkar said. "Still this may help us. Sabatu says that Modran is stubborn and proud. He may not believe that we would dare to challenge him, or that he can be stopped."

"We have less than three months," Trella said. "Now we must set all our plans into motion."

"Yes. I'll summon all the commanders." Eskkar leaned back in his chair. The days of indecision and doubt had passed. Knowing the worst always calmed him down. "It's time to tell them what they'll be up against."

"I'll send word to Sargon," Trella said. "He should be here as well. Draelin is available, if you approve." Trella paused for a moment, no doubt thinking of the dangers her son would soon face.

"Yes, but Draelin must return as soon as possible. He will be needed here to help Alcinor." He sighed. "Sumer and Isin must also be told," Eskkar said.

"I will have messengers on their way tomorrow at first light," Trella said. "We promised to tell them the moment we learned something new."

"What shall I do with Steratakis? There won't be any more messages, and he knows too much." Annok-sur's question caught Eskkar by surprise. He had already forgotten the messenger.

"Send him to Nuzi," Trella said. "Tooraj can keep him under guard for the next few months. After that, it won't matter. But warn Steratakis to keep silent. Not a word of this must get out yet, or there will be panic in the City. I don't even want the name Tarrata mentioned."

Tooraj commanded all the troops guarding the mine and its surroundings. His soldiers protected each shipment of gold and silver that flowed downstream to Akkad.

"And I must tell Sabatu that Chaiyanar will be coming to Sumer," Eskkar said. "I promised him that I would give him the chance to fight against his torturer."

"Orodes must also be told," Trella said. "He must have time to prepare what he needs."

Orodes, for managing the mine at Nuzi, received one part out of every hundred that the mine produced. With that tiny fraction, he had become the richest man in Akkad.

"Are you sure he will do as you ask?" Eskkar knew Orodes had grown used to a life of ease.

"Yes, I'm sure Annok-sur and I can convince him," Trella said. "He does owe us a great deal."

Eskkar nodded. With Annok-sur present, Orodes would understand the message. "Trella, will you be able to obtain everything that my soldiers will need?"

In many ways, Trella had the most difficult assignment of all. It would fall to her and her clerks to obtain and distribute the vast mountains of supplies and weapons Eskkar required. Food, water, swords, arrows, bows, spears, all those were obvious enough. But she also needed to ensure that the soldiers received clothing, sandals, helmets, leather armor, slings, and bronze bullets for them. In short, all the little things that, lacking, could halt an army or bring it to ruin.

"Yes, my clerks are ready," Trella said. "When the time is right, I will call on the all the nobles and traders throughout the land for their assistance. They will deliver what we need."

Eskkar grunted. Yes, they would deliver whatever she asked of them, or they would find themselves waiting for that drop of poison in their cup, or a knife between their ribs. Nor would any dare to risk doing less than his utmost. If Akkad survived, Trella would remember who had not made every effort to support the war.

"Then I will leave Akkad in your hands." Eskkar felt grateful that at least the long period of inaction had ended. "I will begin my inspection of the training camps tomorrow, to ensure that they are ready."

"Take care, Husband. Your soldiers will need you more than ever before."

He nodded. It was still not too late for Elam to try and strike him down. "I'll be careful, Trella. But from now on, you should not leave the Compound for any reason. We're all going to need your help if this plan is to succeed."

8

Orodes stepped off the boat and onto Akkad's dock just as the setting sun touched the horizon. The boat had departed late from Nuzi, and a slow passage down the Tigris had not made up any time, despite Orodes's frequent suggestions to the ship master. At least the boring journey had ended.

Now he looked forward to a fine meal prepared by his incomparable cook, along with some exceptional wine brought all the way from Sumer, offered by his two wives and three slave girls. Afterwards, he would relax in his garden, sip some wine, and let his women take care of his more personal needs.

Tall and lean, Orodes lacked a year before he reached his thirtieth season. Nevertheless, his hair had thinned, and his temples were tinged with gray. Orodes's plain face bore the scars of countless encounters with splinters of rock hacked and chipped from the hard earth. Thanks to the gods, he still had both eyes. Plenty of miners his age had lost an eye or damaged their vision from flying grit and rock fragments.

Slinging his leather pouch over his shoulder, Orodes started down the wharf. His servant, burdened by the weight of his master's tools, struggled to keep pace. Orodes rarely used the hammers and chisels these days, but the richest man in Akkad had grown accustomed to satisfying all his desires, no matter how large or small. Orodes preferred his own tools, and if that meant a servant had to strain his back lugging everything his master might want to Nuzi and back, so be it.

Before Orodes reached the end of the wharf, he found his way blocked by one of the Hawk Clan guards. The soldier motioned him aside, halted the servant with a single glance, then lowered his voice as he delivered the message.

"I have a request from Lady Trella for you, Master Orodes. She would very much like to see you at midmorning tomorrow." The soldier smiled as he delivered the last part of the message. "If it is convenient."

Orodes recovered from his surprise. "Yes, of course." What else could he say? Convenient or not, no one refused an invitation from the Queen of Akkad. "Tell Lady Trella that I will attend her at that time."

The soldier hadn't bothered to say where. The Queen seldom left the Compound, and she conducted her private business in Eskkar's Workroom.

The Hawk Clan soldier spun on his heel and strode off, leaving Orodes standing there, open mouthed. Already the brief message had ruined Orodes's satisfaction at returning home. By the time he reached his large house and passed inside, his mood had turned foul. He snapped at his wives during dinner, and drank too much wine.

While he picked at his food, Orodes wondered why Trella wished to see him. It couldn't be anything to do with Nuzi. He had just come from there, and everything seemed under control. Once again, he thanked the gods for his foresight. By inspecting the mine once a month, Orodes ensured that the operation ran exactly as he ordered. Besides, Orodes reported the numbers from the mine every ten days, not to Trella herself but to one of her senior clerks.

Whatever Trella wanted, it must be important. Members of the Hawk Clan did not carry trivial messages. The soldier could have waited until Orodes arrived home. Meeting him at the dock meant something serious, and something Trella did not want mentioned even in front of Orodes's wives or servants.

Trying to guess what Trella wanted also spoiled his after-dinner recreation with his women. Their efforts produced little gratification, and as soon as Orodes spent his seed into the young and recently acquired pleasure girl, he ordered all of them out of his bed chamber. It took another full cup of wine before he slipped into an uneasy and restless sleep.

Now midmorning had arrived, and Orodes eased himself into the comfortable chair that faced Trella across the table. The Queen wore no jewelry, only the same silver fillet to hold back her hair that Eskkar had given her years ago. She sat with her back to the wall, in the place her husband usually occupied. That told Orodes that the King would not be present.

Two other people also had seats at the table. Wakannh, the Captain of Akkad's Guard, and Annok-sur. As always, her presence lent a grim air to any meeting. People had a habit of disappearing or turning up dead after meeting with Akkad's chief spy. The others' presence confirmed Orodes's conclusion – something important would be discussed.

"Good morning, Orodes," Trella began, her voice as pleasant as always. "I hope you had a successful journey to Nuzi."

Neither Wakannh nor Annok-sur bothered with more than a simple incline of the head, though they kept their eyes fastened on Orodes.

"Yes, Lady Trella. Everything at the mine is running smoothly." He resisted the urge to make his words a question.

"Indeed it is, and as always, our thanks for your skillful oversight. But today we must speak about another subject, one even more important than the mine. Akkad needs your services again, Orodes, as we did once before. Esskkar and I hope that you will be able to help us."

Orodes let himself relax just the tiniest amount. He smiled at the subtle reminder. "I am always ready to help Akkad in any way I can."

Ten years ago, Trella had plucked a drunken young man from the mud of Akkad's lanes. As the youngest son of a family of miners, Orodes had rebelled against his father's old fashioned ways and his older brothers' rigid authority. Despite Orodes's keen wits and mastery of the craft of mining, his kin had expelled him, their youngest and most quarrelsome son, from the family business.

Orodes had fallen into despair and disrepute until rescued by Lady Trella. She'd done so not because of any sympathy for a drunken young sot, but because she needed the best miner in Akkad. And one desperate enough to undertake a dangerous dig deep into the earth.

She had placed him in charge of a newly discovered and very secret gold mine at Nuzi. The moment Orodes reached the site and saw its potential, he abandoned his dissolute ways forever. The challenge to extract the vast amounts of gold and silver crucial for Akkad's war with Sumer had provided all the incentive Orodes needed to regain his self-respect.

In Trella's service, Orodes had accomplished what no other miner could have done. He'd developed new techniques to unearth and separate the various ores from deep within the ground. For his services, Lady Trella allowed him to keep one part by weight of every hundred extracted. Within five years, he'd become the richest men in Akkad.

Trella came right to the point. "You've probably heard rumors of a coming war. I can tell you, in private, that those stories are true. The Elamites intend to invade our lands and capture our cities. We need your help to defeat them."

Orodes leaned back in surprise. Like most others in Akkad, he'd heard hundreds of rumors in the last few months, and discounted most of them. After all, only a fool would contend against King Eskkar and his well-trained army. But an invasion from the east, that changed everything. Such a war would threaten him personally. If Akkad lost, wealthy people like Orodes would be squeezed to death by the victors, eager to seize as much wealth as they could.

She waited a few moments until he had time to comprehend the situation. "Naturally we require as much gold as we can raise to help defeat these invaders. A contribution from you will help us buy what we need to fight."

He sagged back in the chair. Orodes realized he was going to lose his fortune, or most of it. Half his wealth? Three quarters? Perhaps all of it. He glanced at Wakannh. A single word from Trella, and Orodes would be lying dead on the floor. It had happened in this very room before. Wakannh's soldiers could already be at Orodes's house, searching for his secret hiding places.

"How much am I expected to contribute?"

Trella smiled again. "A gift of five hundred gold pieces would be most helpful."

Less than fifteen percent of his wealth. Orodes met her gaze. Something was wrong. Trella likely knew exactly how much gold he possessed. For that small a sum, Trella could have sent one of her clerks, and Orodes would have paid it without a second thought.

"Is there anything else I can do, Lady Trella?"

"Since such a contribution to help save Akkad is so small, we have another request to make. There is a very special task that only you are qualified to perform. We need a Master Miner who knows how to dig in the earth, and clear away obstacles."

Her request surprised him. He straightened up in his chair. Had another mine been discovered?

"Eskkar's cavalry needs a secret route through the southern mountains to the Great Sea." She unrolled a map and spread it on the table. "We've charted a path through the mountains. We'll need a trail wide enough for two horses to ride side by side. You're the only man in Akkad bold enough and skilled enough who can carve a pathway through the foothills in the time we have. Of course I'll make sure you have everything necessary, skilled laborers, soldiers, tools, supplies, food and water. Whatever you need, as much as you require, you have only to ask."

Orodes stared at the map. The route marked by Trella's finger extended through the last third of the mountains. Many miners had explored the area, but never found a trace of anything valuable. Every one of them, however, attested to the rough terrain. As far as he knew, no one had ever reached the Great Sea.

He lifted his eyes. "If I agree to do this, how much time do I have?"

"Three months, no longer," Trella answered.

"It can't be done. Not in that short a time. Such an effort would take at least six months, possibly more."

"For anyone else, I would agree. But you are the Master Miner of Akkad. If anyone knows how to cut through a mountain, it is Orodes. Besides, three months is all the time we have."

Orodes opened his mouth, then closed it. He'd been about to ask what would happen if he refused. Only a simpleton would ask that question, and Orodes was no halfwit. A single glance at Annok-sur provided all the answer Orodes needed.

Most of the fools in Akkad feared King Eskkar's temper. Those closer to the truth worried about Trella, who had probably sent more men to their deaths than her bloodthirsty husband. The presence of Annok-sur, who still hadn't said anything, reinforced the unmentioned threat.

A night swim in the Tigris, Akkadians called it. The innocent saying meant that a dead body might be tossed into the river and carried downstream seven or eight miles before the waters slowed enough to drift a corpse to the shore.

Not that he thought Lady Trella would do such a thing to him. First they would confiscate his fortune. Then it might be just as easy to have a pinch of poison dropped into his stew. Bad food still killed plenty of people every year, and not even the healers could always tell the difference between poison or fouled meat. Especially if the healers happened to be in Trella's service. Orodes shook the gloomy thought from his mind.

"If you do this, Orodes, we will be in your debt," Trella said. "I can promise you that no more of your wealth will be needed. And your effort may help win the war. Besides, we need someone we can trust, someone who can keep his mouth closed, someone with your special skills of mining and digging, and someone who can't be bribed."

Orodes leaned back in his chair. "You are very persuasive, Lady Trella. If it will help Akkad, of course I will do my utmost." Not that she needed to be so compelling with Orodes. He knew well enough what might happen to anyone who disagreed with her.

"Then I am sure you will succeed, Orodes. If you do not, the war with Elam may be lost."

"When do we start?"

"Now. This morning. We will tell you everything we've learned, and the preparations we've already started."

Orodes took a deep breath and nodded. Then he smiled at the dour Wakannh and the grim Annok-sur, both no doubt disappointed by having to let him live. At least Lady Trella hadn't mentioned how much he was in her debt, or how she had rescued him from a filthy lane and saved his life.

Not to mention that Orodes knew what to expect if foreign invaders occupied the land. They'd take all his gold and seize the mine at Nuzi as well, after torturing him and his family to make sure he revealed the location of every last coin and nugget.

And if Akkad were besieged, Orodes might be better off in the mountains. There the only real danger he would face would be getting crushed in a rock slide, and that risk would be slight enough. Of course if he failed, his dead body would be tossed into some rocky chasm, never to be seen again. Yes, that outcome was much more likely.

2

The northern lands, two hundred miles northwest of Akkad . . .

The antelope bounded over the crest of the low hill, running for its life and heedless of the rocks and boulders that littered the hillside. The thunder of hooves against the earth drove the desperate animal, ears flat against its head. A band of six horsemen galloped in pursuit, their fierce cries exhorting the horses onward, regardless of the risk.

Sargon, the son of the King of Akkad, led the chase, though no one in that city would have recognized him. The boy banished by his parents from the City of Akkad had grown into manhood. Dressed and armed like any steppes warrior, he guided his stallion with the skill that proclaimed his origins. Heedless of the danger, Sargon urged his mount ever faster over the rocky ground, where one slip likely meant a broken leg for the horse, and a nasty fall for its rider.

Today the vagaries of the hunt had let Sargon take the lead, pursuing the single antelope that had not managed to reach the safety of the wooded glen. Seeing the hunters riding toward the herd, it had turned away and burst into a run, trying to escape.

Caught up in the excitement of the chase, Sargon was determined to bring the creature down. The heavy breathing of his horse, the pounding of its hooves, the rush of air across Sargon's face, all these added to the thrill of the hunt. However, the powerful beast, its black horns flashing, refused to give up. It leapt over obstacles that forced Sargon to change his course again and again.

So far the chase had lasted over half a mile, and now both hunter and hunted could see another stand of forest ahead that would shelter the fleeing antelope. Once within the trees, it would disappear. Unwilling to let the animal get away, Sargon, in his seventeenth season, urged the big warhorse to its fastest pace, swerving around or jumping over every ditch or large boulder in their path.

A flat patch of ground ahead caught his eye, and Sargon turned toward it, allowing the antelope to increase the gap by a few more paces. But the level ground gave Sargon the brief moment he needed to whip an arrow from his quiver and fit the shaft to the string, a difficult feat that few not born in the steppes could have accomplished.

By now the forest had drawn closer, less than two hundred paces away. Holding the halter rope and the bow in his left hand, Sargon leaned forward against the stallion's neck and pulled the bowstring to his ear.

Behind him he heard his friend Garal coming up fast, the rumbling of his horse's hooves growing ever louder. Both men had drawn ahead of the others. Sargon held the taut bow a few more moments, trying to close the gap by another handful of paces. He heard the snap of a bowstring, and an arrow flashed past his shoulder.

Garal, a master archer even from the back of a galloping horse, had launched a shaft. But either their prey veered or Garal's aim was off, and the missile flew a hand's breadth above the racing animal. Another flat patch of ground, and Sargon let fly his own shaft.

The arrow struck home, burying itself deep into the antelope's shoulder. The creature cried out, even as it stumbled. A few more steps, and the animal tumbled to the ground, mortally wounded.

As soon as he loosed the shaft, Sargon pulled back on the halter, slowing his horse. By the time he eased his steed to a walk and turned it around, he'd traveled almost a hundred paces beyond the fallen antelope. Garal, too, had to slow his mount gradually, before he could reach Sargon's side.

"A fine shot, Sargon. I was just a little too far behind."

Sargon laughed. Garal was far and away the best bowman not only in this group of hunters, but in the entire Ur Nammu Clan. For the last two years, he had also been Sargon's teacher, companion, friend, and fellow warrior. The two young men had fought side by side in two battles, a powerful bond that united them.

"For once the gods put the animal in my path," Sargon said. "Even so, you almost dropped him."

"I thought I could steal the kill from you, but it would only have been a lucky shot."

They walked their horses back to the site of the fallen animal. One of the warriors had already dispatched the antelope. Each man offered some words of praise to Sargon, exactly the same way they would have spoken to one born and raised in their clan.

Two horse boys, riding well to the rear of the hunters, arrived at last. They would see to the gutting and cleaning of the carcass. With a careless wave toward the body, Garal led the horsemen back toward their camp, about fifteen miles away. The boys, learning the way of the warrior, would follow as soon as they finished.

The pleasant ride back didn't take long, and Sargon enjoyed the moment. A fine day, a strong horse, and a successful hunt. Tonight they would eat well, and in the morning they would ride for the main camp of the Ur Nammu, less than a full day's journey away.

They found their campsite undisturbed. Earlier in the day, the riders had brought down two antelope, which the horse boys had half-buried under some rocks to keep the scavengers away. The fresh meat would be welcomed by the clan's women, and tomorrow evening there would be enough food to fill the bellies of every member of the Clan.

Sargon had scarcely finished tending to his horse when a shout floated across the landscape. He turned his eyes to the east, and saw a single rider galloping toward them, waving his arms in excitement.

Garal studied the approaching horseman. "It looks like Timmu."

It took another few moments before Sargon could confirm the sighting. Garal possessed a keen sense of vision, another trait that made him stand out even among the Ur Nammu warriors.

"What brings him here?"

Garal shrugged. "We'll know soon enough."

Timmu, Garal's half-brother, had only thirteen seasons, but he had grown tall, and would soon be accepted into the ranks of the warriors. He galloped into the hunting party's camp, slowing only at the last moment, and jumping down from his mare even before it stopped moving. Garal frowned at the foolish display of horsemanship, but Sargon couldn't keep his smile hidden.

"Sargon! Subutai sent for you. He wants you to return at once."

"Is anything wrong? Is Tashanella well?"

In the two years since Sargon had claimed Tashanella, daughter of Clan Leader Subutai, his young wife had given birth to a daughter, and now was well into the final months of her second pregnancy.

Tashanella had played an important role in reconciling Sargon with his mother, Lady Trella, and his father, King Eskkar.

"No, nothing like that, Sargon. Some soldiers arrived from Aratta, and said they had to speak to you. That's why Subutai told me to find you."

Sargon asked about the men and their message, but Timmu knew nothing more.

A glance at the setting sun told Sargon that he'd best wait for the morning to depart. "I'll leave at first light," he said. "I should be back at the main camp before midday."

Garal nodded. "I'll be there as soon as I can." As the leader of the hunting party, he had to remain with them. "Whatever it is, wait for me. You may need my help."

"I'll wait for you." Sargon smiled. "Who else would keep me out of trouble?"

When Sargon crossed the ridge and saw the Ur Nammu camp, he breathed a sigh of relief. A handful of cooking fires sent long tendrils of white smoke slanting into the air, driven by the gentle breeze. Children played, and women strolled about, so clearly no danger to the Clan had arisen.

At a canter, Sargon rode toward the beckoning water, downstream from the camp. He paused long enough to plunge into the shallow water, and wash some of the dirt and horse stink from his body. Satisfied that most of the powerful horse smell had been rinsed away, he led the stallion, its thirst quenched, into the camp. As he approached the corral, a boy ran out to greet him and take charge of Sargon's favorite mount.

Though he wanted to see Tashanella, Sargon headed straight for Subutai's tent. When the Clan Leader sent for a warrior, that man didn't stop first to see his wife, even if she were the clan leader's daughter. Whatever Sargon's position might be back in Akkad, in the Ur Nammu Clan, he remained just another warrior and as duty bound to obey his Clan Leader.

Subutai waited outside his tent, along with three soldiers from Akkad, all Hawk Clan members by the emblem on each chest. That meant the news, whatever it might be, was important. Then Sargon recognized Draelin, one of his father's senior commanders.

Something of import had happened or the long awaited summons to war had arrived, for Eskkar to dispatch Draelin to carry a message.

Draelin knew enough about barbarian clan customs to hold his tongue until Sargon had exchanged greetings with Clan Leader Subutai.

"Sargon, it's good to see you again," Draelin said. "You grow taller and stronger each day."

"Stronger, perhaps," Sargon laughed, "but no taller. Now, what brings you to Subutai's camp?"

By now Sargon knew he would never be as tall or as powerful as his father. Instead Sargon had learned how to use his speed, agility, even his shorter stature to his advantage. After years of constant practice, his former teacher Garal admitted that Sargon had equaled him with a sword. Nevertheless, Sargon worked hard to improve his skills with lance and bow, as well as with the sword.

Draelin glanced around, and both Sargon and Subutai understood the look.

"Come into the tent. We can talk there. My wives will make sure we are not disturbed."

No one would be allowed close enough to the tent to hear what words were exchanged within. If Subutai's wives couldn't hold their tongues, the clan leader would have beaten that defect out of them years ago.

Soon the three men were seated in the center of Subutai's tent, each with a water cup at hand.

Draelin waited until Subutai nodded to him. "The King sent me to bring both of you the warning that the Elamite invasion is about to begin. Their soldiers are gathering, and they will start their march into the Land Between the Rivers within three months. That's a little earlier than we expected. I delivered the same warning to the camp at Aratta, to the leader of the Hawk Clan there. They assured me that my message will also be received by the Alur Meriki within a few more days."

Sargon exchanged looks with Subutai. The war had truly begun. All the planning and preparations of the last two years would soon be tested.

"The Elamites are sending men through the Jkarian Pass," Draelin continued, "at least six thousand. Perhaps thirty thousand more will come through the Dellen Pass, to attack Akkad directly. Another large force, around fifteen thousand, will approach Sumer from the coast of the Great Sea."

Subutai's eyes widened at the numbers, so large that he could scarcely comprehend them. "So many! Can Eskkar defeat such a vast army?"

"My father always has a plan, Chief Subutai."

"And a trick or two for our enemy," Draelin added. "That's why I have to rush back to Akkad. He says he has a special task for me."

"Does my father wish me to return to Akkad?"

More than two years ago, Eskkar had delivered his rebellious son Sargon to the Ur Nammu. The Clan agreed to teach him the way of the warrior, although both Subutai and Eskkar knew that Sargon's death would be the most likely result. But the headstrong boy found the path to honor. Instead of death or dishonor, he helped save the Ur Nammu from invaders, and at the same time reconciled them with the Alur Meriki, long their bitter enemy.

Accepted as a warrior by the Ur Nammu Clan, Sargon took Chief Subutai's daughter, Tashanella, as his wife. Over the course of time, she helped Sargon make his peace with his parents. Though he remained with the Ur Nammu, Sargon had regained his position as heir to the Kingdom of Akkad.

Nevertheless, relations between father and son remained delicate, and neither wanted to provoke a quarrel.

Draelin, of course, knew the whole story. "He thought you might ask that. The King said you should do whatever you think best, but that he hoped – that's the word he told me to use – you would at least come back with me for the meeting he's arranged with all the commanders. After that, you can return here. Or if you decide to fight at his side, you will be considered a leader of two hundred, under the command of Muta. Or you can ride with Hathor in the south."

Muta was second in command of all of Akkad's horse fighters, under Hathor. The last time Sargon had visited with his father, they had spoken of such an arrangement. Sargon had expected a direct order to return to Akkad, but instead Eskkar had merely said that he trusted Sargon's judgment.

"You will do what is best, Sargon," his father had said at their last meeting. "If you choose to fight with Akkad's cavalry, you will have a real command, with all the responsibilities that go with it."

In the last few months, Sargon had thought long and hard about those words. But in the end, he had chosen to stay with the Ur Nammu. When the time came for battle, no one else would have as much influence with the Clans as Sargon possessed, not even his father.

Eskkar had defeated the Alur Meriki in battle, and won from them a promise to fight Akkad's enemies when called upon. The Alur Meriki would fulfill their oath, but Sargon had managed to transform their pledge into an alliance, one that now benefitted both the Ur Nammu and Alur Meriki.

"If my father wishes me to join the commanders' meeting, I will return with you, Draelin. I will tell him in person that I have decided to ride with the Ur Nammu and the Alur Meriki."

Draelin grinned his approval. "I thought as much. You'll have good hunting, I'm sure."

"Tell Eskkar that the Ur Nammu will be ready." Subutai, too, had a smile on his face. "In two months, I will have almost two hundred and fifty warriors ready to ride."

"I will carry your words, Chief Subutai," Draelin said, bowing his head in respect. "Oh, there is one thing more. I brought a prisoner with me. Annok-sur's guards grabbed him up coming out of a tavern in Akkad. She said Yarna would be happy to teach you the language of the Elamites, and that you could set him free after three months, if he pleases you. Or just kill him. He's so terrified of the Ur Nammu that his knees were shaking. I would have conveyed him here, but I thought it best to give him some time to control his fear. His name is Yarna, an Elamite trader from Susa, and he's waiting with my men."

Sargon had no doubts about the man's willingness to help. A few sessions with Annok-sur and her torturers would make any man eager to follow her bidding. Of course, whenever anyone spoke about Annok-sur, they really meant Sargon's mother. Regardless, Trella believed that learning the Elamite language might prove useful, and Sargon agreed.

By the time Yarna found his way back to Elam, the war would be over. Nor would the prisoner be eager to tell anyone where he'd been or what he'd been doing. "Tell Annok-sur I am grateful," Sargon said. "It may help all of us."

"Then my duties here are finished," Draelin said. "If it does not give offense, I would like to depart as soon as possible. The faster I get back to Akkad, the quicker I can begin whatever assignment your father has waiting for me. He said it's important."

"You may leave whenever you wish," Subutai said. "My men will give you whatever food or provisions you require."

"I will need a few moments to prepare for the journey, Draelin" Sargon said. "With your permission, Chief Subutai?"

"Granted. And Draelin, bring your prisoner to me. I will make sure he is taken care of. In fact, I think Garal should also learn to understand and speak the language of the Elamites. The more we know the ways of our enemy, the better."

"Chief Subutai, please tell Garal why I could not wait for him." Sargon stood. "Now I must talk with Tashanella."

He preferred not to leave his wife, but it would only be for eighteen days or so. Both Tashanella and Sargon knew how important this meeting of Eskkar's commanders would be. She would want Sargon to stand at his father's side before the other leaders. Such a gesture would reaffirm her husband's position as Eskkar's heir.

"Then I'd better prepare as well." Draelin stood. "Good hunting to you, Chief Subutai. May your ride bring you even more honor and glory."

Subutai shrugged. "I have had more than enough glory in my life. But honor, that is something else. We owe much to the people of Akkad, and now we will honor the friendship between our two peoples. Tell Eskkar that we will ride in his service with pride."

10

While Draelin galloped north to find Sargon, Eskkar rode out of Akkad to visit the training camps. In the last two years, he'd spent time at each camp, meeting with the commanders and observing the men, their equipment, and their morale. Eskkar wanted his subcommanders to know that the time for training had passed. War loomed on the horizon, and he wanted to make sure every one of his soldiers had what he needed to fight.

It took fourteen days, but Eskkar visited every camp. He spoke to each commander, inspected the soldiers, and made sure that the men were being properly trained. Now the time had come to start implementing the plans he and Trella had prepared to repel the coming invasion.

Wild rumors of war floated throughout the land, almost all of them carefully nurtured and disseminated by Trella and Annok-sur's agents. Akkad was going to attack Sumer. Akkad would assault the city of Isin. Lagash and Isin had decided to invade Sumer. The barbarians would return from the north and overrun the land.

Other, wilder tales circulated about an invasion from the west, or one from the lands across the eastern mountains. These whispers came and went so fast that soon few of Akkad's inhabitants believed any of them. Conflict of some kind appeared certain, however. The provisioning and arming of the soldiers couldn't be concealed. Every night, the lanes and taverns of Akkad filled with many more soldiers than usual.

The time had come to sow the final seeds of deceit into the minds of any travelers or spies returning to Elam. Annok-sur wanted the last traders leaving Sumer and Akkad to bear witness to the chaos and turmoil in the Land Between the Rivers. By the time these conflicting reports reached the east, it would be impossible for Elam's generals to ascertain the truth. Instead they would have a picture of a confused and frightened Akkad, one without the will to resist.

Meanwhile, Corio and the builders strengthened Akkad's walls, and the city's soldiers trained constantly. Increased numbers of alert soldiers manned the walls or practiced their bowmanship. At the same time, large contingents of men and cavalry moved between Akkad and the surrounding camps.

Eskkar brushed aside all these rumors, refusing to confirm or deny any of them. But the people of Akkad and those from the surrounding farms noted the preparations. The ones who remembered the original siege by the Alur Meriki, or the war against Sumer, nodded knowingly. They watched as the scattered huts and tents that somehow found a way to creep closer to the city's outer walls were torn down.

The wide ditch that encircled the city was once again dug out, and in many places lined with stones from the river. The irrigation masters made their own preparations to flood both the ditch and the countryside around Akkad. At the first approach of the enemy, the water would flow to impede the invaders' efforts.

Nor could the people fail to notice Trella's agents in the marketplace and dock yards, buying grain, and assembling ever larger herds of sheep and cattle across the Tigris, just to the west of the city. Despite the rumors of war, trade flourished, both over the land routes and along the Tigris, as supplies of all types flowed into the city.

Prices rose on food, livestock, and grain driven by the sudden scarcity of these goods, as most were diverted to either Akkad's storehouses or the soldiers' training camps. The number of Akkad's soldiers increased as well. Since maintaining fighting men and their equipment demanded plenty of gold and silver coins, that fact alone warned the people that a great conflict approached.

Fortunately, the Kingdom still received a steady supply of silver from the mine at Nuzi. The bright silver disks, marked with the symbol of the City on one side and the outline of a hawk on the other, flowed from hand to hand, from traders to merchants, from farmers to laborers, and even to the ale houses frequented by the soldiers.

Only one thing remained certain – the many years of peace were coming to an end. Once again war menaced the Land Between the Rivers.

Eskkar continued to ignore the rising tide of questions and kept his attention focused on the soldiers and their training. He knew Trella and her hundreds of clerks and scribes could manage the myriad details needed to prepare the city to withstand an extended siege.

She would see to it that Akkad's soldiers received all the food and equipment they needed to fight. Bantor, as Commander of the city's defenses, prowled the walls every day, searching for the slightest weakness that an opposing army might try to exploit.

In the last year, six training camps had been established, all on the western side of the Tigris, and all within twenty to thirty miles of the city. Spearmen, archers, and slingers practiced their craft in these outposts, less than two days march from Akkad. More camps lay farther to the north. The cavalry trained their mounts and men in these, fighting mock battles and galloping over the countryside.

Horses, ever in short supply, arrived in steady streams from the far western lands. Uruk and Lagash traded with the western desert nomads for fresh animals that soon found their way to Akkad's training camps. The rulers of those two cities also supplied plenty of grain and additional weapons. Trella's envoys had explained the situation to those cities and the need for them to do their utmost. They understood that, while they might not feel the first blows of the invading Elamites, they stood little chance to resist the enemy if Akkad and Sumer should fall.

Trella's supply masters and counting house clerks knew their business. They had, after all, fought two major wars in the last twenty years. Food, weapons, horses, clothing, even ale and wine, poured into Akkad and its supply depots. Arrows by the tens of thousands were crafted, and the sound of new bronze swords and axes being forged and tested echoed in every camp.

Each day Bantor, Annok-sur's husband, worked to improve the City's fortifications. The oldest of Eskkar's commanders, a fall from a horse five years before left Bantor unable to fight on foot or with the cavalry. But his experience with two sieges of Akkad now served him in good stead. Wakannh, the Captain of Akkad's Guard, maintained law and order within the city. Both men were determined to ensure that Akkad's defenses would be well organized and supplied.

When the fighting began, no matter who the enemy might be, Akkad, its soldiers, and its inhabitants would be ready.

Trella's hard work left Eskkar free to concentrate on the army. After years of secret planning, the appointed day to meet with Akkad's senior commanders arrived at last. Until now, only Hathor, Alexar, Bantor, and his wife Annok-sur knew the full extent of the threat and the measures Eskkar and Trella had initiated. Some commanders knew part of the plan, and the others had guessed what might be approaching.

The time had come to tell all the leaders everything that lay in store for them, and the role each would play in the coming conflict.

The morning after Sargon and Draelin reached Akkad, Eskkar summoned his commanders and trusted friends to the Compound. Just after midmorning, on a beautiful summer day, the leaders climbed the stairs to Eskkar's private quarters.

One by one, the commanders filed into the Map Room. They took their places around the long table, its surface covered by a detailed map of the Land Between the Rivers, from the northern mountains to the Great Sea. The women had already taken their seats, with Trella at the far end of the table. Annok-sur and Uvela sat beside her, along with Ismenne, the Map Maker.

Draelin, Daro, Wakannh, Yavtar, Shappa, Drakis, Muta, and Mitrac occupied the center seats. Hathor, Bantor, and Alexar took their places near the head of the table, as Eskkar and his son Sargon entered. Sargon chose a place beside Draelin. Every eye studied the heir to the city, searching for any hint of weakness. But they found none. All they saw was another soldier, tough and battle hardened despite his youth.

Eskkar closed the door behind him. His Hawk Clan guards remained at their station on the floor below, to make sure no one could approach the Map Room.

As Eskkar took his place at the head of the table, he faced Trella at the opposite end. For a moment, he studied their faces, as they in turn studied his. All of them knew the threats of war had once again gathered at Akkad's gates. In the last few months, most had guessed the name and plans of the enemy, but none had talked, either openly or in secret, about the coming conflict. Each one knew the importance of keeping his thoughts to himself.

"The Elamites have been preparing to invade our lands for nearly three years," Eskkar began without any preamble. "In that time, they have dispatched many spies to Akkad, as well as to Sumer and Isin. They have also bribed many in Akkad to provide information about our strengths and weaknesses. To conceal our strength as much as possible, we've kept you and our soldiers moving from camp to camp. It's also the reason why Trella and I kept our plans hidden even from you, the men who must lead the fight in the coming war."

Taking his time, Eskkar outlined the situation that Akkad faced. "We will be greatly outnumbered, by well trained and equipped soldiers. We will also have to fight the invaders on two fronts. However, Annok-sur's spies and Yavtar's traders have collected much information about the Elamites' plan. Through their efforts, we know when and from what directions the enemy will come."

No one spoke, but every man kept his attention focused on Eskkar's words. These were all tough, battle-tested men who had fought Akkad's enemies before, some of them many times.

"The Elamites will strike from three directions, and at nearly the same time. One force, probably horsemen only, will come through the Jkarian Pass to the north. They will send between five and seven thousand men to devastate the farm lands that supply Akkad's grain and livestock, then turn south and move toward our city. On their way, they will collect food and herds for the besiegers. Many of the people will be rounded up and sent back to Elam as slaves."

The commanders glanced at the map. The Jkarian Pass lay almost a hundred and eighty miles north of Akkad.

"The main thrust will be toward Akkad," Eskkar continued, "through the Dellen Pass. These soldiers, between twenty-five and thirty thousand men, will be well prepared to assault Akkad. The Elamites have captured many cities in the east, so they know all about sieges."

That got a reaction from the men at the table. An army that size was larger than any force ever assembled in the Land Between the Rivers, even larger than the armies Akkad had defeated at Isin.

"The most critical attack will come from the south, along the coast of the Great Sea, to besiege Sumer. Our agents tell us that perhaps fifteen to sixteen thousand soldiers will take that route."

Eskkar noted the stunned looks on the men's faces, as they calculated the total number of invaders, between forty-five and fifty thousand, that would have to be defeated.

"Sumer will be the key to stopping the invasion. If Sumer falls, the Elamites will be able to keep men and supplies flowing along the coast. And with so many soldiers to man Sumer's walls, we will never be able to drive them out. Even now, they are gathering ships and storing weapons and food to support that army. If Sumer is taken, Akkad and Isin, and the other cities, will not be able to withstand the greater numbers of the enemy, and sooner or later, we will be defeated. It might take another year or two, but with Sumer as an Elamite base, we cannot win."

The commanders exchanged grim looks. Such numbers were daunting even to experienced and battle hardened fighters.

"But we have made our own plans," Eskkar said, "and we have prepared a few surprises for the Elamites. This time, thanks to Trella's efforts and despite all the rumors of war you've heard, the cities of Sumer and Isin, and Uruk and Lagash, too, will be fighting alongside Akkad's soldiers. Even now, King Gemama of Sumer is readying his city and all his people for the coming siege. He will have to hold out until Hathor, and as much cavalry as we can spare, joins with the horsemen of Isin to break the siege and cut the Elamite supply line to the sea."

"Then all these rumors of war with Isin and Sumer were false?" Draelin reached out his hand and touched the map at the City of Isin.

"Yes. But only King Naxos of Isin and King Gemama of Sumer knew the truth, and they have only been made aware in the last few months."

"Will they have sufficient time to prepare?" Wakannh, Captain of Akkad's Guard, asked that question.

"King Naxos of Isin has always been prepared for war." Eskkar smiled at the looks on their faces. Everyone knew of Isin's constant readiness to wage war. Since the war with Sumer more than ten years ago, King Naxos had prepared for an assault by Akkad.

"But this time, he will turn his eyes to the south, to aid Sumer. And we will provide men and supplies for that fight. Even as we speak, King Gemama has his men working day and night to prepare Sumer for the Elamite onslaught. Uruk and Lagash are already delivering supplies, weapons, and tools to help him, along with a few hundred laborers and soldiers. However, it will be up to us to provide a way to break the Elamite siege of Sumer."

"Who will help Akkad withstand our own siege?" Daro, the recently promoted Commander, raised the question no doubt all the others were thinking.

"No one, Daro, because we are not going to just sit and wait for the Elamites to surround Akkad's walls and grind us down. We're going to meet them in the Dellen Pass, and hold them long enough until they run out of supplies and have to turn back. In the narrow mountain passes, their greater numbers will not be as effective against our men, and they will soon be short of food. They will be marching with only a few days rations, expecting to live off the land once they enter into Akkad's territory. Meanwhile we will have plenty of food, water, and weapons delivered by bearers recruited by Trella and led by her clerks. Instead of a siege lasting months, we need only stop them for five or ten days."

"What if they manage to resupply, and you can't hold them?" Wakannah's voice held no trace of worry, just a question.

"That, too, has been considered. Sargon will make sure the Elamites do not get their supplies. But if we are unable to drive them off, we will simply fall back to Akkad. Trella will make sure we are resupplied with enough food along the way, so we can have an orderly retreat if we have to return here. Meanwhile, Bantor and you will prepare Akkad for an extended siege. Food and weapons for at least six months will have to be stockpiled. But we hope it does not come to that. If we have to fight behind Akkad's walls, it will mean the enemy has driven us back from the Dellen Pass."

Daro had another question. "If the Dellen Pass and Akkad will be the Elamite's main thrust, how will Sargon block the enemy from resupplying?"

"The time has come for the Alur Meriki to fulfill their pledge. Chief Bekka, Sargon, and more than a thousand Alur Meriki warriors will soon be on their way to Elam's northern lands. Once the Elamite army has entered the Dellen Pass, Sargon and the warriors will disrupt any supply lines behind them. With almost all the Elamite soldiers taking part in the invasion, the Elamites will have no force in reserve to deal with Sargon and the warriors."

Everyone's eyes went to Sargon, who nodded. "The warriors of the Ur Nammu and the Alur Meriki are eager for this fight. They will ravage everything they find."

Eskkar went on. "With luck, Sargon and the warriors will only need to stop the flow of supplies for a few days. Without food and water, the Elamites will have to break our ranks, or fall back. And they are not going to break our soldiers. Bantor and Alexar have trained them into the finest fighting force in the land."

"That we have," Alexar said. "Our spearmen and archers are ready."

Eskkar nodded. "Even so, we have considered every possible way to maximize the number of men we can put into the field. We will be greatly outnumbered on every front, and never have we put together such a difficult battle plan. Much depends on events that will unfold in the next two months. Fortunately, thanks to Annok-sur, King Shirudukh of the Elamites believes what we want him to believe, that we are unprepared and without allies. He expects an easy victory with his superior numbers. That is the weakness we will exploit. "

He glanced around the table, and saw no signs of fear or doubt. "Remember, I've been fighting my enemies for nearly thirty years. One lesson I've learned very well is that even a small force, used ruthlessly and with all possible speed, can defeat a more numerous or stronger enemy. Especially if that enemy is not expecting the tactics and weapons we have prepared."

"Some of our men will be worried about the enemy's numbers," Mitrac said, speaking for the first time.

Eskkar leaned forward, his hands resting on the Map Table. "Most of our soldiers are simple men, who place their trust in their leaders. They know that we will not throw away their lives, that we will not fight a senseless battle. As long as we show no signs of worry or apprehension, they will believe they can win. We must not display even the slightest sign of doubt of our victory. There must be no loose talk to give them pause."

Everyone at the table understood that. If the men distrusted their commanders, morale would vanish. And once an army took a single step to the rear, they were as liable to turn and run as stand and fight.

"Will we be using the river to fight those attacking Sumer?" Daro had led the war boats that helped defeat the Sumerians.

"No, Daro," Eskkar said. "This time we have a different surprise for those invading the south. You and Master Miner Orodes will be working together on that. Yavtar has given me an interesting suggestion, and you are the best man to carry it through."

Drakis and a few of the others chuckled at Daro's expression of surprise at the mention of Orodes's name.

"What about the Elamites coming from the north, through the Jkarian Pass? How will we stop them?" Draelin raised the final question.

"That will be your assignment, Draelin." Eskkar grinned at another surprised look, this time on Draelin's face. Then Eskkar nodded to Trella.

"We have a bold plan to hold back the enemy coming through the Jkarian Pass," Trella said. "But it would be best if we do not speak of that now, Draelin. You will learn all about it this afternoon. Now we will spend the rest of today and tomorrow, if need be, to discuss the rest of our plans, and the role each of you will play in the coming fight. All of you have plenty of experience in fighting, and we must all draw upon that knowledge."

Eskkar straightened up and crossed his arms. "For almost three years, King Shirudukh of Elam has planned our downfall. He thinks we are weak, that we will tremble in fear at the size of his armies. But the surprise will be his, when he finds out we are united and ready for his invasion. And when Elam's armies are driven back, I intend to lead an army of as many men as we can raise into Elam, and teach Shirudukh what fate awaits anyone who attacks Akkad."

11

Twenty-five days later . . .

When the order came to halt, Orodes breathed a sigh of relief, grateful to slide down from the horse and give his backside a rest. While the richest man in Akkad knew enough about horses for a man raised inside the city's walls, he lacked both the skill and experience to ride day after day over rough terrain. Still and all, the trip through the steep hills and cliffs offered enough danger even for an experienced horseman. Fortunately, on this expedition, all Orodes had to do was follow the horse in front of him.

Along the long and crooked line of men and horses, riders swung down from their mounts and stretched. Orodes handed his horse's halter to the soldier assigned to care for the animal, and walked the forty or so paces needed to reach the head of the column.

A huge jumble of fallen rocks blocked the way forward. A steep cliff rose up on his right hand side, with a sharp drop on his left. One glance told him they had reached their destination. Or rather the start of their journey. Now the hard work, Orodes's work, would begin.

He recalled the first day he saw the mine at Nuzi, and knew that he alone of all the miners in Akkad understood how to rip the ores from the earth's bosom. Since those days, Orodes's skills had grown even sharper.

Others would have abandoned the Nuzi mine when the easy veins of gold played out, but he had devised a way to extract high quality silver from the ores, digging his tunnels ever deeper into the earth. Without the gold and silver that flowed from Nuzi into Lady Trella's coffers, the Akkadian war against Sumer would have been lost.

Now Orodes was expected to save Akkad a second time. To this end, Lady Trella had plucked him once again, this time from his wealth and comfort, and sent him riding south, with a new challenge.

In his absence, servants and apprentices in Nuzi would keep the silver flowing from the mine. Trella demanded an expert in working with rock and stone, chisel and hammer. Now the time for him to begin his task had arrived.

Orodes reached the head of the column and stared upward at the rocks that had, over the years, cascaded down from the cliff, making what little path they followed into the foothills impassable for the horses. Luka, the young man guiding the expedition, stood with hands on his hips, staring up at the rocks.

Orodes joined him. "Is this the place?"

"This is it." Luka raised his hand and pointed. A bronze chisel protruded from the rock face. "There's my mark."

"Are you sure?"

A few soldiers standing nearby and watching with interest at the first obstacle, chuckled at Orodes's question, and he realized that his words sounded a bit childish. Who else would have hammered a piece of bronze into a rock in the middle of nowhere? Not that Orodes cared what a bunch of soldiers believed or said. With his wealth, he could afford to ignore what others thought about him.

"Yes, this is the place."

Luka looked barely old enough to know how to wipe his bottom, but Orodes knew the man had nineteen seasons, and probably a wife or two back in Akkad. Luka had fought as a slinger in the battle against the Alur Meriki two years ago, so Orodes had to treat him as a veteran. More important, Luka had managed to climb or crawl his way over every jumble of rocks in these foothills until he reached the Great Sea.

At least, that's what he told King Eskkar and Lady Trella. Most travelers thought these hills impenetrable. Orodes still had his doubts about Luka's claim.

"Well, Orodes, we're here." Daro, the leader of the sixty soldiers and twenty supply men that comprised the remainder of the little expedition, moved up to join Luka and Orodes. "Now it's up to you. What do we do next?"

His mind already at work, Orodes ignored the soldier's words. All the same, Daro's presence on this enterprise had aroused Orodes's curiosity. Daro's background as an archer, and his experience with boats should have seen him assigned to some task on the river.

Instead, he had received this command, that of supporting Orodes and his laborers as they dug their way to the Great Sea.

Orodes had attempted to talk to Daro about his orders, but the soldier merely smiled, and repeated the same meaningless words that Orodes had received from Trella. Namely, how important it was for Orodes to be successful. Part of Orodes wondered what Daro's orders would be in the event of failure. But the time for those questions had passed.

Instead Orodes stared at the rocks blocking their way. They looked impassable, but he had dug his way through worse obstacles before. Ripping gold and silver ores from the bowels of the earth had taught him more than once that what seemed impossible at first glance often yielded soon enough to men's concentrated efforts. Especially when directed by a master miner such as himself.

"I need to see what's ahead." Orodes moved to the boulders blocking the way, placed his hands on their surface, and examined the rocks. He recognized the quartz, of course, and more than a few slabs of hematite.

In the last two days of journeying through these foothills, he had seen the concentration of salt-bearing rocks increase, easily visible by the rapid erosion that left cracks and gaps in the cliff and streaks of white scattered across their surface. Over time, those gaps would grow, until a chunk of the cliff wall could no longer support its own weight, and then a section would come tumbling down, usually shattering into hundreds of pieces. Exactly what had happened here.

The good news, if there were to be anything good about this expedition, was that all these types of rocks could be worked. Skill and experience would be needed, but Orodes knew he had both qualities. As for the rest of the soldiers, they'd learn soon enough. He'd endured plenty of their jests and followed too many of their wearisome orders in the last sixteen days. Now they would obey his. He'd make sure they put their backs into it.

"Let's get started." Orodes gestured to Luka.

"Follow me." Luka began climbing. He moved up the steep surface like a mountain goat, scarcely using his hands to help his ascent.

Orodes tried to follow his example. Before he reached a quarter of the way up, he slipped and burned the skin from his hand trying to stop his slide. Back where he started, Orodes took a deep breath, and ignored the glib mutterings behind him. That would stop soon enough. Once the work started, every soldier would be carrying rocks from dawn to dusk.

He climbed again, this time moving with greater care and making sure his feet had a firm grip for every step. Just before setting out from Akkad, Orodes had complained to his shoemaker about the high price of the thick leather sandals protecting his feet, but now he thanked the gods for the sturdy leather. Nevertheless, Orodes kept his eyes on his footing, glancing up now and then to make sure he followed in Luka's steps.

At last Orodes, breathing hard, reached the top, about twenty-five paces above the soldiers below. Luka extended his hand down to help, and Orodes, ten seasons older and in much weaker physical condition, was not too proud to accept.

Looking around, Orodes followed the base of the cliffs into the distance. Perhaps half a mile away, he saw what appeared to be another landslide obstructed the way. They'd have to go over that one, too, but from here it looked passable. He returned his attention to the rocks beneath his feet.

Staring down, he saw the jumble of boulders, large rocks, stones, and even flat chunks of the cliff that had collapsed. About fifty paces of trail, wide enough to accommodate two horses riding side by side, would need to be cleared, perhaps more. Moving these stones would be dangerous, but from what he could see, it could be done.

For this first obstacle, the soldiers would have to start from the top. No doubt some of the subsequent blockages would have to be worked from the bottom, undermining the boulders and slabs of stone. Here, the loose fragments could simply be tossed over the side into the depths below.

Not having to carry the rocks away would save time and labor. The larger pieces would have to be broken up first. Supposedly all these soldiers understood how to use a hammer and chisel, but he knew how often fighting men lied about such claims. For the promise of an extra copper or two, they'd swear they had swum the length of the Tigris. Still, with luck, he might not lose more than a couple of men to falls or injuries.

Orodes turned to Luka. "What else is up ahead?"

"About a mile farther on, around the base of that hill, there's another pile of rocks blocking the way."

Orodes realized he'd asked a stupid question. Of course there would be more blockages. If the way south were easily cleared, someone would have done so years ago. Well, one obstacle at a time.

"Let's get back down." Orodes glanced below at the crowd of soldiers and horses beneath him, all taking their ease and staring up at him, mouths gaping open. The descent, of course, was always more dangerous than the ascent. Still he intended to get down without a fall. "You go first, and make sure I reach the trail in one piece."

With a grin, Luka led the way, sometimes clinging to the stones with one hand while offering his other to assist Orodes. Luka's arms, Orodes noticed, appeared almost as hard and well-muscled as any of the famed Akkadian bowmen. Despite the slinger's help, Orodes found himself again out of breath when he slid down the last few paces.

Daro waited for them. Orodes saw that the rest of the men had already unpacked the sacks from the supply animals.

"Can we get through?" Daro stared upward at the jumble of rocks.

"Yes, of course." Orodes tried to keep the superiority out of his voice. No sense antagonizing one of Eskkar's favorite commanders. Daro had also fought against the Alur Meriki, and in the Battle of Isin as well. "It will take a few days to clear the path. I'll send the first crew up now. We've still got plenty of daylight left. Meanwhile, the second crew can get busy expanding the trail behind us. No sense having them stand about idle."

Some of the soldiers had once worked in quarries or mines. Before the expedition left Akkad, Orodes had satisfied himself that most of them did indeed know how to handle a hammer and chisel, and even how to split a rock. In addition, he'd brought with him five of his finest rock masons, all men skilled in mining and working with stone. Each would direct a team of eight soldiers.

In a way, the soldiers would make better workers than the usual slaves laboring in the mines. These men were stronger and disciplined, and Orodes didn't have to waste time or manpower worrying about them running away or pretending to be ill. And with a regular supply of food promised from Akkad, none of these men would starve to death, a common fate of slaves laboring in the mines. He turned to Luka.

"Next time we climb up like that, you'll go first and string a rope. We don't want anyone falling down and injuring themselves before they reach the top."

By 'anyone,' of course, Orodes meant himself. If another man fell and broke his neck, he could be replaced. Orodes didn't intend to take any more chances with his own skin.

Time to get to work. He gathered his five masons and gave them their orders. They broke out their tools – finely crafted bronze hammers and chisels, thick pry bars, stout wooden pegs to help split the rocks, ropes, and sturdy shovels. With their usual efficiency, Trella's minions had ensured that only the finest equipment, and plenty of it, traveled with the special expedition.

Standing well back, Orodes watched Luka ascend the landslide once again, this time carrying a hammer, chisels, and a length of rope. After Luka had fastened the climbing rope, Orodes instructed the men about his first rule of climbing. Once the way to the top was secured, Orodes would always be the first one up, so he could fall on something soft, like the man behind him, and Orodes would be the last one down, so that no one could fall on him.

At the top, Orodes showed his men where to start, what to do, and what not to do.

"It will take a few days to clear this mess, so work with care. Get rid of all the loose shale first."

The men broke into teams and started. In moments, the crash of stones landing fifty paces below echoed through the hills. The most senior mason took his eight soldiers and began cracking the larger pieces of rock. First they wedged the stone in place, to hold it steady. Then a few blows from the hammer often sufficed to split the rock. For the harder stones, the men employed a chisel. In moments, dust and rock chips were flying through the air.

The hot sun, reflected off the cliff walls, soon had every man sweating. With no trees and precious little shade, the work would be even more difficult. Water, too, would be in short supply, packed in on horseback from the last stream. But Daro had assured Orodes that livery men would be arriving with fresh water every day.

Orodes supervised every activity. He'd have to do that, until he learned which men he could trust, and the extent of their abilities. Still, unlike the usual lot of sullen slaves who worked in the Nuzi mine, these soldiers were willing enough. They realized that Orodes knew what he was doing.

By mid afternoon, the men tired. Orodes ordered them down, and the next work crew sent up. Once again he instructed them on what to do, watched them work, and studied their skills. The second crew lasted until the afternoon shadows began to lengthen. He ordered a halt. No sense risking an injury by working in the fading light. As soon as the last man started down, Orodes followed, using the rope all the way.

Once again Daro waited at the bottom. "How long to clear this pile?"

Orodes knew the question wasn't really about this obstacle. "Two or three days. Assuming the rest of the men are as competent as the first two crews who worked today. But whether we can get to the Great Sea in the next seventy days, who knows? Luka claims there are forty-four rock piles that need to be cleared."

"Luka should know. He made the trip all the way to the sea."

Orodes still had his doubts about that, but decided now wasn't the time to bring them up. "Luka did it last year, Daro. New landslides may have blocked other parts of the trail, or made existing ones larger. We're likely to bring down a few ourselves."

"What causes these rock slides?"

Orodes lifted his hands and let them drop. "Wind, rain, snow, heat, cold, who knows? Perhaps all of those things. Or it could just be some angry demon living in the mountains, turning over in his sleep and shaking the rocks loose." Orodes didn't really believe in demons, but he'd seen enough strange things happen beneath the earth to not discount anything.

"It doesn't look like you made much progress today."

"Don't worry about it, Daro. We'll get as far south as we can."

No sense trying to explain quarry work to a soldier. Orodes walked away, searching for the pack horse that held his personal baggage. He still had some bread and honey in his pouch, and he wanted to find a comfortable place to spread his blanket and enjoy his supper alone. Then he intended to get a good night's sleep.

Two days later, the men broke through the last of the rocks, and Orodes nodded in satisfaction. He even offered a gruff word or two of praise for the men's labors. As soon as the soldiers swept the last of the rubble off the trail, the little caravan collected its tools and resumed its march.

"Will we make it in time? If it took three days to get through this blockage . . ."

Orodes, riding at Daro's side, considered ignoring the question. But the soldier had been pleasant enough, and Orodes didn't want to be arguing with everyone for however long the dig lasted.

"I can't say yet, Daro. This was the first obstacle, so we learned quite a bit about the rocks and how to move them. All the men now know what to do, so our work will go faster. Remember, not all the passages will be as difficult as this one. Some will go quicker than others. Meanwhile, when we reach the second blockage, we'll send a small crew on ahead to the third, to begin work there. That way we'll always be working on two obstructions at a time."

"It still seems impossible. I mean, to get all the way to the Great Sea in such a short time."

"Well, that's why I'm here." Orodes laughed, a grim sound that rolled against the cliff face. "To make it possible. You just make sure the men have what they need, and do what they're told."

The soldier grunted, ending the brief conversation.

Despite his bold words, Orodes had his own doubts. After what he'd seen today, he should have started at least twenty or thirty days earlier. But Trella undoubtedly had her reasons, whatever they might be. Still, these were good men, and not afraid of hard labor. Time and the gods would tell. One down, and forty three to go.

12

Eskkar swung down from his horse with a grunt of satisfaction. Behind him, the twenty Hawk Clan guards did the same, all of them just as grateful to be off the back of a horse. For almost a month, the King and his guards had ridden from sunup to dusk, visiting the foothills and passes of the Zagros Mountains. Eskkar had sworn to himself that he would study every patch of ground between Akkad and the Jkarian Pass.

Whatever happened in the coming war with the Elamites, he intended to know the best places to fight or defend well in advance.

For this expedition, Eskkar had brought with him Mitrac, Akkad's Master Archer. Mitrac had wanted one more look at the Dellen Pass, in particular the place where the battle would most likely take place.

But now the day's traveling had ended, and for once the sun still stood high in the afternoon sky. Eskkar hadn't visited the village of Nuzi in many months. But since his return journey from the northern lands brought him within a half day's ride of the mine, he'd allowed Mitrac to convince him that they should stop and visit both the garrison and the source of Akkad's gold and silver coins.

So Mitrac had commanded the guards and ridden at Eskkar's side. Mitrac had looked forward to the stop at Nuzi, since he had friends there. In any case, Eskkar had grudgingly admitted that too many months had passed since he last inspected the troops at Nuzi. Another day or two, added to the nearly thirty days since Eskkar had departed Akkad, wouldn't make much of a difference.

Trella would be pleased as well. She depended on the mine's output, which she turned into gold, silver, and copper coins, to recruit, arm, train, and pay Akkad's soldiers. The more time her husband spent at Nuzi, the smoother the operation would run.

Because of its value, the silver mine at Nuzi remained one of the most heavily guarded places in the Land Between the Rivers. The original find and initial excavation had yield plenty of gold, but those thick veins had faded away to mere threads. Many of the miners had expected to exhaust the ores years ago.

However the ancient upheaval that lifted the heavy metals close to the surface had proved to be far more extensive than Master Miner Orodes or anyone could have imagined. While most of the surface nuggets and veins had already been mined, the ever-deeper shafts into the earth continued to produce acceptable quantities of silver, as well as smaller amounts of gold and copper.

Over the years, ores of lead, copper, tin, iron, azurite, malachite, and other minerals extracted from the earth had proved nearly as valuable as the silver and gold. Almost by accident, Nuzi had become Akkad's main source of the bronze needed by its soldiers and craftsmen.

Forges sprang up around the mine, and the smoke from burning charcoal and heating metal hung in the air from dawn to dusk. The wealth of Nuzi paid for more than half of all of Akkad's expenditures.

With so much of value to protect, the garrison of soldiers stationed there had grown as well, and before long, a training camp was established nearby. Now hundreds of archers and spearmen trained at the new camp. Women, of course, accompanied their men, and soon children increased the population. Now three good-sized villages, with their outlying farms and herds, surrounded the mine and smelting pits.

Orodes and his senior apprentices still directed the operation of the ore pits and smelters, but lately the Master Miner spent most of his time in Akkad. With the vast wealth he'd earned from Nuzi since the war with Sumer, Orodes had become the richest man in Akkad. These days he much preferred the company of his wives and pleasure slaves in Akkad, where he lived in a large house surrounded by a stout wall, and protected by a sizeable contingent of personal guards.

The mine, the soldiers' garrison, and the training camps were under the command of Tooraj. One of the older members of the Hawk Clan, he'd lost an eye in the final battle against the Alur Meriki, when they sought to overwhelm the city's wall.

Tooraj, too, had been at Nuzi since its beginnings, and his responsibilities had grown as steadily as the mine. He also provided security for the villagers and craftsmen who dwelt near the excavation. They were represented by a small council of elders, who made sure that the miners and soldiers treated them fairly.

"Lord Eskkar, it's good to see you again." Tooraj, a few seasons older than Eskkar, looked just as fit. A patch covered his left eye socket, to keep out the dirt and dust. "Welcome to Nuzi."

"What, you can't remember your Captain?" Eskkar laughed, and hugged the soldier until he pleaded for mercy.

Tooraj nodded at the compliment. "It's been a long time, Captain, since you've been here. I was out on patrol during your last visit."

"Well, this time you can show me everything you accomplished. My men need a rest, so we'll remain here tonight and tomorrow." Eskkar nodded toward Mitrac. "You remember Tooraj?"

"Oh, yes, he fought at my side when the barbarians attacked Akkad's walls. I understand he's been most helpful in making Deltin at ease. I would like to see Deltin and give him a message from Daro."

Tooraj clasped arms with Eskkar's companion. Hawk Clan members did not forget the oaths they'd sworn to their fellow clansmen. "Deltin's a good man, Mitrac. Daro did well to rescue him."

Nuzi held one additional secret, known only to a few. A prosperous Akkadian also lived near the mine, a man named Deltin. Only a handful knew his real name – Sabatu. Lady Trella had insisted on the name change. She and her agents remained most cautious in their handling of the Elamite refugee.

"I suppose Mitrac would like to meet his friend at once," Tooraj said. "What would you prefer to do, Captain?"

"I'll accompany Mitrac," Eskkar said. "He's very interested in Deltin's progress."

"He lives on the other side of the garrison," Tooraj said, "upwind of most of the smelting ovens. Not a long walk, if you would like to stretch your legs."

They did. Leaving their horses behind, the three men set off at a brisk pace. Tooraj explained that Sabatu occupied a large house of his own, just a few paces from where the old Hawk Clan soldier had established his own headquarters. A wall as tall as a man surrounded Sabatu's dwelling, but the open gate was unguarded, and they passed into what Eskkar expected to be the usual garden. Instead, he found himself at a small archery range.

Tooraj called out Deltin's name, and the Elamite emerged from the house, surprised to find that he had visitors. As soon as he saw Eskkar, Deltin bowed low.

"No need for that," Eskkar said. "You look well."

After Sabatu decided to help Akkad's cause, he'd spent almost a month at Eskkar's Compound, working with the senior commanders. Sabatu also worked with Trella, Annok-sur, and especially Ismenne, Akkad's Master Map Maker. Ismenne had married Daro a few years ago. She spent several days with Sabatu, Eskkar's scouts, and some of the city's traders. Afterward Ismenne had devoted almost ten days to creating maps of Elam's western lands, and the mountains and passes of the Zagros Mountains.

While the Map Maker drew sketches of the land, Eskkar and his senior commanders had spent almost as much time with Sabatu, talking about King Shirudukh and his generals. Tactics, training, weapons, every facet of Elam's war machine was discussed and analyzed. Sabatu knew all about the likely contingents that could be summoned from various regions.

The information about the size of the armies Elam could field had sobered everyone. Nevertheless, by the end of that hectic month, Eskkar had learned all he needed to know about his enemy.

By then Trella and Annok-sur had arranged for Sabatu to move to Nuzi. The mine's close location – a full day on the river, coming down the Tigris, and less than two days going upstream from Akkad – meant that Sabatu stayed close at hand, but out of sight of the people of Akkad.

In the months since Sabatu's rescue, Yavtar's spies regularly brought back word from Sushan, but there was never a mention of the man's escape. No doubt the incident had proved too embarrassing for Grand Commander Chaiyanar, who must have blanched under the wrath of King Shirudukh over his failure to torture Sabatu to death.

Nevertheless, neither Yavtar nor Daro would ever dare tread on Sushan's docks again. The risk of finding Chaiyanar's soldiers waiting for them far outweighed any possible gain.

The last time that Eskkar had seen Sabatu, the man had not fully recovered from his injuries. But today, Eskkar saw a soldier, with powerful arms and thick muscle across his chest. The scars had faded, and he had recovered as much as he ever would. Sabatu's hands, however, yet told the story of Elam's torturers.

Sabatu's thumbs still appeared twisted, and the last three fingers on his left hand were bound together with a strip of leather.

While Mitrac and Sabatu exchanged greetings, Eskkar strode over to the table placed at the head of the archery range. The targets, two bales of hay standing close together, rested against the wall at the other end, about thirty paces away. He glanced down at the table, and saw three bows stretched out, their grips well-worn from use. All were small, curved, and quite thick, a horse fighter's weapon. Then Eskkar noticed the grip.

He picked up one of the bows. "What's this?"

"I asked Mitrac to fashion a bow that I could use, My Lord," Sabatu said. "That was before I left Akkad. Together, we carved out a bow that I can use despite my weak hands."

"All I did was talk to Sabatu about archery," Mitrac said. "Daro suggested it. The next time I was here, I spent two days with Sabatu. I really enjoyed designing a bow for him. I've never seen one like it. Then one of your Hawk Clan warriors at Aratta constructed the first weapon. He was very skilled."

When steppes warriors grew too old or injured to fight, they took up weapon making to provide for their families and to help the clan. Several Alur Meriki fighters from the original Hawk Clan had joined Eskkar after the Battle at the Stream. One of them had constructed the unique weapon for Sabatu.

Eskkar examined the bow. The oversized grip felt unbalanced to his hand. A hole, more a slot in the wood, appeared just large enough to accept the three fingers of Sabatu's left hand. When Eskkar tried to grip the bow properly, his hands didn't fit.

"It was designed for my hands, My Lord, which are smaller than yours," Sabatu said. "Instead of gripping the weapon with my left hand, I slip my three fingers into the slot. My thumb and first finger slide into the groove. The grip pushes back on the center of my palm. The arrow rests on the carved projection, to keep it close to the center of the limbs. Then I push out with my left arm to hold the bow steady. My right thumb is just strong enough to help draw the arrow. It took a month or so for the muscles in my wrist and arm to toughen up, but now I scarcely notice it."

Sabatu demonstrated. Facing the targets, he fitted his left hand into the grip, nocked a shaft, then drew it back. The muscles on his arms rippled as the thick limbs of the bow resisted the pressure. Eskkar recognized a powerful weapon, almost as difficult to draw as the ones Akkad's bowmen used. The arrow hissed through the air, and drove deep into the center of the target.

An impressive shot for a man with two crippled hands, Eskkar knew. "Can you use the bow on horseback?"

"Not very well, My Lord. "I'm still trying, but I've fallen twice already, so I think I'll always have to dismount to shoot. Perhaps in time, I'll get better at it. But for now, I'm working on my marksmanship. I've hit a mark at a hundred and twenty paces, but I'm most accurate at sixty to seventy paces."

Eskkar, always interested in weapons of any kind, hefted the bow in his hand. "I'd like to try this. Show me again."

For the rest of the afternoon, the four men took turns shooting the three weapons. Tooraj was the first to give up, and Eskkar soon followed. But by the time dusk arrived, Mitrac could use the unusual bow almost as well as Sabatu.

"You've done well, Sabatu," Eskkar said, "better than well. That's fine shooting for any archer. Let Tooraj know if there is anything else you need, and you'll have it."

He turned to Tooraj. "Come, we'll leave these two alone, while you take me around."

Eskkar and Tooraj left the house and started back toward the mine. "What do you think of Sabatu? Can he be trusted?"

"I worried about that, too," Tooraj said. "But any time in the last few months, Sabatu could have taken a horse and ridden back to Elam. By now he knows all about our plans and numbers, so he gains nothing by remaining here. I believe he's beginning to see that he can have a new life in the Land Between the Rivers. After Sabatu satisfies his desire for revenge on this Elamite Chaiyanar, that is. Until that is settled one way or another, Sabatu will never be at peace with himself."

Eskkar had believed much the same, but felt reassured hearing Tooraj confirm his opinion. "He does know about some of our ideas to defeat the Elamites. There was no way to keep that knowledge from him."

"In the beginning, Sabatu probably thought he would be killed after we'd learned what we wanted to know. But he trusts Daro and Lady Trella, so that's no longer an issue."

"Daro suspected as much, so he asked Trella to speak to him. I think she eased his mind."

"In a few months, it won't matter," Tooraj said. "By then he'll be more than deadly with that bow. I've watched Sabatu out on the archer's range, day after day, from dawn until dusk. He can shoot as well as any of our bowmen, and almost as far. Grand Commander Chaiyanar better keep his distance."

"I hope Sabatu gets close enough to take the shot," Eskkar said. "We will need every man who can bend a bow."

"Captain, when the time comes, I would like to fight alongside you and the Hawk Clan once again."

Eskkar shook his head. "I don't know of anyone who could command this place half as well as you. Besides, Trella would be dismayed if you left us. You've already given more than most men in Akkad's defense. You've no need to risk more."

"A soldier always wants to fight one last time, Captain."

"If we can't hold back the Elamites, you'll have your chance to fight. But until then, Nuzi's silver and gold production is far more important than any fighting man, even one as brave as yourself."

Tooraj grunted in disappointment. "I suppose I am getting too old."

"As am I," Eskkar said. "As am I."

"Tonight we'll dine at my house," Tooraj said. "But tomorrow, we'll have to hold a feast in your honor. They always complain that they seldom see the King."

Eskkar shrugged. That meant another night of too much food and drink, followed by a long ride the next morning. Tooraj spoke the truth. Both men were getting old when the thought of a long night of drinking and eating held only dread.

The next day, Eskkar, Mitrac, and Tooraj inspected the mine, the smelting pits, the sluices where the impurities were washed away, forges, furnaces, and all the other processes that turned rough ores into silver and bronze. Slaves and criminals worked in the mine itself, and operated most of the fire pits.

Except for serious crimes that called for execution, Akkad sentenced all its criminals to work in the mine at Nuzi. The threat of being forced to labor there helped keep many of the petty criminals and thieves out of the city.

Slaves didn't last long working in the mine. Few survived more than a year. Most would die at their labor, either by injury or from breathing the fumes. Even so, some of the criminals would serve their sentences and be given their freedom. Soldiers guarded the mine, its output, and the laborers. Fresh soldiers had to be rotated into Nuzi every few months, as the boring task of guarding slaves and protecting the silver tended to wear down even hardened soldiers.

After touring the mine, Eskkar visited the adjacent training camps. He met with commanders and subcommanders, talked to soldiers and men in training, and visited the main archery range. As the day drew to a close, he spoke with the village leaders and farmers, sympathizing with their problems and listening to any complaints. But those were few enough. Everyone who lived near Nuzi shared in its wealth.

The night's feast took place behind Tooraj's residence, and several hundred soldiers and their women, as well as villagers attended. Eskkar let himself relax, as he always did, around fighting men. As the evening's festivities ended, Eskkar said his goodbyes, and entered Tooraj's house to spend the night. Inside, Eskkar found Mitrac and Sabatu waiting for him.

The two men had sat side by side during the meal, good friends sharing pleasant conversation and an enjoyable dinner. Now Mitrac looked serious, and he excused himself, leaving Eskkar alone with Sabatu.

"My Lord," Sabatu bowed again, "As you must know, I've done everything that you and Daro have asked of me, and I have never asked for payment. But now I wish you to grant me a special favor."

"No need for that, Sabatu," Eskkar said. "Whatever it is you want, if it's in my power, I'll try to give it to you. It is we, after all, who are in your debt."

"When the war comes, My Lord, I want to join the fighting. I want to face Chaiyanar in battle, and kill him myself, if I can. Most of all, I want him to know who it is he faces. Give me that, and I will forever be in your debt."

A simple request, but Eskkar considered his reply with care. He'd seen such situations before. Fanatical men fixed only on revenge tended to make poor decisions in a fight, sometimes risking the lives of those around them. Eskkar stared into Sabatu's eyes, searching for the hatred that would lead to fatal mistakes. But the man, now fully recovered, met the King's gaze without flinching.

Eskkar saw the determination in Sabatu's eyes. "You can have your chance at revenge, Sabatu. But you must place yourself under the orders of one of my other commanders who will face Chaiyanar. You must swear to obey his orders, even if it means postponing your chance for vengeance. For your own good, and for ours, you must not take any foolish chances, at least not until the battle is decided one way or the other. If Chaiyanar catches you alive . . ."

Sabatu nodded. "I will obey the commands of the one who faces Chaiyanar, and I will take care, My Lord. No matter what happens in the battle, you have earned my thanks."

"You are a good soldier, Sabatu. But remember, the first duty of every soldier is to help his side achieve victory and to survive. That is, after all, the best revenge."

"Yes, I suppose it is, My Lord. If I may, there is one more request I would make. If I do survive, and you achieve your goal of driving back Elam's armies, then I would like to join you and your family, be part of Akkad."

"That is one request I gladly grant. No one will be more pleased than Daro to hear of your decision. He already thinks of you as his brother."

"I am sorry that you did not bring Daro with you. Will he be joining the battle at Sumer?"

"Daro has left Akkad on another, possibly more important task, Sabatu. But I am sure he would wish you good hunting."

"My Lord, you know it is likely that neither of us will survive the coming battle. I know the numbers of your soldiers. How can you hope for victory against such odds?"

"Well, Sabatu, we're not dead yet. I have fought in so many battles I've lost count of them. And in every one, I was outnumbered. Yet I am still here, and my enemies are vanquished. There is a chance for victory, I promise you that. Don't throw your life away needlessly."

"If you say we can win, then I will believe you and heed your words."

"We can win, Sabatu. It won't be easy, and we'll need some luck. But luck favors those who are most prepared for battle, and when the time comes, Akkad will be more than ready. And I for one, would not like to face you and your bow in battle. Until the day arrives, keep practicing your archery."

Sabatu bowed. When he lifted his head to meet Eskkar's gaze, all the strength of the soldier within had returned. "That I will, My Lord, that I will."

13

Sargon swung down from his horse and tossed the halter to one of the swarm of young boys who rushed to greet him. He needed only a few steps before he joined the circle of warriors who'd gathered in front of Subutai's tent. Sargon's arrival at the Ur Nammu camp was two days late, but he didn't bother to explain. They would have endured the same rains that slowed his ride north.

His escort of fifty Akkadians hadn't even settled into their campground. Sargon had ridden straight in, pausing only long enough to rid himself of most of the grime and mud of the journey. Despite the invasion already on the move toward Akkad, Sargon wanted to deliver his words in person. Nor was now the time to allow any possible insult to a free and proud people like the Alur Meriki and Ur Nammu. He would not send an underling to order them to give battle.

He knew all the chiefs waiting for him. Subutai, Fashod, and Chinua of the Ur Nammu. Bekka and Suijan and Unegen from the Alur Meriki. The chiefs, and all their warriors, had gathered at a campsite agreed upon months ago. Far to the north, and at the base of the mountains, its location would save many days of riding when the ride east began.

Sargon bowed to those present, but ignored the usual pleasantries. "The Elamites are on the move. Our spies inform us that they are massing their soldiers and making their final preparations before marching west. Their plan is cross the mountains in two fronts at nearly the same time, to sow confusion in our lands. By now the eastern mouths of both the Jkarian and Dellen Passes have been sealed off to our scouts, and no more word of their actions will be coming through. I expect they'll start moving toward these lands soon, if they haven't already started."

"Then it is time for us to ride east." Subutai turned to Bekka. "I am ready to join Chief Bekka's forces."

In the last two years, the leaders of their respective peoples had grown closer. Much of the old resentment between the two Clans had died out. The food and supplies from Akkad had helped bring them together, of course. But in the last few months, the knowledge that they would soon be again confronting a common enemy had drawn the Ur Nammu and Alur Meriki into something more than a fragile peace.

The old steppes saying had proved true once again – the enemy of my enemy is my friend. The Elamites held only hatred for all the steppes warriors.

Bekka nodded approvingly to Subutai. "My warriors are ready. I am bringing almost eleven hundred warriors and boys with me. As well as many extra horses, though I expect we'll find enough of them in the east."

"I have readied two hundred and thirty warriors," Subutai declared. "Together we will strike a heavy blow against the Elamites."

"The warriors of the Alur Meriki and Ur Nammu are brave," Sargon said, "but my father asked me to remind you that you need not risk your men's lives in unnecessary battles, or challenge their forces directly. Your presence in their rear will do much to disrupt their preparations and cut Modran's supply line." Sargon took a deep breath. "My father also said to tell you that he wishes he could ride with you into battle."

Sargon knew his father meant the words. All his life, Eskkar had wanted to ride to war with his warrior clan. But Eskkar, after the murder of his family by the Clan's sarum, had fled his people before Eskkar had the chance. Now, once again, the opportunity would be denied him.

"You will ride in his place, Sargon, and do us much honor." Bekka, too, meant his words. A king's son would face the same dangers as his warriors.

Sargon bowed again. His father had reluctantly accepted that decision, but now was not the time to bring it up again. Sargon had insisted on riding with his adopted Ur Nammu kin, and none of Eskkar or Trella's arguments had changed his mind. Sargon might have grown up and accepted his parents and his responsibilities, but in their eyes, he remained as stubborn as ever.

"You will be a great help to us." Subutai knew of the many heated discussions between father and son. "You know your father's plans, as well as the minds of the Elamites. And you now speak their language. That will prove useful."

Sargon, along with his friend Garal, had spent more than two months learning the Elamite's main tongue.

"I am glad that I can ride in my father's place." Sargon didn't trust himself to say more. Subutai knew that Eskkar would have preferred Sargon stay behind, or at least join him defending Akkad. But Sargon had declared that he could be the most help to Akkad by riding with the warriors. In the end, Eskkar had shrugged his shoulders and given in.

The King's son had turned into a man, and was entitled to make his own choices, even if that meant riding into battle in a distant land against a mighty empire.

"The supply arrangements for your women and children are in place," Sargon went on. "And I'm leaving my fifty men behind to guard the supply camp, along with the older Hawk Clan warriors. Most have too many seasons to fight in this campaign, but they should do well enough to help guard your camps."

"Both our clans will keep scouts out far and wide," Bekka said. "If an enemy approaches, we will fall back to your supply camp."

Soldiers and laborers had established a large campsite surrounded by a palisade, a small village, really, to store the food and herd animals needed to support the two Clans while their warriors rode to war. The fortified village would also provide protection in case of the sudden appearance of some enemy.

"My mother's people have created a new map to guide you, Chief Bekka." As leader of the majority of fighters, the Alur Meriki sarum would command the raid. Sargon drew the cloth from his pouch and spread it out on the blanket. "Remember, you should avoid the Elamites in the Jkarian Pass. If they find their way blocked, they may turn back."

The chiefs exchanged glances, but no one spoke for a long moment.

"You still believe you have a way to stop that force?" Subutai asked the question that all the clan leaders wanted to ask.

Until recently, only Sargon knew of Alcinor's plan to topple a mountain, which might or might not succeed. It wasn't that Eskkar didn't trust his allies, but the fewer who knew the details the better. Any man could be captured and tortured into revealing what he knew. But the time for that secrecy had passed.

Sargon told Subutai and the others of the plan to seal the Jkarian Pass. "If our Engineer can't close the pass, we at least hope to slow the invaders down enough to keep them out of the fighting for a few days. If they do get through, they can devastate the countryside. Or they might even attack my father's supply line. They should be no threat to your people. General Jedidia won't bother coming this far north. His plan will be to isolate Akkad and loot the countryside."

When Sargon finished, no one spoke. The idea of moving a mountain didn't come easily to such men.

"I know Master Engineer Alcinor well," Sargon said, breaking the silence. "If anyone can accomplish this task, it is he."

Sargon's words would carry more weight than his father's. "No man can be certain of such things, but, yes, I believe Alcinor will find a way to block the pass. For how long, I don't know. Hopefully long enough to make them turn back to resupply their men."

"How many Elamites do you expect your father to face in the Dellen Pass?" Bekka had heard the earlier estimates, but he knew that Sargon would have the latest information.

"Between twenty-five and twenty-eight thousand men. Over five thousand mounted."

"And Eskkar will have how many to oppose them?" This time Subutai asked the blunt question.

"A little more than six thousand," Sargon answered. "Plus another thousand or so for a rear guard and to deliver supplies to the battleground."

None of the chiefs met his gaze. The numbers foretold a grim story. Finally Subutai lifted his eyes. "Can you stop them with so few?"

Sargon shrugged. "It is all that we have. My father does not need to defeat them, just force them to turn back. With your help, he should be able to hold them off." Sargon wasn't as confident as he sounded, but he had no intention of voicing any doubts.

"And the enemy force that marches toward Sumer?"

"King Naxos of Isin and Hathor have ridden south with five thousand horsemen to deal with the invaders. Our cavalry will be greatly outnumbered, but all they need to do is make sure the siege of Sumer is broken."

"What happens if this King Naxos is defeated, and Sumer falls?" Subutai persisted.

"Then the war is lost. Isin and Akkad will fall in turn, and after them the rest of the Land Between the Rivers. If that day comes, the Alur Meriki and Ur Nammu will be alone."

"The situation then is grave." Chief Bekka of the Alur Meriki added his worries to those of Subutai. "There is much that can go wrong."

Again, Sargon nodded. These leaders knew as well as any of Akkad's commanders that battle plans drawn up months in advance and far from the actual fighting often led not to victory, but disaster. All the same, he had little more to offer them. But every clan leader there had reason to respect Eskkar's ability to plan where and when he gave battle.

"Yes, it is true that much can wrong. But Sumer will not fall easily, not with a large army of our fighters loose in the countryside and striking at the enemy's rear. My father will only need to hold the Dellen Pass for ten or fifteen days. If Chief Bekka can disrupt their supply caravans, then Lord Modran and his army will have to fall back, and the invasion will have failed. My father can then move south and deal with any Elamites still besieging Sumer. By then, even if the enemy gets through the Jkarian Pass, they won't have enough numbers to attack Akkad."

Bekka nodded. "Your father will face the heaviest fighting, Sargon. He will indeed need the blessing of the gods."

"It is a way of fighting that my father has learned well," Sargon agreed. "His men are well prepared for this fight. Now much depends on whether we can get into the Elamite lands in time."

"When should we leave?"

"At once, Chief Bekka," Sargon said. "The enemy appears to have moved his forces a few days earlier than we expected."

"Then tomorrow, we will also begin our ride," Bekka said. "At least we are well prepared with food and horses along the way. I will dispatch messengers to gather the men. We will have a long ride before we reach the lands beyond the mountains."

"My father's last words to me were to bid you both good hunting, Chief Bekka, and you, Chief Subutai." Sargon rose. "Eskkar said that it may be some time before he speaks to you again, but he knows that you will strike a heavy blow. And that Akkad will not forget your help in our time of need."

The three men knew that it was likely none of them would ever see Eskkar alive again.

After a moment of silence, Subutai turned to Sargon. "You will stand in your father's place during our battle. Of that, I know he would approve."

"We will begin our journey tomorrow, at dawn," Bekka said. "The Alur Meriki and our allies ride to war together, and the Elamites will feel our wrath."

"Then I will return to my tent and make my own preparations." Everything Sargon needed waited there. He wanted one last evening with Tashanella. This was the first time since their marriage that he rode to war.

14

Fifty days after Orodes and his diggers went south to clear the way to the Great Sea, Engineer Alcinor, son of Master Builder Corio, accompanied another troop of men and soldiers. This caravan also departed the city in secret, collecting men, supplies, and pack animals waiting at farms well away from Akkad. Once assembled, they headed north, toward the mouth of the Jkarian Pass, just over a hundred and eighty miles to the northeast.

The Elamite invasion loomed, but at least now the city's inhabitants knew the name of the enemy that threatened to destroy them. Talk of war had long disturbed the peaceful lives of the people of Akkad. Fresh rumors swept through the lanes and ale houses, each story contradicting another. The Elamites would be outside the walls tomorrow. The Elamites were attacking Sumer. The Elamites were rampaging through the northern lands.

The tales spread so rapidly that few could keep up with them. One fact remained – Akkad's soldiers trained from dawn to dusk, as they prepared for the coming invasion.

For the second time in his life, Alcinor left a troubled city and rode toward danger, when every instinct urged him to turn the horse around and run for his life. Of course Alcinor knew there was no place to flee.

The Elamites would overrun the Land Between the Rivers, and no city or village would be safe for long. Not to mention that he would be recognized wherever he went. Still, the irrational impulse kept reappearing, disrupting Alcinor's sleep and adding to his private doubts about his mission.

Thoughts of his wives and children stiffened Alcinor's resolve. He'd risked personal danger before, at the Battle of Isin, and survived. For his family, his city, and his own sense of honor, he would risk it again.

Alcinor had helped make the victory at Isin possible. He remembered how, at Lady Trella's request, he'd visited Isin a year earlier, to secretly study its defenses. While examining Isin's walls and surrounding terrain, Alcinor had conceived the idea to flood the city.

When Eskkar and his army reached Isin, with the vast Sumerian army in pursuit, Alcinor personally supervised over a thousand soldiers who dug the great ditch. The day before the battle, when Eskkar rode out to meet King Naxos under a truce, only Alcinor had accompanied him.

Alcinor had described his plans to move the river and destroy the city to Isin's King. For a few moments, Alcinor thought that Naxos in his rage would attempt to kill both Eskkar and himself. Instead Isin's ruler had yielded to Alcinor's all too real threat to drown Isin, and Naxos remained neutral in the Great Battle that took place the following day.

By that stroke, Alcinor had nullified over two thousand soldiers of Isin, whose presence surely would have meant the difference between victory and defeat in the close-fought battle that destroyed Sumer's attempt to invade Akkad's lands. After seeing the aftermath of the bloody fighting, bodies torn asunder, the overpowering stench of blood and worse, and the wretched cries of the wounded, Alcinor felt relief that he had lessened the carnage for the soldiers of Akkad.

At Isin, Alcinor had relied on Eskkar and an entire army of soldiers to protect him. Now he rode into the Jkarian Pass with an escort of only one hundred cavalrymen. If they encountered anything larger than an Elamite scouting party, the Akkadians stood a good chance of ending up dead. Alcinor had to hope that for the next fifteen or twenty days, the soldiers of Elam continued to ignore the Jkarian Pass, until he had time to seal the passage.

Despite the danger, Alcinor looked forward to the challenge. If he succeeded, he would be the first man to move a mountain, truly an achievement worthy of Akkad's foremost Engineer.

Now the time to make good on his boast had arrived. Alcinor was returning to the Jkarian Pass for the third time. But this expedition included an enormous pack train of supplies, as well as an assortment of artisans and laborers. The war with Elam would start in thirty or forty days, and he'd known all too well that he might need much of that time to accomplish his mission.

Instead, bad luck dogged the expedition from the start, as Alcinor's caravan encountered one delay after another. They had started later than he wanted, waiting for the oak logs, now carefully trimmed, to dry. After only two days on the road, heavy rain held them up for three days. A day after they resumed traveling, a bout of illness, doubtless from some food supplies contaminated by the downpour, swept through half the men. That cost the cavalcade another two days.

Nine more days of slow traveling ensued before they reached the primary supply site. There, too, they encountered another setback. The same rains that had impeded Alcinor had also prevented some of the supplies he needed from arriving early. Gritting his teeth, Alcinor endured another three days of waiting before the expedition resumed its progress.

Even then, the caravan, burdened with the odd supplies he needed for this task, moved slower than Alcinor wished. Nevertheless, they finally reached their first destination, the mouth of the Jkarian Pass, which lay at the base of the Zagros Mountains. They turned east and entered the pass, beginning the gradual climb into the foothills, along the oldest known trade route to the Indus.

As soon as Alcinor's caravan headed east, they were moving directly toward the lands of the Elamites. The enemy might easily have dispatched their own soldiers to guard the pass. In that case, Alcinor would be lucky to get back to Akkad alive, and the intricate plan he had concocted would be in ruins.

Alcinor forced himself to ignore his worries. The soldiers trusted Eskkar, and the King and his wife trusted Alcinor. It would not do to show fear or doubt in front of Commander Draelin and his men. While Alcinor might not have the courage of a soldier, to stand and face an enemy with a sword, at least he knew he had the respect of the men. Some of them held him in awe, remembering what he had done at Isin.

Draelin commanded the one hundred cavalrymen, and the presence of one of Akkad's senior commanders indicated the importance of this mission. Eskkar obviously anticipated they might run into trouble, so Draelin's horsemen were comprised of some of the finest cavalry in Akkad's army.

The day they departed the city, Alcinor had stood beside Draelin when the soldier received his final orders from King Eskkar – get

Alcinor to the Pass, safeguard him while he worked, and supply him with whatever physical labor he might need to accomplish his mission. The Jkarian Pass must be closed.

To achieve that end, a pack train of forty horses plodded along behind the soldiers, filled not only with the usual sacks and skins holding food and water, but an odd collection of tools and lumber. Alcinor also had four men each carrying a ladder of various size. There would be few trees inside the pass. Thirty six supply bearers struggled alongside the beasts of burden, carrying another collection of special supplies required by Alcinor and his apprentices.

Nevertheless, the most important burden – sixteen oak logs, each about ten paces long, an arm length wide, and as straight as an arrow – rested on the shoulders of another hundred and forty porters and seventy-five mules.

Trella had scoured the countryside all the way to Akkad's borders to find those mules, better animals than horses or oxen for hauling the unusual and unwieldy cargo. Each log rested in a skein of sturdy ropes that formed a sling supported by four mules, and assisted by eight husky laborers. They used smaller poles of oak passed under the log, to help carry the weight, and to support the mules over the rough terrain. Both men and beasts grunted under the heavy logs, as they struggled along.

At least the men enjoyed the luxury of cursing the brutal task, especially when the cavalcade entered the Jkarian Pass and started the long ascent toward the crest. The mules couldn't swear at their burdens, but they did get to rest part of each day, when some of Draelin's cavalry used their horses to take the animals place. The sweating bearers had no such relief, as they stumbled along from dawn to dusk.

Five days after starting the ascent into the Jkarian Pass, and just after midday, the heavily burdened cavalcade reached its destination. Even the final leg of the journey had taken longer than expected. A fast moving merchant caravan could cross the Pass through the Zagros Mountains in anywhere from six to ten days.

But the ever increasing slope of the trail had strained horses, mules and men. To Alcinor's eye, they had arrived just in time to avoid complete exhaustion and collapse.

Thankfully, since the Akkadians first entered the Pass, they'd encountered only one caravan coming west, and Alcinor had been grateful to see that they were in fact only merchants and their armed guards. While there might be a spy or two mixed among them, he thought it highly unlikely that anyone would suspect his intentions. Even the odd cargo of logs would be ignored. After all, what could one do with a handful of logs in the middle of the mountains?

The engineer and the soldier rode side by side. "This is the place, Draelin." Alcinor pointed toward the right. "Behind that boulder is a narrow path that leads away from the trail and into the mountains. It only lasts for about eight hundred paces before it comes to an end against the cliffs. There's no other way in. But at the far end, there's a good place to make camp. It's large enough to hold your men and the supplies, and it's far enough off the trail so that no one will see or hear them."

"I don't like the idea of being trapped in these rocks." Draelin sounded dubious. "But at least we'll be out of sight."

"I'll tell the men where to stack the logs. No sense carrying them all the way into the rocks."

"As soon as they're unloaded," Draelin said, "I'm going to send the mules, bearers and any men we don't need back to Akkad. The sooner we're rid of the filthy beasts and the extra mouths to feed, the better. Then I'll clean up our trail and send out the scouts."

Alcinor led the men into the rocks, told them where to camp, and returned nearly to the mouth of the trail. Two hundred paces into the rocks, the cargo of precious logs and equipment had already been unloaded. Alcinor had only a few moments to thank the porters and bearers, before both men and mules had departed, anxious to get out of the Pass before the Elamites arrived.

Draelin's soldiers were busy sweeping the ground clear of any tracks that indicated a large party had turned aside and ventured into the mountains. Before the last of the mules was out of sight, Draelin's men had collected the animal droppings and carried them into the cliff, where they would be buried under piles of loose rocks.

"I've sent out four scouts, two toward the east and two on our back trail." Draelin pointed to a pair of men moving east, just as they disappeared behind the rocks. "They're on foot because we can't take a chance on leaving horse tracks or droppings. Still, they should be able to run back and give us enough warning if anyone happens along the trail."

Alcinor nodded at Draelin's plans, though he had little interest in

the soldiers' activities. "I'm going to examine the cliff wall. Do you
want to come along?"

Draelin glanced up at the rock face towering over them. "Not
really, but I suppose I must."

Alcinor led the way, moving back deeper into the cliffs for a
hundred paces, then turning eastward. A few moments later, both
men were scrambling over rocks and around boulders as they
steadily climbed higher. When Alcinor reached a flat slab of rock, he
halted to catch his breath.

Draelin glanced around. "Is this the place?"

"No, but you should see this."

Alcinor crawled out along the top of a formation until he reached
its edge, with Draelin following. A drop greater than two tall trees, at
least a hundred paces, lay directly beneath them.

Flat on their bellies, both men peered out at the rocky vista spread
out below them. About a hundred and thirty paces away lay part of
the Jkarian Pass, with a good stretch visible from their vantage point.

"The highest part of the Pass is less than two miles east," Alcinor
said. "You can just glimpse it from here."

Draelin crawled closer to the edge and stared. "I can't even see
the scouts. But I'll take your word for it." He twisted his head
upwards. "Is that the cliff?"

"No, it's a little further ahead, and a bit closer to the trail. But we
have to climb even higher." Alcinor wriggled away from the
precipice and regained his feet. He led the way, moving higher and
deeper into rock walls that towered overhead, following marks that
he had scraped on the stones on his previous visit. Finally he
stopped. "This is the place."

Draelin's eyes widened as he glanced around. "I can't even see
the main trail. How can you block the Pass from here?"

"Look up."

The soldier did so, and Alcinor smiled at the look of amazement
that appeared on Draelin's face. Overhead a massive slab of rock
towered over them, leaning at a sharp angle. It looked as if it waited
for them to arrive, poised to crush them to death for daring to stand
beneath it.

"Ishtar mother of the gods!" Draelin's mouth stayed open, and he
made a sign to ward off the evil spirits.

"Don't worry, Draelin. It's been standing here for many years, perhaps hundreds of years."

"If you say so." Draelin continued to stare at the rock wall leaning over them. "When Eskkar first told me you were going to bring down a mountain, I didn't believe it. But looking at that thing, it looks ready to collapse at any moment."

"It won't come down, not yet."

"I'm not so sure. I never felt fear run through me like that, not in my whole life. By the gods, how much does it weigh? It's the size of a village! Bigger, even!"

"I've no idea," Alcinor admitted. "More than we can imagine."

Sounds of men climbing toward them reached Alcinor's ears. The first of his workers had unpacked their loads, gathered their tools, and mounted the cliff in search of their leader. Mouths agape, they, too, kept glancing at the massive overhang.

Alcinor nodded in sympathy. The cliff did indeed appear threatening. "Well, Draelin, there's no need for you up here. Go back down. Tell your men to send up water, at least three skins. My men are going to need a lot of water."

"May the gods be with you," Draelin said, "but I'm not coming back up here again, not unless you need me."

Alcinor ignored Draelin's parting words. Instead the engineer strode deeper into the rocks, so deep that the sunlight scarcely penetrated. He reached the place where he'd left another mark scratched on the cliff face, a circle with a line through its center. Yes, this was where they would start.

Alcinor spread his fingers and pressed them to the rock surface. He rubbed them hard against the stone, then touched his fingers to his lips. He recognized the gritty taste of the limestone, and the faint hint of salt. The cliff's surface, composed mainly of quartz and limestone was strong, very strong, but buried within that strength were tiny flecks of salt.

Those slight grains of impurity accounted for the occasional white streaks scattered over the cliff. If he were right, those impurities would be just enough to weaken the stone.

"You have stood proud and high for many years." Alcinor spoke to the cliff face as if she were his mistress. "But you'll come down when I ask you. You'll struggle and resist, but in the end, you will yield."

His assistant Jahiri, a few seasons older than the Engineer, joined him. On the journey up, Jahiri had ridden with the log bearers, watching over the precious cargo. His cheerful attitude set him apart from most of the builders. Unlike his master, Jahiri stood tall and broad, and the thick muscles on his shoulders and arms seemed more suitable to a common laborer.

Nevertheless, he had proved himself the most amenable to the Engineer's new ways and methods. "Is this the slab?"

Alcinor moved a few paces deeper into the shadow. If he stretched himself upright and raised his arm, he could almost touch the massive slab of stone that leaned over his head. "Yes. This is where the cliff is tallest, and hopefully, weakest. We'll start here."

Jahiri squatted down and examined the rock surface beneath their feet. "We'll have to level the footing first." He lifted his eyes up. "And trim the beam to match the angle of the overhang."

"Use the strongest and straightest log we have," Alcinor said. "This one will carry the most weight, and will be the key to bringing down the mountain."

Jahiri glanced up at the mountain towering over him. "Looking at this weight of stone, I wish we'd brought thicker beams."

"These will have to do. If the logs were any thicker, we'd never have been able to carry them."

The first work crew arrived, and Alcinor told them to begin. Under Jahiri's direction, they started chipping the rock away. Another senior apprentice directed ten of Draelin's soldiers, who grunted under the burden of man-handling the awkward size and bulk of the first heavy oak log.

They used ropes and brute strength to haul it up the rocks, cursing their bad luck the entire way. They fought against the massive bulk heavy weight which kept threatening to slide back down the slope, or crush their fingers and toes as it shifted with each movement.

The wood had come from the northern forest. Jahiri had travelled almost to the steppes. There the master apprentice selected twenty of the finest oak logs from the crafty woodmen who dwelt in the foothills. They had recognized the opportunity to demand a high price, and Jahiri had paid almost double what such lumber would usually cost.

Two ships had floated the logs down the Tigris, to a farm just north of Akkad. The logs were trimmed and inspected for soundness, then dried in the shade. When Alcinor and Jahiri had finished their preparations, sixteen logs remained, each one about ten paces long and each perfectly straight.

"Better to have to cut them down when we're at the Pass, than try to make do with a shorter one," Alcinor had declared at the time.

As soon as Jahiri and his men finished preparing the footing, Alcinor took his measurement with his special staff, nocked and marked along its length for different distances. He indicated where the log should be cut, and a wood cutter and his assistant started the sawing, using a bright new bronze blade made by the finest toolmaker in Akkad. Trella had indeed spared no expense.

The two men took their time with the saw, one man pulling the blade, while the other guided it from the other end. Then they reversed roles, with the second man pulling the blade back. The labor took skill and patience, but Alcinor wanted a straight cut, and these men knew how to deliver it.

Again and again the saw rasped its way through the thick log, cutting into it by tiny fractions. The hard wood fought the blade, and other men took turns at the labor until they completed the cut. Then the oak had to be trimmed with hammer and chisel to sit flat on the ground but angled on the top to match the slope of the overhang. The entire task would have taken a day or two back in Akkad, but Alcinor had the services of over ten skilled artisans, and the work proceeded rapidly.

Three times they attempted to raise the log and fit it against the cliff, but each time the oak beam needed further adjustment.

At last the log rested snugly at top and bottom. Jahiri selected a special tool he'd ordered made, a thick bronze strip as wide as his hand and formed into a half circle, to avoid damaging the log. Two men held the band in place, while Jahiri used his hammer against the metal surface, each blow wedging the log tighter and tighter against the overhang. The log resisted, and sometimes it took five or ten blows to move it the tiniest of fractions.

When Jahiri finished, sweat covered his brow and dripped onto his chest. Alcinor gave the order to halt. The heat under the cliff drained the men's strength. "Enough for today. We'll start again at dawn." He led the tired and thirsty men down the hill. As soon as they reached the bottom, the laborers headed toward the camp and their supper.

Alcinor, however, found Draelin waiting for him.

Draelin said nothing until the others had gone on ahead. "A messenger just arrived from Akkad. Lord Eskkar says the Elamites are on the move toward the Jkarian Pass. Considering how long it took before the news reached the King, and the four days it took for the messenger to reach us, the enemy could be here any day now. How soon can you be ready?"

Alcinor's satisfaction at today's progress vanished. Frowning, he turned to stare up at the cliff face. "I need to put at least ten more support logs in place before we start chipping away at the cliff. They must be placed exactly straight so as to take the strain. If we're rushed . . . if we're off in our calculations, then the whole cliff could come down the wrong way, or not at all, and we'll accomplish nothing."

"So we've another five days, before you're ready?"

Alcinor shook his head. "After the beams are in place, then we have to chip out more of the cliff wall. It's like cutting down a tree. The first cut, the deepest, is at the base of the rock wall. That points the way the cliff should fall. Then the second cuts, well above the first, will cause the weight of the stone to shift onto the logs. That may take another two or three days."

It took Draelin a moment to add up the days. "Damn the gods and that cursed rain. So we've got to be here at least eight days. What if the Elamites come before you're ready?"

"Then we hide here in the rocks, Draelin, and hope they don't find us. Unless you can hold them off until we finish?"

"Six thousand men? Maybe more?" Draelin snorted. "I don't think so. Why didn't we start sooner?"

"Because Lord Eskkar said that we had to seal the Pass at the last possible moment, so that the Elamites don't find out about it and change their plans. Then they could just turn around and march back east, to join their other armies coming through the Dellen Pass. Remember, the logs took longer to arrive, and because of all the delays that held us up."

"And now we may be too late. Well, let's hope Ishtar smiles on you, and your plan works." Draelin glanced up at the cliff towering over them. "Is there anything more my men can do to speed up the pace?"

"No, I don't think so. This is not a job for unskilled workers, like digging a hole in the ground. I'll keep my men working as hard and fast as they can. If we rush, we may accomplish nothing. It will take how ever long it takes to bring down the mountain."

"Damn." Draelin shook his head. "I'll send my scouts deeper into the Pass, and double the guards on the camp."

"Good. That should give us plenty of warning."

"A warning may not mean much."

Alcinor lifted his hands and let them drop. "We'll do our best."

The two men walked back through the maze of rocks that led to the camp. Neither would enjoy their supper much tonight.

Alcinor wondered if Lord Eskkar and Lady Trella had cut the time to finish the job too close. Draelin had told the engineer that the first Elamite invaders into the Land Between the Rivers would use this route. Their goal, according to Trella's spies, was to ravage the lands north of Akkad, and hopefully draw Eskkar's cavalry northward into a fight, weakening the city's defenses.

A good plan, Alcinor had decided, as soon as he grasped the implications. Faced with so many threats, Akkad just did not have the manpower to fight the Elamites coming through the Jkarian Pass. Eskkar would be hard pressed to hold off the invaders' main army.

Still, all of this meant little now. Alcinor had a task to do, and that was all that mattered. He glanced at the cliffs towering all around him, and wondered if he would get out of this place alive.

15

The next morning, Alcinor led all five of his craftsmen up to the slope. He wanted each of them to see the first beam set into its place, so they would understand what they had to do next.

As he spoke, the day's first crew of soldiers arrived, grunting under the weight of another log. Alcinor wanted all the beams carried up to the cliff face today, since he didn't know when he might need one. Soon all the artisans were at work.

"You know what we need to do, Jahiri." Alcinor had whispered the news of the approaching Elamites to his master apprentice last night. "We may have to take more chances than we planned."

"I'll work them as fast as I can, Engineer."

Alcinor and Jahiri returned to finish their work on the first beam. Using a plumb bob made from a smooth cord and a pointed, finger-sized length of polished bronze, they made sure the beam stood perfectly straight. Once again they used the half circle tool, this time tapping gently with the hammer, to adjust the base of the log. The hammer struck with a ringing sound, again and again, until the plumb bob, attached to a small nail at the top of the beam, hung down in a straight line and nearly touched the ground.

Satisfied at last, Alcinor and Jahiri moved onto the second beam, locating this one exactly five paces from the first and deeper underneath the cliff wall. Before midday, the second log had been fitted into position. The crews managed to get a third beam in place before darkness fell.

For the next three days, Alcinor's men labored from earliest light until the sun set in the west. He worked as hard as any of them, moving from crew to crew, helping or making suggestions, and ensuring that they accomplished every task as soon as possible. Nevertheless, setting the beams required an unusual amount of precision. Any mistakes would be costly in both time and effort, or even take a man's life.

That resulted in many delays, but Alcinor insisted that every task be done with all the skill each man possessed, exactly as he and Jahiri had demonstrated. His craftsmen labored and sweated in the heat of the rocks, but they never stopped their efforts. They, too, understood what was at stake in the Jkarian Pass.

The morning of the fourth day, under Alcinor's watchful eye, Jahiri tapped the twelfth and last beam in place. This one, smaller than the others, stood over sixty paces from the first, near the deepest recesses of the overhang. A few paces farther, and the overhang curved down and merged with the rock floor. Alcinor told his men to drag the four unneeded logs aside, out of the way.

The twelve beams formed a portico that stretched overhead and in as straight a line to satisfy any rich merchant in Akkad.

"Well, that's done, then." Jahiri climbed onto the ladder, stretched up, and unfastened the plumb bob. Coming down, he wrapped the cord around the bronze, and handed it to the Engineer.

Alcinor shoved the plumb bob into his pouch, retrieved a piece of chalk, and turned to face the cliff wall. He marked an outline on the rock about two paces wide, directly behind the twelfth beam. "Start the men working here."

Jahiri, standing beside him, studied the rock face, his hands on his hips. The cliff wall, where it merged into the overhanging shelf, already had multiple cracks and even a few open rifts. "This section will be the most dangerous. If the cliff is going to come down by itself, it will be here. I'd better start the chiseling myself."

"Take care, Jahiri. Stop at the first sign of danger." If this were any other task, Alcinor would have let some less experienced man take the risks. But his master apprentice understood the danger, and the need.

"I'll start my crew chipping away at the rock face. As soon as I'm sure they know what they're doing, I'll move back toward the slope."

Alcinor nodded. Each blow of a chisel would weaken the rock face, and his men understood all too well the peril hanging over their heads. If part of the cliff faced collapsed prematurely, at least Jahiri would have a chance to scramble back to safety. Most of the laborers would not.

All the same, they put aside their fears as much as possible, and continued on with the work. Only Alcinor and his master apprentice, however, knew exactly how dangerous it really was.

The two men returned to the staging area just outside the overhang. The crews stood ready with their hammers and chisels. Alcinor ordered all the unneeded workers away from the cliff, and told Jahiri to start.

With a crew of four men, Jahiri disappeared under the overhang and went to work. Using hammers, chisels, and pry bars, they began to attack the back wall of the cliff, where the overhanging portion met the ledge. Soon chunks and splinters of stone flew off the rock face, weakening the cliff wall with every stroke.

Alcinor stood well away from all of this, watching. This was indeed dangerous work. The stone cutters might chip away too much of the cliff, and part of the rock face might collapse on Jahiri and his men. While Alcinor didn't expect that to happen with the first effort, the risk would grow as they chipped away more and more of the limestone.

Jahiri and his crew spent the rest of the day weakening the cliff wall behind the twelfth post. The men all gave sighs of relief when Jahiri led them out into the fading sunlight.

The first part of the overhang had been chipped away. Alcinor ordered the crew out and back to camp. Then he and Jahiri went back to inspect the work before the last rays of the sun disappeared.

"It looks deep enough." Jahiri rubbed his jaw as he studied the rock face.

Alcinor examined the last beam, the one farthest from the opening. At the top and bottom, the tiniest trace of splintering had appeared. He touched the top of the log, where a small crack had appeared. "This wasn't here this morning." He knelt down and studied the ground, where the beam rested. "Give me the hammer."

Jahiri hesitated. "Are you sure you want to do that? Anything could shake the cliff loose."

"I don't think so." Alcinor took the hammer from his assistant's hand and tapped the base of the log, softly at first, then harder. "It feels different from the other logs, denser. It's holding some of the weight of the rock."

Jahiri glanced upward, then shivered. "Then let's get out of here."

"Yes. Tomorrow, before we start work on the next section, have your crew bring in the fire wood. Better to get that out of the way. Use only two men, ones you can trust."

"I'll do it myself. I don't want anyone making a mistake now."

"It will get worse with each section, Jahiri."

Jahiri looked at him and shrugged.

Alcinor rose and the two men hurried from the gloomy recess of the cliff. Neither took a deep breath until they made their descent all the way to the trail. But at least the end of their labors was in sight, and still Draelin's scouts hadn't reported seeing any Elamites moving toward them. Alcinor considered today's extensive progress a good sign.

Over a meager supper that night, Draelin disagreed. "We arrived almost twelve days late. We don't know how much time we have before the Elamites arrive. Eskkar believes that they will probably send men through this Pass first, since they've got the farthest to travel."

"We're going as fast as we can," Alcinor said. "We should be able to chip away at the cliff's wall more rapidly now. But it still will be two or three more days before we're ready.

Draelin shook his head, but said nothing. There was nothing to say.

In the morning, Alcinor kept the crews waiting at the opening while Jahiri built a fire base of kindling and wood staves the thickness of a man's arm around the twelfth beam. Only two men carried the firewood, an armload at a time, to the master apprentice. Working with care, Jahiri arranged the dry wood around the base of the beam, layering the sticks and making sure every section of the upright log would feel the effects of the fire.

When he finished, Jahiri returned to Alcinor's side. "The wood is in place, and I set out a line of stones. I've ordered the men not to cross that line. We'll do the beams one by one, as we chip out each section."

"Then let's get on to the next one," Alcinor said. "Make sure the men take care with their chisels. I don't want to gouge a large chunk of stone out of the overhang now. Just have them slice it away, a little at a time."

Midday approached when Jahiri ordered the laborers out from under the overhang. Alcinor, watching from the opening, saw the fear and relief on the men's faces as they trotted past him. Chipping away at the cliff, all the while knowing that the next blow from the hammer might bring the entire cliff wall crashing down on their heads, made for nerve-wracking work.

When the men were all out, Alcinor and Jahiri made their way in. The men had chiseled their way deep into the cliff, and Alcinor nodded in satisfaction. He stepped over the line of stones and examined the farthest beam, but saw no further signs of splintering.

"It looks good, Jahiri. Bring in the next load of firewood."

"Will it be enough?" Jahiri kept staring at the rock face just over his head.

Now was not the time to reveal his own doubts, Alcinor realized. "Yes, the fire will work for us when the time comes."

"I'll start them on the next section at once. This is one job I want to finish as soon as possible."

"It won't be any too soon," Alcinor agreed. "Draelin is getting more and more worried. He thinks the Elamites will be here any day now."

The next day passed, and the next, while the men, divided up into work crews, risked their lives again and again by entering beneath the overhang and chipping away at the base of the cliff. The men scarcely spoke any more, afraid that the least sound might drop the massive slab of rock upon their heads, crushing them to death in an instant.

Alcinor and Jahiri, standing a hundred paces away, felt the men's eyes watching them. "They think we're safe out here," Alcinor said, "while they're risking their necks."

"That's what they're getting paid for," Jahiri answered. "Once this is finished, none of them will have to work for a year."

Trella had assured the laborers triple wages, with a bonus when the cliff wall came down. Of course, that assumed any of them got out alive to return to Akkad. More important, in the event of their death, the coins would go to their families. Lady Trella had also given that promise to them.

"Another two days, and we'll be finished." Alcinor, too, felt the fear from the cliff. "The sooner we're away from this place . . ."

A shout interrupted him, all the more dramatic since the men working on the cliff seldom spoke above a whisper. Alcinor turned to see Draelin scrambling up the ascent path.

The soldier wasted no words. "My scouts have seen the Elamites approaching."

Alcinor felt a wave of despair pass over him. He needed more time. "Are you sure? Maybe it's just a scouting party."

"Well, scouting party or the whole army, there are horsemen coming down the trail, and they'll be here soon enough. How much longer before you're ready?"

Alcinor considered. "Even if I worked the men as long and hard as I can, it's going to take at least another day and a half."

"Curse our luck. We'll just have to hope it is an advance party and pray to the gods that they don't find us. When I send word, you stop working. Meanwhile, send anyone you don't need as far back into the rocks possible. I don't want to hear a sound, not even a cough, until they're past."

"We'll be quiet, though I don't think they can hear this far from the trail."

"Horses have good ears, and can smell, too," Draelin warned. "Just keep everyone quiet."

"And if they find us?"

"Then I'll bring my men up here, and we'll try and hold them off as long as we can, or until you bring the mountain down. Better to die fighting or beneath the cliff than under torture."

Alcinor watched Draelin move back down the cliff. The soldier had his own problems. He had to keep more than a hundred men and horses quiet.

Word spread to cease working. Alcinor made all the men set their tools down gently, then sit on the ground. They could only whisper among themselves. After a few moments of staring at the cliffs, Alcinor crawled out along the ledge, to the same place where he and Draelin had lain the first day.

The part of the Jkarian Pass Alcinor could see remained empty. Looking around, he couldn't detect any sign of Draelin or his scouts, though the soldier must be watching from some hidden vantage point.

"Is anything happening?" Jahiri slid alongside. "Some of the others wanted to join you, but I ordered them to stay behind and keep silent."

Alcinor smiled at his apprentice's eagerness. "Nothing on the trail yet. Let's just hope they don't see us."

"Why would anyone stare into these rocks?"

"They're soldiers. Who knows what they stare at."

"Look!"

Three horsemen, shields slung across their backs and wearing swords on their hips, rode into view. They didn't look particularly alert, but they did glance around from time to time. They rode leisurely, little more than a slow walk. Alcinor reminded himself that they had been traveling uphill for at least three or four days.

The enemy disappeared from sight, but it wasn't long before more Elamites appeared. Riding in a double column, the horsemen soon filled the trail from end to end.

"Count them, Jahiri."

The column seemed endless as it plodded across Alcinor's field of view. At last he saw the pack animals that carried the men's supplies. Two livery men, each leading a string of three horses loaded down with bulging packs, brought up the rear. They, too, finally disappeared from view.

Alcinor realized he'd been holding his breath and he let it out. Obviously a scouting party, but comprised of a lot more men than Alcinor expected.

"One hundred and ninety-six, including the packmen," Jahiri said.

The sun moved overhead, but no word came from Draelin to resume work.

"We're wasting time," Jahiri said.

"Draelin will tell us when it's safe to resume."

A few moments later, Alcinor heard Draelin's voice as he climbed to the base of the cliff.

"Did they see us?" Alcinor couldn't keep all the anxiety out of his voice.

Draelin grinned. "If they did, we'd be fighting them off right now. But they're only the advance party for the main force, which can't be more than a day behind." The smile faded from his lips. "You've got to work even faster."

Alcinor glanced up at the sun. Only a little past noon. "So the main force could be here by midday tomorrow."

"Don't count on it. They'll probably make camp at the crest, which means they'll reach this place earlier, perhaps by midmorning." Draelin sighed. "Can you still do it?"

The man was nothing if not direct, Alcinor realized. "Perhaps. We'll have to work through the night, by torchlight. It will be more dangerous."

"The Elamites may see the glow of your torches." Draelin took a deep breath. "That doesn't matter now. Get your men to work, and let me know if any of my men can help."

"You heard him, Jahiri." Alcinor didn't like this. He, Jahiri, and all their men would have to work on the cliff face at the same time. If anything went wrong, they would all be dead, crushed by the unimaginable weight of stone overhead. And if the cliff didn't come down, they were likely to die from the swords of the Elamites. Either way, they would be just as dead.

Alcinor had to appeal to his men. None of them wanted to work at night, let alone all of them up there, crowded underneath the shadowy overhand, bumping into each other and the beams. In the end, he had to promise them more coins. They finally agreed, but by then Draelin had sent ten of his bowmen up to the ledge, ostensibly to guard the workers.

The grim soldiers looked just as capable of shooting Akkadians as Elamites. The craftsmen and laborers understood the silent message, and Alcinor didn't bother to ask what the soldiers' orders were.

Torches, water, oil, the rest of the firewood, four stout ropes, and the two heavy bronze chains soon arrived, lugged up the ascent by sweating soldiers. Jahiri placed the men and got them started. This time neither he nor Alcinor dared watch from the safety of the ledge. Only the presence of the Engineer and his master apprentice convinced the workers that it was still safe to work.

By sunset, they had gouged out a considerable portion of the cliff. The tap-tap-tap of the hammers striking the chisels seemed almost continuous now. More soldiers were pressed into service, and they used empty sacks to sweep away the debris carved out of the solid rock, saving the workers one task.

As soon as it grew dark, Alcinor ordered the torches lit and the hammering continued. In the torchlight, with the shadows flickering through the rock dust, the overhang looked like a demon's pit.

No man liked to work at night, when the spirits of the evil dead emerged from their subterranean lairs to wander the earth, seeking to steal men's souls. He heard the faint muttering of prayers to Marduk and Ishtar. Whether the men asked the gods to protect them from the demons, or to keep the cliff from coming down, he didn't know.

Alcinor paced back and forth the length of the overhang, constantly inspecting the beams. Even in the torchlight, all the logs now showed signs of the weight of the mountain they supported. Alcinor wondered if he should have used more beams. Alcinor knew oak was the strongest of the woods, but even he couldn't guess if they would hold.

He thanked the gods that he and Jahiri had taken the extra time to get the beams properly positioned. If any of them weren't perfectly vertical, they would have already split under the weight.

Jahiri did his share, moving from group to group, making sure they chipped where he wanted, and that they did not go too deep into the rock. By midnight, even the presence of their masters couldn't overcome the fear of the workers. Coated with dust, hands and arms bloody from the flying chips of stone, the men labored on, and by now influenced more by the sight of the armed soldiers than by any idea of possible reward.

Alcinor ordered a rest period, but didn't let the men leave the overhang. Water and food were brought to them by the soldiers. He knew if his workers ever got out, not even the soldiers could force them back. However the rest helped restore their strength.

The endless hammering soon resumed. Post by post, section by section, the cliff was being weakened. Twelve, eleven, ten, nine, eight, seven, six, and five were finished to Jahiri's satisfaction a little before dawn.

"Time for another rest," Alcinor said. The men looked ready to drop. Wielding a hammer and chisel continuously was exhausting work, and he didn't want some weary man to make a mistake. "It'll be morning soon, and the men will be able to see better."

With the first rays of dawn, Draelin arrived. "Well?"

One look told Alcinor that Draelin had not slept either. No doubt the soldier had spent the evening preparing defenses against the Elamites.

"Only four more sections to dig out," Alcinor said. "We should be ready before midmorning."

"I think that's all the time you're going to get," Draelin answered. "One of my men crept far enough up the Pass to see the enemy's night camp. He got close enough to make out their fires. I'm just hoping they didn't see your torches."

"We'll be ready." Alcinor tried to make his voice sound convincing.

"How long will the fire take?"

"Not long." Alcinor uttered the lie smoothly. He had no idea how long it would take for the fire to weaken the support beams.

Draelin swore at the vague answers, but turned away without another word.

Jahiri moved to Alcinor's side. He'd been close enough to hear the conversation. "I'll get the men back to work."

With the first ray of daylight, the hammering resumed, the men chiseling away at sections four and three. The rock appeared to flake away more easily, which made sense to Alcinor. The overhang had eroded more at this end of the cliff, so the rock must be softer. Which also, he realized, meant it would be weaker.

He glanced up at the massive weight of stone towering above him. Gods above, please hold together a little longer.

Finally Jahiri ordered the workers to move on to the last two sections. Even the men sensed that the end was near, and they managed to keep up the pace, though by now Alcinor knew their arms must be burning in agony from the continuous work.

"I think we're going to make it." Jahiri wiped the sweat from his eyes. His face, his entire body was coated with rock dust.

"Well before midmorning," Alcinor agreed. "We'll even have time . . ."

A loud crack sounded from the rear of the overhang. The noise, like the grinding of two giant stone hammers and magnified by the cliff, panicked the men. They dropped their tools and fled to the entrance, their eyes wide with fear. Only the soldiers, either braver or unaware of how much danger lurked overhead, sprang to their feet and prevented the work crew from scrambling down the rocks and abandoning the site.

Alcinor and Jahiri looked at each other. Alcinor felt his heart racing in his chest, and Jahiri appeared just as frightened. They stood waiting, but no more noise came from the overhang. The rock had shifted, but hadn't come down and flattened them all. Not yet.

"Let's see what happened." Alcinor whirled around and faced the soldiers. "Keep everyone here. Nobody leaves."

He and Jahiri picked their way through the rock chips beneath their feet, their eyes searching the cliff wall for any sign of weakness. They found it soon enough, between the sixth and seventh posts. A crevice wide as a man's arm ran up the cliff surface and continued onto the overhang, reaching nearly to the front face before it disappeared.

"Ishtar mother of the gods," muttered Jahiri. "It's going to come down any moment."

Alcinor studied the mass of stone above his head, trying to envision the shifting direction of the various forces struggling within the cliff. "I'm not so sure. The crack has relieved some of the stress in the stone here, but increased it in other places."

Still, he knew a good breeze on the upper surface might bring it down, but not in the way Alcinor wanted.

"Look at the post!" Jahiri clutched Alcinor's arm with one hand, while he pointed with the other.

The seventh post had shifted from the vertical by at least a hand's width. The wood had also cracked, a long seam now showing on the inner side. For a moment, all Alcinor could think of was that the oak logs were strong indeed. He realized he was holding his breath. Drawing air into his chest, he clasped Jahiri on the shoulder.

"Get the men back to work," he ordered. "I'll start the fires going. We have to do it now."

They trotted back to the opening and found Draelin there, shifting from one leg to the other, left hand clutching the hilt of his sword. "What happened? Why did you stop working?"

Alcinor ignored him. He grabbed two of his men. "Each of you gather two oil pots and follow me." He shoved them on their way, and the force of his words kept them moving.

The battering resumed as Jahiri snatched up a hammer and pushed his crew back beneath the overhang. Meanwhile, Alcinor led his two men into the shadows, all the way down to the twelfth post.

"You, open the pots and saturate the wood. Be careful to not waste any oil. Make sure it all goes onto the wood." He ordered the second man to do the same on the eleventh post. Alcinor stood between them, making certain the black liquid spread over the dry wood, and didn't trickle away on the dusty rock.

The oil that burns would saturate the carefully arranged firewood, and form a pool at the base of the beam. When set afire, all the heat from the flames would be concentrated on the log itself.

Post by post, Alcinor supervised the application of the oil pots, two to each post. Even before the last set of pots was emptied, he collected a fresh torch and set it alight from the small fire that the soldiers had kept burning during the night and into the morning.

Alcinor walked calmly to the twelfth post, the one deepest into the mountain. For a moment, he just stared down at the wood. "May Hephastor move this mountain," Alcinor prayed to the god of every builder, then touched the flickering end of the torch to the still dripping oil.

With a whoosh, the flames engulfed the post. Taking his time and ignoring the heat, he repeated the process, working his way, post by post, until he reached the front of the cavern. The flames would set the beams afire, he knew, but the oak was strong and would take time before it weakened.

Jahiri, on his knees beside the first post, struggled with a specially made, heavy bronze chain. The thick links surrounded the base of the log, but in a wide loop that was a long pace from the beam. Jahiri wanted to keep the links out of the worst of the fire, to maintain their strength.

Alcinor waited until his apprentice completed the loop and then carefully dragged the other end of the long chain, which stretched about twenty paces, out from underneath the overhang and into the sunlight. If the fire did not weaken the beams enough to bring down the cliff, men and horses would try to rip the weakened timber of the first beam from its position.

"I'm ready," Jahiri called out.

Alcinor tossed the torch at the base of the first beam, then walked out. When he rejoined Jahiri and Draelin, the frightened laborers wanted to descend the cliff, but the soldiers still blocked the way.

Alcinor turned to face the flames. All twelve beams were ablaze, flames licking and crawling their way up each post. The fire created a black cloud of oily smoke that curled and twisted its way along the bottom of the overhang until it could reach the open sky. The heat, partially trapped beneath the rock, surged like a wave toward them. Alcinor could see the air flowing, even without the streams of smoke rushing up from the rock.

"Well, the smoke will tell the Elamites where we are." Draelin had to shout to be heard over the crackling of the flames. "What happens now?"

"The oak beams are strong, and it will take awhile before they lose their strength. As the beams fail one by one, the weight of the rock will shift to the remaining logs. When that happens, the cliff will become more and more unstable, until it topples from its own weight."

"Should we be standing here?"

"It will take a few more moments," Alcinor said. "And we may need to use the chain to weaken the first post, which is the strongest. Keep your men ready."

The flames, fed by the oil and the dry firewood stacked around each post, roared up with a sound that echoed out over the rocks. Two years ago, Alcinor had watched in fascination as a large swath of houses in Akkad burned to the ground, but never in his life had he seen flames like these. Meanwhile, dense black clouds boiled out from beneath the overhang, a living snake of reeking smoke that stormed up into the heavens.

"I think it's time to go," Jahiri said, rubbing his jaw.

Alcinor stared at the burning inferno. He'd built this pyre to bring about the death of the mountain, and now he found himself transfixed in spite of the danger. Still, Jahiri was right. The weight of the rock should make it topple toward the trail, but large chunks of the cliff would be flying in all directions.

"Draelin, send your soldiers down first. As my men come down, make sure everyone stands by the chain. We may need every man hauling on it."

No one needed any urging to descend, the soldiers and laborers scrambling down as fast as they could. Only when all the others were gone did Alcinor start his descent, but he stopped when his head was level with the base of the rock. He stared at the burning cliff, a sight no man had ever seen before. Even the demons who dwelt deep below the earth in their pools of fire would be in awe.

Alcinor glanced below, and saw workers and soldiers grasping the chain wherever they could. The last link of the chain had been threaded with two stout ropes, and these fastened to leather traces attached to two horses. A soldier stood beside each animal, a leather lash in his hand. Both animals shifted nervously, ears jerking back and forth, worried by the smell of burning oil and the crackling of the nearby flames.

A snapping noise jerked Alcinor's head around. One of the beams had failed. Others would soon collapse under the additional strain. Because of the smoke, he could only see the first few beams, burning as furiously as a funeral pyre.

The chain, meant to help break the keystone beam if the flames failed to do the job, wouldn't be needed. One last look, and he resumed his descent. Hands reached up to help him down. He tried to speak, but his chest was full of smoke. He coughed as he waved the men away, until he cleared his throat.

"Run! Forget the chain. Run!"

The men needed no further urging. They fled for the safety of the rocks. The soldiers unhooked the traces from the horses, and the animals bolted. Alcinor, supported by Jahiri on one side and Draelin on the other, stumbled after them toward the safety of the rocks.

Before they could get behind the massive boulders, the cliff broke loose from the mountain with a deafening boom, magnified by the rocks, that struck the men like a blow. The ground shook, and the three were knocked to the earth.

Alcinor landed on his back, and he glimpsed the death of the mountain. The massive slab of stone, sixty paces long and at least that many in height, separated from its base with a deafening crack. The wall of rock turned halfway as it fell, striking the lower cliff wall that also leaned out over the trail. Falling from a height of more than forty paces, nothing could resist its impact.

The lower wall collapsed under the additional weight and snapped in two. The ground shook again and moved, in the same fashion as an earthquake. A whirling cloud of dust rose up, to mix with the flames and smoke, and the entire cliff came down with a demon-like rumbling that went on and on, carrying an unbelievable mass of stone that choked the Jkarian Pass.

It took a long time before the shaking stopped. Jahiri recovered first. "You did it! You moved the mountain!" He threw his arms around the Engineer and hugged him.

Alcinor started coughing from the thick dust that hung in the air, but nothing could keep the smile from his face.

"By Ishtar, I never thought it would work," Draelin said, "but you've done it!" He slapped Jahiri on the back.

Alcinor climbed to his feet, surprised to find that his legs trembled so much he could scarcely stand. "I knew she'd come down. She protested, but she succumbed at the last moment."

"If the trail is truly closed, you may have saved Akkad," Jahiri said.

That took the smile from Alcinor's face. "Let's hope that Eskkar and the others are as successful."

"We still have to get you and your men back to Akkad," Draelin reminded them. "Remember, there's that Elamite scouting party that already went through the Pass."

"They won't all linger at the mouth of the Pass, will they? Don't you have enough men to drive them away?" Alcinor had forgotten about the enemy scouts.

"Yes, but I have to leave some behind, to watch the Elamites and make sure they don't somehow find a way through your landslide. But I don't think I'll need to keep too many here. The mountain you moved should be enough to hold them back for a few days, even if it doesn't send them all running back to Elam."

Draelin clasped Alcinor and hugged him until he gasped, then did the same to Jahiri. "Take care of your master. I'm going out to see what the Pass looks like, and make sure it's completely blocked."

"It is," Jahiri asserted. "Master Engineer Alcinor is the first man to ever move a mountain."

And that, Alcinor decided, would be his contribution to the war.

16

Half a mile away, General Jedidia guided his big stallion, a rangy black brute with a single splash of white on its forehead, as he led the two-mile long column of Elamite horsemen through the Jkarian Pass. Yesterday his troop had crested the route's highest point, and now the final leg of the journey to the Land Between the Rivers lay before him.

While the Pass still held many twists and turns, the gradual descent would continue. In two days, three at most, he would reach the open grasslands that lay to the northeast of Akkad.

Once there, Jedidia would unleash his ruthless fighters, and they would loose terror on the helpless villagers and farmers. More important, his soldiers would destroy Akkad's main source of food and supplies. No matter how determined or violent a resistance King Eskkar offered from his city's wall, the destruction of the northern countryside meant, sooner or later, the end of the conflict.

To achieve that goal, General Jedidia commanded an army of almost six thousand horsemen. He had received a simple set of instructions from King Shirudukh – destroy any Akkadian force he encountered, devastate whatever countryside he traversed, cut any supply lines, and bring his horsemen down to the city of Akkad, killing or capturing any that tried to flee the doomed city. Once Jedidia reached Akkad, he had orders to place himself and his cavalry under the command of Lord Modran.

That part of Jedidia's instructions still rankled. The fawning sycophant Lord Modran had obtained the coveted assignment of capturing Akkad with all its wealth, the task that Jedidia knew he deserved. To humiliate Jedidia even further, Grand Commander Chaiyanar – the pompous title never ceased to grate on Jedidia's nerves – had received the second most desirable objective, the rich City of Sumer. Their machinations had left Jedidia, Elam's most experienced and efficient soldier, with the smallest army and the least profitable mission.

Lord Modran's victory was assured. He led enough soldiers to overwhelm the entire Land Between the Rivers by himself. It was just a matter of time. Chaiyanar, whose only military skill consisted of laying siege to cities, would easily pluck the second and far weaker apple from the tree – Sumer. He, too, had more men than he needed. Jedidia, however, had only six thousand men, not enough to capture Akkad or face King Eskkar's army.

Jedidia understood King Shirudukh's cunning decision. The King knew his generals could never be completely trusted. He wanted no strong commander in the field who might someday rival his own glory, or perhaps even threaten his rule.

Only twenty years ago, King Shirudukh's father, after assassinating his liege lord, had seized the crown of Elam. What had happened in the past, could yet happen again, and so the present King of Elam trusted none of his commanders with too much power.

Despite their repeated oaths of fealty to his rule, Shirudukh knew that none of his three most senior generals could be allowed to grow too powerful. If any of them tried to seize the throne, the other two would unite against him. The balancing of power between them meant far more than any mere pledges of loyalty. After all, a successful revolt absolved the oath giver of all guilt or punishment.

Zathras, Jedidia's second in command, guided his horse alongside. "General! Do you see the smoke rising from the cliffs?" Zathras raised his left arm, pointing toward the left side of the Pass.

Jedidia put aside the gloomy thoughts that had eaten at his guts for the last few months. He lifted his gaze, following the direction Zathras indicated. For a few moments he observed the dark plume of greasy smoke billowing into the air.

"What could be burning so fiercely in these rocks, General?" Zathras's voice held more curiosity than concern.

"I don't know, but whatever it is, it seems too far from the trail to be a problem."

Jedidia studied the cliffs that had risen higher and higher on either side of the Pass in the last few miles. The trail had narrowed here as well. Less than sixty paces separated the towering rock faces. "But this might be a good place for an ambush."

Zathras turned to one of his subcommanders, riding a few strides behind. "Ride ahead, and warn the advance guard to be alert. The Akkadians may try to slow us down."

Jedidia had considered the possibility of either an ambush or a delaying attack long before he entered the Jkarian Pass. Months ago, his scouts had ridden the length of the Pass from Elam to Akkad's northern lands.

They'd found several places where small groups of men might lie in wait, but none, as he recalled from studying the maps, near this particular part of the Pass. And even if a few hundred enemy attacked, they would soon be driven off.

Nevertheless, Jedidia had sent almost two hundred men on ahead yesterday, to scout the trail, and they had not reported any activity. Even if his scouts had been ambushed, they would have sent a warning back to the main column at the first sign of trouble. Nonetheless five hundred riders formed Jedidia's vanguard, riding a few hundred paces ahead.

A shout made him lift his eyes. He saw two riders galloping toward him, and guessed something was amiss. They slowed just long enough to speak to their subcommander, then resumed their rapid pace toward their leaders.

The two scouts pulled their snorting horses to a stop. "Enemy soldiers are up ahead, General. We counted at least twenty of them, hiding in the rocks on the left hand side of the trail. They shot arrows at us, but the range was too great."

Jedidia frowned at the foolish report. Of course the scouts had no real idea of how many men might be hiding in the rocks, waiting to attack. Not that it mattered. Unless Eskkar had sent his entire army to the Jkarian Pass, Jedidia's fighters would brush them aside.

He had more than enough men to deal with any lesser resistance. No, this was more likely some scouting party that had slipped past his advance scouts, or perhaps a small force thrown together in desperation to try and defend the Pass and slow his advance.

"We'll soon find out how many there are." He turned to Zathras. "Take command of the vanguard, and clear the trail."

In moments, Zathras had raced ahead, and reached the head of the leading column. Orders were shouted, and suddenly five hundred heavily armed men were in motion, riding at a fast canter and readying their weapons. The thunder of the horses' hooves echoed against the walls of the Pass. Jedidia nodded in satisfaction. His second in command had more than enough men to deal with any ambush.

Jedidia kept the main column at its usual pace, letting the gap widen between him and the vanguard. He had no need to rush, and he would soon see for himself what mischief the Akkadians had prepared. The barbarian king of Akkad might be famous for his battlefield tricks, but Jedidia knew that overwhelming force was the best trick of all.

As he rode, he glanced again at the smoke pouring up into the sky. The thick gray ribbon appeared to have grown denser, turned into a cascade of flames, shimmering in the heat as it twisted its way into the air. From here, it appeared as if the cliffs themselves were on fire. The breeze shifted, and he breathed a hint of the oil that burns. Perhaps a subterranean stream of oil had breached the surface and somehow caught fire, though usually such pools were found only in the lowlands.

The advance force, weapons at the ready, slowed as they approached the part of the trail level with the smoke. Suddenly a deafening clap of thunder echoed between the walls of the Pass. At the same moment, the ground shook.

Jedidia's horse stiffened its legs and dug its hooves into the ground. The general clutched at his horse's halter, and with a firm yank, managed to bring the frightened animal under control. Earthquake. It must be an earthquake.

Men cried out in fear, and shouts made him glance once again toward the column of smoke. He glimpsed a massive slab of rock falling through the air, before it slammed into the cliff wall that bordered the Pass.

The sound of snapping stones and rumbling rock filled the air. The ground continued to tremble, and the horses closest to the landslide panicked. Jedidia saw men dumped from their seats, while others fought to control their wild-eyed mounts. The soldiers' shouts had turned into a babble of excited voices, and loose horses galloped away from the danger, scattering or knocking aside anything in their path.

A huge cloud of dust floated in the air ahead, obscuring the trail, some of it drifting towards the Elamites. At least the ground had ceased shaking. The gray cloud slowly settled, and Jedidia's mouth opened in astonishment.

The trail through the cliffs had vanished. The opening, at that point no more than fifty or sixty paces wide, had disappeared under a massive rock slide. Boulders the size of houses were piled on top of one another, much like a child would stack a pile of stones. In some places the barrier stood almost thirty paces high.

The advance force had narrowly missed being crushed by the slide, and now they scattered. Frightened horses, many of them riderless, whinnied in fear at the trembling earth. Jedidia rode up as close as he could get without risking his horse in the debris. The last of the dust blew away, and he could see that the slide extended some distance down the Pass. Obviously it would take time to clear the way. Still, it would take more than an earthquake or landslide to stop him.

Zathras rode back, covered in dust from the shattered rock. "The Pass is blocked, General." He had to pause to clear his throat. "And we heard men shouting from behind the rocks. The Akkadians may have done this."

Jedidia clenched his jaw. Of course it was the Akkadians. Who else would be lurking in the Pass.

"Take five hundred men forward on either side of the pass. Work your way through the rocks on foot until you reach the other side. Kill anyone you find. If you meet any resistance, send word and I'll give you as many men as you need."

Zathras nodded, whirled his horse around, and galloped off.

General Jedidia glanced up at the sun. Only a little after midmorning. Well, his men would find a way through the rubble. Still, he knew they weren't going any farther today, and decided there was no sense standing around in the sun. He dismounted and ordered his men to make camp and his servants to set up his tent.

That attended to, Jedidia turned to one of his messengers, riding a few paces behind. "Send for the Builder."

The General had with him a handful of men trained in dealing with walls and fortified villages. Jedidia had nearly left them behind, thinking he would not need them for this invasion. Now he blessed his foresight. They would be useful in clearing a way through the pass.

He waited impatiently until the Master Builder and his five assistants rode up from the rear of the column. Jedidia pointed at the slide, told them to find a way through the rocks, and ordered them on their way.

Noon came and went without any word from the Builder. The sun continued to move across the sky. Messengers from his second in command returned and reported that they could not find a way through the rocks on either side of the pass. Jedidia frowned at those reports, and told them to keep searching.

With nothing to do, his thoughts returned, as they so often did, to his humiliation. In the last few years, many had noticed Jedidia's successes and ever increasing popularity with his men. And so for this campaign, King Shirudukh had tossed Jedidia the hardest bone to gnaw on, and the one with the least flesh.

Nor was Shirudukh the only one who had noticed Jedidia's rising star. Both Modran and Chaiyanar had grown jealous of his accomplishments. They wished to add glory to their names and wealth to their Houses, so Jedidia would receive little opportunity for either plunder or battlefield victories. Together the two generals must have groveled before the King, and whispered lies about their rival into his ear.

Regardless, the orders General Jedidia had received from King Shirudukh should be easy to carry out. The main thrusts of the invasion would be toward Sumer and Akkad. The Akkadians and their allies, if indeed they had any, would be busy defending those cities, and would have no soldiers to spare for their northern lands. If any dared to ride against him, Jedidia had more than enough well trained horse fighters to deal with Eskkar's cavalry.

Before the invasion started, such ideas had troubled Jedidia. Now he could only hope that he could achieve some significant victory over the Akkadians. A more pleasant thought, one that often soothed his mind at night, was that perhaps by some lucky stroke Lord Modran would die in battle, fall from his horse, eat tainted food, or any of the other countless ways men could perish in a campaign.

Such things did happen. Some in Elam's Council of Advisors thought that the barbarian king Eskkar would prove a formidable opponent. If that turned out to be true, well, even a dying snake could still strike a lethal blow. But as for himself, without the favor of the gods, Jedidia could do little to change his fate. He would have to endure this humiliation, and hope for the best.

Unlike the other two prongs of the Elamite invasion, all of Jedidia's fighters were mounted. Though in the last two years he had trained and equipped almost ten thousand infantry, those soldiers had been taken away from Jedidia and given to Modran and Chaiyanar.

That meant Jedidia had no foot soldiers stumbling along, slowing him down and struggling to keep pace. His baggage train consisted of a mere two hundred pack animals carrying only enough food to last until he established himself in Akkad's lands.

And his men, recruited from all over the Empire, comprised some of the best horse fighters in the land. They could ride hard all morning and then fight all afternoon. With their own homelands ground to dust under King Shirudukh's heel, these renegades, traitors, and nameless men were loyal only to Jedidia and the King. At their General's command, they would slaughter any in their path without a hint of remorse.

Not that Jedidia expected to meet any real resistance. The barbarian Eskkar, faced with overwhelming numbers, would fall back and hide behind his city's walls. Or he just might flee, abandon his city and run for his life, taking only his wives and as much wealth as he could carry.

Jedidia, with more horsemen than the entire city of Akkad could field, expected to encounter nothing more than terrified refugees fleeing north, clutching with them any gold or whatever pitiful valuables they possessed. He intended to take the gold, kill the old and the young, and turn the rest into slaves, thousands upon thousands, that he would sell back in Elam.

While he might not capture as much loot as the other generals, Jedidia would still add much wealth to his coffers by the time this campaign ended. Within a year Jedidia expected to return victorious to Elam, and with even more horsemen under his command. Once the Akkadians collapsed and King Shirudukh had imposed his rule, Jedidia would absorb the fittest survivors into his cavalry.

Mid afternoon arrived before the Builder returned. One glance, and Jedidia knew he had a problem. The man, thin and nervous, bobbed his head in deference. Gray rock dust covered almost every part of his body. Jedidia saw fear on the man's face, all the usual signs of someone obviously afraid to deliver bad tidings.

"What is it?"

The Builder flinched at the snarl in Jedidia's voice. "General Jedidia, the Pass is completely blocked. Part of the mountain toppled, and the trail is buried for at least a hundred and fifty paces."

Jedidia had seen as much for himself. "How soon to clear it?"

The Builder shook his head. "I . . . I don't know, Master. We'll need digging tools, hammers and chisels to break up the boulders, carts to remove the rubble, ropes to climb up the rocks. Ten or fifteen days, perhaps longer."

Fifteen days! Jedidia had expected to hear the task would take a day or two at most. Of course the fool standing before him knew they had none of those items with the expedition. Jedidia led an invading force, not a construction gang. He restrained his anger.

"Very well, then how long will it take to clear a pathway. We don't need much, just one wide enough to accommodate a horse."

The man swallowed. His face, caked with dust, showed his thirst, but Jedidia had no intention of offering him a chance to drink.

"Master, the rocks are large and piled up on top of each other. To carve a trail through the rubble wide enough to accommodate a horse, it would take almost as long. In a few days, we could probably clear a way for men to scramble through to the other side, but horses . . . not without ropes and chains. We need hammers and chisels, and plenty of men to labor moving the rocks. If we had lumber, we might be able to construct a plank bridge over the rubble."

Jedidia gritted his teeth. The nearest source of wood lay sixty miles behind them. He took a deep breath and softened his tone. No sense terrorizing the man any further. "Look, Builder, there must be a way through these rocks. The Akkadians, they did this. They found a way to bring down the mountain, didn't they?"

"Yes, Master, but the place where the cliff tumbled leads right into the heart of the mountains. Your soldiers are searching the rocks on either side, but I do not think they'll find a way through. Men, yes, but not horses."

"Can't you dig your way through, or under the blockage?"

"We are in the mountains, Master. The dirt we see underfoot is shallow, with solid rock beneath. There is nothing to dig into."

The Builder's hands trembled in his fear, and rightly so. If any of this proved to be false, Jedidia would have the man whipped to death. Jedidia's lips clamped shut. No, that was too quick. He would make sure the fool suffered for at least three days before he died.

The General turned his back on the Builder and stared at the blocked pass. A sense of dread settled on his shoulders. He had worked with the Builder and his kind before. He knew their estimates tended to be optimistic. The reality always took much longer.

Jedidia's men had only enough food and water left for four or five days. Of course that could be stretched if the men went on half rations. But even if he had tools and food, the Builder claimed they couldn't get through the rocks in that short time.

They could eat a few horses, of course, but there was almost no wood to build fires. He could send foragers back to the east to find food, but carrying enough supplies for his army back up into the Pass would be impossible. His horses were already short of grain and water. Jedidia hadn't concerned himself with that, since he expected to reach grassland and water in a few days.

As for taking his men through without the horses, that was out of the question. Even if they climbed past the rubble, and made it all the way through the Pass, Jedidia's men would be on foot, a hundred miles from nowhere, and without food or water.

He had expected to live off the fertile lands of the Akkadians. Long before he found and collected enough to eat, his force of soldiers would have disintegrated, and what remained would be little more than a hungry rabble. Not to mention that Jedidia didn't intend to walk into enemy country, or face the famous Akkadian bowmen on foot.

Slowly, the realization sank in. Either his men would find a way around the blockage, or he would have to turn back. If he did that, by the time he crossed back over Elam's border, resupplied his men, and followed Lord Modran's footsteps through the Dellen Pass a hundred miles to the south, the war might well be over. Modran would have collected all the glory and all the loot.

Jedidia would be the laughingstock of the Elamite army, the great warrior who let a handful of Akkadians block his path with a few stones. Not to mention what King Shirudukh would say about that.

Or do. His exalted cousin had no sympathy for failure, even from his relatives.

Jedidia's teeth ground together in rage. He would send a few messengers back to Zanbil, to see what supplies there might be useful in getting through the landslide. That would give his men a few days to attack the problem. Perhaps they would find another way, or the stupid Builder might come up with some plan to get the horses through.

Jedidia decided not to have the man killed. Better to let King Shirudukh himself hear the man's words and excuses. Then the Builder could be properly tortured by the King's skilled jailers and publicly put to death for incompetence.

Still, Jedidia could not shake the gloom from his thoughts. The Akkadians were no fools. They wouldn't have bothered toppling the mountain here if there were any easy way around. He would need luck to find such a way, and luck, as his advisors had warned him before setting out, always seemed to favor the King of Akkad.

Thoughts of the Barbarian King made him clench his fists and smite his chest. Eskkar had taken Jedidia's already gloomy prospects and ruined them completely. He might end up being tortured alongside the Builder. "Damn you, barbarian! Damn you and your cursed tricks!"

17

The soldiers' garrison at Nuzi . . .

S abatu stood in his garden, practicing his archery, when he heard the sound of hoofbeats. A rider galloped past his home, and through the open gate Sabatu heard the labored breathing of the horse. A few moments later, the hoofbeats stopped abruptly, which most likely meant an important message had arrived from Akkad for Commander Tooraj. The solder in charge of Nuzi's garrison lived only a hundred paces from Sabatu's own residence.

Nevertheless, Sabatu refused to speculate on what message the horseman might carry. Instead he continued with his training, whipping a shaft from the quiver, fitting it to the string, and launching the arrow at the target. One after another, Sabatu loosed his shafts, stretching the rock-hard muscles in his arms. For more than a year, he'd worked with his bow, improving his eye, strengthening his muscles, and teaching his reluctant hands to master his custom-made bow.

Each repetition sharpened his skill and honed his eye, and Sabatu had grown quite proficient with his weapon. While he did not have the long range skill of Mitrac or even Daro, he could match his skill with the best of Akkad's horsemen. Sabatu varied the routine often, moving about, shooting without bringing the arrow to his eye, dropping to one knee, even loosing a few shafts while running toward or backing away from the target.

But now Sabatu's aim and attention wandered, and not every missile struck the center of the target. His thoughts lingered on the horse and rider that had raced past his gate, wondering if today the long-awaited summons to war had arrived.

The sun settled closer to the horizon, and as more time passed without any further sounds or activities, Sabatu dismissed the idea of war from his thoughts. His arrows once again found their mark in the center of the target with each snap of the bowstring. Then he heard footsteps, and a moment later, Commander Tooraj stepped through the gate.

"Just got word from Akkad, from the King." Tooraj wasted no words. "The Elamite army under Grand Commander Chaiyanar is moving against Sumer. Their forces are likely to arrive in the next ten days or so. If you're still wanting to join that fight . . ."

The long-awaited day had indeed arrived. Sabatu never hesitated. "Yes. How can I get to Sumer?"

"The soldier who carried the message is returning to Akkad by boat tomorrow morning. You can travel downriver with him. Once there, I'm sure Lord Eskkar will tell you how to get to Sumer."

"I will be ready before dawn."

"I'll be sorry to see you go," Tooraj said. "I could use a master bowman here. The King is taking half my men, and I'll be short handed."

"You won't be joining the fight?"

Tooraj shook his head. "Too old. Besides, we can't risk bandits plundering the mine. Or soldiers, either."

"Nuzi could be in no better hands." Sabatu smiled at the veteran fighter. "But if things go wrong at Sumer, or when the fighting ends, I promise to return here."

Sabatu meant every word. He'd come to like and respect Tooraj.

"Good hunting, then, Sabatu. May your arrow bring down your enemy and ours. I'll keep your house ready for your return." Tooraj glanced at the sun. "I have to go. The men are eager to learn who's going and who's staying." He extended his brawny arm to Sabatu.

Sabatu clasped the man's arm with even more force. "Good fortune to you, Tooraj, and all the people of Akkad."

At dusk the next day, the setting sun's rays sent waves of light across the Tigris when Sabatu stepped onto Akkad's dock. He went straight to the King's Compound, only to find that Eskkar had departed the city and left no word for Sabatu. He tried to speak with Queen Trella, but she, too, was unavailable. The guard at the gate refused to admit Sabatu. After wasting the rest of the evening and most of the next day trying to find Daro, Sabatu had encountered Yavtar in the lane outside the King's Compound.

Explaining his plight, Sabatu asked for Daro.

"Daro?" Yavtar scratched his chin. "He left Akkad some time ago. Don't know when he'll be back."

Sabatu caught the glint in Yavtar's eye, but the old sailor refused to admit that he knew anything at all about Daro or his whereabouts. However, Yavtar agreed to get Sabatu to Sumer by way of one of the supply boats destined for the southern city. The next day, Sabatu sailed from Akkad.

After almost three days on the Tigris, the slow-moving ship reached the trading port of Kanesh, the fort that marked Akkad's southern border. Even as he stepped ashore, Sabatu heard the dockside guards talking among themselves. The Elamites had already reached Sumer's outskirts and sealed off the city. Meanwhile their cavalry had continued moving north.

Suddenly the voyage for Sabatu's supply boat had become too risky. The nervous ship master refused to proceed further south. He unloaded his cargo of weapons and grain, turned his boat around, and set out for Akkad. Sabatu stood on the dock and cursed his bad luck.

The Elamites had moved against Sumer sooner than anyone in Akkad anticipated. The invaders had already surrounded the city, and done their best to cut off all river traffic to its dock. Now only Akkad's sleek and fast war boats had any chance of reaching the besieged city. The Elamites hadn't come in force as far north as Kanesh yet, but their cavalry patrols had ridden boldly almost within range of its alert archers.

Fuming at his bad luck, Sabatu discovered that he now had to wait for one of Daro's fighting ships to arrive. With Sumer under siege, these were the only boats that dared try to slip into and out of the city under the cover of darkness. It took another two days before one of Yavtar's fast-moving boats arrived from Akkad, bound for Sumer. The ship's cargo consisted of forty bows and two thousand arrows, weapons that would soon be needed by Sumer's garrison.

Sabatu pleaded his case with the frowning boat captain, clearly unwilling to transport a useless passenger.

"Well, I'm a man short," he said. "But unless you can row and use that bow, I won't take you on."

"I promise you, I can row, and I can fight."

The boat had departed Kanesh after dark, and the gruff ship master declared they would make landfall at Sumer just before dawn. He handed Sabatu an oar, and sat him down at the last rowing position in the rear of the craft, where he would have little chance to do anything wrong.

Sabatu didn't care. He would have clung to the side of the boat for the length of the journey if need be.

Now Sabatu stared at the glistening water that carried the crew and cargo racing down the Tigris. The boat would make the entire journey under the cover of night. At last he traveled toward a goal of his own, the City of Sumer. There he would have his chance, however slim, to confront in battle Grand Commander Chaiyanar – the man who tortured Sabatu and had his family murdered in front of him.

The fighting boat had covered half the distance to Sumer when the Elamites attacked. Sabatu, like the rest of the river boat's crew, had no warning. One moment the small craft had been moving swiftly down the Tigris, the silvery water reflecting the soft light from the nearly full moon.

Then a flight of arrows struck the boat, the individual shafts striking home with dull thuds that broke the night's silence. With a loud splash, one of the rowers went overboard. Another man dropped his oar and started cursing, and Sabatu saw an arrow had passed through the fleshy part of the man's arm, the bloody barb point exposed. The nine man crew, now reduced to only seven, responded fast enough, crouching low and paddling with all their strength.

Sabatu responded rapidly as well. He thrust his oar deep into the river and dragged it through the water with a grunt of exertion. The boat leapt forward despite the arrows that hissed overhead or splashed into the river.

The moment the arrows ceased, Sabatu dropped his oar, snatched up his bow, and strung the weapon. Pulling an arrow from the quiver resting beside his feet, he searched the east bank of the Tigris for the Elamite soldiers. But the boat, moving faster now, gave him no time to locate a target among the black shadows of the shoreline, at least seventy paces away.

The boat traveled a quarter of a mile before more arrows smacked against the hull, and Sabatu heard another man cry out. The remaining rowers worked their oars with all their strength, the prow of the boat cutting through the gleaming water with a relentless hiss. They were almost out of range when the second, and unnoticed, disaster struck.

The commander of the boat, acting as the steersman, took an arrow right through his neck. He never cried out, or if he did, no one heard him. Dead or dying, he loosened his grip on the steering oar. Without a steersman, the boat turned hard toward the western bank. By the time the arrows ceased and the rowers caught their breath, the boat, driven at top speed, had nearly reached the opposite shore.

"Someone take the oar!" One of the soldiers, a man named Harnos, had taken command.

Sabatu was closest, and one quick glance told him the steersman, slumped back against the stern, had died instantly. Sabatu dropped his bow and lunged toward the steering oar.

Instinctively, he pulled the tiller oar inward, then realized that motion only turned the bow of the craft even more toward the western bank. With a savage jerk, he shoved the oar outward as far as he could reach, feeling the force of the river thrusting against the oversized tiller. The boat, still with plenty of momentum, swung slowly back toward the center of the river. Sabatu saw the darker shoreline looming only a few paces from the ship.

"By the gods, I thought you'd run us aground!" Harnos, second in command – the entire crew consisted of Hawk Clan soldiers – moved to the stern to take control of the vessel.

But before Sabatu could yield the tiller, the ship lurched to a sudden halt, accompanied by the sound of wood snapping and men tumbling over the thwarts. The noise of the collision rang out loud enough to be heard across the river. The boat had missed running aground on the west bank, but not the tree that had collapsed into river.

"Damn!" This oath came from the crewman nearest the bow. "We've hit a tree limb!"

The boat, impaled on the nearly submerged log, lost all headway. The craft's stern swung toward the center of the channel, twisting the ship's frame and widening the hole below the water line. Sabatu heard the river rushing into the craft. A moment later, and the cool water reached his feet.

The experienced crew reacted swiftly.

"Curse our luck! The boat's going down."

"At least we won't have far to swim."

"Take your weapons. We may need them."

That last came from Harnos, who clearly knew how to think fast. Men swung over the side, clutching bows, quivers, and swords. It took Sabatu a moment longer to realize that the ship was lost, and it was time to leave. The water had already reached his thighs, and the gunwale barely remained above the flowing river.

Snatching up his bow and a quiver of arrows, he stepped into the water and half-swam, half-waded his way to shore. Slipping and sliding on the mud, he struggled to climb the bank and would have fallen back into the river, but a powerful arm reached down, grabbed his tunic, and pulled him out of the water.

"What are we . . ."

"Quiet, you fool." Harnos was definitely a man used to giving orders. "Can't you hear the horses?"

The soft drum beat of hooves reached Sabatu, and he heard voices, too. With a shock, he realized the words were the language of Elam. They must have cavalry on both sides of the river.

"Follow me," Harnos whispered. "We've got to get away from here. They'll spot the boat and come looking for us. And if you make another sound, I'll slit your throat myself."

Without a glance back, the soldier led the way into the darkness, the rest of the men, as ghostly as shadows, trailing behind in single file. They moved into the trees that followed the river's course and vanished.

With a muttered curse, Sabatu ran after them, already worried that they had moved out of his sight. But he soon caught up with the last man. After that, he never let them get more than two paces ahead. Soon enough Harnos led his little detachment out of the trees, and into the open fields.

As his fright at nearly drowning passed, Sabatu clenched his teeth in frustration, angered by yet another delay in his journey to Sumer. This disaster might well thwart Sabatu's chance for revenge. Nor could he complain to Harnos, who had received no special orders concerning the passenger.

Sabatu considered striking out on his own and trying to reach Sumer on foot. But if Chaiyanar's cavalry had reached this far north and on both sides of the river, there would be little chance to avoid being caught. The city would be ringed with horsemen, and Sabatu would never be able to slip through their cordon.

No, Sabatu realized he would have to stay with these Hawk Clan soldiers. They knew the land, and with luck would eventually get back to Kanesh. There Sabatu would have to plead for passage on another ship. He refused to consider that he might not be able to reach Sumer and miss the opportunity of personally killing Chaiyanar.

The Akkadian boat had run into Elamite cavalry, and an unlucky arrow had sent the vessel to the bottom of the river, leaving Sabatu stumbling through the darkness. Now the best that he could hope for was a quick return to Kanesh, and the chance to board another fighting ship on its way to Sumer.

He had to get there before Chaiyanar captured the city, which he would surely do. Once ensconced within Sumer's walls, the Grand Commander would be too well protected. No, Sabatu knew that he needed the confusion of the final assault on Sumer to slip amongst the Elamites and take his shot at Chaiyanar. In the chaos of the city's fall, Sabatu hoped that he could make his way close to his hated torturer. Speaking Elam's language should be enough to open the way.

One shot, that's all he prayed for. If he could put an arrow into Chaiyanar, Sabatu would thank the gods and gladly fall on his sword.

18

Fifty-six days after Orodes cut through his first pile of rubble, and the same day as Alcinor brought down the cliffs and blocked the Jkarian Pass, Orodes clung to his perch atop a boulder and stared at the landscape before him. For once, he could see something besides another god-cursed winding and narrow trail, a heap of rocks, or a gaping chasm.

The long days of endless labor in the mountain's foothills had drained both his strength and his energy. By now he no longer cared about Lady Trella, Akkad, or even the coming Elamite invasion. All that remained was a dogged determination to complete a task, and prove once again that Orodes of Akkad was not only the richest man in the city, but also its greatest miner.

Even so, he knew that he would have failed, except that as he and his men had worked their way farther south, the hills and cliffs had gradually diminished in size. And the obstacles, though more frequent, had decreased in both height and the weight of rock that needed to be cleared. Now, looking ahead, Orodes saw the end to his labor, less than a mile away.

He glimpsed something else in the distance. A patch of blue glistened under the sun. Wrinkling his nose, Orodes caught the scent of the Great Sea. He heaved a vast sigh of relief. He had done it. Despite all the obstacles the mountain gods had heaped in his path, Orodes had vanquished them all. He took another, deeper breath of the salt-scented air. Yes, the end of his journey was in sight.

Luka joined him atop the boulder, wriggling his way to the edge. "I told you it was here! I told you."

"You're sure this is the last one?" Orodes thought he could follow the trail through the end of the hills, but he couldn't be certain.

"Yes, this is it." Luka pointed to a pair of grooves scratched on the rock beside them. "This is the mark I made when I returned from the Sea. You did it, Orodes, you did it!"

Orodes resisted the temptation to take all the glory for himself. Every man in his crew had worked hard, of course, but Orodes knew no other man – miner, builder, or digger, not even Master Engineer Alcinor – in the Land Between the Rivers could have accomplished what Orodes had done, not in so short a time.

"We did, indeed, Luka." Orodes accepted Luka's words of praise, as he stretched out his arm to the south. "So that is the beach itself?"

"No, you can't see it from here. But when you emerge from the hills, there is about three hundred paces of sandy grassland, then about another hundred or more paces of sand to the water's edge."

All Orodes could spy from here was the green strip of earth, and the small patch of blue water. But the Great Sea waited just beyond, no doubt about that.

"Pick a few men and go take a look," Orodes ordered. "Make sure no one sees you. The soldiers will be here by morning, and the more we know about what awaits them the better."

The impatient horsemen in the vanguard of the cavalry had caught up with Orodes and his men eight days ago. After wasting half a morning answering foolish questions and watching his men get distracted, he'd told Hathor and King Naxos to remain a full day behind.

Daro, the commander of the expedition, had shaken his head and accepted Orodes's decision. Neither the King of Isin nor Hathor of Akkad had enjoyed being ordered to remain in the rear.

"I'll send a messenger back to Hathor at once," Luka said. "How long will it take to break through?"

Orodes already had that answer. After clearing forty-three blocked passages, he could estimate the time to clear this one easily enough. He glanced up at the sun, which had just moved past its midday peak in the sky. "If we work until dark, we should be able to clear the way by midmorning."

Luka called down orders to his men. Soon he and two others were scrambling through the rocks. They reached the other side, and set off at a trot for the beach.

Orodes slid back down and faced his men, scattered about as they lay on the ground and grateful for any chance to rest. All were dull-eyed and near exhaustion. Dust covered arms and legs, where it had worked its way into the skin. Every one had at least a double handful of cuts on their face, hands, arms, and chest, the result of too many sharp bits of flying rock.

Orodes had as many himself. He'd worked almost as hard as any of his men, supervising the crews, selecting the best way to work each obstacle, often times picking up a hammer and chisel himself. Gazing at the bodies sprawled about, he wondered if he appeared as haggard to them as they did to him.

Orodes took a deep breath. "Men! We've reached the sea. This is the last barrier. Once we break through here, we can return to Akkad and you can collect your pay."

No one cheered. Only a few bothered to glance up at their master, but even they showed no excitement or enthusiasm. Almost two months of back-breaking labor had extinguished any such sparks. By now even thoughts of the additional coins Orodes had promised meant little.

"Daro and the soldiers will be here by nightfall," Orodes continued, "and they have extra supplies, so we'll eat well tonight. They can help clearing the trail and with the digging tomorrow. Let's get to work."

Orodes ignored the weary groans that answered his words. Instead he reached down and found his pack. Removing his hammer and chisel, he turned, strode to the rock wall, and started work. One by one, with the usual accompaniment of grunts and sighs, his weary men climbed to their feet and followed his example.

Soon the noise of hammers striking chisels, rocks being tossed aside, and men swearing at the hard labor resumed its usual song. One more, Orodes thought, one more passage cut through the rocks and he could rest.

When he returned to Akkad, he intended to sleep for the first five days, then spend the next five floating in the Tigris, washing and scraping away the rock dust imbedded in his skin. And eating. He would treat himself to fresh meat every day, perhaps at every meal. Visions of roasted chickens, thick steaks, and hunks of steaming mutton passed before his eyes.

And wine. Orodes intended to get decently drunk every night. He would just lay in his bed and let his wives and slave girls climb all over him.

'The fantasy continued as he labored, and lasted until dusk arrived and it grew too dark to see anything. The exhausted men dropped their tools and slid to the ground wherever they happened to be. Nobody bothered searching for any scraps of firewood. His crew had not built a proper campfire in five days. Instead, they slipped into sleep as only the physically spent and emotionally drained can.

"Wake up! Wake up, I say."

Orodes, his head resting against a boulder, opened his eyes, and pushed himself to a sitting position.

"Who is it?"

"It's the King of the Elamites, who do you think it is?" Daro squatted down beside Orodes. "Leave you alone for a few days, and look at you. A child could have slit all your throats."

Orodes rubbed the sleep from his eyes with the back of his hand. Daro and most of his soldiers had fallen back with the cavalry, to help keep Naxos and Hathor from annoying the digging crews. "None of us would care, as long as he didn't wake us up doing it. Are the soldiers here?"

"Any moment now," Daro said. "King Naxos and Hathor are right behind. I came on ahead, as soon as Luka's messenger brought us the news."

"Good." Orodes couldn't force himself to put any enthusiasm into his words. "We can use the help."

"Where's Luka?"

Orodes told Daro about the sea, and that he'd sent Luka on ahead.

"It's true you can see the Great Sea?"

"Almost," Orodes said.

Both men turned at the sound of horses approaching. One of Daro's men had just finished with flint and stone and started a small fire from wood scraps and tinder the soldiers had brought with them. The man touched a torch to the tiny flame, and after a moment, held it high, revealing two tall figures striding toward them.

Daro helped Orodes get to his feet. "King Naxos, Orodes has succeeded. He's cut his way through the mountains."

Even in the torchlight, Orodes felt the penetrating eyes of King Naxos of Isin studying him. "Doesn't look much like the richest man in Akkad right now, does he?" Naxos grunted at his own joke. "How far are we from the sea?"

Orodes, awake now, reacted the way most men did to the King of Isin – with annoyance. "About fifty paces, Lord Naxos. In the morning, after we cut through the last of this rubble, you'll be able to see the beach from here. Less than a mile, I'd guess."

"You've done well, Orodes, though you don't look any more cheerful than the last time I saw you."

Orodes turned to the second man, and recognized Hathor's gaunt figure even in the flickering light. "Did you have any trouble along the trail?"

Hathor shook his head. "Lost a handful of horses, and two men to falls. But it took us much longer than we thought. We're about out of food and water, and there won't be much in the way of supplies coming down the trail for a few days."

"How much food and how many horses do you have with you?"

Naxos, obviously unwilling to let Akkadians lead the conversation, answered that one. "The last of our forces caught up with us two days ago. We've almost five thousand horsemen strung out behind us, most of them wondering where in the name of all the gods they're going. You'd better get us to the sea, Orodes, or I'll send you back to Akkad in pieces."

"You can depend on Orodes, King Naxos." Daro's voice showed his confidence. "If he says we'll reach the water tomorrow, we'll be there."

"Have you sent any scouts on ahead?" Naxos paid no attention to Daro's assurance.

Orodes again felt glad for his foresight. "Yes, Luka and two of his men went on ahead. They haven't reported back yet. Luka probably went up the coast."

"Or they're prisoners of the Elamites, spilling their guts out under torture. If they're not back here by morning, I'll send out some scouts of my own."

"By midmorning you can ride to the beach and see for yourself." Orodes decided he had enough of the King of Isin.

If Naxos detected the hint of disrespect, he ignored it. Instead, he snorted and stalked away, the soldier carrying the torch accompanying him.

"Don't hold too much against him, Orodes," Hathor said. "We've been riding and walking the horses for sixteen days, creeping and twisting our way through these mountains. All that without knowing if your plan was going to work. It's enough to put any man on edge."

Orodes shrugged. "Well, by midmorning, he'll be your problem. Me and my men, we'll be heading back toward Akkad. All I want is enough food and water to get home. "

"With most of our supplies gone, we've more than enough extra horses for your men. I'm sure we can spare you some food, enough to last until you meet up with the next supply train."

Orodes knew that Lady Trella and Akkad's efficient system of distributing supplies continued to send food and water through the mountains, to keep the soldiers and Orodes's men supplied with the essentials as they carved the trail to the sea.

"Then if you don't mind, I intend to go back to sleep. You and Naxos can ride to war and glory." Orodes, weary and drained from his efforts, no longer cared who won the battle or lost it. He was going to start for home in the morning. If the Elamites reached Akkad's walls, he would worry about that when it happened.

Muttering a belated prayer to Carsindar, the god of miners and diggers, Orodes slumped down along the rock, threw his dirty blanket over his chest, closed his eyes, and dropped back into the exhausted rest he'd so recently left.

19

The next morning, Daro glanced up, and saw that the sun had climbed high in the blue sky. Mid day approached, as he, King Naxos, and Hathor emerged from the last of the hills and strode onto the grassy dunes that bordered the beach. The commanders left their men and horses back in the hills, hopefully out of sight and out of earshot of anyone on the sandy shore.

The expedition's long journey through the foothills had ended, only six or seven days later than planned. For better or worse, the first part of Eskkar's plan to save the City of Sumer from the Elamites had begun.

A few hundred paces away, the low waves rolled gently onto the white sandy shore, broken here and there by a scattering of black rocks spattered with bird droppings. Daro led the way toward two large boulders that marked the end of the hill country. Luka stood there, waiting for them. The slinger had just returned from his second scouting mission. Now the time had arrived for King Naxos and Hathor, as leaders of the expedition, to see and hear for themselves what lay before them.

The four men clambered to the top of the westernmost boulder. While not very high, it overlooked the tall grass, and they could see a mile or more of the shore in either direction. Both the shoreline and the gently rolling sea remained empty of life, except for the noisy gray and white sea birds that circled raucously overhead searching for food, swooping and gliding over the land.

The intoxicating sea smells washed over the four men, a blessing after the baking sun and horse stink that had accompanied their slow journey through the mountains.

Daro nodded to Luka. The two men, thrown together for the last two months, had become friends. The taciturn Orodes, in charge of breaking through the mountains, had kept to himself. Without a

backward glance or a word of goodbye, let alone mention of good
luck in their coming battle, Orodes and his men had departed just
after midmorning. They would retrace their steps through the
mountains and hopefully reach Akkad before the Elamites could lay
siege to the city.

"What did you see?" King Naxos's gruff voice cut short Luka's
greeting.

"The cove where the Elamites landed is a little less than three
miles to the west, right where Yavtar said it would be." Luka pointed
with his arm. "The beach here was empty yesterday afternoon, so I
waited until dark and then went along the coast. The Elamite camp
was easy to see. I counted four or five campfires, so it must be big. I
didn't try to get too close. But I could see that supplies are piled up
all over the beach."

"Did you see any ships?" Daro, unlike Hathor, King Naxos, and
their horsemen, had a very different mission.

"Not last night. I couldn't be sure from the light of the fires. But
this morning when I went back, I counted eight or nine boats
beached on the sand, just above the water line. They look big, too,
bigger than what we usually see on the Tigris. Each vessel had at
least one tall mast. But no ships have passed this way today."

Many of the boats that plied the Tigris and Euphrates boasted a
small sail, but those that sailed over the Great Sea often relied on
taller and stronger masts to harness the wind.

"So many boats!" Daro couldn't keep the surprise out of his voice.

"I thought that would interest you," Luka said.

Boats that made the journey along the coast line of the Great Sea
had to be bigger and more rugged than the river boats that plied the
relatively tame waters of the Tigris, Euphrates, or the other countless
streams that crossed the land. More than a few river sailors had
drowned until they recognized the fact that waves on the Great Sea
could swamp the smaller boats.

That necessitated constructing larger and sturdier boats, which
carried heavier cargoes and manned by larger crews, probably ten or
twelve men to each ship. Even so, the boats hugged the shore as
much as possible.

When Daro had first heard the term, "hugging the shore," Yavtar
had explained that meant riding the sea anywhere from a half mile to
two miles off the beach, to avoid the low lying rocks and powerful

breakers. Not to mention the shallows near the shoreline where waves might roll a vessel over.

"If we can capture those boats," Daro said, "we can help cut the Elamite supply line."

"You know we won't be able to come back for you if you get into trouble." Hathor made it a simple statement, not a warning.

Daro grinned at that. "You'll likely find more trouble than I will."

"What about the Elamite forces at the camp?" Naxos, impatient as ever, ignored Daro and kept his gaze on Luka.

Daro knew the boats meant nothing to Naxos, nor did the King have much interest in Daro's plan for them. Still, Daro felt some sympathy for Naxos. The man had a daunting task of his own to deal with, and it had nothing to do with ships. The King of Isin had to worry about the twelve thousand or more enemy soldiers who might already have captured Sumer. Or if the Akkadians had been betrayed or detected, the Elamites might be just out of sight beyond the cove, waiting for Naxos and his soldiers to appear.

With luck, however, the enemy would believe their spies' latest reports, and think that King Naxos and his horsemen had departed toward the west, to attack the city of Lagash.

"From the campfires, King Naxos," Luka repeated, "I think they have less than three hundred men at most. Probably more than half of them sailors."

King Naxos, in charge of the cavalry, had brought twenty-six hundred riders with him, nearly every mounted fighter he and his city could muster. Hathor and Akkad had contributed fifteen hundred more, almost half of all the Akkadian horse fighters. Another eight hundred horsemen came from Sumer, dispatched to the northern lands in small groups long before the enemy arrived.

All together, close to five thousand cavalry lay hidden in the hills behind the Akkadian leaders. If Eskkar's luck still held, the Elamites knew nothing about this unseen force at their rear.

It also meant that these Elamites guarding the beach must be overwhelmed before they could send warning to their companions of the Akkadian presence.

Daro knew that for Naxos to have any chance of success, he needed to catch the enemy by surprise. The Elamite army, now encamped around Sumer's walls, far outnumbered Naxos's fighters. The cavalry he led might be behind the invaders, but should the

Elamites discover this danger lurking in their rear, they would whirl around fast enough, and then Naxos would be the one with the sea at his back.

If that happened, it wouldn't take much misfortune for the combined horsemen of Akkad and Isin to be trapped against the seacoast and destroyed.

Naxos stared at the empty windswept beach. As the moments passed, Daro wondered whether the King of Isin wished he and his men had remained safe behind their city's walls. Even now, he might be considering turning around and retracing his steps through the foothills. Hathor and the Akkadians would stay, of course, and probably the Sumerians.

Hathor finally broke the silence. "The soldiers guarding the ships matter little. If we can finish them off before they can send a warning, the Elamites won't know we're here."

Naxos shook off whatever gloomy thoughts had troubled him. "You're right. We need the food and water anyway. At least we'll be finished with these damned hills. We'll move out as soon as the men are ready."

The King of Isin, away from the treacherous mountains at last, seemed more relaxed. The prospect of fighting against a superior force apparently didn't bother him.

As Daro watched, Hathor and Naxos scratched out lines on the top of the boulder, and went over the assignments and the order of march one last time. When they finished, Luka dashed off back into the hills, to bring the vanguard of the cavalry down to the beach. It would take time for the entire force to work its way through the last part of the narrow trail and assemble here.

Hathor turned to Daro. "Are you and your men ready? You'll be on your own."

"Better that, than galloping across the country," Daro laughed. "My men are archers and boatmen, not horse fighters. As long as we can capture at least two boats, we'll take our chances on the sea."

"Then we'd better get moving." Naxos turned his face away from the sea. "Hathor, post lookouts, and let's get the men formed up as soon as we can. The quicker I get away from these damned hills, the better."

"Remember, we just need to make sure that none of the boats get into the water," Daro said. "If even one of them escapes to the sea, it will put all of us in danger."

"We'll do our best," Hathor said. "You'll ride with us?"

"Oh, yes. I need to see the boats, and I might have to get two or three of them into the water as quickly as possible. If any do escape, I might have to pursue. Hopefully, by the time we're ready, no more will be arriving so late in the day."

By mid afternoon, the last of King Naxos's force finally emerged from the hills and joined the march westward. The long column of horses plodded along, not on the sandy beach, but farther inland, along the grassy belt that sprouted at the base of the hills.

A refreshing sea breeze in the men's faces marked a dramatic change from the hot and still air of the mountains. For the first time in many days, the soldiers felt at ease. Even the prospect of a fierce battle against a numerically superior force didn't seem to give them any concern.

The horsemen rode in two thick columns, with riders four abreast in each column. Despite the eight man wide front, the double line of horsemen stretched back almost a mile and a half.

Naxos wanted a slow pace, which made sense to Daro, who rode beside Hathor at the head of the column closest to the water. The Elamite army had trodden this same path, and hopefully the men at the beach would think this new approaching force just another, late arriving, part of the army. After all, Daro reasoned, enemies would not approach at a walk.

Soon the enemy camp could be seen, and Daro took a quick count. Eleven boats, far more than he had expected, lay in a jagged line on the sandy beach, out of the surf and well above the high water mark.

He saw no signs of crews loading or unloading cargoes, so the work must be finished for the day. Some of the empty boats likely would push out to sea and set sail for Elam at first light tomorrow. No doubt the others waited for Sumer to fall, so they could stuff their holds with captured loot before returning home.

Now, however, the boat masters and their sailors rested from their long voyage. With any luck, Daro prayed, half of them would be swilling wine or ale stolen from the cargo. The more he thought about it, Daro decided that many of them would be drunk. Sailors had uncanny skills at tapping into and skimming portions of the kegs, skins, or jars that carried ale and wine intended solely for the army's commanders.

The blue waves topped with white foam of the Great Sea beat and fell upon the shore, moving back and forth with a powerful regularity that drew the eye. The sounds of the surf rumbling onto the sand added to the pleasant ride. Cool air blew off the water, refreshing soldiers who had sweltered among the rocks during the long journey south. Even the horses showed more spirit, apparently enjoying the softer mix of sand and grass beneath their hooves.

By now Daro could see the entire cove. No one in the camp paid any attention to their approach. He reminded himself that thousands of Elamite soldiers had made the same journey along the coast, and this would appear to be just one more contingent of soldiers joining the campaign.

Daro kept his position alongside Hathor. The column closest to the water was comprised of Akkadians. Naxos led the second column. All the men had been ordered to ride slumped on their horses, and to look both weary and bored, as if they had just completed a long journey. The King had also warned them not to gape like fools at the sight of the water, the first time most of these men had ever seen the Great Sea.

"Might as well turn toward them," Naxos called out. He led the column closest to the hills. "We'd be expected to stop and talk."

By now they were within five hundred paces of the camp. Two pennants flew about fifty paces apart, one yellow with black trim, and the other crimson with some emblem stitched in its center. As Daro watched, two men swung up onto horses and trotted out to meet them.

Without turning his head, Hathor gave the first order. "Pass the word. No one is to reach for a weapon until I give the command."

The two Elamites cantering toward them suspected nothing. One wore a brightly colored cloth wrapped around his head, with a glistening gemstone set in the fastening band. A sword hung from his waist. The other, unarmed, looked more like a servant than a guard. Daro surmised they were used to seeing strange folk in their empire. They halted their horses twenty paces from the head of the column. Naxos raised his right arm, and the vanguard eased their horses to a stop.

The leader of the Elamites spoke, his words an odd combination of gutturals and higher pitched sounds. Daro, though fluent in the language of southern Elam, had trouble understanding the meaning. Naxos didn't bother to reply to their incomprehensible language. Instead he kicked his horse into motion, drawing his sword as the same time.

For a moment, the man just stared at the horse and rider rushing toward him, flashing death in his hand. The Elamite didn't know whether to draw his sword or turn to flee. Before he could do either, Naxos's sword swung down, striking at the base of the man's neck.

Hathor, too, had urged his horse forward. But he reached for his lance, swinging it up in a smooth motion that bespoke years of practice. The servant, his eyes wide with shock, whirled his horse around, but before he could get it to a gallop, Hathor's powerful arm flung the bronze tipped weapon, and Daro saw it bury itself into the man's back.

With a roar, the entire column surged forward. Daro saw horses flash by him on either side, as the better riders overtook him. Nevertheless, he followed Hathor who headed directly toward the gap between the water and the boats. The Akkadians had their orders – to seize those vessels and kill their crews.

Naxos, meanwhile, led his horsemen straight ahead. The first few hundred riders would swing past the Elamite camp, to prevent any chance of their fleeing toward Sumer and their allies. Only when that escape route was closed would he and his men turn and attack.

The riders had nearly reached the camp before the Elamites grasped the horror approaching them. Many were sailors, porters, and camp followers. Little more than a hundred fighting men found themselves facing thousands of fast charging horsemen.

Panic reigned, as the Elamites rushed about. Some reached for weapons, others tried to get to their horses. But by then, hundreds of Akkadian cavalry had galloped past, cutting off any way of escape. A few of the Elamites tried to fight their way through, while others rode into the surf, but they never had a chance. Akkadian bowmen soon brought down all those attempting to flee. Soon blood stained the sands, as the Elamites died, most without ever striking a blow against their attackers.

The crews of the ships reacted faster than the soldiers. They rushed back to their boats, frantic to get them into the water and away from the shore.

But they, too, had no time. Hathor's men tore into the gap between the surf and the boats resting high on the beach, the Akkadian horses kicking up great gouts of sand. Lances and arrows flew through the air, striking down any man that moved.

This was not battle, just the easy slaughter of the ships' crews, most of whom knew little about fighting. Some Elamites fled up the beach, gaining a few more moments of life before the horsemen rode them down. Others dashed into the surf, but the waves pushed them back, and the Akkadian bowmen finished them off.

The Akkadians had their orders. Kill everyone in their path. Daro wanted all those sailors dead, and Hathor had issued another order to his commanders – thrust a lance into every throat. None of their foes could be allowed to fake death, or hide beneath the bodies of others.

Daro reached the first of the boats, his horse splashing in the wet sand behind the craft. He continued on, until he'd ridden past every one of the vessels, sword in hand and peering into each one, to make sure no Elamite sailors could get a craft into the water. He ignored the clash of weapons and cries of the dying that continued further up the beach, where Naxos and his men finished hunting down the last of the invaders.

Daro finished his quick examination of the boats. By then, his one hundred and twenty Akkadian bowmen had arrived and surrounded the ships. Though all of them knew how to ride, they were not experienced horse fighters, and Hathor had ordered them to the rear.

Daro hadn't minded. The arrangement meant that none of his carefully selected archers, all of whom had experience on river boats, had risked an injury in the fighting.

As the first of his men dismounted, Daro sent them onboard the vessels, to make sure no Elamites hid among the ballast. Meanwhile, he selected the three largest and sturdiest boats, and ordered them to be dragged closer to the water. Daro wanted them ready to be launched at a moment's notice.

Each boat he selected stretched longer than any river boat in Yavtar's fleet, with a wider beam and taller sides as well. All three looked sturdily built, strong enough to withstand the waves of the

Great Sea. Unlike the clumsy *Apikin,* Daro recalled, as he nodded in satisfaction.

"Leave the rest of the boats where they are, but stave out the bottoms. Make sure none of them ever goes to sea again. Keep the hulls intact, but rip out every plank and board within. Collect every paddle, rope, and sail, too. We'll need them."

By now all of Daro's bowmen had reached the water's edge. He had more orders for them. Their supply of extra bows and shafts, laboriously transported all the way from Akkad, were to be divided up and loaded onboard the three captured craft.

That finished, his bowmen formed a line to carry water skins, food, and anything else needed to keep the three boats afloat and ready to fight. Fortunately, the stacks of fresh supplies that covered the beach, intended to support the Elamite army at Sumer, provided everything Daro needed for his small force, and in more than sufficient quantity.

Next he divided up his men, forty to each ship. That was a large contingent, but since the boats carried no cargo, there should be just enough room for that many to work the ship and fight. With so many extra men plying the oars, the boats would race through the sea, faster than any cargo vessel.

Hathor rode up just as the initial frenzy of loading supplies and weapons ended. "I see you found more boats than you expected."

Daro grinned. "These three," he pointed toward the boats now resting on the wet sand, "are bigger and better than anything I expected. My sailors will need to learn how to handle ships this size."

"Well, don't drown them all at once." Hathor gestured toward the cavalry. "Naxos is already regrouping the men. We're pushing on ahead. There's still plenty of daylight left, and Naxos doesn't want to risk anyone getting by us after dark."

"Any word on the Elamites?"

Hathor nodded. "Yes, the last of the army passed through here six days ago. By now, the entire army is outside Sumer."

Sumer lay less than a full day of hard riding from here.

"Leave us a few horses," Daro said, "so we can get word to you if any more Elamites show up."

"I'll do better than that. Naxos wanted to take all the extra horses with us, but he agreed you can have five. I told him it would look odd if someone shows up and there were no horses about."

Sixteen horses had been in a rope corral, which had somehow remained intact.

"Good. We can use them to drag the bodies away."

"I never thought about the dead bodies." Hathor shook his head. "There's always something you don't think of, isn't there?"

"Well, I can't leave them lying about. No boat master with eyes in his head would land his ship on a battlefield."

"I'll leave you the prisoners we found. We took two men alive, and the older one looks like some kind of merchant or trader. See what you can wring out of them. If it's anything useful, send word." Hathor whirled his horse around. "I've got to get back to Naxos. He wants me to stay close, so he can keep an eye on me."

"Don't forget these." Daro handed him the two pennants that had flown over the camp. "My men picked them up. They're a little dirty, but you might find a use for them."

"Ah, good idea." Hathor reached down and grasped the pennants. "And to think that Yavtar told me you couldn't find your prick in the dark."

,Daro laughed. "Good hunting, Hathor."

With a wave, the Egyptian touched his heels to his horse and rode off in a flurry of sand.

In moments, the last of the cavalry, now moving at a respectable canter, disappeared behind the sand dunes to the west. Four of Daro's men arrived, pulling along two prisoners at the end of a rope, their hands bound before them. His bowmen looked annoyed, no doubt unwilling to be guarding insignificant prisoners.

Daro glanced at the two captured men. Both had blood splattered over their tunics, though neither appeared to have more than minor injuries. Neither bothered to keep up any pretense of courage. Fear gripped them both, and the older one couldn't control the occasional shiver that made his arms tremble.

"Keep them apart," Daro ordered. He had no time for them now. "Make sure they don't talk or escape."

He climbed into one of the beached boats, and gazed around the cove. Bodies littered the beach, and the roiled sand would tell anyone at a glance that a battle had been fought here. The dead needed to be concealed. The best place for them would be the Great Sea, but the bodies would soon wash up on shore, or float along the coast, as likely toward any approaching Elamite ship as not.

Daro sighed. Lifting his eyes from the shoreline, he stared across the grassy belt that butted up against the low hills, about five hundred paces away. Damn the gods, why couldn't the camp have been closer to the hills.

"Get all the ropes you can find, and bring up the horses. We're going to drag the dead inland, behind the grass and those hills."

Months ago, at Eskkar's war council in Akkad, Daro had first learned of the daring plan to save Sumer. Yavtar had also attended the meeting. The old sailor had provided estimates of the numbers of boats that would be needed to keep the Elamite supplies flowing until Sumer could be taken.

The discussion of the coastal shipping had given Yavtar an idea to strike a hard blow against the enemy. Seize a few boats, destroy the rest of them, and use the captured ships to patrol the sea and prevent further supplies from landing. If successful, the lack of supplies would help weaken the invading enemy.

The war council talked about such a venture for most of the day, before Eskkar agreed to it. Daro, the logical choice for such a daring plan, had joined Orodes's expedition, commanding the small force of soldiers accompanying the Master Miner. Now Daro, by patrolling the seacoast, would try to help King Naxos and Hathor in their coming fight. Unlike the rest of the cavalry force, Daro had brought with him a troop of one hundred and twenty archers, almost all of them with some experience on Akkad's fighting river boats.

"As long as they can keep up with us, they can come," Naxos had declared at the war council. "If they can cause some mischief with the enemy supplies, so much the better."

Daro recognized the doubt in King Naxos's voice. The King of Isin had little expectation that Daro's efforts would amount to much.

And so the river archers had walked their horses all the way from Akkad to the sea, following the cavalry, and stepping through endless piles of horse droppings the entire distance. Daro's small troop of bowmen wouldn't be of much use in the coming battle north of Akkad or even at Sumer, but here, on the beach, they just might fulfill a much larger role.

As Daro glanced around at the ruins of the enemy camp, he knew the first part of the plan had gone perfectly. His men had captured three large and sturdy ships, vessels capable of moving with ease through the powerful coastal flows of the Great Sea. Just as important, they also had all the weapons, food, and water they might need. The more difficult part had just begun – putting the ships into the water and preparing them for war.

By nightfall, Daro could barely stand. He'd raced his horse back and forth across the beach too many times to count. Fifty paces behind the dunes his men found a small ravine, and soon began dumping the bodies, with the help of the horses. Daro had to order a few men into the pit with the bodies, to arrange them as close together as possible, so that no space was wasted.

When the last Elamite body slid into the ravine, the men scooped and kicked sand over the dead. It wasn't much of a grave, but they managed to at least cover the corpses. In the morning, Daro would have them do a better job, collecting more sand and tossing as many rocks as possible over the bodies. He didn't want a flock of sea or carrion birds screaming and circling over the site, alerting any observer that something was amiss.

Daro finally trudged over to the two prisoners, starting with the common sailor first. Daro sat down on the sand facing the man, his face still streaked with dried blood.

"What's your name?" Daro spoke in the common language, used by sailors and traders along the coast of the Great Sea.

"Pettraka, Lord."

"Would you like some water?" The prisoner looked as dry as the sand beneath him.

"Yes, Lord. Please."

Daro glanced at the guard and held out his hand. The bored soldier tossed over a water skin. Daro quenched his own thirst, but made no move to share any with the prisoner.

"Tell me about the boats. When is the next boat coming?"

"I . . . I don't know, Lord. I'm just an oarsman. All I do is row."

"Show me your hands."

The man lifted his bound hands. Daro saw the thick calluses that covered his palms and fingers, and the powerful muscles in his arms. A simple rower.

With a few questions, Daro learned all he needed. The man's ship had arrived in the early afternoon, carrying food and grain for the horses. The sailor knew nothing else of value.

Daro stood, and handed the man the water skin. "From now on, you will row for Akkad, if you wish to live." He let the man have a few swallows, enough to quench his thirst, then pulled the skin from his grasping hands. Daro didn't want the prisoner to regain his strength just yet.

The beach still bustled with activity. The ships, their bottoms hacked out, remained useful as a source of fire wood. Their deck planks would also make excellent shields. The men had discovered two saws, and were busy cutting the wood.

Daro strolled over to where the second prisoner sat. One look at the man's tunic, and Daro knew Hathor had indeed captured either a ship captain or one of the beach commanders. Again he eased himself to the sand, this time stretching out his legs. He glanced at the man's parched lips and jiggled the water skin.

"Your name?" This time Daro spoken in the language of the Elam.

The man, of about forty seasons, licked his dry lips and glanced around the beach, as if searching for help. Matted sand still clung to his hair and beard, both speckled with gray. His once fine tunic revealed that he had soiled himself, either from fright or because the guards hadn't allowed him to move since he'd been captured.

"If you won't talk, then you're of no use to me. I'll have you beaten to death."

"And if I do talk to you?"

The hoarse words, spoken in Akkadian, came out in a rasp, and with only the slightest trace of an accent. Daro smiled at his good fortune. "First, you'll have some water to drink. Then, if your words are helpful, you may live. Otherwise . . ."

The man didn't take long to decide. "Water. Please."

"Your name. I'll not ask you again."

"Kedor of Sushan. I am the owner and master of that ship, the one with red eye painted on the bow," he inclined his head towards one of the three intact vessels. "You selected well. It is a fine craft."

Daro handed him the skin, and let the older man quench his thirst. "Well, Kedor of Susa," Daro used the Akkadian name for that distant city, "I thank you for your ship. My name is Daro, and I command these men."

"Akkadians, yes, I've visited your fine city several times. A pity the King of Elamites intends to enslave it."

"King Shirudukh may find that Akkad is not an apple waiting to drop into his hand. Those who wage war on King Eskkar usually end up dead."

"You know the barbarian King?"

"Oh, yes. I have fought twice at his side." Daro shifted his legs to a more comfortable position. "But now I need your help, and I am willing to let you live in exchange. After the Elamites are defeated, your kin in Elam can ransom you."

Kedor shook his head. "I am from Sushan, not the land of Elam. Once it was a free city, but years ago King Shirudukh established one of his palaces there. He's there now. He plans to visit Sumer as soon as it is taken, to see for himself the fertile countryside of the Land Between the Rivers. No doubt he will be even less merciful here than he was at Sushan."

"We look forward to his visit," Daro said. "As much as I enjoy talking to you, now I need the knowledge that is in your head. Tell me all about the supply boats, when they come, what they carry, how they are defended. You see, Kedor, I intend to capture as many of them as possible, and sink the rest. By the time I am finished with Elam's supply craft, you may be the only ship master still alive on the Great Sea. Think how well you'll do after the fighting ends, and when you're ransomed and returned home."

20

The next day, a little after noon, a well-rested Daro surveyed the placid and peaceful beach. The debris from yesterday's brief battle had vanished. The last of the churned sand had been smoothed with a dragged mast, and no evidence remained that a large body of horsemen had charged through the area.

A cheerful driftwood fire burned, the sharp breeze from the sea whipping the flames and whirling glowing ashes into the air. Several of his men lay scattered about on the sand, taking their well-earned leisure.

Others, their bows and shafts hidden in the broken hulls, strolled about the camp, leisurely moving supplies from place to place. Every man had worked without ceasing long after dark, to mask every trace of the Akkadian attack.

The camp looked, or so Daro hoped, like a woman waiting for her lover, or in this case, the next Elamite ship to arrive. Kedor, the captured Elamite sea master, informed Daro that ships seldom arrived before midday. They preferred to leave themselves plenty of daylight as they covered the last leg of their difficult journey along the coast.

Whatever the prisoner's reasons, either fear of death or a real hatred toward the Elamite rulers, he had decided to cooperate completely with his captors. Or perhaps Kedor had considered the possibility of being the only surviving shipmaster in his home port of Sushan. With his help, Daro had prepared the camp. Now nothing remained except to wait, to rest, and enjoy whatever brief respite the gods allowed them.

"Sail to the east!"

The lookout, positioned on board the proud craft that had once belonged to Kedor, waved his arm toward a faint smudge of white far out to sea. The winds and waves must have pushed the ship far from shore before it could turn its bow toward the beach. Daro watched as it turned toward land, and he saw the vessel lose the favor of the wind.

The craft's sail came down, and the crew of the boat struggled at their oars, driving the craft through the waves toward the camp.

He glanced up at the sun. It had just moved past its highest point in the sky, so Kedor had spoken the truth about that, at least.

Kedor, his tunic washed in the morning surf and spotless once again, looked every bit the wealthy ship owner. His three rings, stolen by his captors, had been returned to him, and the red gemstone on his right hand flashed in the bright sunlight. He even carried a sword on his waist, though the blade had been broken off close to the hilt, leaving only a dull stub inside the scabbard.

"Remember," Daro said, "act as if you are in charge of the camp, and I am merely your faithful bodyguard. Make sure they come all the way in. If they suspect anything is amiss . . ."

"I understand, Daro." Kedor smiled grimly. "You don't need to threaten me any further."

Nevertheless, Daro made sure that two of his archers stood close by, ready to take up their bows.

Side by side, Daro and his captive stood on the beach, two men enjoying the fresh sea air as they watched the ship pulling its way toward them.

"The men will be tired when they land," Daro commented.

"Yes, the last pull is the hardest. You don't want your boat to lose its way and get swamped trying to make land." Kedor raised his hand to shade his eyes from the brilliant sun reflecting off the blue water. "Your men will be expected to help beach the boat. Still, you're in luck. Many times several boats sail together, for safety. This captain must have pressed on ahead."

The boat drew closer. Now it caught the swell of the waves washing ashore and speeded up, as the onrushing tide made the crew's job less taxing.

Suddenly the boat loomed up. Daro shouted to his men, and they dropped their burdens and leisurely waded into the surf, waiting to assist the vessel's crew. He heard the captain's booming voice as he ordered the oars in. The ship flung itself through the last of the waves, bottom hissing against the sand.

It stopped with a lurch, tilting slightly to the right, but by then the Akkadians had reached its side, and before it could float off again, they dug their feet into the swirling sand and heaved the vessel farther onto the sand, grounding it.

A man wearing a large hat with a wide brim to deflect the fierce sun strode along the length of the ship, staring at the men on the beach.

Daro turned to Kedor. "Tell the captain to surrender, or I'll put his crew to the sword."

Kedor repeated the commands, and Daro saw the look of shock on the captain's face. Twenty archers rose up from the nearest hulk, bows drawn and shafts aimed at the rowers. At the same time, the men who helped beach the craft swarmed up its sides. Only a few had swords, but the rest carried knives, and they far outnumbered the stupefied crew.

In moments, the Akkadians had the crew of fifteen off the ship and under guard. Daro and Kedor confronted the shocked captain, who had already lost his fine hat and whatever jewels he might have been wearing. Daro's men could strip a body, alive or dead, of all its valuables in the briefest of moments.

"What's your cargo?"

"What is this? Who are you?"

Dargo grabbed the man by the throat and jabbed the tip of his knife into the man's stomach. "Answer my question, or I'll spill your guts on the sand, and let you watch yourself die."

The man's knees turned to water, and the words spilled from his mouth.

Soon Daro nodded in satisfaction. A food ship, destined to resupply the men attacking Sumer. A good catch.

"Sail, ho! Another ship to the east!"

"You did well, Kedor." Daro could afford to be generous. "Now let's see what the next one brings us."

The second boat, a little smaller, was taken as easily as the first. This one, with a crew of twelve, also carried food for the soldiers, and a good supply of grain for the horses. Daro had no use for the grain and most of the food, so he decided to give his archers some practice at sea.

Just before the tide turned, they loaded the second ship that had arrived with all the unneeded supplies, and launched it back into the surf. Kedor's old ship – the men had already renamed it the *Akkad* – followed, and soon the two craft were more than half a mile off the shore.

As Daro watched from one of the beached vessels, the crew of the smaller boat broke open the hull. The ship began to sink, and the crew swam over to the *Akkad*. In moments, the stricken ship slipped under the waves, taking with it the supplies that would soon be needed by the Elamites.

The *Akkad* remained offshore, rowing back and forth, as the men familiarized themselves with their prize and the way it handled.

Just before dusk, another ship was sighted. Daro signaled the *Akkad* to return, and soon welcomed its laughing crew back in the camp. The third vessel, rowing hard to reach the camp before nightfall, proved to be the catch of the day. Larger than the others, it contained a good supply of weapons – swords, spears, as well as bows and sheaves of arrows.

Daro rubbed his hands together in satisfaction. He had three ships ready to fight, plenty of food and now a vast supply of arrows. At the first hint of danger, he could put to sea and be out of reach of the Elamite army.

Even Kedor appeared impressed. "You've done well, Commander Daro. I thought you might catch one or two ships' crews by surprise, but not three. What do you intend to do with the crews? You'll soon have too many to guard."

"In the morning, I'll send them on their way toward Sumer. Whether they find any safety in that direction is up to them. As long as they don't try and go east. I don't want them warning approaching ships. If you like, Kedor, you can go with them."

The former captain considered his choices. "I believe I would prefer to stay with you. Sooner or later, I'd like to get my ship back, and if I leave, it's unlikely I'll ever see her again. I'm sure I can help you deal with the Elamites. Even when you're captured or killed, I should still be able to convince the Elamites that I was forced to work for you."

Daro nodded. "And when Eskkar drives these Elamites back to their own lands, you could find yourself enjoying a pleasant welcome in Akkad and a suitable reward. The King will need men who know the Elamites' ways."

"Then until the gods bring either of those happy days upon us, I will continue to help you. But please, make sure your men still consider me a prisoner."

"Indeed I will, Kedor. But I think Ishtar and Marduk, the gods of Akkad, will bring you good fortune." Daro laughed. "And meanwhile, we'll starve the Elamite army as much as we can."

"You think they will not capture Sumer? The soldiers talked as if taking the city would be as easy as plucking a ripe berry from a bush."

"Well, I think they'll find that Sumer is much better prepared for a siege than their spies reported. King Naxos and his five thousand riders will give the Elamites more than they can handle. By now, that battle may have already begun."

Daro clapped his hand on Kedor's shoulder. "Come, we should celebrate our new alliance with some wine."

"Thanks be to the gods," Kedor said. "I was beginning to think that none of Akkad's leaders had a taste for fine spirits."

Daro laughed as he led the way toward the supplies stacked up upon the beach. "We'll drink to our next capture. I wonder how King Naxos is doing?"

21

After leaving Daro and the supply cove behind, the Isin and Akkadian cavalry covered twenty miles without incident. As the last of the day faded into dusk, the scouts returned and reported no sign of the Elamites. Hathor, riding at the head of the column beside Naxos, decided not to press their luck.

"Let's make an early camp," Hathor suggested. "The Elamites are bound to have patrols to the north and west, and they'll likely be returning to Sumer before dark. If we get too close to the city, we may run into one of them."

"We could make a few more miles before nightfall," Naxos agreed, "but there's no sense wearying the horses."

They had reached a small stream, an offshoot of the Tigris, that also found its way to the Great Sea. Too shallow for the large, seagoing vessels the Elamites used to transport their supplies, the branch was also the closest source of fresh water to the cove. The Elamites, traveling in three separate armies so that the ships could resupply them along the way and at the cove, had reached Sumeria a few days apart.

Each army would have come up this same trail, then followed the stream north until it joined with the Tigris a handful of miles south of Sumer. The debris and human waste scattered about indicated that the Elamites had indeed camped here as well.

The combined force continued another half mile north, until they found a relatively clean place to halt for the night. Sliding down from his horse, Hathor ordered his commanders to join him. Issuing the night orders didn't take long. His men understood they were in enemy territory, and they knew what needed to be done.

With so many men and horses, even stopping to make camp presented its own challenges. The mounts came first, of course. They had to be fed a few handfuls of the precious grain captured at the cove, then rubbed down, and corralled for the night. Units of one hundred men, each under the leadership of a subcommander, comprised each group. Fortunately, the forces of Akkad and Isin had ridden together for almost thirty days, and every man knew his task.

"Make sure the sentries are posted," Hathor said. "Double the guard on the horses, and I want fifty men ready to mount up at all times." Then he strode through the camp, as the evening fires were lit. Hathor stopped at every small gathering, talking and laughing with his men, much the way Eskkar always did.

Hathor understood the need to stay close to his men. Soldiers fought, he knew, not just for a cause, but because they believed in themselves, their companions, and their leaders. And the more they saw their leader concerned with their welfare, the harder they would fight.

As he moved among them, Hathor saw no signs of fear or worry, though everyone knew they might be fighting for their lives tomorrow. Sumer, besieged by thousands of Elamites, lay only twenty miles or so to the north, and the men knew it.

During the march through the mountains, Hathor and Naxos both had to deal with the usual petty frictions of large numbers of soldiers jammed together. Quarrels had broken out nearly every day, but there had been only a few incidents occurring between the men of Isin and Akkad. Where the blame fell upon his men, Naxos had been harsh in his punishments, and Hathor had followed the King of Isin's example.

Both commanders knew they had to make their forces cooperate, or the entire expedition might fail. But the shared suffering that the men had endured during the long and difficult journey had softened everyone's rough edges, and by now, to Hathor's satisfaction, the men worked willing together. Even the dimmest witted or most quarrelsome bully understood that the enemy would kill the soldiers of Isin and Akkad indiscriminately, and that bond kept the men close.

In his rounds, Hathor did take in all the usual complaints – too much riding, contrary horses, not enough food, and stiff and sore muscles – the list was endless. Soldiers had grumbled about such things as long as men had gone to war, and with much the same result – another hard ride the next day, a desperate battle, and a good chance of ending up dead.

Still, if the soldiers had any real misgivings about their mission, Hathor would have glimpsed it in their eyes or heard it in their voices. Instead they splashed about in the stream, or relaxed in the warm and breezy evening air, still smelling of the sea, a happy change from the endless days and stifling heat in the foothills. They might have been children playing, instead of men about to go into battle.

Satisfied with his men's good spirits, Hathor took one final walk around the perimeter of the camp, checking on the sentries. He'd heard too many of Eskkar's stories about stealing horses and night stampedes to leave anything to chance, especially this close to the enemy. Both he and Naxos wanted their men and horses to be fresh when they reached the city. They might all be fighting for their lives before the sun cleared the horizon.

Only then did Hathor drop down on the soft ground. The gurgling of the water against the rocks lulled him to sleep, almost as quickly and deeply as any of his soldiers.

In the morning, Hathor and Naxos woke their men well before dawn, in case the Elamites had learned of their presence and planned a morning attack. By the time the leading edge of the sun lifted over the horizon, every fighter stood beside his mount, ready to ride or repel an attack. But sunrise brought only empty horizons, with no sign of any enemy scouts observing their position.

Naxos gave the order, and the cavalry formed into its usual columns and resumed its journey. The open terrain, mostly sand with large clumps of bright green grasses, promised easy riding for the men. The two pennants taken from the beach, each fastened to a lance tip, waved in the breeze just behind the two leaders.

"They haven't discovered us yet," Hathor said, riding at Naxos's side. "We'd have seen their scouts by now."

"Or they're baiting a trap for us closer to Sumer," Naxos argued.

Hathor laughed. Naxos's gloomy words didn't carry conviction. "In that case, we'd better hurry north. It wouldn't do to keep the Elamites waiting."

Naxos swore, then laughed.

They continued north, following the stream. The day promised to be another hot one. Hathor didn't mind, having been raised in the Egyptian desert. As midmorning approached, the Akkadians had their first encounter with the enemy. Still traveling at a comfortable pace to conserve the horses, they came across an Elamite supply party returning to the beach, to collect food and supplies from the boats.

Fifty pack animals, twenty Elamite handlers, and ten guards comprised the supply gang. Either because of the captured pennants, or perhaps because they didn't expect a hostile force between Sumer and the beach, they rode right up to the slow-moving Akkadians without the slightest suspicion. As he had yesterday, Naxos killed the leader himself. The rest of the Elamites died almost as fast, taken by surprise and cut down in a hail of arrows.

"Collect all the horses," Hathor shouted when the killing stopped. "We don't want any riderless horses returning to Sumer."

Naxos, a splash of Elamite blood on his right arm, appeared as ferocious as any of his men. Isin's King, Hathor decided, enjoyed killing people. Certainly the man showed no fear of death of fighting. Hathor prayed to the gods that Naxos's eagerness for battle wouldn't turn to some reckless action.

The Akkadians left the dead where they had fallen, and continued their journey.

"Not many guards," Naxos commented cheerfully.

Maybe, Hathor decided, the King should kill a man or two every morning, if it would keep him in a good mood. "Nothing of value to guard," Hathor said. "Just empty packs to fill with supplies at the cove. Still, you're right. These Elamites seem very confident. I expected we'd be spotted by now."

Keeping their horses to a slow walk, Hathor and Naxos rode together at the head of the army, with only a few scouts out ahead. The Akkadian cavalry still followed the well-beaten track that Elamites had created on their march from the beach.

A few miles beyond, Hathor came across an even more visible sign of the enemy's passage. Eight bodies, six men and two women, lay naked alongside the trail. The men, hacked to pieces and covered with blood, had probably died fast enough.

The women, their faces covered with so much blood that Hathor couldn't even tell if they were old or young, showed large bruises on their thighs and breasts, the usual signs of repeated rape. Both had wide belly wounds that would have killed them slowly. One had a clump of sea grass shoved into her opening.

Swarms of the fearless black sea flies nearly covered the corpses, as they feasted on the still fresh meat. Hathor wondered how many men had taken the women before they died. Even death might not have stopped the most brutal of Elamites.

Most likely farmers, Hathor guessed, harmless and helpless before the Elamite swords. Hathor knew that every man would stare at the bodies as they rode by. Behind him, the laughter and loud talk faded into sober words.

Hathor wasted little more than a look at the dead. Helpless farmers had suffered at the hands of soldiers and marauders since the beginning of time, and he'd killed more than a few of them himself.

After a brief glance at the bodies, Naxos, too, had ignored the sight. Dead Sumerian farmers meant nothing to him. "So, Hathor, what do you think we will find?"

"The last of the invaders reached the city three or four days ago," Hathor replied. "By now they've sealed the approaches and started preparing for the assault. I expect that we'll find them spread out, with the largest concentration of men north of Sumer, in case anyone tries to reach the city or break the siege. They're obviously not watching the south, or we'd have seen their patrols."

"What do you suggest we do when we get there? What would the mighty Eskkar do?"

Hathor took his time before answering. He knew the King of Isin's pride still rankled that he had agreed to follow Eskkar's battle plan. All the same, Naxos already knew what Eskkar would do.

Long before the expedition set out, Eskkar, Hathor, and Naxos had prepared several plans of action, depending on whether or not the Akkadians were discovered, even when they were discovered. If the element of surprise remained intact, the leaders had already agreed on what to do.

"My Lord Naxos, King Eskkar asked you to take this command. He told me to follow your orders as I would his own. He asked only that I take no foolish chances with my men's lives. You've no need to compare yourself to him. The command is yours."

"Bah! I know Eskkar well enough. He'd sacrifice Isin and Sumer, too, for that matter, to save his city."

"Perhaps he would. But he did not. As Eskkar told you, the fate of the war is in your hands. Even if he wins a victory over the Elamites, it will be of little value if Sumer and the southern lands fall."

"We're still outnumbered three or four to one," Naxos said. "The Elamites may swallow us whole."

Hathor laughed. "Eskkar once told me that in every battle he ever fought, he was always outnumbered. It's the will to victory that wins battles. The Elamites are confident of their numbers and sure of their conquest. That will be their weakness. Lead your men with honor. No man can do more."

Naxos digested that for a moment. "You like Eskkar, don't you?"

For the first time, Hathor heard only honest curiosity in the King's voice. "Yes, I do. We are friends. Fifteen years ago, he gave me back my life when a single word could have ended it. Since that day I have found nothing but honor in the man. He cares naught for glory or gold, only for the life of his city."

Hathor remained the only survivor of the hated Egyptians, who had once fought against the soldiers of Akkad. Hathor and others had seized control of the city after a night of bloodshed. But the Egyptians ruled Akkad only for a few days, before Eskkar returned and led a small group of followers over the wall to rescue his wife and child and reclaim his city.

When the battle ended, Eskkar had fought and captured Korthac, the leader of the Egyptians. Attempting to flee, Hathor had taken a wound that left him unable to fight or escape. Only Trella's plea to her husband saved Hathor from the torturers and death.

In the years since, a bond formed between Eskkar and Hathor. Both men started life as outcasts, and both found themselves alone in a strange land. Eskkar understood what Hathor had faced in those first few years, before the people and soldiers of Akkad had, grudgingly at first, accepted the role that Eskkar had given him.

Over time, Hathor received many gifts and honors from Eskkar and Trella, but by far the most valuable was his wife, Cnari, who had given him his first real family.

Naxos broke the silence. "Yet Eskkar builds an empire that threatens to swallow Isin and all the other cities of the Land Between the Rivers."

"You would prefer the constant battles between cities, like the Sumerians did? Or more attacks from the steppes warriors, or this invasion of the Elamites? Perhaps, King Naxos, the age of empires is upon us all. Rather than resist its coming, you might find it more pleasing to become a part of it."

A shout ended the conversation. One of Naxos's scouts had returned, galloping his horse until he pulled up at Naxos's side.

"We saw Sumer's walls and the Elamite army!" The excited scout waved his hands as he spoke. "We're less than three miles from the city."

Even Naxos's dour face showed excitement. "Were you seen? Did they spot you?"

"No, my lord. Their camp, thousands of men, is spread out in a ring around the city. I ordered my men to stay and keep watch. I came back at once."

"Good." Naxos turned to Hathor. "What do you think?"

Hathor had further questions for the scout, but the man had seen little more than the enemy camp and the city.

"Well, it doesn't look as if they know we're behind them." Hathor kept his voice calm. "Let's ride ahead and see for ourselves what's there. Meanwhile, I think we should keep our men moving ahead. If we stop here, and someone sees us, it may look odd. If we keep moving ahead, they may think we're just more reinforcements from Elam."

Naxos rubbed his beard for a moment. "All right. We'll take a look." He ordered his commanders to keep the men going at the same slow pace, told the scout to lead the way, then urged his horse into a gallop.

Hathor touched his heels to his horse, and followed. A mile sped beneath their hooves, and the two leaders soon reached the four scouts waiting for them at a stand of palm trees. The men had tied their mounts to a bush, and now lay on the ground beneath the northernmost stretch of trees.

Hathor dismounted and calmly fastened his horse to a nearby tree, deliberately taking his time. Naxos must have taken the hint, for he slowed himself down. Together the two leaders moved forward, until they reached the others, hugging a small rise in the earth.

Dropping to the ground beside the scouts, Hathor peered beneath some low hanging palm fronds. He took in the grassy countryside that encompassed Sumer. The farmhouses that had once surrounded the city had vanished, knocked into a rubble of mud bricks days ago by the city's defenders. Anything useful to an invading army had been removed or destroyed. He saw no herds of sheep, goats, or cattle. Black scars covered the land, where Sumer's defenders had torched the crops and grasslands.

Closer to Sumer, he saw smoke from many fires rising into the air. The fires followed the rough curve of Elamite soldiers that had encircled the city on three sides, from the northern riverbank to the southern riverbank. Both leaders stared at the sight, studying the ground, the enemy, and the lay of the land between. The nearest Elamites were at least a mile away.

Naxos broke the silence first. "A lot of men."

"Yes, but we don't have to fight all of them." Hathor pointed to the well beaten track that led to the city. "We can come down the road until we're almost at the city. Then we sweep to the left, and attack the enemy on the south side of the city. Either we drive them into the river or up against the walls."

"This is better than we'd hoped," Naxos agreed. "Where is the fording place?"

In the war against Sumer, Hathor had studied all the approaches to the city and the surrounding countryside. That personal knowledge of the terrain had been one more reason why Eskkar gave Hathor the responsibility of command. During the long ride through the mountains, he and Naxos had discussed the many possibilities of what could await them when they reached the cove, on the ride to Sumer, and even what they might find when they arrived at the city.

Of course they had hoped to take the enemy by surprise, but every eventuality had to be considered. The worst situation, that they failed to take the Elamites by surprise, would have resulted in their facing a slightly more numerous contingent of enemy cavalry. While the Elamites had a larger force of horse fighters, a sizable number of these would likely be scouting the north, to prevent any reinforcements or attacks from Isin and Akkad.

So even a direct attack by the enemy might not prove disastrous. And Naxos and Hathor could always slip across the Tigris in relative safety.

But the surprise appeared complete. Now the long planning sessions allowed the two commanders to make rapid decisions.

"The fording place is over there, about a mile south of the walls." Hathor pointed toward the river on their left. "You can just make out the two sandbars that divide the water. We can safely ford there."

"Once we cross over, we should be able to hold the west bank, at least for a time."

"There's a good chance we can ride right up to them." Hathor couldn't keep a hint of excitement from his voice. "With the captured pennants from the cove, even when they see us, they may take us for more reinforcements.

Naxos took another long look at the enemy position. For perhaps fifty heartbeats, he said nothing, just stared at the enemy encampments. "I've fought many fights, Hathor, but I've never led so many men into battle, against so many." He took a deep breath. "What do you suggest?"

Hathor understood the man's pride, and his reluctance to take advice from another. But Naxos wanted to win, and obviously he knew now was not the time to spurn the wisdom of others.

"King Naxos, I think we should just continue up the trail, until we're ready to attack. Then hit the enemy south of the city." Drawing his knife, Hathor scratched lines in the dirt. Soon Naxos added his own ideas, and the two men worked out the battle plan. It didn't take long, and when they finished, both men were smiling.

They slipped away from the edge of the trees, and returned to the horses. Hathor swung onto his horse. "Now we just have to tell the commanders. They can tell the men as we ride. I want every man to know what's going to happen."

"That won't take long." Naxos mounted his horse, but ordered the scouts to stay behind and keep watch, until the Akkadian cavalry arrived. "Our men have trained for this kind of battle, and they're ready for a fight. They only need to know where to ride and who to kill."

22

G rand Commander Chaiyanar sat on a cushioned and comfortable chair atop a small grassy knoll that gave him a good view of Sumer's walls and its main gate. The chair had accompanied him on the ship from Sushan. Not trusting such a valuable possession on a pack animal, one of his personal guards had carried it, grunting under the weight, all the way from the beach.

Short in stature and with more than a hint of an expanding belly, Chaiyanar had participated in or directed numerous sieges in the last ten years. Early on he'd learned the importance of a comfortable place to sit.

Overhead, a reasonably clean white awning, fastened to four tall stakes driven into the ground, provided the only patch of shade. The Sumerians had cut down every tree, and burned every bush within miles of the city's walls. But Chaiyanar expected the usual petty inconveniences, and no longer let such things bother him.

A small table stood at his left hand, holding pitchers of water and wine, as well as a platter containing dates, honey, and bread, everything covered by a white cloth to keep off the bothersome flies. His chief servant hovered nearby, eager for the chance to do his master's bidding. At Chaiyanar's right, a naked girl knelt, waiting to perform more personal tasks.

Commander Chaiyanar had less than thirty-two seasons, but had already demonstrated both his skill and his loyalty to his Uncle Shirudukh, the King of the Elamites. In the last five years alone, Chaiyanar had besieged three cities, and captured every one.

The walls of Sumer impressed him not at all. His men had surrounded the city four days ago, to make sure no one escaped, and that no reinforcements could join the defenders. After his first inspection, Chaiyanar estimated that it would take about twenty days to breach the walls and storm the city, certainly no more than thirty. Since then, nothing had caused him to change his schedule.

The spies who revealed information about Sumer, its strengths and weaknesses, had gauged it well. No unexpected surprises, no hidden defenses, no increased numbers of defenders on its walls. If the city proved as wealthy as the spies declared, Chaiyanar would use its gold to gratify his every need for the rest of his life. Sumer, King Shirudukh had promised, would be his to rule.

Meanwhile, his men, nearly sixteen thousand strong, knew what to do, and they had their orders. Some dug trenches, to protect them as they worked their way closer to the city's defenders. Others made shields and ladders, while some sharpened digging sticks to help weaken the walls.

A siege remained a complicated affair, and Chaiyanar had no intention of simply starving Sumer into submission. That might take months, and he didn't intend to delay the conquest of the other Sumerian cities. He inspected his men's progress twice daily, at midday and again just before sundown. In between, he took his ease or amused himself with his slave girls.

His men had captured only eight women since they reached Sumer's outskirts, and, following his standing order, the soldiers brought all of them to him first, so he could choose however many he wanted for himself. This time he had selected two. One had long blond tresses, a rarity among his own people.

She had proved most satisfactory last night and again this morning. Now she waited at his feet, to bring him food or wine or anything else he needed. Later he would have her suck his rod while he watched his soldiers sweating under the fierce Sumerian sun.

A hundred paces away, his senior commanders had set up three tables, where they issued orders and resolved the usual problems with any siege. The commanders went about their business quietly, so as not to disturb their general. He'd made it clear to them years ago that he did not want to hear the endless details of every decision as the siege progressed.

Chaiyanar sipped wine and contemplated his future city. He would have to rename it in honor of his uncle. But aside from that courtesy, the city and lands of Sumer would belong to him and his descendants for all time, a generous gift from King Shirudukh. No doubt Chaiyanar would have to return to Sushan yearly, to prostrate himself before the king and renew his oaths of fealty, but that minor inconvenience could be borne.

He took another sip of the well-watered wine, then reached down and stroked the girl's blond tresses, before tightening his grip on her hair and twisting her head so he could see her eyes, wide with the pain. Chaiyanar enjoyed hurting his concubines, watching their expressions change when he inflicted pain on their bodies.

The fact that they dared not resist or even protest made their suffering all the more pleasant. Yes, soon it would be time for her to pleasure him again.

One of his commanders walked over and bowed, keeping his head down until given permission to speak.

"What is it?" Chaiyanar didn't bother to conceal his irritation. Interruptions always meant some kind of trouble.

The commander lifted his head, and shifted position to face his general. "My Lord, one of our sentries just returned. He reports a force of cavalry approaching from the south." He raised his arm and pointed. "You can just see them from here."

Chaiyanar frowned. He had all the men he needed, and wasn't expecting any reinforcements. He'd led the last troop of cavalry up to Sumer's walls himself, after joining them at the beach. Setting down his cup, he stood, lifted his head, and gazed toward the south. Yes, Chaiyanar saw the soldiers, a long column, moving slowly up the road. Two pennants flew behind the lead horsemen.

The approaching riders certainly were not hostile. No enemy force would travel at such a plodding pace. It was possible that King Shirudukh, at the last moment, had diverted some more forces away from Lord Modran or General Jedidia, and dispatched them toward Sumer. Nevertheless, it did seem odd that no messenger had brought word of such action.

"I think I recognize the red pennant, my Lord. It's the emblem of Sushan."

The line of men continued to grow, the men leading the column now less than a mile away. The end, however, remained out of sight. Then a shift of the wind turned the pennant broadside, and Chaiyanar indeed recognized the familiar emblem of the port city of Sushan. He frowned again, and wondered if his uncle had decided to burden him with another general.

"Send a rider out to see who they are," Chaiyanar ordered. "Tell their commander to report to me at once."

He slipped back into his chair, picked up his cup, and drained it in his annoyance. Still, the additional cavalry might prove useful. He could extend his patrols halfway to Akkad. With so many extra men, perhaps the siege could be shortened.

"It's working." Hathor kept his voice low, though there was no need.

"They've seen us." Naxos, too, tried to conceal his excitement. "Look, a rider is coming our way."

"Better a messenger than a call to battle."

Naxos laughed. "It's too late for that, I think."

Hathor glanced around. They had nearly reached the outskirts of the Elamites' camp. Any farther, and they would be too close for an effective charge. "Then perhaps you should give the order, King Naxos."

"Good hunting to you, Hathor of Akkad." Naxos twisted on his horse. "Strike those pennants, and sound the charge."

A grinning soldier a few ranks back took a deep breath and raised a ram's horn to his lips. A moment later, the deep boom of the horn floated over the land.

Naxos didn't wait for the sound to end. "Attack! Attack!" He kicked his horse forward, drawing his sword at the same time.

The city of Sumer possessed four gates, all hastily reinforced in preparation for the Elamite siege. The largest, used by the majority of traders, farmers, and visitors, faced the east. Atop the wall beside the Eastern Gate, Jarud, Commander of Sumer's Guard, stood beside King Gemama.

The height of the wall gave them an excellent view of the rolling farmlands that surrounded the city. Jarud had ordered the destruction of every dwelling within two miles. Both Jarud and Gemama could clearly see the billowing awning that covered General Chaiyanar's head, and even the naked girl kneeling at his feet.

Now, however, they ignored the thousands of soldiers who ringed Sumer. Instead, they stared with dread at yet another column of horsemen approaching from the south.

A moment ago, King Gemama and Jarud had cursed their luck at the arrival of still more invaders. The besieging forces already surrounding Sumer were daunting enough. Then the lowing call of the ram's horn changed everything. The pennants vanished, tossed aside as the men urged their horses to a gallop. Weapons suddenly glinted in the bright sunlight.

For a moment, Jarud stared in shock at the wave of horsemen bearing down on the Elamites. Then he heard the war cries of Akkad and Isin rising over the pounding of the horses' hooves. Comprehension came. "By every demon burning below, I didn't think they'd get here this soon!" He clapped Gemama on the shoulder, a blow strong enough to knock the breath from the King's portly body.

Gemama scarcely noticed. "Thank the gods! Look at the Elamites!"

Just out of range of Sumer's defenders, the enemy host had surrounded Sumer's walls, except for the narrow stretch along the river. Since their arrival, the Elamite soldiers had stacked their weapons for the eventual attack. Then they joined the hundreds of laborers, those skilled in digging and building platforms, all working together to prepare for the assault.

Now those soldiers and workers on the southern side of the city rushed about in panic, searching for their weapons, as an irresistible river of fierce horsemen engulfed them.

Realization of what was happening swept along the walls. The defenders erupted in cheers, their mood shifting from despair and gloom in an instant.

"Damn me for a slow-witted fool," Jarud said. "Stay here on the walls, and keep the men alert." He turned and dashed down the parapet steps two a time.

"Where are you going?" King Gemama shouted the words at Jarud's back.

"To get into the fight," Jarud called over his shoulder, "before it's too late."

Hathor led nine hundred Akkadian cavalry, every man screaming his war cry, straight ahead for the first three hundred paces, as if he intended to attack the entire Elamite force. Then he guided his horse to the left, and turned toward the southern walls. Behind him rode

the finest mounted bowmen in his command. They followed his
path, and as they made the same sweeping turn, they shot arrow after
arrow at the main force of the invaders, those positioned in front of
the eastern wall.

Each man launched four or five high-arcing shafts, and that arrow
storm struck confusion into the scrambling enemy. The shafts, not
aimed at any particular invader, rained down on men and horses.
Two small herds of Elamite horses, likely mounts for the enemy
commanders, bolted, adding to the panic. Hathor didn't intend to
engage them, merely keep them away from Naxos and the rest of the
Akkadians until the King finished his slaughter.

Hathor and his riders had divided the enemy encircling the walls
in two. The largest part of the Elamite army lay to the east and north
of the city, but those who had taken up their station on the southern
side of Sumer now found themselves cut off and encircled.

King Naxos led the rest of the men, four thousand strong, straight
into the enemy's confused ranks. Trapped between the river, Hathor,
and Naxos, more than three thousand Elamite soldiers, many still
scrambling for their weapons, were ridden down in a fury of blood.

Outnumbered at the point of attack, caught unprepared, and
swarmed from all sides, Chaiyanar's men never had a chance to offer
any real resistance. Most just ran. Some in their fright sought to
escape to the safety of their companions on the eastern side of the
city, but Hathor's men turned their deadly bows away from the main
force and directed their weapons at any fleeing toward them. Now
the Akkadians aimed their arrows with care, loosing shaft after shaft
into the panicked mass of besiegers.

Other Elamites tried to move up closer to Sumer's walls, but the
moment they came within range of the archers atop the parapets,
flights of arrows from the defenders tore into them. Some Elamites
fled toward the river, hoping to escape into the waters. But many
couldn't swim, and for them the river proved as deadly as the
approaching horsemen. Those who could swim, tossed away swords
and any other impediments in a desperate effort to plunge into the
river and get out of range.

Hathor guided his men down a line that he guessed would be just
outside the range of Sumer's arrows. By now his wild charge had
reached the river. His bowmen eased their horses to a stop, and
started picking off those in the water. Soon enough, the river cleared,

as the dead, arrows protruding from their bodies, floated away to the south on the blood stained waters.

Even before the slaughter ended, Hathor ordered the destruction of the enemy supplies to begin. Akkadians flung themselves from their horses and began stacking anything that would burn. The Elamites had several fires going at the time of the attack, and some of those still smoldered. Now fresh smoke rose into the air as shields, clothing, tools, anything that would burn was heaped into the flames. Stacks of arrows, waiting ready for the Elamite attack on the city, were the first to be tossed into the fire, after the cavalrymen had replenished their own quivers.

Hathor, with three Akkadians as his guard, picked his way through the dead and the debris. He shouted orders and pointed with his sword to any piles of goods that should go into the fire. But the Akkadians had not missed much.

The ram's horn sounded again, this time with a different note. Everywhere men raced back to their horses. Hathor glanced to the east. The main force of Elamites had regrouped, and now advanced toward him, a thick double line of infantry carrying shields. They had recovered faster than Hathor expected. Behind them he saw archers forming up as well. Even farther back, the Elamite cavalry, at least three thousand of them, had raced to their horses and now prepared to confront the Akkadians.

"Time to go!" Hathor's bellow carried over the battlefield. "Let's get out of here, unless you want to give those bowmen a target."

Laughing, the Akkadians cantered southward and toward the river, moving faster once they cleared the fields of the dead. In moments they were out of range of the approaching archers. The Elamite cavalry, however, had finally collected enough of its force to launch a counter attack.

But first they had to catch the Akkadians. Hathor, riding at the rear of his men, kept glancing back at the enemy horsemen. They were closing the gap, but Hathor's men needed to cover only little more than a mile. By the time he reached the ford, Naxos had already ordered most of his men into the water. The King, always eager to demonstrate his courage, waited at the river until Hathor reached his side.

"They're at your heels," Naxos shouted, as he turned his horse into the stream.

Hathor didn't bother to look behind him. With a touch of the halter, his stallion slid down the now slippery bank, roiled into loose muck by nearly five thousands horses, and splashed into the muddy water. More than a hundred paces ahead the first of the two islands that divided this part of the Tigris waited. Hathor caught up with Naxos, and the two men churned their way through the warm water, their horses kicking up walls of spray.

Twice Hathor thought he might have to cling to his horse's mane and swim for it, but each time the big warhorse, holding its head high, found its footing. Then he and Naxos were scrambling up onto the first island. Hathor patted his horse's neck, then turned toward the eastern shore.

The first Elamite horsemen to arrive at the fording place were already dead or dying, multiple shafts riddling their bodies along the river bank. The Akkadian bowmen had just enough range with their weapons to drive the enemy away from the shoreline.

"Well, that will teach them." Naxos laughed at the sight.

An arrow splashed into the water at the King's feet.

"They do have a few bows," Hathor said. "Let's keep moving."

Naxos, bellowing commands that floated over the river, ordered the men to continue the crossing. Soon the entire force was strung out between the two islands and the western bank. When Hathor, breathing hard, finally reached the far side of the river, he swung down from his horse.

The enemy hadn't attempted to pursue. They knew they would run into an arrow storm as they struggled through the water. They just sat there, watching the Akkadians.

"They won't leave their rear unguarded again," Naxos said with a grin.

"That they won't," Hathor matched the King's grin with one of his own. "Which will be even better for us, since we're not going south. Now it's time to teach them a few other lessons."

23

Jarud raced down the steps from Sumer's eastern wall, ignoring the sudden chaos that had erupted within the city since the Akkadian attack. He ignored, too, the sounds of battle outside the wall. Jarud knew what the Akkadian cavalry would do to the unprepared Elamites, and he intended to take advantage of the temporarily hapless enemy.

He leapt the final four steps to reach the ground, nearly colliding with his second in command, returning from his rounds. Jarud grabbed his shoulder. "Strip a hundred archers from the southern wall, and send them to the gate. We're going out there to finish what the Akkadians started. Hurry!"

Without waiting for acknowledgement, Jarud rushed through the lanes, twisting and turning until he reached the Southern Gate. About twenty soldiers and laborers were there, mouths open at the sight of the Commander of the Guard running toward them. "Open the gate! Collect as many axes and torches as you can find. We're going out!"

For a moment, the men just stared at him. "Damn you, don't just stand there, get that gate open! We don't have much time to destroy the Elamites' supplies."

The work gang, assigned to reinforce the soldiers on the wall in the event of an assault, burst into motion. More than twenty men hurled themselves at the gate. First they had to free the braces that kept the logs immobile. Swinging oversized mallets, they knocked loose the tapered wooden blocks, hammered into place, that prevented the massive panel of the right side from opening.

As soon as those were out, ten or more men seized the lower log and struggled to heave it out of its sockets. By then a second crew waited, and as soon as the first gang moved aside, they seized the upper log.

The first handful of archers arrived, hurriedly stringing their bows and clutching arrow quivers. They moved into position beneath the gate. Jarud recognized his nephew, Jaruman and his ten bowmen.

More laborers arrived, carrying axes of every shape and size, waiting for the gate to open. The babble of voices rose, until Jarud jumped onto a cart. "Silence! Be still, damn you!"

The din abated, and Jarud grabbed one of the gate's guardians. "Collect the black oil and torches. I want to burn as much of their weapons and tools as possible."

The defenders had stored pots of the oil that burns near the gate, to use against any attackers. Stacks of the thick torches, freshly bound and soaked in oil, were also at hand, to provide illumination in case of a night attack.

With a wrenching creak, the heavy gate swung free. Jarud snatched an unlit torch leaning against the wall, and as soon as there was room enough to pass, Jarud led the defenders through the opening. The Elamites had dug almost two hundred paces from the walls, just out of bowshot and a long run for Sumerian archers. Although Jarud was the first one out of the gate, the faster and braver of his men overtook him before he'd gone twenty paces.

Caught up in the excitement of the invaders' destruction, the soldiers and work gangs of Sumer poured through the gate, raced across the open space, and dashed in among the dead and dying Elamites. By the time Jarud, breathing hard, reached what remained of the Elamite position, his men were already finishing off the wounded, collecting weapons, and using their axes on the large shields.

The Akkadian cavalry had started several fires that still roared, sending thick smoke rushing upward into the heaves. All the same, in their haste, they had missed plenty of material that would burn.

Spreading out, the Sumerians collected lumber, shields, ladders, even clothing ripped from the dead, and heaped them into piles. Discarded swords, knives, spears, and bows were snatched up, and soon men stumbled back toward the gate, each struggling under a load of captured weapons and tools.

Those Sumerians with torches thrust them into the burning fires left behind by the Akkadians. Jarud joined them, shoving the torch he'd carried into the nearest fire. The oil-soaked torch flared, snapping and smoking. One of the soldiers snatched it from Jarud's hand and moved to the first pile. Another man splashed some black oil on the dry wood. In moments, the first new flames caught and rose. Soon fresh fires joined those started by the Akkadians.

All around Jarud, axes rang as men attacked the shields and planks, breaking them apart. Others scooped up the jagged shards and tossed them to the nearest fire.

"Quick as you can, before the enemy returns," Jarud shouted as he ran among his men. "Bring everything that will burn and toss it into the fire!"

He glanced around. More men still streamed from the Southern Gate, hurrying to add their efforts to those of their companions. By now more than two hundred Sumerians scrambled and searched through the Elamite position.

"Elamites! Look, they're coming!"

Jarud whirled toward the east. A small group of Elamites had collected their weapons and moved toward the Sumerians. "Archers! Keep those men at bay."

Another detachment of archers had joined with Jaruman, who now had thirty men under his command. They formed a small line of bowmen facing the advancing Elamites. Jarud watched as the archers launched the first flight of arrows toward the enemy.

Other Sumerian soldiers dropped their loads, took up their bows, and extended the rough skirmish line, widening the bowmen's position on either side. Soon they were launching shafts as fast as they could at the approaching Elamites, halting their progress for the moment. Still, Jarud knew it wouldn't take the enemy long to regroup, but every moment was precious now.

A shift in the wind sent a hot wave of air from the nearest fire over Jarud. A quick glance showed at least twenty fires of varying size consuming the enemy's supplies. Several of the pyres loomed taller than a man. All of them flamed and crackled, gathering strength as his frantic men continued to add ever more combustibles.

By now men were tossing sandals, swords, cooking pots, clothing, anything they could snatch up into the blaze. The heat forced Jarud back a few more steps, as the crackling tongues of fire roared into the sky.

Another gang of men arrived from the city, and Jarud shouted at them to collect anything they could find and toss it onto the bonfire. Some lugged more pots of oil, to spread the fire ever faster. By now the Sumerians had stripped the Elamite position on the southern side of the city nearly clean.

"More enemy soldiers! More soldiers!"

Jarud turned toward the enemy. Every Elamite who could find a horse had joined the pursuit of the Akkadians, ignoring the Sumerians. But the invaders had plenty of infantry. About three hundred of these had formed into a cohesive force which now advanced with raised shields toward the Sumerians. His archers still launched shaft after shaft at them, trying to slow them down, but Jarud knew it was time to go.

"Back to the city! Back inside the walls!"

Every man turned and raced for the safety of Sumer's walls. Every man except Jarud's nephew, Jaruman, and his handful of archers, who kept shooting arrows, even as they slowly backed their way toward the safety of Sumer's walls. Jarud watched as enemy shafts began to rain down on the last of the bowmen.

Some fool started laughing, and soon the sound spread through the men rushing back within the walls. Jarud found himself grinning as well. But when he reached the gate, he glanced over his shoulder and glimpsed a handful of his men still working their bows.

"Get back here! Now!"

The archers launched one more ragged volley before they turned and broke into a run, heading for the open gate and following Jarud's men.

He shoved the last man inside. "Damn fools!" Jarud took a final look around, to make sure his remaining soldiers passed through the entrance. Everyone had returned.

He stepped inside. A gang of carpenters waited there, hammers and levers in hand. "Seal the gate!" The ponderous gate creaked to a close, and the laborers swarmed over it, dropping the beams into place, and hammering the bracing blocks tight.

A cheering crowd of Sumerians – men, women, soldiers – waited just inside the gate to welcome them. Those who had followed Jarud outside the wall had wide grins on their faces, as they caught their breath. Some of them still laughed, and to Jarud's surprise, he joined them. The raucous chorus swept through the defenders. He climbed atop a supply cart, and waited until the din died down.

"With the help of our Akkadian friends and allies, we taught the filthy Elamites a lesson today," Jarud shouted. "That will slow them down!"

A roar of support echoed against the walls and gate, a sound that would be heard by the invaders. Jarud, even more than the jubilant crowd, knew the truth of his words. The Elamite siege effort had taken a heavy blow. If Hathor had destroyed the enemy boats along the coast, the loss of supplies would hinder the invaders almost as much as the loss of men.

More important, the Akkadian cavalry's attack, combined with the efforts of Sumer's own forces outside the wall had strengthened the resolve of every man and woman in the city. The gloom that had hung over the city since the enemy's arrival would dissipate like the smoke from a campfire in the southern breeze.

The people of Sumer now knew they didn't fight alone any longer, and that a large force of friendly fighters had arrived and already started harrying the Elamite invaders. And that, Jarud decided, was almost as important as the number of enemy dead lying outside Sumer's walls.

Chaiyanar guided his warhorse through the debris and dead that, only this morning, had comprised his forces facing Sumer's southern walls. His guards, retainers, and senior commanders followed behind, hanging as far back as they dared, and each one hoping the blame for the disaster would not fall upon him.

Corpses littered the ground, almost all Chaiyanar's men. Nearly three thousand soldiers and siege workers had stood in this place, and the Akkadians had ripped through them like a whistling scythe through a field of ripe wheat. Despite the briefness of the assault, the Akkadians had been thorough.

At least four thousand Akkadian cavalry had overwhelmed Chaiyanar's unprepared men, and now nearly twenty-five hundred Elamites lay dead, in exchange for a few handfuls of Akkadian corpses.

The rest of the Elamites had managed to escape, but the savagery of the raid would haunt the survivors. The easy siege had turned into something else. Now every man in Chaiyanar's army would keep glancing over his shoulder, in fear of another surprise attack. And when they next rode into battle, awareness of defeat and death would ride with them.

He saw the hand of Eskkar of Akkad in all this. Chaiyanar had been warned about the King of Akkad's tricks, but he expected nothing so brazen at Sumer. He knew the cities of the Land Between the Rivers had little love for one another, and the spies had reported only bickering between Isin, Sumer, and Akkad. In fact, the fools claimed that the squabbling had increased in the last few months. Now that lie stood exposed.

Today's surprise attack from the south seemed like one of the barbarian king's cunning tricks. Chaiyanar's scouts, spread out in a line more than fifty miles long to the north and west, had reported nothing. The Akkadians must have swung far to the west, before turning toward Sumer.

Chaiyanar stared at the still burning fires, then glanced toward Sumer's walls. The defenders had sallied forth from the city within moments of the attack, almost as if they expected it. The Sumerians had added their efforts to the destruction caused by the horsemen, and wreaked still more havoc on the supplies abandoned by his men. He'd heard the laughter and cheering from within the city.

Chaiyanar's men tried to put out the fires and salvage what they could, but the heat drove them back. Of course there was no water to douse the flames. The largest bonfires would smolder long into the night. Whatever remained beneath the ashes would be useless, melted and twisted by the heat. His men had lost almost all their weapons, tools, and lumber, much of it irreplaceable.

By the time Chaiyanar had organized the rest of his horsemen, the cowardly Akkadians had fled to the south, crossed the river, and jeered at his men from the opposite bank. Then they rode off into the west, no doubt boasting about their success.

Now Chaiyanar had to deal with the mess. The cursed Akkadians had set back his schedule for capturing Sumer. Worse, he now had a large enemy contingent to deal with. This was no mere raid, to harry his efforts. With a force that size, he knew the Akkadians would be back, and they would seek to break the siege. He wondered why the Akkadians hadn't persisted in their attack, instead of fleeing south at the first sign of opposition.

Fortunately, he yet had plenty of soldiers left. His cavalry would ring the doomed city, and the next time the Akkadian filth returned, he would be ready for them. Once the city fell, he would hunt down the Akkadians and slaughter them to the last man, to avenge today's losses. There would be none of the usual assimilation of conquered soldiers. The Akkadian victory today would not be allowed to infect his army.

Still, he would need new supplies. Chaiyanar remembered the supply train that had gone south this morning. His pack handlers probably had run straight into the approaching horsemen. By now the bodies of the guards, porters, handlers, and, much more important, all the pack animals littered the way to the supply cove.

The more Chaiyanar thought about his situation, the angrier he grew. Damn the gods, he needed the supplies arriving each day from Sushan. He turned to one of his cavalry commanders.

"Take a thousand riders and as many extra horses as you need, and ride to the cove. Escort all the supplies you find here at once. Send word back to Sushan that we'll need more food, weapons, and grain. Don't forget to warn the commander at the cove about the Akkadians. Have the ships put to sea at the first sign of trouble."

"Yes, Lord Chaiyanar. At once."

The man wheeled his horse around and galloped off, no doubt glad to be away from his grim commander.

Chaiyanar turned toward the leader of his cavalry. "You'd better send word to the horse camp. If the Akkadians know about it, they may be headed there."

The man blanched. He'd forgotten about the verdant valley where many of the Elamite cavalry had encamped, to have access to food and water for the horses.

'Yes, Grand Commander!" The man started bellowing orders to his men.

If the filthy Akkadians rode straight to the camp, they would fall upon a small force of Elamite cavalry with as much surprise as the Akkadians had delivered at Sumer.

Chaiyanar turned his gaze back to Sumer's walls. He hadn't expected the haughty men from Isin and Akkad to ride to Sumer's aid. After all, the two cities had fought a bloody war ten years ago. Still, if Eskkar's horsemen were this far south, then Akkad itself would be undermanned. Unless Eskkar had some other trick planned for Lord Modran, who should even now be moving toward Akkad.

Thoughts about Lord Modran enraged Chaiyanar even more. If Modran could manage to capture Akkad before Chaiyanar could take Sumer, then Modran might lead his troops down to take command of the Sumerian assault. That would mean disaster and humiliation for Chaiyanar. King Shirudukh might even award Sumer to Modran.

Chaiyanar decided to redouble his efforts to take Sumer, no matter how many lives it cost.

"Damn all the gods, you'll suffer for this, Eskkar of Akkad!"

24

As soon as the men regrouped on the west bank of the Tigris, Hathor dispatched the messengers. Two groups of four men, each rider leading an extra horse, dashed off to the northwest, angling apart as they rode. They would take different routes to the same destination, an uninhabited strip of rocky watershed that stretched along one of the Tigris's many tributaries.

One of Yavtar's messenger boats would be waiting there, ready to carry the news of Hathor's activities to the north. The extra horses should allow them to escape any Elamite war parties they might encounter. At least one of the riders had to get through. The survival of Hathor's force depended on making contact with Yavtar's fleet.

While Hathor dispatched the men, Naxos sent out scouts ahead of the Akkadian cavalry and on either flank. Hathor and Naxos then led their force north, in three main columns, always keeping the Tigris on their right.

They rode hard, pushing the horses. The animals hadn't had much work during the long and plodding journey through the mountains, so they remained fresh enough. However, there had been little forage in the mountains, and Hathor's men had emptied the last of their grains sacks just before they arrived at the cove.

The Elamite supplies at the landing site had provided each horse a few mouthfuls of grain, but the creatures needed to graze to maintain their strength.

"Do you think the Elamites will follow?" Naxos had to raise his voice to be heard over the drumming hoof beats.

"They'll be fools if they don't," Hathor replied. "What else are they going to do with their cavalry?"

The Elamite cavalry at Sumer numbered at least five or six thousand horsemen, a force fully equal to the Akkadians. Hathor had to engage and destroy as much of that force as he could, if the siege of Sumer were to be broken. But first the Akkadians needed supplies and some fresh horses.

By mid afternoon they were almost twenty miles from Sumer. They turned west, following a small branch of the Tigris. A mile later, they crested a low hill, and saw a wide valley of rich farmland ahead.

Naxos took one look at the bright green grass and grinned. Three separate horse herds grazed placidly in the warm sun. "At the gallop, men," he shouted, and kicked his horse to the forefront.

The men spread out into a line of battle, stringing bows as they rode. Now the earth shook under the hooves of the horses, and the din of hoof beats overwhelmed the shouts of the riders.

The Elamites had quartered at least a thousand cavalrymen in the valley, for the same reason that drew the Akkadians. The thick grasslands and pastures, watered by a wide stream, could easily support a large number of horses. The Elamites planned to feed and rest part of their horses there for a few days. Then the detachment would return to Sumer, while another force arrived to take advantage of the plentiful grazing.

"They must not have gotten word from Sumer yet," Hathor shouted, over the pounding of the horses.

The Elamites saw them coming, but even so they were slow to react. Men dashed about, gathering their weapons or chasing after their mounts. But the war cries of the Akkadians, mixed with blasts from the ram's horn, affected the enemy horses. They milled about, many eluding capture and adding to the confusion.

By then it didn't matter. The Akkadians, scattered over a wide area, overran the enemy's main encampment. Attacking at full speed, nothing could stop the assault. The Elamites had no time to prepare a defense.

The killing began. Once again, the Akkadians used overwhelming force against a much smaller number of the enemy. While the surprise might not be as complete, the turmoil kept the Elamites from putting up any real resistance. Those who could reach a horse, fled. The rest were ridden down and killed, in groups of twos and threes.

The fight lasted longer than the one at Sumer, and the Akkadians suffered more than a few causalities, but the enemy lost more than half their men before the remainder escaped. Even as the last of the killing ended, Hathor swung down from his horse in front of the largest farmhouse.

From the standard waving in the breeze just outside the entrance, Hathor guessed that the same structure had previously been used by the Elamites as their headquarters. Soon Akkadian patrols were riding out in every direction. Other parties went out to round up the horses left behind by the fleeing men.

By the time Naxos returned, Hathor had the horses grazing, the captured food and grain distributed, and the men cleaning their weapons and seeing to their mounts. Three prisoners, their hands bound behind their backs, knelt in the dirt outside the farm house.

Hathor shook his head as Naxos dismounted, but Hathor couldn't keep the smile from his face. "How was the hunting?"

Naxos laughed. "I only killed three. One of them actually attacked me."

"Only three? I thought you would have at least ten to your credit."

Naxos glanced around sheepishly. A long table, brought outside from the house, had two Elamite maps spread over its surface. Subcommanders stood beside it, setting up the night camp and issuing any needed instructions. "Good thing I've got you to look after things," Naxos said.

"Just try not to get yourself killed chasing after helpless fools."

"No need to worry about that." Naxos clapped his hand on Hathor's shoulder. "These men are poor fighters. If the rest of the Elamites are as bad, we'll have no trouble beating them."

After the fight outside Sumer's walls, and the reports of his men, Hathor had much the same opinion. But men caught by surprise were one thing. The Elamites might prove tough enough in a real battle.

Both men took the time to wash up, and wolf down some captured food. Afterward, Hathor made the rounds of the camp. Tonight, however, Naxos joined him. Hathor did most of the talking with the men, but he noticed right away the difference Naxos's presence made, especially to his own soldiers.

"The men were glad to see you," Hathor remarked, as they returned to the command post at the farmhouse.

"It's not something easy for me," Naxos said. "Talking to the men, encouraging them, asking about their needs. I see how it affects them, but . . . I'm always afraid I'm going to say something stupid."

"It is difficult," Hathor agreed. "For me also. But it's something I learned from Eskkar."

"Him again. The great Eskkar."

The two men stepped through the doorway. For a moment, they had the place to themselves. Hathor unbuckled his sword and leaned it against the wall.

"Do you remember Gatus? The man who helped train so many of Akkad's men?"

Naxos nodded. "I met him once, long ago, when he was just a member of the guard. But everyone knows how he trained the archers to fight on Akkad's walls."

"He told me a story about Eskkar, how in the beginning, Eskkar seldom spoke more than a handful of words in a month. Eskkar, too, had trouble speaking to the villagers and soldiers. Even the thought of speaking to a group of villagers terrified him. Eskkar had to force himself, and hated every moment."

"Really? Eskkar always seems to know what to say. He spoke easily enough when the two of us met outside Isin's walls."

"Ah, I missed that meeting. I didn't arrive at Isin until the next day, right before the battle."

"I know now why he sent word for me to come out from my city," Naxos said. "Eskkar could have shouted his threats from outside the city's walls, or sent messengers to carry his words. Later I realized he didn't want to embarrass me before everyone in Isin. Part of me wanted to kill him just for that. But his words rang true. After the destruction of Larsa, I couldn't take the chance he would do the same to Isin."

"Gatus told me that most people, in the beginning, thought Eskkar too ignorant to speak, much less lead the city. And when Eskkar and Trella started working together, everyone thought she was a witch who summoned a fiend from the pits below to take over his mind and put words on his lips."

Naxos laughed. "I never heard that. But I can believe it."

"It's more than a little true. Trella helped him, of course. She encouraged him to talk with at least a few of the men every day. In time, Eskkar got better at it. Perhaps like sword fighting, the more you practice, the more skillful you get."

"I take your point, Hathor." Naxos unbuckled his sword belt and tossed it on the flimsy table. "If you don't mind, I'll join you again for tomorrow's morning rounds." He took a deep breath, and stretched out his arms. "Perhaps by the time we get done with this campaign, I'll be as good a talker as Eskkar."

25

The morning after the raid by Naxos and Hathor at Sumer, Eskkar rode out of Akkad just after dawn, with the feel of rain on his face. A glance at the thick clouds above warned him to expect more of the same during the day, which meant a slower pace for the horses. Rain had fallen on the city for the last three days, and Eskkar had remained within the city, hoping that the weather would clear.

When the rain persisted, Trella had ordered the priests in Ishtar's temple to pray for fair weather. Nonetheless the useless priests or indifferent gods had refused to stop the storm showers. At last Eskkar could delay his departure no longer. Akkad and its King rode to war, and now more than ever, Eskkar had to share the discomforts of the trail with his men.

Drakis, riding at Eskkar's side, ignored the light drizzle. His always cheerful voice floated over the already cursing men who followed behind their leaders. Before they'd gone a mile, mud had splattered every horseman. "Another beautiful day for a ride, you lazy sons of whores! A little rain will toughen you up."

Eskkar smiled at his commander's words. Forty of the toughest horsemen in Akkad provided security for the King of Akkad.

A ragged chorus of groans greeted Drakis, as he picked up the pace. Nothing bothered the man. The more conditions worsened, the more upbeat his words would become. The man had, after all, survived enough deadly wounds to bury a handful of soldiers. Some of his men called him The Invincible for just that reason.

Eskkar reached into his pouch and removed a hunk of bread. Better to eat it now, before it grew too soggy and fell apart. The rain, which had thankfully slowed to an occasional sprinkle, didn't appear to affect the men. Eskkar, however, felt the stiffness in his old wounds. In the last few years, bad weather made his leg ache

painfully, the same injury that had nearly killed him when he first
limped into Akkad, supported by Bracca's arm.

His left shoulder twinged, too, another painful remembrance of a
sword tip that had reached the bone. In his youth, Eskkar had often
smiled at the older warriors who struggled against stiff joints and
complained about old wounds, especially during the rain or cold
weather. Now, to his chagrin, he had joined them.

These gloomy signs of advancing age did little to cheer Eskkar's
disposition, but he shrugged them off, after muttering a curse or two
beneath his breath. Soon enough he'd be fighting for his life, and a
few aches and pains would mean little.

This morning Eskkar had said his goodbyes to Trella, neither of
them dwelling on the chance that he might be defeated and dead in
the next few days. As she had done often before, Trella merely urged
him to hurry back, and said she would be waiting for him.

Both mother and father had said more painful goodbyes to Sargon.
He had departed five days earlier to join Akkad's allies – the Ur
Nammu and Alur Meriki. The likelihood of Sargon's survival wasn't
much better than his father's. Eskkar had clasped his son tight, while
Trella stood by with tears in her eyes, as her oldest son went off to
war.

Nevertheless, Eskkar put all thoughts of wife and son out of his
mind, and forced himself to concentrate on the current task – guiding
his horse through the wet earth. Like Eskkar, each of his forty riders
led a second horse, a precious gift from the last of Trella's herds. The
extra horses would allow Eskkar to make up some of the lost time,
assuming, of course, that the gods didn't pour more rain down upon
his head. The Dellen Pass and the approaching Elamites awaited his
arrival.

Despite its personal discomfort, the wet weather could be
considered a gift from Ishtar, the Goddess who oversaw Akkad's
welfare. The rains came from the east, and would have likely slowed
the Elamites as well, burdened with food and weapons, in their
march toward the Land Between the Rivers. The Akkadians,
traveling across a much shorter distance and less rugged terrain,
would not be as affected.

The dark clouds stayed overhead during most of the day's
miserable ride and the evening's wet camp. The next morning,
however, the gods finally answered the priests' prayers, and the sun

shone bright in a cloudless sky. By noon the ground had dried enough for a quicker pace, and the Akkadians pushed their horses.

Two more days of hard riding and fast walking followed, but by alternating horses, Eskkar's troop made good progress over the rough ground. They traveled almost a hundred and twenty difficult miles as they headed for the eastern mountains and the Dellen Pass.

Just before noon of the fourth day after setting out, Eskkar reached the top of a small hill, and saw the looming foothills and the mouth of the Dellen Pass in the distance. He smiled in satisfaction, and thanked the gods for the speedy trek. Only two animals had gone lame during the journey, forcing their cursing riders to fall behind and catch up when they could.

From his vantage point, Eskkar studied the approaches to the Dellen Pass. The mouth of the Pass splayed out from the foothills, spreading wide, the ground appearing as if the gods had poured the liquid earth from a pot, letting it scatter across the ground. The trail itself disappeared into the foothills, wending its way eastward. It finally emerged, more than a hundred miles later, on the far side of the mountains.

On this side, after exiting from the Pass, the traveler had a choice of three trails. One, the least used, led to the northwest. The second went due west, the favored approach for those traders heading for the Euphrates. The third, and most traveled, wended its way southwest. On that path lay Akkad, the gateway to the Tigris and the southern cities. And the intended destination of the invading Elamites.

Gazing toward the foothills, Eskkar watched what appeared to be an endless caravan creeping toward the Dellen Pass. The army of Akkad had arrived as well, strung out for miles to the south. Soldiers and their supplies made up the brunt of those on the march, but there were hundreds of pack animals and even more porters and livery men trudging along, mixed in with the fighting men.

The army had followed the main trail from Akkad. However Eskkar and his men had taken a shorter, though more difficult route to the same destination.

"We couldn't have timed it any better, Captain." Drakis guided his horse alongside. "Doesn't look like much of an army, though."

Eskkar smiled. "No, more like a village on the move. There may be more porters than soldiers."

"Well, they wouldn't be here if they weren't needed." Without conscious thought, Drakis rubbed the scar on his cheek, just below his left eye. He'd taken an arrow in the face during the battle to recapture Akkad from the Egyptians, and nearly lost his eye.

"No sign of the Elamites," Eskkar said, scanning the countryside. A few hundred enemy horsemen could tear to shreds the clumsy, strung-out column. "Better uncover the pennant, before our men think we're an enemy patrol." He eased his horse ahead, angling his approach to meet the head of the column.

Eskkar's eight personal guards closed up behind him. Their duties had returned, guarding the King from any and all danger.

Meanwhile, Drakis ordered the Hawk Clan pennant uncovered, and the weary troop made its way toward the Akkadian army. By the time they reached it, Alexar, in command of the slow-moving Akkadian force, had galloped up from the rear of the column and waited to greet them.

"Good to see you, Captain. We were starting to think you weren't coming." Alexar moved away from the line of march and eased his horse to a stop. "The men were starting to worry. Is there any word from the north?"

River boats could carry information faster even than the speediest horse. "Yes, Sargon left to join the Ur Nammu and ride with them. They should be nearly through the mountains and into Elam soon. All is well with you?"

"Other than being at least a day, maybe two behind schedule, everything is as we expected. Lady Trella's preparations were so thorough that the soldiers haven't started complaining yet."

Eskkar glanced down the column. "Where's the cavalry?"

"Already in the pass," Alexar said. "I sent Muta and most of the horsemen on ahead, with orders to hold off the Elamites until we arrive."

Muta, Hathor's second in command during the war with Sumer, had charge of Akkad's remaining cavalry. Nevertheless, his eighteen hundred horsemen weren't going to stop the Elamite army for long. Still, if Akkad's luck held, only a few more days would be needed for Eskkar to get his men into position.

"Are we staying with the column?" His voice as cheerful as ever, Drakis clasped arms with Alexar.

"No, Drakis," Eskkar said. "You take twenty of my guards up into the Pass and join Muta and his men. Tell them I'm on my way. But tonight I'll stay with Alexar and the infantry."

With a wave, Drakis turned aside, shouting to his men to follow. They rode off toward the Pass, facing another stretch of hard riding.

"I'll take the lead, Captain," Alexar said. "You probably should spend some time with the men. They've been wondering about you."

Both men understood how important it was for Eskkar to be seen by his men, and even the porters. He would have preferred to ride on ahead with Drakis, but it would be the infantry that would bear the brunt of any fighting, and they needed to see their leader.

Eskkar touched his heels to his horse and rode toward the irregular column. As he approached, the soldiers struggling under their heavy burdens of weapons and supplies recognized their commander and gave a ragged cheer. The sound followed him as he paced his horse down the line of march, waving to the men. His presence gave them reassurance and confidence. They knew that where he led, others could follow.

As he rode, he studied the faces of the soldiers and laborers turned toward him. A company of spearmen marching together, strong and husky, carrying shields and spears. Archers, tall and lithe, with powerful arms, bearing bows and at least two fat quivers of arrows. Slingers, who appeared to be little more than boys, each laboring under the weight of two sacks of bronze bullets and struggling to keep up with their taller and stronger companions.

Aside from their primary weapon, each soldier carried a sword or in the case of the slingers, a long, curved knife. Sacks of bread and dried meat hung from wide belts that sagged under the weight. Armies, Eskkar knew, needed food and water as well as weapons if they were to fight effectively. Fortunately, thanks to Trella's meticulous planning and effort, a vast amount of supplies traveled with the army, with more already on the way from Akkad.

Such planning and preparation had helped win the war against Sumer. Since then, Trella and her clerks had grown even more efficient. Eskkar and his soldiers would have all the supplies they needed for this campaign.

Eskkar smiled and waved at each company of men, making eye contact with as many as he could. He knew the names of more than a few leaders of ten and twenty, and he called out to those as he moved down the line. Despite their youth, these men would soon be fighting and dying under his orders, and he recognized the debt he owed them. They would be the ones who saved Akkad, though he doubted many of them understood the hard decisions that had brought them to this day.

He saw none of the subtle signs of fear, the wide eyes, the trembling hands, the licking of lips. They had come to fight, and if they had their private dreads, they concealed it well. No man wanted to show apprehension in front of his companions.

Most of them had been soldiers in Akkad's army for more than a year, and many were veterans of the war with Sumer. For most, recruitment into the army had given them an honorable occupation, an escape from the drudgery and near-slavery of hard labor on the farms and in the villages.

From the smallest cluster of mud huts to the grandeur of Akkad, every gathering place of men struggled under the excess numbers of its restless young men. On the farm, fathers and older brothers pushed aside their younger siblings, leaving them few opportunities.

Women, too, were denied them. Older and more prosperous men had the pick of available women, often taking three or four as wives. That left a shortage of women, and those who remained available had little interest in joining with a younger son who had no prospects and nothing to offer in the way of a bridal price.

Without the army, many of these restless young men would have turned to banditry or petty theft, stealing and robbing from others until the city's guards caught up with them. Then death, mutilation, or forced labor as slaves would have been their lot.

The military gave them status and purpose, even as it provided for them. They didn't receive much in the way of payment, a few copper coins every ten days. Even so, Eskkar knew his men earned every coin, sweating under the hard training of their leaders and learning the trade of war.

And now, for the pittance these soldiers received, Akkad and its leaders expected them to fight for their country, and if necessary, to die for it. As always, Eskkar felt somewhat humbled by the trust they placed in him.

These men, along with the people of Akkad and its surrounding villages, had made him king. They fought because he and their commanders ordered them to fight, and because they knew, most without fully understanding, that the decision to take a people to war was the most important responsibility of any leader.

Foolish and unnecessary wars could destroy any city, even in victory. Akkad's soldiers trusted Eskkar to lead them into battle. Whether against Sumer, Larsa, or even Isin, the enemy mattered little. Soon they would contend with an enemy most of them, until recently, had never heard of, the Elamites.

Raised among the Alur Meriki Clan, as a boy Eskkar had never considered the reasons men went to war. You fought because your clan leader ordered you to fight. Surrounded and supported by your kin, you followed your clan's orders and did your utmost because that was every warrior's duty.

Whether you lived or died meant nothing. Only honor mattered. To die failing in your duty meant a mark of shame on your family. To die in battle meant glory, or at least honor.

During the great siege of the Alur Meriki against Akkad, Eskkar had learned a hard lesson – that he needed to convince others to follow him freely into battle. Villagers required a reason to go to war. You had to do more than order them to fight. To win their trust, he'd learned to appeal to their own needs to survive and protect their families. Once they understood that, they became willing fighters.

Trella had always comprehended that the men of Akkad needed a reason to risk their lives and wage war. She helped provide that motivation, influencing the city's women who then appealed to their menfolk to face up to their obligations. For this coming conflict, the women spread the true stories of what had happened to many cities in Elam, and about the enemy's plan to reduce all the people to the level of slaves.

These subtle maneuverings always seemed a little un-warrior like to Eskkar, but he'd learned long ago to accept them. As the city's ruler, he no longer disdained using fear, terror, lies, or even murder to protect Akkad and its people from harm, even though many deplored such devices. A leader needed to use every possible tool, however devious, however ruthless, to protect the majority of his followers.

Thanks to Trella, Eskkar never took either the peoples' support or their loyalty for granted. As she worked each day with the men and women of the city, Eskkar did the same with his soldiers. He made sure that he spoke with every man, regardless of rank, as often as possible.

And so today Eskkar decided that as many soldiers as possible should know the name and see the face of the man who ordered each of them into battle. He owed that one duty to the men.

Unlike the war with Sumer, where army faced army across an open field, the coming battle with the Elamites would be different. The inhabitants of Akkad had a major role to play, though far from the city's walls. The porters and bearers were, he knew, as brave or braver than the soldiers marching beside them. Many of the common people had volunteered despite their fear, eager to do something, anything, to defend their city and their families.

It took courage for untrained and unarmed men to follow an army into battle, knowing that death might easily overtake them. But Trella had appealed to every city dweller to defend Akkad. She entreated them to serve not by hiding behind its walls, but by accompanying the army into the field, and giving it the support, supplies, and weapons it would need to do battle.

To acknowledge their bravery, as Eskkar rode down the column, he gave the pack men, horse handlers, porters, laborers, and craftsmen as much respect as he gave to the soldiers. They, too, needed to know the face of the man who ruled them. The city of Akkad was going to war. Its inhabitants, like Eskkar, were risking their lives and those of their kin because Eskkar and Trella had told them this was the best way to save themselves, their families, and their future.

Before he reached the rear guard of the ragged column, Eskkar had ridden more than three miles. Near the end of the column, he found a surprise. A small contingent of Hawk Clan soldiers, Lady Trella's own guards, were riding behind the soldiers. One of them led a horse that lifted its shaggy head and whinnied as it caught the scent of its master.

"A-tuku!" Eskkar face brightened at the sight of his favorite horse. He'd left the animal in Akkad, not wanting to wear it down on a long ride to the north and back. Trella, of course, had sent it on with her guards, to make sure her husband rode his best horse into battle.

And not just his horse. Trella had insisted that Eskkar donned his finest armor and helmet, and carried the strongest and lightest shield. Her fate remained entwined with his own. If Eskkar fell in battle, even in victory, Trella might find the city of Akkad slipping from their family's grasp.

The lead elements of the army camped that night at the mouth of the Dellen Pass. A nearby stream delivered fresh water, and that luxury was far too precious to ignore. Their journey had not ended. In the morning, Esskar intended to take his Hawk Clan guards and move as fast as possible deep into the Pass.

The place he'd chosen to defend remained thirty miles away, well up into the mountains, and he wanted to get there before sundown. As for the bulk of his forces, they would arrive as best they could.

Esskar spent much of the evening walking through the ranks, accompanied by his guards. He wore his cloak, as much to impress his men as to ward off the cold. Many of the soldiers, and more than a few of the laborers, reached out their hands to touch his arm or even his cloak. Often unable to find the words to respond to such devotion, he nodded his head again and again in thanks for their efforts.

When he finally lay down to sleep, Esskar felt the weariness in his legs. Pulling his warm cloak over him, he fell asleep in moments. His last thoughts were of the Elamites, even now moving toward him. He wondered what concerns, if any, lay in the mind of Lord Modran, the leader of the army Esskar would soon face across the battlefield.

26

The next day, just before midafternoon, a weary Eskkar slid down from his horse, and this time even he could not avoid a sigh of relief. Days of arduous riding had worn him down. Once he would have shrugged off the effort, but as each year passed, Eskkar had to struggle ever harder to maintain his stamina. He knew the time had already passed for campaigns such as these. But war made no provision for the old or the young, or those whose bones ached from incessant traveling.

Awake well before dawn, he'd left Alexar and the infantry behind and started for the Pass with just his twenty Hawk Clan guards. It had taken most of the day to cover the thirty miles over the hilly slopes that led deeper into the Dellen Pass and reach Muta's position, despite using an extra horse.

Eskkar turned over A-tuku and the other nearly exhausted horse to his guards. At least A-tuku remained fresh. Eskkar had ridden the second mount most of the way, wanting to keep the powerful bay as rested as possible. If there were going to be any fighting on horseback, he wanted to be on his best warhorse. Eskkar had time for one quick glance around before Muta and Drakis strode over to join him.

"Any sign of the Elamites?"

Muta laughed. "Oh, yes, Captain. Late yesterday afternoon about five hundred of their cavalry came down the trail. I swear, you could see the shock on their faces. They had no idea anyone would be in the Pass, waiting for them."

"For awhile I thought they were going to attack us," Drakis said, "but they hesitated when they saw our numbers. We even killed a few fools who rode too close to our line."

If the Elamites had been surprised, then Trella's spies had spread their false information well, Eskkar decided. "If they were the vanguard, then the rest of their army isn't far behind. Alexar and the infantry won't be here until midday tomorrow, with the rest of the men straggling in after that. The damned rain slowed everyone down."

"I think we have time, Captain." Muta grinned at Eskkar's questioning look. "We captured one of their scouts. His horse took an arrow and he knocked himself unconscious when he went down."

At this stage of the campaign, even the lowliest captured enemy soldier could provide plenty of valuable and up to date details about the Elamite army. Trella's agents had gleaned much information about Lord Modran's forces, but now Eskkar would have a current source of news. Eskkar nodded approval.

"Have you questioned him yet?"

"Not really. We roughed him up a bit," Muta said, "just to find out how far away their army was. He says his cavalry troop was about twenty-five miles ahead of their main column. So even if they pick up the pace, they won't be here before noon tomorrow, at least not in force. The Elamite army travels slowly, it seems. Still, Captain, you'll want to talk to him. He did say it's the largest army he'd ever seen. Said the column stretches out for thirty miles."

Eskkar shrugged at the news. Bracca's message had warned that Lord Modran's army would be comprised of at least twenty-five thousand men. But if the Elamites were indeed spread out along the trail, they would have to concentrate their forces before launching an attack.

"I'll want to talk to him. But let me take a look around first, and speak to the men. I haven't seen this place in six months." The prisoner could wait a little longer.

Almost two years ago, as soon as Eskkar and his commanders had devised their plan for the defense of Akkad, Drakis and a handful of Hawk Clan guards had ridden through the Dellen Pass from end to end. Searching for the best place to give battle, they had selected this location. After inspecting the site himself and reviewing all the reports from the scouting parties, Eskkar had confirmed their choice.

The Pass itself stretched its way more than a hundred miles through the mountains, from the gateway to the Indus and Elam, to the Land Between the Rivers. That distance, however, did not account for the constant ups and downs of the trail, as it writhed between the peaks and cliffs. The highest part of the Dellen Pass lay closer to the western side of the mountains, about ten miles east of where Eskkar now stood.

That meant the Elamites had been marching mostly uphill for more than sixty miles. But this location, despite being on the general downslope into Akkad's lands, had a favorable slope for the Akkadians. The approaching Elamites would wend their way down the trail, until they reached a spot about two miles away, where the ground flattened for more than a mile. After that, the trail climbed again for the next few miles before starting its final descent to the mouth of the Pass, some thirty miles away.

This carefully chosen place ensured that Eskkar's soldiers possessed the high ground, a major advantage for any army. The Elamites, when they attacked the Akkadians, would be charging uphill.

Now the time had come for one last look at the place he had chosen to fight. Eskkar called for A-tuku, and swung onto the bay. He guided the horse to the center of the trail. At this point in the Pass, the width was less than a quarter mile wide. Facing east, he stared down the slope, visualizing the enemy soldiers advancing toward this position. Their legs would be weary as they marched into battle.

Eskkar turned his gaze to his right, toward the southern wall of the Dellen Pass. He saw only the towering cliffs, which even Shappa's agile slingers had declared were impossible to climb or flank. He grunted in satisfaction. His right flank would indeed be secure.

Turning to his left, the northern cliff face rose almost as high. But on that side of the Pass, a massive jumble of large boulders and chunks of the mountain itself littered the ground beneath the northern wall. The cliff's debris extended almost a hundred paces into the Pass, restricting the trail's breadth even further.

His Akkadian soldiers would stand between those two points, a solid line of infantry and archers. For this battle, the Elamite army would have no way to flank their enemy.

Eskkar's men would be greatly outnumbered, but the narrow width of the trail through this part of the Pass meant only a portion of the enemy could be brought to bear against his soldiers. As Eskkar had reminded his commanders, they didn't need to defeat the Elamites, just hold them off. As long as the Akkadians could stand their ground, the Elamites would have to destroy Eskkar's army if they wanted to get through the remaining thirty miles of the Pass.

Thanks to Trella's agents, for the last few months every Elamite spy had reported to his masters that Akkad continued to prepare itself for a siege. Finding the bulk of the city's forces facing them in the Dellen Pass would be the last thing Modran and the Elamites expected. Or at least Eskkar hoped they had swallowed the bait. Forcing the enemy to fight here, in difficult terrain, would nullify much of their advantage in numbers.

Despite its vast size, the enemy army would have little in the way of food and water with it, and only a slender chain of supplies coming behind it from Elam. Modran's invasion plan anticipated crossing the mountains and marching unopposed up to Akkad's gates. He intended to besiege the city and live off the countryside, supported by food and herd animals collected by General Jedidia.

And just as Eskkar had defeated the Alur Meriki at the Battle of the Stream by blocking access to any water for their warriors, he now intended to do the same to the Elamites. The nearest water available to the enemy was a mountain spring about forty miles to their rear, which meant that any water needed by their soldiers and animals had a long way to travel to reach this place of battle.

Men and horses would be forced to ride back forty miles, fill as many water skins as each horse and rider could carry, and then return to the battle site, struggling under the heavy weight.

For each trip, Eskkar knew almost as much water would be wasted as reached the Elamite camp. Skins would leak or break, reducing the amount of water available. There was just no way to supply thirty thousand men with enough water over that distance. A shortage of water would soon be Lord Modran's most pressing problem.

Meanwhile, the stream where Eskkar and Alexar's army had camped the night before, close to the mouth of the Dellen Pass and over thirty miles to the rear, provided all the water the Akkadians needed. Porters and liverymen would deliver fresh water skins to Eskkar's army every day, from dawn to dusk. But if the Elamites wanted to reach the next source of water along their invasion route, they would first have to defeat the Akkad's forces.

Food, except for a few mountain goats, was nonexistent in the mountains. The invaders would have carried enough provisions with them to get through the Pass, and perhaps a few days after that. Their limited supplies of food and water meant they would have to get through as quickly as possible. Every day that Eskkar's men could delay the enemy's advance would make them that much weaker.

Nor was there much grass for the Elamite cavalry. No army carried enough grain to feed so many mounts. The animals needed to graze, and hardly any grass grew in the rocky and shallow soil of the Dellen Pass. Eskkar guessed that the enemy horses had already started to feel the first pangs of hunger and thirst.

Unless the Elamites turned back, they would have to break through Eskkar's position if they wanted food and water. However he had no intention of letting them do that. He would fight them here, in the mountains, on a battleground that he had chosen, until the last man. Even if the invaders overran his position, every enemy soldier that Eskkar could kill here in the Pass would add a bit more strength to Akkad and its remaining defenders.

All the pieces, laboriously planned over the last year, were now in place. The only task that remained was for Eskkar and his men to hold back the onslaught.

Eskkar touched his heels to A-tuku, and paced the horse toward the southern cliff wall. The impassable, sheer cliff rose several hundred paces high. Back and forth he rode, studying the rock face, making certain once again that there was no way his position could be flanked from that side.

Tugging on the halter, he guided his mount toward the northern wall. On his last visit to the site, Eskkar had measured the distance himself, just to be sure. From north to south, the width of the Pass was fewer than three hundred paces, less than a quarter of a mile. A narrower opening would have been even better, but this location had its advantages. No battleground, Eskkar knew, was ever perfect.

At the northern side, gigantic boulders lay strewn about the base of the cliff wall, and rising up into cliffs that grew ever taller until they backed into the mountain wall itself. On his first visit, Eskkar and five of his guards had spent most of a day wandering through the substantial chunks of rocks and pieces of the cliff wall.

He learned that a man on foot could, with difficulty and enough time, make his way through the maze, climbing over and squeezing around the boulders. But one of his guards sprained an ankle, and another managed to scrape his knee so hard that it required bandaging. For soldiers carrying shields or bows, it would be even more arduous. The Elamites would try it, of course, but Eskkar felt confident he had the answer to that.

Guiding A-tuku away from the rocks, Eskkar returned to the center of the Pass. A small cairn of stones marked the spot. He halted his horse, and looked back up the trail that had brought him to this place. The ground continued to slope upwards for just over two hundred paces, before it flattened out and disappeared behind a curve in the Pass.

Shifting his gaze to the east, Eskkar stared down the slope, at the path the Elamites would have to take. Yes, this place would do very well for a fight to the death.

Eskkar dismounted and turned A-tuku over to one of his guards, gulped some water, and walked back to the center of the Pass.

Drakis now waited there, sitting on the cairn. He pointed downward with his finger. "This is where we think the first battle line should be, Captain. The men can line up in good formation, and it's nearly level from side to side."

The first row would be the infantry, Akkad's spearmen, at least four rows deep. Twenty paces behind them would stand the archers, three rows deep. Even at close range, the bowmen would take advantage of their slightly higher position on the slope to shoot over the heads of the infantry.

With the extra height, the Akkadian archers, shooting downhill, should be able to outrange any Elamite bowmen. Mitrac's bowmen would loose six or seven volleys, which meant thousands of arrows, before the attackers could reply.

The third Akkadian battle line consisted of Muta's cavalry. Their task would be to hurl back any Elamites who broke through the first two ranks. Even so, most of the cavalry would fight on foot, using their smaller bows to augment the Akkadian archers, or their swords to reinforce the spearmen.

In planning for this battle, Eskkar and his commanders quickly realized that a large number of cavalry wouldn't be that useful in the Dellen Pass, and would merely create another supply problem. That decision had freed up the rest of the Akkadian cavalry. Hathor now led those men, along with Isin's forces, in their campaign against Grand Commander Chaiyanar and the Elamites attacking Sumer.

Eskkar had brought with him only enough horsemen to help hold the line, and to cover any retreat. Still, if Modran's soldiers forced the Akkadians to withdraw, Eskkar knew that any attempt to fall back would likely turn into a rout. If the nearly ten thousand enemy cavalry joined the attack, Muta's men would be overwhelmed and cut to pieces.

To stop the invaders, Eskkar had twenty-four hundred infantry men, sixteen hundred bowmen, eighteen hundred cavalry, and six hundred slingers. All in all, sixty-four hundred Akkadians would have to hold off more than twenty-five, and perhaps as many as thirty thousand Elamites. Those were daunting numbers, but at least here, in the Pass, Modran's cavalry would be almost useless.

Eskkar took one last glance around, and nodded in satisfaction. The time had come to talk to the prisoner. He strode over to where the captured Elamite sat on the ground, guarded by two soldiers. Drakis followed. Muta was already there, glowering at the captive. Slight of build, dried blood covered the left side of the man's face. His fear showed by the trembling of his hands and lips.

"Drakis, translate my words exactly."

Both Eskkar and Trella had insisted that all the senior commanders learn at least the rudiments of the main Elamite language. Drakis, because of his good grasp of several dialects spoken in the Land Between the Rivers, had become fluent in the prisoner's language.

Eskkar stopped less than a pace away from the captive, close enough to smell the man's fear. "Do you know who I am?"

The Elamite had to swallow before he could get out the words. "No, Master."

"My name is Eskkar, and I'm the King of Akkad, the city you came here to loot and destroy."

The man flinched at hearing the name. "Master, I'm just a soldier. I was ordered . . ."

"I want to learn everything you know about your army, and I may want to send a message to Lord Modran. So I'll give you one chance to talk. If you tell me the truth, you may yet live to carry that message. If I think you're lying, or holding anything back, I'll have every bone in your body broken, cut out your tongue, then tie you to a horse and send you back to Modran as a warning. Do you understand?"

Eskkar's size and bulk, towering over the helpless prisoner, would have frightened a much stronger man. "Yes, Lord. I'll tell you everything I know."

The interrogation proceeded, with Drakis and Eskkar asking questions and demanding answers so fast that the Elamite had no time to make up a good lie.

Only once did Drakis have to use force, a brutal kick in the face that probably broke the man's nose, and sent a fresh stream of blood trickling down the prisoner's chin. After that, the information came forth in a rush. Thirty thousand men, more than half of them infantry. Nearly five thousand archers, and perhaps nine thousand cavalry.

"That's a lot more horsemen than we expected," Drakis said, after he and Eskkar had moved away from the prisoner. "They must have pulled some cavalry from Jedidia's force."

"I'm more concerned about the number of bowmen," Eskkar said. They're going to unleash an arrow storm against our line."

"Still, with so many archers, they could have swept Akkad's walls clear of defenders." Drakis rubbed the scar on his face, the wound he'd received years ago fighting on those very walls. "Better to meet them here."

Drakis spoke the truth about the futility of trying to defend Akkad. Early on, Eskkar and his senior commanders had realized that they could not put enough bowmen on the walls to resist such numbers – not when the enemy could mass thousands of archers against a single point of the wall.

Eskkar shrugged. Right or wrong, they were committed to fight here, in the Dellen Pass. "Let's just hope the rest of our men and supplies reach us before the enemy can attack in force."

By midmorning, a large force of Elamite cavalry appeared, at least a thousand strong. They held their position at the base of the trail, well out of range, and stared up the slope at the Akkadians. Muta ordered half his horsemen to mount up, just in case the Elamites decided to attack.

But then the first of Eskkar's soldiers arrived. Not the bowmen, or even the infantry, but the slingers, still staggering under the weight of bronze and stone missiles they carried. Eskkar rode out to meet Shappa, leading the ragged column. If the slingers had managed to get here, the rest of the army couldn't be far behind.

With a sigh of relief, Shappa dropped his sack of stones, and let his shoulders sag for a moment. "The archers are only a few miles back, Captain. My men decided they didn't want to miss the fight, so we got up in the middle of the night and pushed on ahead. You should have heard the spearmen cursing us when we passed them by."

Eskkar smiled. He could indeed imagine the language. No part of the army wanted to arrive last and even worse, be led to the battlefield by a force of boys and young men. "Well, I'm glad you're here. The Elamite cavalry is just down the slope. As soon as they get a few more reinforcements, I'm sure they'll attack."

"Where do you want my men? In the rocks?"

"No. For now, split them in half, on either side of the Pass. That should give you a clear field."

Shappa nodded. "And Captain, this morning a messenger caught up with me. Luka sent word that Daro and Orodes broke through the mountains and reached the sea, with Hathor's cavalry right behind them. That was," Shappa had to use his fingers to count, "five days ago."

"So the battle for Sumer may have already started," Eskkar said. "Let's hope Hathor and Naxos catch them by surprise."

"Luka will be coming here as soon as he gets a horse." Shappa laughed. "He won't want to stay in Akkad while his men are here. Besides, Luka is probably sick of Orodes by now."

Eskkar could smile at that, too. Orodes might be a Master Miner and the richest man in Akkad, but he remained an unpleasant and annoying person. Eskkar clasped Shappa on the shoulder. "You and Luka have both done well. Now get your men in place. Tell them they'll have to wait for food and water until the supply men arrive."

Six hundred slingers weren't going to be as effective fighters as an equal number of archers, but they would still be a force to be reckoned with. At close range, their missiles would be almost as deadly as an arrow.

Eskkar rode back to the cairn marking the center of the trail. More enemy horsemen had arrived, but they observed the steady trickle of men coming to reinforce the Akkadian cavalry. The Elamite cavalry showed little inclination to attack a mixed force of horsemen and foot soldiers.

And so the two sides, little more than half a mile apart, watched each other until almost dusk. As the shadows darkened in the Pass, Eskkar knew the likelihood of battle for the day had ended. Clearly, the Elamites wouldn't find the prospect of charging uphill in the darkness appealing.

Before the light faded against the high cliff walls, Mitrac and the first elements of Akkadian bowmen arrived, stumbling along, bent over beneath their loads of weapons and stocks of arrows. Eskkar greeted the late arrivals, until it grew too dark for anyone to see much of anything. But by then he had most of his archers, and even a few hundred of Alexar's infantry.

At last Eskkar turned away to get some rest, leaving Drakis and Muta to take charge of the camp, and distribute the newly arrived men. Just before Eskkar fell asleep, he had time for one satisfying thought. Without a day to spare, he'd managed to assemble his men before his enemy. Either his luck, or more likely, Trella's planning, had held up once again.

27

In the morning, Lord Modran and his commanders rode up to the vanguard of his army. Reports had come in until well after dark last night, so he knew he faced a sizeable force of Akkadians. But one look up the slope of the Pass, and he realized the full extent of the situation. The Akkadians had chosen a favorable place to fight, and Modran could see a thin line of enemy reinforcements continually arriving.

Better, Modran decided, to attack now in case even more Akkadians were coming. He turned to his second in command, General Martiya. "We'll attack at once. Collect the archers and have them provide cover. Use Jedidia's rabble to lead the charge. That way they can prove themselves to our men."

King Shirudukh, at the very last moment, had assigned the invasion targets for each of his generals. At the same time, in a clear sign of disfavor, the King had transferred seven thousand of Jedidia's foot and horse soldiers to Lord Modran. General Jedidia, left with only his cavalry force of six thousand men, found himself assigned to invade the countryside north of Akkad. As everyone knew, there were no cities or even large villages of significance, and nothing much worth looting.

With those simple orders, Shirudukh had weakened General Jedidia's power, and bestowed the King's favor on Modran. Even Grand Commander Chaiyanar had benefited, assigned the easily-plucked city of Sumer. Needless to say, Jedidia's protests had gone unheeded.

"The northern lands are very important to us." King Shirudukh could scarcely keep the smile from his face. "You will have other chances to distinguish yourself in the future, General Jedidia."

The King's soothing voice did nothing to lessen Jedidia's humiliation, visible in his flushed face and clenched teeth.

Even now, Modran smiled at the memory of Jedidia's repressed fury. Modran had control of Elam's largest army, and received the most valuable target, the city of Akkad. He would come out of this campaign with unimaginable wealth and power, so much so that Jedidia would never again be a threat.

But first, Modran would have to brush aside these Akkadians seeking to delay his passage through the mountains. While General Martiya shouted orders, Modran found a rocky hillock off to the side of the column that provided a good view of the enemy, only a half mile ahead.

The early reports had mentioned a large number of cavalry, but Modran now perceived that the Akkadian front line consisted of ranks of infantry, with archers formed up behind them. Further back he could make out the horse fighters, clearly intended to be used as a reserve.

Despite Modran's impatience to close with his adversary, it took until midmorning before the bowmen and Jedidia's former soldiers, both contingents marching near the rear of the column, could get in position. During the delay, an impatient Modran watched the steady arrival of men that continued to swell the Akkadians' ranks. These latest arrivals, however, seemed different. Not as many bore weapons. Indeed, most carried sacks or what looked like water skins.

"Our men are ready, Lord Modran." Martiya pulled his horse to halt beside his general.

Modran, his eyes fixed up the slope, decided to change his tactics. "Hold the cavalry ready. Order the rest of the men to follow behind Jedidia's infantry. When we attack, I want all our men brought into play. We'll crush these Akkadians with the first charge."

Martiya glanced up at the Akkadians. Obviously he, too, had seen the battle line taking shape and growing in numbers. "Yes, Lord Modran. Better to take our losses and break through their ranks as quickly as we can."

This second delay didn't take as long, as Modran's men had readied themselves for battle, and by now every man knew his station. At last Martiya waved his sword in readiness.

Lord Modran took one last look up the slope, and gave the order. "Begin the attack!"

As Eskkar watched the Elamites massing below, more Akkadians continued to arrive. In groups of ten or twenty, archers and spearmen swelled the ranks. The final march into the Dellen Pass had sapped their strength, but every man had gotten a good night's rest.

All of them felt grateful that the long march from Akkad had finally ended. Directed to their positions by Alexar's impatient subcommanders, the infantry and bowmen shuffled into their places. By now, Eskkar knew, his men would prefer a tough fight rather than any more hard marching over the rough and hilly ground.

After the last of the infantry arrived, Alexar and Drakis had formed up their men in four ranks of four hundred men each. That presented a solid front that stretched the width of the Pass. Every spearman, in addition to his spear, wore a short sword at his waist.

Each man carried a large, but surprisingly lightweight shield just thick enough to stop an arrow or deflect a sword. A leather vest covered his chest and a bronze helmet protected his head. Thick leather gauntlets covered each wrist and forearm. Sturdy sandals, laced up high on each calf, provided firm footing.

Every Akkadian possessed not only a dependable weapon, but also the finest clothing and leather armor. Trella's supply clerks had done their job well. They had outfitted sixty-four hundred men for battle, and at the same time ensured that each soldier had enough food and water to last at least ten to fifteen days.

Nor had all those supplies burdened the men. More than a thousand porters and livery men, volunteers from Akkad and its neighboring villages, had delivered those supplies, gathered from the many storage depots along the way.

About a quarter of the infantry, usually the strongest men, carried spears nearly three paces long. The rest carried weapons about half a pace shorter. Every spear was tipped with a bronze point, its slim, leaf-shaped blade riveted to the shaft. All the weapons had a long strip of leather wrapped tight around the grip, to make certain the wood didn't slide through the man's hand on impact.

Twenty paces behind the infantry, Mitrac had assembled his sixteen hundred archers, also in four ranks. They wore leather vests and caps, as well as a leather guard on their left arm. On their right hip, a short sword hung from every belt. Each man wore a quiver of fifteen arrows on his left hip, and another slung over his shoulder.

Between each pair of bowmen rested a linen sack containing an additional fifty arrows, carried to the battle site by Trella's porters.

Twenty paces behind the archers stood twelve hundred dismounted cavalry, also arranged in four ranks. They carried the shorter horseman's bow that lacked the range of Mitrac's archers. But at close range, up to sixty paces or so, the weapons were just as deadly. The rest of the cavalry tended the horses and kept themselves ready as the reserve, with each man holding fast his own mount plus three others.

Eskkar, sitting on his second-best horse just behind the archers, watched his spearmen ready themselves for the coming attack. Years of training, intensified over the last two years, had turned these men into the fiercest foot soldiers in the Land Between the Rivers. He had no doubt they would soon demonstrate their fighting skills to the Elamites. In the Battle of Isin, the Akkadian infantry had torn apart their far more numerous adversaries.

For his personal guard, Eskkar had ten Hawk Clan fighters protecting his front, and another ten, mostly archers, protecting his back. The remaining Hawk Clan soldiers had taken positions with Alexar and Drakis. The rest of Eskkar's command staff consisted of ten messengers, two drummers, and two clerks. The task of the scribes was to keep track of the enemy's forces, and the Akkadian dead and wounded.

The rising slope gave each of the Akkadian contingents a clear and unobstructed view of any approaching enemy. From their elevated position, each bowman's shaft would fly at least twenty or thirty paces farther than the enemy, who would be shooting uphill.

Both the men and the plan were in place. The time for doubt and worry had passed. The strength and skill of Eskkar's men, with the help of the battle gods, would decide Akkad's fate.

A commotion down the trail began, and Eskkar saw the Elamite bowmen, at least three thousand strong, moving forward, with a dense mass of horsemen behind them. The moment for the assault had finally arrived.

"Make ready!" Alexar's voice boomed against the cliff walls.

Eskkar ignored the shifting ranks and cursing men all around him. His soldiers moved with purpose, forming and adjusting the battle lines, and readying their weapons. Each man inspected his companion's gear as well, looking for anything out of place or overlooked. Eskkar kept his eyes on the Elamites as they moved into position. Alexar and Drakis, helped by their subcommanders, checked and rechecked the infantry lines, confirming that each man knew how to place their shield for the coming arrow storm.

Mitrac's archers flexed their bows, inspected bowstrings, and made sure the spare arrows stood close at hand. His subcommanders readied the archers, making certain they formed even lines with enough room between each man so that he could work his bow without interference.

Muta, standing with the cavalry, had one of the most critical assignments. His task was to reinforce any weakness that developed in the lines, and if it appeared that the enemy might break through, to deliver a counterattack with his horsemen.

Despite the activity, Eskkar had little to do with the preparations. For months, the men had trained to form similar battle lines, all without knowing the true reason for the odd formations. Now, within the narrow width of the Pass, that training reassured the men. Eskkar felt confident that the infantry understood both their role and how they were to fight.

With a loud shout that echoed up the Pass, the enemy archers started forward. Eskkar dismounted and handed the horse's halter to one of his guards. Surrounded by thousands of soldiers on foot, any man riding a horse would be targeted. Eskkar had already donned his bronze chest plate and helmet, and he wore the same cloak he'd worn when he met with the Alur Meriki.

While not needed, it identified the leader of the Akkadians to his men, and he wanted to be sure that today of all days he was recognized. If the enemy also picked him out, so be it. Eskkar would not try to hide from their arrows.

Eskkar carried his round bronze shield, and his short sword, better for close-in fighting. His long sword waited with A-tuku, should he need to fight from horseback.

Looking down the slope at the mass of men surging forward, he nodded in grudging approval. The enemy had not wasted either time or men in a probing attack. Instead, Modran was hurling his entire force, or as much of it as he could bring to bear in the confines of the Pass, as soon as he could get them into formation.

Even so, Modran had made his first mistake. The presence of so many horsemen near the front ranks showed that he intended to attack with his cavalry. They paced their horses up the slope behind the mass of archers, and would charge after the Elamite bowmen weakened Akkad's battle lines and cleared the way.

But those horses, would soon work in Akkad's favor. Eskkar felt confident that his bowmen could not only stop a cavalry charge, but turn it to his advantage.

Mitrac gave his first order, and a drumbeat began, the distinctive pattern immediately echoed by two more drummers equidistant from Mitrac's position. At the sound, Akkad's archers planted their feet, fitted their first shaft to the string, and waited.

Mitrac, his own bow in hand, stood at the center of the line, just behind his men. He needed no orders from Eskkar as to when to begin. As soon as the enemy drew within range, Mitrac would unleash his archers. The keen-eyed Master Bowman studied the approaching Elamites and took one last gauge of the wind.

"Draw!

The drummer changed his beat, and Eskkar heard the rasp of sixteen hundred arrows. Every bowman raised his weapon to achieve maximum distance. Except for the drum, still repeating the same notes, the Akkadian ranks fell silent, waiting for the final command.

"Loose!"

The Battle of the Dellen Pass had begun.

The twang of the bowstrings mixed with the hiss of the shafts in flight, louder than any flock of birds taking wing. The first cloud of arrows rose up into the still air of the Pass, the missiles aimed to strike the front rank of the Elamites, and timed to arrive just as the enemy entered extreme range. Well before the first missiles arrived, a second volley took flight.

"Keep the count," Eskkar ordered Zerla, the senior of his two clerks.

The Elamite archers, still out of range with their smaller bows, slowed their advance as they watched the arrow cloud descending upon them. Because of that hesitation, Eskkar guessed more than half of the Akkadians' first volley fell short, the arrows clattering and bouncing off the hard ground.

Even so, enough struck into the advancing mass to slow further the approaching front ranks. Then the second volley landed, this time with many more shafts reaching the formation of Elamite bowmen.

Eskkar saw that the enemy archers wore little defensive leather. Without shields to protect them, the long Akkadian arrows slammed home into flesh, disrupting the line. The Elamites would have to advance at least another hundred paces to get within range of their opponents. The enemy commanders urged their men forward, knowing they had to endure the arrow storm.

Without thinking, Eskkar realized he'd also been keeping count of the volleys. Mitrac's men launched sixteen flights of arrows before . the first ranks of the Elamite archers drew close enough to raise their bows.

Twenty paces away, Alexar's voice boomed out, and another drummer raised his sticks and echoed the commander's order. The front rank of infantry went down on one knee, placing their shield on the ground directly in front of them. The second rank closed up, and set their shield atop those of the first rank. The third and fourth ranks raised their shields and turned them sideways, to provide protection from any arrows arching down from above.

His usual bodyguards, Pekka and Chandor, moved into position in front of Eskkar, raising their shields to protect the King. At his left side stood Saruda, and on his right were two more of Saruda's men, their own shields raised. Eskkar lifted his shield, holding it just below his eyes. He needed to see the battle as it progressed.

Arrows began to strike the ground in front of the Akkadian infantry. A few reached the shield wall. By now Mitrac's archers had loosed twenty four ragged volleys, as the faster bowmen plied their weapons more efficiently than the slower. Mitrac's men needed no urging to continue the arrow storm. They had little enough armor, and the longer they could keep the enemy bowmen at a distance, the safer they would be.

Despite heavy losses, the sheer numbers of Elamite archers kept pushing the front rank forward. More and more arrows began striking the Akkadian infantry's shields. Eskkar glanced behind him, but Muta had already given the order. The first volley from the dismounted cavalry, eight hundred of them, rose up into the sky. The shorter bows might not have the reach of the Elamite weapons, but from the greater height, they would strike the front line.

Eskkar grunted in satisfaction. The Elamites were dropping, struck down by the long shafts that slammed into the ranks, their sharp bronze tips still moving fast enough to tear through flesh and bone.

Now smaller arrows began to arrive, falling almost straight down, to strike heads and shoulders. Eskkar glanced at Mitrac's archers. As far as he could tell, not a man had been killed, though Eskkar saw one bowman had taken a shaft in the arm.

This was the way to win a battle, Eskkar knew. Killing large numbers of the enemy at long range would take the fight out of the invaders. No man likes to stand and die without being able to inflict a few blows of his own.

He saw the confusion in the Elamite ranks. No doubt their leaders wondered when the arrows would lessen, when the Akkadian bowmen would run out of missiles. But the bundles of arrows were being steadily replaced. Hundreds of men had carried many thousands of those shafts, spears, and bronze bullets all the way from Akkad, and even now, during the fight, Trella's porters continued to distribute them. Mitrac's bowmen would drop from exhaustion before they ran out of arrows.

In the last two years, Trella's supply clerks had accumulated and hidden tens of thousands of the missiles in supply depots throughout the land. Akkadian volunteers, following the path of the soldiers, had carried their bundles all the way from the city and surrounding villages to this place in the Dellen Pass.

With no slackening of the arrow storm, the Elamite commanders abandoned their initial plan. Their bowmen fell back and to the sides of the Pass, clearing the way for their cavalry to advance.

Mitrac's drummers sounded the call to halt, and the arrows ceased to fly. Every left arm dropped down, the men grateful to have even a few moments rest. The Elamite cavalry had to pick its way through the dead bodies strewn in its path, before it could gather itself for the charge.

"Draw!" The drums echoed Mitrac's command.

Eskkar turned to Zerla. "What's the count?"

"Twenty-six!" The man's excited voice brought a few chuckles from the men nearby.

Sixteen hundred bowmen had each launched twenty-six arrows. That calculation was beyond Eskkar's ability. He glanced at the other clerk, Enki, who as a young boy had helped save Trella's life. She had trained him as a clerk, and soon discovered that he possessed a unique skill in calculations. Now he knelt almost at the King's feet.

"Enki, how many arrows is that?"

Moving his lips and fingering his counting beads, the young clerk took only a few moments. "Forty-one thousand, six hundred, My Lord."

A staggering sum, one Eskkar could barely comprehend. Each bowman had nearly emptied the two quivers he had carried into the Pass. Now they would be supplied by the bundles brought by Akkad's inhabitants. He swiveled his head, making sure that each archer still had a plentiful supply at hand.

Then Eskkar realized that Enki's total didn't count the volleys shot by Muta's eight hundred dismounted cavalry. No wonder the Elamite archers had been driven back. No fighting force could withstand such an arrow storm.

Now the Elamite cavalry would have their turn. Even at this distance, Eskkar could see the jerky movements and hesitations that signaled fear in their ranks. The enemy could see the trail before them, strewn with their dead and wounded, thousands of arrows protruding from the hard ground like so many blades of tall grass. Modran's cavalry knew they would have to endure the same devastation.

"Loose!" The enemy horsemen had surged forward, and Mitrac's order launched a fresh wave of destruction on them. Once again, sixteen hundred shafts flew up into the sky. The frightening hiss of the arrows in flight echoed against the rock walls, as the bolts reached their peak and, with a whistling sound, began to descend.

This time the Akkadians had the range, and almost all arrows struck home against the enemy cavalry just beginning to surge forward. Horses and men went down, and the shrill shrieks of the wounded animals overpowered the shouts and screams of their riders.

All the same, the charge was underway, urged on by the Elamite commanders. The enemy horsemen galloped over and around their dead and dying, or trampled them underfoot. The protruding Akkadian arrows slowed the enemy riders, as the horses sought to avoid stepping on those as well. Yet more and more horsemen flooded up the trail, like a rising river, the shouts from their riders driving the horses forward.

The Akkadians ignored the mass of horses rushing toward them. Arrows flew as fast as each archer could work his bow, and Eskkar saw their left arms lowering as the enemy drew closer, until they

were shooting straight down the slope. For a moment, Eskkar
wondered if the Elamites could ride through the flights of missiles,
but then Muta's men launched their shafts and increased the carnage.
Screams from the wounded or dying horses added to the confusion,
and the injured animals fought their riders.

The charge broke. Hundreds of the enemy, both horse and rider,
had taken more than one shaft. Now many Elamites dragged on their
halter ropes, turning their mounts around, unwilling to ride into the
certain death that never ceased streaking toward them. And they
could see the four ranks of spearmen waiting patiently, the spears
glinting in the sunlight. Even as the Elamites tried to fall back, the
Akkadians continued to shoot, every archer working his bow as fast
as he could.

The retreat turned into a rout, and with what seemed like a single
motion, every horse turned toward the rear. The deadly shafts
continued seeking out their targets until the last fleeing Elamite was
out of range.

"Halt!" Mitrac's drummer sounded the notes that told the bowmen
to stop.

Eskkar watched as the men lowered their bows. Some archers sank
to their knees, too exhausted to stand. It didn't matter. The cheers
sounded from the infantry, as they rose up from behind their shield
wall. The Elamites had been driven back.

Examining the slope, Eskkar observed that no enemy rider had
reached within fifty paces of the Akkadian front line. A few riderless
horses still milled about, but most of those had retreated back down
the Pass. Already he saw a handful of the slingers darting forward,
trying to catch as many of the loose animals as they could.

The cheering grew even louder, and finally the noise turned into a
single word that made Eskkar glance about in astonishment.

"Eskkar! Eskkar! Eskkar!"

The men were giving him credit for the victory, though he had
done nothing but stand there and watch the battle. This was, Eskkar
realized, one of those moments when he had to reach out to his men.
He drew his sword and held up his arms, turning from side to side to
face those around him.

"Men of Akkad!" Another roar greeted his words. "You've won a
great victory, but the fight is not over. You will be challenged again,

but again we will stand firm against them, like the very walls of Akkad. The enemy will not pass!"

Another roar went up, a crescendo of sound that boomed and echoed against the walls and hurled itself down the slope. The infantry banged their spears against their shields, adding to the din. Half a mile away, the exhausted enemy turned to stare at the Akkadian battle line even as they heard the noise that marked their defeat. The first battle of the Dellen Pass had ended.

28

Lord Modran's rage had left him speechless. The fleeing soldiers had finally halted their retreat. In their flight, the demoralized Elamites pushed back upon the vast number of men still moving up from the rear, trying to join the battle. Once again more than half a mile separated the two armies, and but now confusion mixed with shocked surprise swept through the long column that comprised his soldiers.

As soon as the chaos ended, Lord Modran had summoned his senior commanders. They stood before their leader, eyes downcast, stunned looks on their faces. Hundreds of his men, perhaps thousands, had been slain before his eyes, and without ever coming to grips with the jeering Akkadians. Modran had lost men before, but never so many so quickly, and never in defeat.

General Martiya pushed through the silent ranks, shoving aside any man that blocked his path. A thin trickle of blood ran down his cheek. "Where did they get so many bowmen? You told us Akkad had less than a thousand archers!"

Modran clenched his teeth at Martiya's boldness. But now was not the time to confront his senior commander's rage. "That's what our spies said."

"Then our spies are fools, or men who can't count above ten. I counted almost two thousand archers loosing at us. And the arrows. They never ran out of arrows!"

"They can't have many left," Modran said. "The next attack will break their ranks. Once we come to grips with them . . ."

Martiya shook his head so hard that some of the blood on his cheek flew off. "Even now, men continue to reinforce the Akkadians. Not soldiers, but laborers carrying packs or water skins or weapons. During the fight, I saw them arriving, delivering more stocks of arrows to their archers. And more porters still come down the slope. They're not going to run out of arrows, My Lord."

"We'll need to build a shield wall, so our own bowmen can close with them. Then we can attack."

Martiya opened his mouth, then closed it. He took a deep breath. "My Lord, there are almost no trees in the Pass. To construct shield walls, we'll have to use every shield we have. That will take time to collect and fasten them together."

Modran eyed his commanders. He saw the defeat in their eyes, and realized they were in no mood to launch another attack today. "Very well. We'll have to clear away the bodies anyway. We'll attack again at dawn. Meanwhile, get every man with a shield and send them to the front. And we'll hold the cavalry in reserve. We won't break through Eskkar's line with cavalry, not as long as he has those bowmen."

Once the first few horses went down in the narrow confines of the Pass, their carcasses slowed the momentum of any charge. Wounded animals caused even more chaos, running about in their fright. In one action, thousands of dead men and animals already littered the slope between the two armies.

Martiya turned to the commanders, and started giving orders. In two's and three's, they moved off, glad to be away from their angry general. At last only he and Modran remained.

"We were warned about the Akkadian bowmen," Martiya said. "Eskkar must have stripped the city to bring so many here. This is no holding action, no attempt to delay our passage. He's not going to fight us from Akkad's walls. He's brought the walls to the Dellen Pass. He's chosen to challenge us here, to the death. If Eskkar tries to retreat, he knows our cavalry will slaughter his entire army, bowmen or not."

"That means the city will be undefended. And we outnumber the Akkadians here at least six to one. Once we break through, they will have nothing left to face us."

Nevertheless, Modran didn't like the idea of an undefended Akkad. If Chaiyanar learned Akkad's defenses were weak, he might move his forces north toward Akkad at once, possibly even capture it. That humiliation would be worse than anything Modran could imagine.

"I don't have the body count yet, My Lord, but we've lost at least fifteen hundred dead, maybe more, and more than a thousand wounded. And hundreds of horses, too. The Akkadian position is strong. We may lose half our men breaking through, and it may take days. Before we attack again, we'll need every last man ready to fight. We're going to need more supplies, too, My Lord. Food, water, perhaps even more men."

Modran ground his teeth. He would look like a fool if he sent word back through the Pass that he needed more men and supplies to brush aside the Akkadians blocking his path. Already he could hear King Shirudukh's contemptuous words.

Still, better to ask for the supplies now. His army hadn't planned to spend any length of time in these mountains. Food and water would soon be in short supply. Once his men broke through, the request for extra supplies would mean nothing.

Modran glanced around and saw his clerks standing nearby, nervous expressions on their faces. "All right. I'll send messengers back to Zanbil, and order them to send as much food and water as they can, and to start collecting all the wood they can find. We'll make shields for our men. Meanwhile, drag those dead horses out of the pass. The men can eat them if they get hungry."

Raw horse meat didn't appeal to Martiya, but then he wouldn't be eating any of it. He still had plenty of good food in his personal supply. "We need to clear the path anyway, My Lord. But even so, I don't think we'll be ready by dawn tomorrow."

Modran had reached the same conclusion, though he refused to admit it yet. "See to it, then."

"Just make it clear, My Lord, to our men at Zanbil that we require all the water skins and food they can carry, as well as any extra shafts for the bowmen. We may be here longer than a day or two."

The small village of Zanbil, just a few miles east of the mountains, had served as the collection and supply depot for Modran's army. Supplies would have continued to flow into the village, awaiting word from Lord Modran that the Elamite army had crossed the mountains and moved toward Akkad.

Modran's teeth ground together. He hated the idea of looking up the Pass and watching Eskkar's battle line for even one more day. "Zanbil will send everything they have, or I'll order the village burnt to the ground and kill every man in it."

"I wonder what other surprises this Eskkar has for us." Martiya rubbed his jaw, and for the first time, noticed the blood.

"An Akkadian's arrow?"

"No, My Lord. One of our men nearly poked my eye out with a sword in his rush to get out of range."

Modran grunted at the idea of losing his top commander to some lowly, panicked soldier. He took a deep breath, and tried to regain his habitual calm. "We'll get through this, Martiya. Use whatever time it takes to get the men ready. What about those boulders on the right side of the Pass? Can we get our men through them?"

"Perhaps. If we attack there in force we might be able to get through," Martiya said. "If we could get a few hundred men on their flank, we could break their line. I'll send some scouts to see if there's a way."

"Find a path. The longer Eskkar holds us up, the harder it will be to brush him aside."

As soon as Eskkar realized the Elamites weren't going to attack again today, he told his commanders to stand down the men. Alexar kept one rank of spearmen in place, just in case, and Mitrac did the same with his bowmen. The rest of the soldiers broke ranks. Some just slumped to the hard ground, too tired to move. Others sought out the water skins, or trotted off to the canyon's walls to relieve themselves.

A babble of voices filled the Pass, as the amazed soldiers examined the dead bodies stretching from one side of the cliffs to the other. Eskkar understood their emotions. They'd just fought and survived a bloody battle, and the sound of their own voices helped reassure them that they were still alive.

He turned away from the battlefield, and glanced up the slope. The porters and bearers from Akkad continued to arrive, their eyes wide with fear, and all of them struggling under their goods. Everyone rushed to deliver their burden and depart.

One particular group caught Eskkar's eye, and he waved his arm in recognition. Builders, carrying their tools, and laborers grunting under the weight of planks. The man in charge saw Eskkar's gesture and paced his horse toward the King.

"Greetings, My Lord."

"Good to see you again, Franar," Eskkar said. Franar was one of Corio's younger sons.

"I'm sorry for arriving so late, King Eskkar," Franar said. "But I did not want my men to get separated. It would have been too easy for one or two to drop out or disappear, and then all my work might have been wasted. They're as scared as rabbits, and so am I."

"You've come just in time," Eskkar said. "We've driven off their first attack, but tomorrow they'll be back, and in greater force."

"Then I'll set my men to work, My Lord," Franar replied. "We've brought torches, and if necessary we'll work through the night. I'm sure every one of my men will be eager to leave the Dellen Pass as soon as possible and get back to Akkad."

Eskkar nodded. The men would be glad to rush home, all the while praying to every god they could think of that they reached the safety of the city in case the Elamites broke through.

"Then I'll leave you to your work, Franar. When you return to Akkad, give my thanks to your father."

Eskkar found Alexar, Drakis, and Mitrac waiting for him. Shappa and Muta joined them a few moments later. The Akkadian leaders moved away from the ranks, to plan for the next battle. When they were settled on the ground, Eskkar turned to Alexar. "How many did we lose?"

"Not many, Captain." Alexar's voice held a hint of pride. "Sixteen spearmen were struck by arrows, seven dead. Mitrac lost just over twenty dead, or wounded and unable to fight. Shappa had twelve killed and five wounded. Muta had three men wounded."

Insignificant losses, compared to the dead and dying Elamites scattered the length of the slope. Eskkar glanced at his commanders. "Next time we won't be so lucky. Send any wounded who can travel back to Akkad with the supply men. Give them the horses we captured."

Those too injured to travel would have to take their chances. Whether they lived or died depended on the gods. At least they would have food and water to ease their suffering.

"Now, let's talk about the battle. You first, Shappa." As always, Eskkar started with his youngest commander. He'd learned years ago that allowed the younger commanders to speak freely, without worrying about contradicting the more senior commanders.

"My men have worked our way all through the rocks, Captain," Shappa began. "We know the paths the Elamites will have to take. This time they only sent a few into the rocks, and those struggled until we drove them off. We didn't have much time to prepare, but the hammers and chisels we need have just arrived. We'll start carving out footholds and scaling the rocks. My slingers and bowmen should be dug in and ready by midday."

In the last year, at Eskkar's suggestion, the slingers had added a new weapon to their capabilities. A small bow, smaller even than those of the Akkadian cavalry, had become the primary weapon of over two hundred slingers. The rocks and boulders of Eskkar's left flank favored such a small weapon, intended to be used only at close range. Its smaller size made it easier to use in the rocky confines, and the bearer did not need to expose too much of himself to utilize it.

"You will have your men in the rocks tonight?" Eskkar didn't think the enemy would try that tactic soon, but he didn't intend to take any chances.

"My men will move into the rocks as soon as it gets dark," Shappa said. "I'll have thirty scouts out in the Pass, in case any Elamites try to sneak up on our position. We'll give you plenty of warning if they do."

"Good." Eskkar turned to Mitrac. "Your men fought well today. Give them my thanks. Do you have sufficient arrows for the next attack?"

"Yes, Captain. Bundles continue to arrive, and we've almost as many shafts as we had at the start of today's battle."

"Franar and his builders are here. He says he will construct the fighting platforms by midmorning. You will have to man those as well."

Eskkar had wanted to anchor the two flanks of his infantry line. Corio, Franar's father, had suggested building a small fighting platform at either end. The wooden structure, carried plank by plank up into the Pass by Franar's workers, would provide an elevated position for twenty archers in each structure. Saw-tooth boards at the top would allow the bowmen some measure of protection and enable them to shoot arrows at any threat to the infantry's flanks.

Franar's platforms had first been constructed months ago, then disassembled and taken to one of the supply depots north of Akkad.

Muta had already chosen smaller bowmen who could work their weapons in close quarters. He placed them under Mitrac's orders. All were excellent shots at close range. They would unleash their shafts at any threatened breakthrough, as well as target enemy commanders.

"We'll be ready as soon as Franar and his workmen are finished," Mitrac said. "Meanwhile my archers are ready, too. They've come to like shooting at such close range."

Eskkar nodded. He'd watched them train. At Eskkar's signal, Muta spoke next, then Drakis and Alexar. But the two infantry commanders had done little in today's fighting.

"Today's battle was a good victory," Eskkar began, "but I think we made a mistake. We hurt the Elamites, hurt them badly, and now they are forewarned about our strength. When they come tomorrow, they will be fully prepared."

"Our position here is very strong," Drakis said. "As long as they can't flank us, we can fight them man to man."

"When their cavalry broke and turned," Eskkar said, "we missed an opportunity. I know you and Alexar have prepared and trained your men to hold the line, but I want you to ready your men for a counterattack. The next time the Elamites look ready to break, I want to hurl our spearmen down the slope. If they crowd up again, as they did today, we should be able to slaughter hundreds more."

Alexar laughed. "Twenty-four hundred men against twenty-five thousand. Charging downhill, over a battlefield filled with the dead and dying. My men will love that."

"Your men won't be the only ones surprised. It's the last thing the Elamites will expect," Eskkar grinned. "As we've learned, anytime you can surprise your enemy during a battle, you can break him. Surprise leads to confusion, which turns to fear and spreads."

"You want us to charge them after their next attack?" Drakis sounded dubious.

"No. I want them to attack and retreat, attack and retreat. Let it settle into their heads that they can retreat in safety. Only when I think we can really hurt them will we counterattack." Eskkar looked at his commanders. "So talk to your leaders of ten and twenty. Prepare them to attack with everything they have. When the spearmen go down the slope, we'll need everyone to move as one, with the archers and slingers following behind. If we can beat the

Elamites, hurt them badly, they'll find an excuse to retreat all the way back to Elam."

Drakis laughed. "We'll give them the excuse, what's left of them. After today's fight, they won't be so eager to attack Akkad again."

"Captain, is there any word from the Jkarian Pass, or Sumer?" Mitrac asked the question that lingered in every man's mind.

Eskkar knew Mitrac had kin riding with Hathor.

"No, only that Hathor and Naxos have reached the sea. No matter what happens at Sumer, they will make sure that Chaiyanar is too busy to move north. Nor have any reports arrived from Draelin at the Jkarian Pass. As soon as I learn anything, I'll pass the word."

Everyone understood. All of them had friends or kin fighting with the other forces.

"And after we drive this scum back to Elam," Eskkar said, his voice suddenly hard, "we will march down to Sumer and finish off Grand Commander Chaiyanar."

29

S argon and Garal rode side by side, each leading a spare horse. In the last two years, Sargon had often led a second horse. Each time always reminded him of his first battle against the Carchemishi invaders and then the wild ride to the Alur Meriki caravan.

Since those days, Sargon had proved his competence as a horseman. Months on horseback with his friends had toughened his legs and thighs. Today he sat astride his horse with the same ease and assurance as Garal or any of the Ur Nammu and Alur Meriki warriors surrounding him.

In less time than the three and a half days that took Eskkar from Akkad to the mouth of the Dellen Pass, Sargon and Garal had ridden almost twice as far. The barbarian war party numbered over thirteen hundred well armed fighting men. Traveling light, with food and supplies awaiting them along the trail, the fast moving steppes warriors covered long distances with each day's journey.

Sargon and two hundred and fifty Ur Nammu warriors had joined with eleven hundred Alur Meriki fighting men. For this campaign, Chief Subutai of the Ur Nammu had placed himself and his men under Chief Bekka's command. That decision was not made lightly. Honor and pride aside, Subutai was the older and probably wiser war leader. But in battle, only one can command, and Bekka led a far greater number of men.

Both leaders had recognized the significance of the gesture. For the Alur Meriki, it acknowledged their leadership and the role they would play in honoring their blood oath to Sargon's father. For the Ur Nammu, it declared their willingness to honor their debt to Chief Bekka and the Alur Meriki for saving their Clan from the Carchemishi.

In addition, another hundred or so young Alur Meriki boys and older men rode with them, carrying extra food and supplies, and leading forty more spare horses. Last night, those too young or old to fight had handed over their sacks and horses, and turned back to the west, leaving only warriors to continue their journey eastward.

But the old and young men who returned to the west still had one more task to perform. They would gather additional food and fresh horses, and once again ride back into the mountains, to this very place. Here they would wait until Chief Bekka and the warriors finished their raid.

On that day, all the returning warriors would likely be in desperate need of food and fresh horses. Even more likely was the possibility that an avenging force of Elamites might be right behind, chasing the warriors.

In the last year, Sargon, Eskkar, Subutai, and Bekka had worked together preparing for the coming war. Almost eight months ago, the Great Raid, as Eskkar called it, had taken shape. In Eskkar's absence, Sargon helped guide the planning and coordination with the Alur Meriki and Ur Nammu.

For the first time in a campaign, the steppes warriors received the benefit of Akkad's efficient supply masters. Sargon assumed command over all the clothing, weapons, food, and tools that during the last six months, quietly and without fanfare, had trickled north to Akkad's outposts. He made sure the supplies were distributed or stockpiled, and available at a moment's notice.

Meanwhile, a small Alur Meriki scouting party had ridden back through the mountains into Elamite territory, quietly marking out likely campsites, grazing grounds, and watering holes. These scouts, after reaching into Elam's lands, returned by way of the Jkarian Pass.

With the routes mapped, the leaders knew in advance what routes to take, where to make camp, and the best watering places. Just as important, the warriors knew exactly how much distance they needed to cover each day.

As the looming Elamite invasion drew near, the wagons of the Alur Meriki moved closer to Eskkar's northern outposts, to place themselves under their protection. With plenty of food in storage for their women and children, the steppes warriors awaited only the final delivery of weapons and grain.

During those months, Bekka and Subutai had improved Eskkar's basic strategy, adding the wisdom of the steppes and its tactics. With Sargon's help, the chiefs calculated the precise number of days of riding needed to reach the Elamite supply village. Trella's maps had aided that process greatly.

The small force of warriors would be no match for the vast cavalry of the enemy, so careful timing would be required to avoid early discovery. Again and again, Sargon studied the maps, and satisfied himself that the warriors could, in fact, maintain the pace that they had set for themselves. And that they understood the necessity of following the plan. Then he made sure that every warrior had whatever he needed to ride to war. No man would lack a good horse or fine weapons.

"Remember," Eskkar had said to Bekka and Subutai at their last meeting, "you do not need to face them in battle. You will strike a heavy blow just by disrupting their supply lines and stopping the flow of men into the Dellen Pass."

Both Subutai and Bekka had nodded gravely, too polite to contradict Akkad's leader. Sargon soon realized that neither clan chief intended to accept such a minor role. When the warriors of the steppes went to war, they expected blood to flow. To avoid conflict with an enemy, despite its greater numbers, did not fit into their own designs.

Just into his eighteenth season, Sargon had also not corrected his father. Eskkar might have grown up in the clan, but Sargon had lived and worked side by side with clan leaders for the last few years. By now he knew more about their way of life, including the ways of their leaders, than his father ever learned.

Nevertheless, Sargon always deferred to his father. Only when asked did Sargon offer his opinions or suggestions. Over time, as the boy-turned-warrior showed his wisdom, Eskkar relied more and more on his son's advice. Little by little, Eskkar gave Sargon more authority to deal with the clans. With sage counsel from Subutai and Bekka, Sargon had fulfilled that task well beyond Eskkar's expectations.

Sargon had also developed lasting friendships with many of the chiefs from both clans which gave him a depth of knowledge about the warriors and their ways. And they, in their turn, had come to trust Sargon more and more. He might be the son of the King of Akkad, but in their eyes, Sargon remained a warrior first, and an Akkadian second.

A year ago, Chief Bekka had formally adopted Sargon into his Clan, to the cheers of the Alur Meriki people and the approval of his parents.

Father and son now maintained an aloof but trusting relationship. Ten months ago, Eskkar had accepted his son as his heir, and Trella had made the public announcement to the people of Akkad. Whatever their feelings once might have been for their son, Sargon's trials with the Ur Nammu had turned him into a man. He'd proved himself worthy of one day becoming the ruler of Akkad and its people.

More important, at least in Eskkar's eyes, was that Sargon had made peace with his mother, and welcomed her role as a counselor and advisor. In the long run Eskkar knew that would prove more vital than the father and son relationship. They did not always see eye to eye on every issue, but both had learned to listen to the other, a major accomplishment for any father and son, warrior or village bred.

Tashanella and her mothers, by their careful maneuverings, had helped restore the mutual trust and respect between Sargon and his parents. Working subtly, wife and mothers ensured that Sargon set aside his bitterness toward his mother, Lady Trella.

Sargon and his wife had visited Akkad twice, and both times Trella had openly embraced her son and daughter-in-law. Only then, when Sargon felt secure in his mother's treatment of his chosen wife, had he let go of the last of his anger.

Sargon, again following Tashanella's suggestion, had journeyed to Akkad with his wife, where she gave birth to Sargon's first born, a daughter. When the proud parents returned to the Ur Nammu, Trella had accompanied them, to spend more time with her new granddaughter.

Time had changed Sargon. He'd grown into manhood even as he won the respect of the Ur Nammu for his quick wits and good sense. The Alur Meriki trusted him, too. He often spent time in their camp, visiting Chief Bekka or Den'rack, who had grown into another of Sargon's friends and mentors.

Last year Bekka had promised one of his daughters to Sargon as a wife, as soon as she completed the rites. Once Sargon might have refused such an offer, but both Tashanella and Trella had advised him to accept the gift. Anything that joined the Ur Nammu, the Alur Meriki, and the Akkadians had to be considered carefully and treated with respect.

Not to mention that Sargon still had no son of his own. A year after he'd taken Tashanella as his wife, she had given him a girl for his first born. Less than a year later, a second child came, this time a boy, who died soon after birth.

None of that mattered now. The time for the endless planning and subtle diplomacy, so much a part of Lady Trella's maneuverings, had passed. The warriors of the steppes rode to war. For them, this was a time of joy. Unlike Sargon's civilized parents, the Alur Meriki relished the chance to strike a hard blow at their enemies.

By the end of the third day, the warriors had ridden far to the north, and entered deep into the foothills of the Zagros Mountains. Turning eastward, they followed the same path that three years earlier, the Alur Meriki had traversed when they departed the lands of the Indus and the Elamites.

The combined force of warriors continued the arduous journey, rapidly retracing the slow steps of the Alur Meriki, back toward the northernmost lands of Elam. Three days after the boys and old men turned back, Bekka and his men completed the journey through the northern foothills.

When the warriors climbed the last hill at the place where the high passes opened up to the south, they enjoyed a vista that revealed the vast and mostly barren high plains. Sargon had never beheld such an expanse. He estimated he could see more than four miles to the south and east.

But the land was empty, save for two Alur Meriki scouts who waited there to receive them. Sargon noticed that their horses were played out. These warriors had ridden hard. He recognized the markings on their lances. These were men from Den'rack's clan, who had traveled in secret into the Elamite lands almost a month ago.

Sargon and Garal, taking their position just behind Bekka and Subutai, heard the scout's words.

"Chief Bekka . . . Chief Subutai." The rider, a veteran warrior with more than forty seasons, nodded to Sargon as well. "Den'rack is waiting at the Jkarian Pass. We only just reached this place, to await your arrival, and to give you the news. Den'rack spotted a large force of Elamite cavalry, more than five thousand, as they rode toward the Jkarian Pass. Unless they stop, by this time tomorrow they'll have entered the Pass. More of our scouts have ranged far to the south, and observed the village where the dirt-eaters were assembling to go through the Dellen Pass."

Sargon heard Bekka's grunt of frustration. "Have they started west?"

"Through the Dellen Pass?" The scout nodded. "Yes, three days ago. Den'rack said they move slowly, because there are so many of them."

Sargon heard the bad news. His mother's spies had estimated that the Elamites wouldn't be starting for the two passes for another few days. That extra time would have given Bekka's men plenty of time to get into position. Obviously the Elamites had moved sooner than expected. They, too, understood that Akkadian spies were everywhere.

Bekka turned to Sargon, who knew much more about how dirt-eater cavalry operated. "The soldiers going through the Dellen Pass do not concern us now. But how long would it have taken for the Elamites to reach your Engineer's place in the Jkarian Pass?"

"At least three days, Chief Bekka," Sargon said. "They would see no reason to hurry."

Sargon saw the frown on Bekka's forehead, and did the same calculation the Alur Meriki leader had just completed. Riding hard, it would take Bekka's warriors two days to reach the mouth of the Jkarian Pass.

If Eskkar's plan to block the Pass succeeded, the Elamite cavalry could already be on the way back. That meant the Alur Meriki warriors might soon have a large enemy force behind or even in front of them.

Sargon offered his own thoughts. "Chief Bekka, even if the trail is blocked, they will probably spend some time trying to get through. They will not likely just turn back at once."

"It matters not." Bekka, too, had come to the same conclusion. "We ride south, as planned."

The march resumed, the warriors beginning the long descent to the valley floor. They continued moving at their usual pace, a combination of fast walk and occasional canter. At least two or three times each day, depending on the terrain, Bekka would give the order and the riders would dismount, to lead their horses on foot. At those times, Chief Bekka would set the pace, either a fast walk or a gentle jog that kept the ground passing beneath their feet.

From dawn to dusk, they rode, eating on the move, and resting only enough to keep the horses strong. By noon on the eighth day after setting out, the warriors reached the mouth of the Jkarian Pass. Standing atop a small plateau and less than a quarter mile from the mouth of the Pass, Den'rack and twenty of his men waited there to greet them.

For a man who had been riding through hostile lands for the last twenty-plus days, Den'rack seemed relaxed. He greeted Bekka, and the other war chiefs with his quick smile. The clan leaders gathered together – Bekka and his chiefs, Suijan, Prandar, Virani, and Subutai, along with Chinua and Fashod of the Ur Nammu.

While not actually a leader, Sargon took his usual place beside Bekka and Subutai. Garal and the other warriors crowded close around their commanders. On the trail, there were no secrets.

Den'rack waited until all the chiefs had taken their places. "King Eskkar's plan to close the Pass has succeeded," he said with a smile. "Two days ago, three riders galloped out of the Pass, messengers from General Jedidia, the Elamite who leads the expedition. We captured them and put them to the torture. They were more than willing to tell us what happened, in exchange for a quick death."

Sargon had no trouble visualizing that interrogation. He'd seen warriors extract information from prisoners before. The three riders would have been separated, tortured, and questioned. If the three stories did not agree, the torture would resume, increasing in intensity, until the men pleaded for death. Only when their reports agreed would they have received a quick dispatch.

"They carried messages for both Lord Modran and for King Shirudukh, advising of the delay. This Jedidia claimed he would attempt to force his way through the landslide and continue his march. If not, he would send word that he was returning to Zanbil to resupply and follow Lord Modran's soldiers through the Dellen Pass."

"And nothing since then?" Bekka asked.

"No. My men watch the Pass very closely. No one has tried to enter it since General Jedidia's soldiers went in. Only the three messengers we captured have come out."

Bekka considered the information for a moment, then glanced at Sargon.

"He must make a serious effort to get through the blockage," Sargon said. "He will have to stay until his supplies run low. To just give up would be too humiliating, and the Elamite King might not be pleased. My mother's spies say that there is little trust among any of these Elamite leaders."

"Then if the Pass is truly blocked," Bekka said, "this Jedidia could come back through as early as today or tomorrow."

"Perhaps." Sargon shrugged, in much the same way as his father. "I think it more likely he will spend a few more days. But he will soon be behind us."

"Then I will leave three men here to keep watch, and bring us warning when the enemy leaves the Pass."

If Jedidia's army emerged. Sargon heard the doubt in Bekka's voice. Sargon also worried about Alcinor's ability to close the Pass for more than a short time. But that didn't matter any longer. Bekka gave the orders, and the great war party continued their way south, now deep into the lands of the Elamites and aiming for the Dellen Pass.

Despite the need for urgency, Bekka slowed the pace somewhat. So deep in hostile territory, the warriors dared not push their horses too hard, not when they might need their strength at any moment, either to attack or withdraw. They halted more often, to graze the animals. Fortunately Den'rack had traversed all these lands, and had already located the best sources of grass and water.

As for food, the warriors' supply was running low. They had consumed more than expected, and Sargon knew that after tomorrow, the last of the food would be gone. If they didn't find the supplies they needed, many of the spare horses would have to be butchered. No matter what the cost, the warriors needed to maintain their fighting strength.

Riding and walking, the warriors moved south, keeping the mountains and foothills on their right. They travelled on what Den'rack called the Upper Trail, a track that hugged the crest of the low foothills. About four miles to the south, another trail also led to the village of Zanbil.

The Upper Trail offered the most direct route, and would cut a day or so off the journey, versus the Lower Trail, which traversed mostly level terrain with more plentiful grasslands.

While the terrain of the Upper Trail might not be as favorable to dirt eaters, it presented little difficulty to the experienced horsemen of the steppes. And it took them straight toward their destination. Every warrior felt grateful for that. They had endured enough of the endless hills in their ride through the mountains.

By mid morning of the fourth day, the riders had covered more than two hundred miles, an incredible distance for such a large force. From their high vantage point they could see their destination. Directly ahead, no more than three or four miles, lay the opening to the Dellen Pass. Even if Den'rack had not pointed out the jutting ridgeline that extended down from the mountains, there was no mistaking the broad trail that descended to the plain. Thousands of men and horses had trampled the earth flat across a wide swath of ground.

"There is the village," Den'rack swung his arm toward the southeast. "The dirt eaters call it Zanbil, about thirty or forty huts, two corrals for holding horses, and a third full of cattle. A small stream borders the village, flowing down from the foothills. All of Modran's army passed through here, and a few soldiers still remain, guarding the supplies."

Sargon craned his neck. Zanbil lay about three miles away, closer than the opening of the Pass. Everything seemed peaceful. No guards or scouts rode patrol around the depot. It meant, Sargon realized, that no one had detected the Alur Meriki warriors in their rapid journey.

That situation would not last long. By now someone must have seen the long column of riders heading south, and soon the word of a large force of barbarians would reach even this place.

To better study the landscape, Bekka, Suijan, and Subutai dismounted and moved on ahead, accompanied by Den'rack. For this engagement, Bekka had announced to the assembly of warriors that Suijan would be second in command, and Subutai would be third.

This arrangement satisfied the honor of both clans, and the Alur Meriki warriors understood they would not have to follow the orders of an Ur Nammu leader unless both Bekka and Suijan were dead. And by then, Sargon knew, whoever led the remaining fighters would matter little.

Sargon followed Bekka's example. None of the clan leaders ever gave him direct orders. In battle, however, he would be expected to follow Subutai's commands. .

Standing in the shadow of a large boulder, the clan leaders studied the landscape. Den'rack identified the various landmarks, and pointed out the trails that led to the village from both the south and the east.

Sargon resisted the urge to offer suggestions. He knew that Bekka would give him an opportunity to speak, and if Sargon disapproved of the plan, he would make his thoughts known.

Chief Bekka didn't take long to grasp the situation. "We need to cut the village off, so that no word of our attack escapes. Den'rack, you know the countryside best. You and Prandar will ride with Suijan, and guide him. Encircle the village to the east and south. Subutai and Virani will take their men straight toward Zanbil. Unegen and I will follow the foothills, and get between the Pass and Zanbil. We will make sure that no riders can slip past us to warn Modran."

"Yes, Chief Bekka." Den'rack couldn't keep the excitement from his voice. "We will need time to get into position."

"Hurry, then," Bekka answered. "Remember, not one man can escape."

Out of sight of Zanbil, the warriors made their preparations. Soon nearly six hundred men departed. They would backtrack for nearly a mile. From there, Sargon knew they would turn east, keeping out of sight of the village, until they were in position.

Bekka leaned back against the boulder. "At least our men will get a chance to rest their horses. Once Suijan launches his attack, we will have to ride like the wind."

Sargon stared at the village. It seemed peaceful enough, the soldiers there unaware of the terror that would soon be upon them. Still, this was war, and these men planned to destroy Akkad and the other cities in the Land Between the Rivers.

"Are you worried about something?" With the chiefs making their preparations, Garal had rejoined his companion.

Sargon smiled at his friend's concern. "No, not any longer. During the ride, I had my doubts that we would arrive here unopposed. But it seems we will surprise the Elamites after all."

"Perhaps some of your father's luck now guides your footsteps."

References to his father no longer troubled Sargon. "I hope it does. This campaign, there is much that can go wrong. Even if we drive the Elamites back, they may return again in a year or two, this time better prepared."

"Did we not smash the Carchemishi, beat them so badly that few escaped our riders? They have withdrawn all the way to Carchemish, and who knows if they will ever have the stomach to ride into our lands again."

"The Elamites are stronger than the foolish Carchemishi, and more cunning. But you may be right. My father thinks so, too. Beat them hard enough, show them they can't win, he says, and their will to fight again will vanish."

"The Alur Meriki, and the Ur Nammu, too, have fought many battles. But your father knows how to win. He has fought alone many times, like the day he slew Thutmose-sin. Out here, in these lands, if something goes wrong, we can just ride away. It takes much courage to stand in one place and face an enemy five or six times your number. And Subutai says Eskkar will have little chance to fall back if he is defeated. Yet he rode into the Dellen Pass to confront his enemy."

"My father once told me that courage follows once you've picked your course of action. If the Pass can be held, he will hold it. His soldiers are both tough and skilled."

The waiting continued. Bekka and the other leaders paced among the warriors, confirming that each man knew what he had to do. The horses were examined yet again, to make sure each mount had the stamina for one final charge. Men strung their bows and tested their draw. Arrows were loosened in quivers, and everyone sharpened their swords and knives. The tasks helped fill the time until Suijan and Den'rack completed their encircling movement.

Sargon heard a murmur pass through the warriors, as they caught sight of Suijan and his riders. Even before Bekka gave the order, men swung themselves up on their horses, everyone impatient to launch the attack.

Subutai, too, appeared more than ready to ride. Sargon and Garal mounted their horses, and took their place behind Chinua and Fashod.

Chief Bekka called out to Subutai and Virani, who acknowledged the command.

"We ride." With those two words, Subutai led the way. The horses descended the final slope to reach the level ground. In moments, the Ur Nammu warriors spread out, dividing into three main groups. Now Chinua took the lead, with Sargon and Garal riding just behind the clan leader.

Glancing to his right, Sargon saw the long column of Bekka's warriors also on the move. The terrain that led to their destination, the mouth of the Dellen Pass, was more rugged, and it would take them longer to reach their position.

Virani and Subutai's men, now spread out in a wide line, kept the already excited horses to an easy canter. They held that pace for the first mile. Looking ahead, Sargon saw no signs of alarm, no Elamite soldiers scurrying about. Clutching his lance, Sargon watched the distance between the riders and the village close, until only a half mile remained.

By now, even the most careless of sentries would have heard the horses approaching. Subutai flashed his sword over his head, and the warriors burst into a gallop. At the same time, they voiced their war cries, the dreaded sound of the steppes warriors riding into battle.

Looking ahead, Sargon now observed the panic sweeping over the villagers. Some of the soldiers reached for their weapons, but most, after one look at the nearly five hundred warriors descending upon them, turned and ran, desperate to get to their horses.

But the Elamites had no chance. Even those who leapt onto their horses could already see the column of warriors approaching from the east, a long line of men that would stretch across the trail that led south. Suijan's riders would extend that line until it reached the base of the foothills, blocking any chance of escape.

Subutai's warriors thundered into the village. Sargon had expected the Elamites to resist, but there were far fewer soldiers than he anticipated, and only a handful tried to put up a fight. The horsemen, still screaming their war cries, launched arrows at anything that moved.

Standing or fleeing, the Elamites were cut down. Those who could not reach a horse ducked into the houses to hide, but the warriors were already swinging down from their mounts, to search each hut. When they emerged, blood streaked every sword blade.

Sargon ignored the chaos and the screams. He rode straight through the village, halting only when he reached the other side. No more than ten or fifteen Elamites had galloped away, but even as he watched, he saw Suijan's men angling toward them. The desperate Elamites tried to dodge this new threat, but they were far too late. Within moments, Sargon witnessed the last of the fleeing riders riddled with arrows.

Satisfied that no enemy had slipped away, Sargon turned his horse back to the village. Screams now filled the air, not the sounds of men dying in pain, but those of the women. Captured, they would be raped before they found their own release in death. Sargon slipped down from his horse in front of the largest hut in the village. Subutai was there, and three Elamites, their hands tied behind their backs, knelt in the dirt before him.

Glancing at the prisoners, Sargon saw that they were all soldiers. One had taken a shaft in his left arm, another had a large bruise on his forehead.

Fashod and Chinua strode over, both smiling grimly. "Our men are searching the village," Chinua said. "Every body will have a lance thrust into its throat, to make sure they are truly dead."

"Are there any more prisoners?" Subutai glanced around what had once been the center of the village.

"No, Chief Subutai." Fashod gestured toward the kneeling men. "Only these three, and the women."

"Sargon will want to question them," Subutai said. "Chinua, have some of your men help him. Tell our warriors to leave the women alive. They may be of use."

The captured men did not speak the language of the steppes, but they realized that they were being discussed. Sargon saw the fear in their eyes. If they'd been standing, they would have collapsed to their knees. He moved to face them.

"I am Sargon, son of King Eskkar of Akkad. You are my prisoners, and you will answer my questions."

He saw the surprise in their eyes that anyone riding with steppes warriors would speak their language. But for the last few months,

Sargon had studied the Elamite tongue from a captured Elamite trader, snatched up from an ale house late at night, and taken to Annok-sur's farm for interrogation. In exchange for his life, the prisoner promised to teach the Elamite speech to the Akkadians. When he'd finished that task, Annok-sur had sent the man north to the Ur Nammu, to teach Sargon.

Sargon had a good grasp of several languages, and he knew these men understood his words. "You will be separated, and I will question each of you. At least one of you will have a chance to live, as I intend to send a message to King Shirudukh. But anyone that hesitates, or if one of your answers does not match what the other two say, that man will go to the torture."

Sargon gestured toward Garal, standing a few paces away. "The Ur Nammu prefer to let their women torture prisoners, but these warriors know the ways of pain. A pole sharpened at one end will be buried in the earth, and anyone who displeases me will sit on it. The pain will be intense, and it will take you at least a day before you die. Do you understand?"

"Yes, Lord." The oldest of the three, and only one not injured, bowed his head. "I will answer your questions."

"Then I will see." Sargon turned to Garal, and explained what he wanted.

The Elamites were dragged across the open space, until each was at least fifty paces away from one another. A warrior stood behind each of them, a club or stick in his hand, to ensure that answers would be both forthcoming and rapid.

Sargon started with the oldest. The man's name, where he came from, why he went to war, how many men were with him, those easy questions established the pace. When he asked about Modran, the prisoner hesitated the slightest moment. Sargon nodded to the guard standing behind the man. The warrior, using both hands, swung his thick stick, likely part of a tent pole, across the Elamite's back.

The blow knocked the man forward, wrenching a cry of pain from his lips. At first Sargon thought the guard had broken the captive's back. With a grunt, the guard pulled the stunned soldier by his hair back onto his knees.

"There won't be a next time," Sargon remarked. "If I think you're lying, or trying to hide information, you go on the stake. Once your companions hear your screams, they'll be only too glad to tell me what I want to know."

The interrogation took the rest of the afternoon. But before the sun began its descent, Sargon had all the information the prisoners possessed.

Bekka returned, and the clan chiefs gathered around. "The entrance to the Pass is secured," Bekka said. "I ordered twenty riders into the Pass, to go in about three miles, and watch for anyone coming in either direction. If they see only a few riders heading for Zanbil, they'll let them pass. If it's a large force, they'll return as fast as they can ride, to warn us. I've also stationed another twenty right at the entrance. They'll stop anyone who tries to enter."

Suijan spoke next. "I've ringed the village with riders. They'll remain concealed, at least half a mile away, so that anyone trying to come to this place from the south won't see them. No one will get in or out without our knowing it."

Bekka turned to Subutai.

"There were sixty-four men and sixteen women in the village," Subutai said. "We killed them all, except for the three Sargon wanted to question and nine women. None of our men were killed or wounded. The village is full of supplies, including grain and bread. There are ninety head of cattle in the pen, so we have more than enough to feed our men for five or six days. We captured thirty horses. I've everything under guard, until you decide how to dispose of them."

Loot taken in battle belong to the clan leader. He determined how to distribute or destroy the material.

Bekka grunted. "We'll eat our fill. Sargon can choose what to do with the rest."

Eyes went to Sargon. "The three prisoners have told me what they know. Lord Modran's army entered the Pass three days ago, around midday, with somewhere between twenty-eight thousand and thirty-thousand men. At least nine thousand were mounted, but the army travels slowly. Once in the Pass, with its steep hills, they'll be unlikely to make more than fifteen or twenty miles a day."

"Even so, by now they have probably encountered Eskkar's forces. If they sent their cavalry on ahead, they would have found the Akkadians even sooner," Bekka said. "That might cause Modran to pick up the pace."

"Perhaps, but the prisoners said most of the horsemen were at the back of the column," Sargon answered. "Still, even a few scouts might have encountered my father's men by now."

Armies comprised of foot soldiers and cavalry usually marched in two separate columns. In the narrow confines of the Dellen Pass, the soldiers would have led the way, so as to not be constantly stepping and slipping on horse dung.

"Well, that doesn't concern us for now," Bekka said. "Our task is to close the Pass and keep any supplies or men from entering. And that's what we're going to do, for as long as we can."

30

The morning after the battle in the Dellen Pass, Eskkar woke well before the dawn, as did his men. When the sun appeared in the sky, every Akkadian stood ready to repel a new assault. But dawn came and went, and even by midmorning, Eskkar observed no signs of another attack in the making. The Elamites, he decided, must be licking their wounds while they prepared for their next attempt.

Also, with so many men crammed into the narrow confines of the Dellen Pass, even moving a single troop from one position to another obviously required both coordination and time. No doubt Lord Modran wanted to be sure of his men and his plan before the next attack.

Whatever the reason, by midday Eskkar decided that the Elamites would not come against him today. The gods could have sent him no greater gift. Eskkar fed and rested his men, inspected their weapons, and made sure every man remembered his position. Only Shappa's fighters kept busy, using the extra time to chisel and carve more steps and handholds into the cliffs. They widened some ledges as well, to take even more advantage of the cliff walls.

Supplies continued to arrive from Akkad, the exhausted porters dumping their loads as fast as they could. Most appeared too afraid for more than a single glance down the slope at the invaders. After receiving their payment token from the scribes, they turned around and headed for home.

Trella's supply men had prepared enough food and weapons for fifteen days, though no one expected that Modran could stay and fight for so long, even if he were resupplied from Zanbil. But as Trella reminded Eskkar and his commanders, better to have too much on hand than too little.

During the war with Sumer, Eskkar had learned one lesson well. Victories could be won by the side that best maintained its supply lines, and ensured regular deliveries of food, water, and weapons. Trella's efforts, even though she remained behind in Akkad, might do as much to win this battle against Modran as the sword arms of Eskkar's men.

Alexar and Drakis kept a careful watch on the Elamites throughout the day, lest they suddenly launch a surprise attack. The long day faded into dusk, and a new worry emerged. While none of the Akkadians expected a night attack, the possibility existed. Which meant the men would sleep in their formations, weapons at the ready.

After dark, slingers would slip out into the empty space between the two armies, to keep watch on the Elamites. During the day, Eskkar had found time to grab some sleep, knowing that the night would be a long one, and that a major attack might come with the dawn.

The night passed slowly, with many alerts and challenges issued. Men imagined they heard the enemy on the move, or claimed they saw movement in the Pass. But Eskkar trusted Shappa's sentries, skilled in moving through the darkness, to provide plenty of warning.

The first glow from the morning sun again found Eskkar fully accoutered and staring down the slope toward the Elamite position.

"They'll come this morning," Eskkar told Alexar and the other commanders.

"A whole day and a half to prepare, and they still aren't ready to attack." Drakis spat to show his contempt. "The longer they mill around, the weaker their will to fight. They've had plenty of time to think about dying."

Eskkar grunted. The Elamites were brave soldiers accustomed to victory. They would find the strength to hurl themselves against Akkad's soldiers.

"Perhaps you should talk to the men, Captain," Mitrac suggested. "It might help them with their own preparations."

"Yes, I suppose," Eskkar said. He'd meant to do this yesterday, but hadn't had time to prepare.

Nonetheless, he wanted to speak to the Akkadians, to rally them for the next encounter. However, before he did that, he needed some quiet place to think. Although with men coming and going, always asking questions or bringing reports, Eskkar knew he would have little time or private space to compose his mind. Then he thought of the one place where he could arrange his thoughts without distraction.

He summoned his guards, always standing nearby. "Petra, Chandra, come with me."

With Petra and Chandra following a few steps behind, Eskkar strode through the ranks of spearmen and out into the Pass. He continued down the slope until he reached the first of the enemy dead, their bodies already stinking and starting to bloat. Flies crawled over the bodies, into the open mouths and blood-crusted wounds.

As he walked among them, he saw their sightless eyes, their hands raised up and frozen in death, lips drawn back, and their faces surrounded by pools of blood already turned black. All the familiar postures of violent death lay at his feet.

He recalled seeing the same poses after the Battle of Isin, when thousands of dead, dying, and wounded lay scattered across the long battle line. Here the corpses were close together, many piled up two and three deep, where men had died even as they tried to scramble over their fallen companions, either to continue the attack or seek safety.

The dead Elamites had already been stripped of their weapons and valuables, and all the usable arrows recovered by Eskkar's soldiers. The dead always gave all their possessions to the victors. Swords, bows, arrows, knives, shields, anything useful had been carried back to the Akkadian lines. Only the bodies remained, along with the harsh smell of human waste, everything covered with flies.

Eskkar felt no sympathy for the enemy dead. Unlike these men, he had not gone to war seeking loot or glory. Elamites had come into his lands to wrest from Akkad everything and anything they could. Better that they died here than outside Akkad's walls.

And here, in front of the Akkadian battle line and among the Elamite dead, Eskkar could find the privacy he wanted.

Ignoring the flies that buzzed around his head, Eskkar collected his thoughts as he paced back and forth across the killing ground. His soldiers deserved . . . no, needed to know why they had been brought to this place to fight and possibly die. Until now, they'd followed orders without question, proof enough of their trust in Eskkar and his commanders. Today, before the next battle, Eskkar wanted to find the right words.

Petra and Chandra, mystified by their Captain's behavior, trailed behind, probably wondering what thoughts were in his mind. Nevertheless their commander, walking through the enemy dead, found the silence he needed to prepare his words.

For more than a year, Eskkar had studied everything he could about the enemy's tactics. Nothing he had gleaned from the merchants, informers, travelers, and spies suggested the Elamites possessed any exceptional or predominant fighting techniques – they relied primarily on their superior numbers, flanking maneuvers with their cavalry, and a brutal frontal attack driven home by their ruthless commanders. They preferred giving battle when they outnumbered opponents three or four to one, overwhelming any opposition by quick charges and flanking attacks.

Eskkar glanced down the slope, and allowed himself a grim smile as he watched the Elamites push and shove their men into position and ready themselves for another assault. By choosing to fight in the Pass with its high cliff walls, he had eliminated the threat of being encircled or attacked from the side.

As the first skirmish proved, his enemy had never encountered a situation where they couldn't sweep an opponent's flanks. Their greater numbers would prove to be less effective as long as he could match them man-to-man along the battle line.

No, only the direct frontal assault remained for the Elamites, and Eskkar's Akkadians would have to withstand that. He and Trella had done everything they could to provide their soldiers with all the food, water, and weapons needed. Most of these men had trained for this battle for more than a year without knowing why. Now everything would be up to the few lines of infantry and archers that stood between the Elamites and the city of Akkad.

His men had another slight advantage. The enemy troops, made up from so many disparate sources, lacked the training to work together as a cohesive whole. Because Elamite soldiers lived apart and trained separately, each contingent would prefer to see another in the front ranks. After the last encounter, no one would want to lead the attack against Eskkar's position.

That lack of unity and discipline now showed as the enemy jostled about, taking far longer than they should to form up into proper ranks. Akkad, with most of its forces raised and trained near the city, had none of those problems.

All warfare, Esskar understood, relied to some extent on deception. And so Akkad had spread rumors about disagreements in the Land Between the Rivers, its lack of men and resources, and its quarrels between the cities, and their unwillingness to fight. Faced with such situations, the Elamites had assumed an inevitable victory. Instead, they suddenly found themselves committed to battle on Esskar's terms, and not their own.

Those rumors and lies had guided the Elamites for many months, and brought Lord Modran to this place. If he retreated, his campaign would be lost, no matter what happened at Sumer. Nor would he keep his command very long, or even his head, should he return to King Shirudukh without a victory.

Esskar had offered Lord Modran the bait, setting the battle line here in the Dellen Pass. As soon as Modran encountered Akkad's soldiers in the last place he expected them to be, Modran should have turned his army around and retreated back through the Pass. If he'd returned to Zanbil at once, he could have gathered enough shields and supplies, before re-entering the Pass. If he had done that, even if it took a month to reassemble and march back, Modran and his army would likely have prevailed.

Instead, after the encounter of two days ago, Modran now had to press ahead, whatever his casualties. He dared not retreat after such losses. He had to break the Akkadian line, or face King Shirudukh's wrath. Today would decide whether Modran and his men had the will to overcome Akkad's discipline and training.

Midday approached, and Esskar smiled at the enemy's slow preparations for the coming attack. He had expected to fight early this morning, with the sun in his eyes, but the Elamites had taken far longer to arrange their forces, and before long the sun's bright rays would have little effect.

His own men had greeted the dawn in their battle lines, in case Lord Modran's forces chose to attack at first light. Since then, the Akkadians remained at their posts, sitting or standing as they pleased, their weapons strewn about the rocky ground at their feet. Many soldiers moved about, stretching tense muscles, or sharpening their swords. Some of the spearmen, likely to cover their nervousness, stepped into the open space and practiced with their weapons.

Regardless, the Elamites would soon be advancing, and Esskar decided the time had come to talk to his soldiers. He wanted them to know not only what to expect in the coming battle, but more important, the reasons why they fought. And he'd wanted to tell them at the last moment, so that no one could forget his words, or what was at stake – the very life and death of Akkad.

Today was, as Trella had reminded him, one of those special times when he had to address his troops, and give his men a reason to fight. Most soldiers, Esskar knew, fought only as hard as required. No fighter wanted to die attempting to do more than necessary. For this battle, however, Esskar knew his men would have to fight beyond even their own expectations.

His thoughts arranged, Esskar left the field of the dead. Walking briskly, he returned to the Akkadian lines, passing through the infantry and archers until he reached the place where the commanders' horses waited. Esskar swung onto A-tuku's back.

He took a moment to arrange his cloak so that it draped properly over his shoulders. A bronze breastplate, with the image of a desert hawk etched upon its surface, protected his chest. Another plate covered his back, fastened to the breastplate by leather laces over his shoulders and around his waist.

The bronze armor, thick enough to stop an arrow or turn aside a sword stroke, fitted Esskar's tall frame perfectly. Trella had seen to that. Countless sessions with Akkad's best metal workers ensured that the armor hugged Esskar's body without restricting his movements.

Thick leather gauntlets guarded each forearm, from wrist to elbow. Last, Esskar slung his long horse sword across his back, the hilt jutting up over his right shoulder. A bronze helmet completed his armor, but for now, Esskar left it with his guards, letting his long hair frame his face.

Taking his time, Esskar guided A-tuku back through the ranks of cavalry, archers, and infantry. The soldiers moved aside to give the King room to pass. Once past the formation, Esskar let the horse take a few more steps before he guided it around and faced his men.

Silence fell over the ranks. Slowly the shuffling of feet ceased, and every eye turned toward the King. Since Eskkar preferred talking to his soldiers in small groups, his men knew to expect something important.

Eskkar understood that the right words might inspire the men. He also understood that the wrong words might weaken their resolve. More than a few of his soldiers had no fighting experience, and fear would be gnawing at their hearts. To fight against so numerous an adversary took both courage and trust. Words could make a difference.

At such critical times, Eskkar had often struggled to control his nervousness at addressing so many. But now he felt calm, and he knew the words would come without hesitation.

With a final pat on A-tuku's shoulder, Eskkar took a deep breath. From his position at the center of the line, his voice would carry to either side of the Pass.

"Men of Akkad." He looked left and right, and saw that everyone had given him their attention. "Today we fight to save our city, and our lands, from the Elamite invasion. Many of you have wondered why we chose this place to give battle, instead of waiting behind our walls with our friends and families."

"And in the alehouses!" The rude words came from one of the archers, leaning on his bow.

The men laughed, and Eskkar smiled broadly, despite the interruption. This was no crowd of farmers or tavern keepers, sheep to be ordered about in silence, but brave and independent fighters. He had fought and trained with these men, some of them for years, and they had earned the right to speak their minds, even if only in jest. In his turn, Eskkar would tell the truth to them, and they would understand.

"The alehouses will be waiting when we get back home. But to save Akkad, we must first drive these Elamites back down the Pass. Your commanders and I, and Lady Trella, have planned many months for this day. We knew more than a year ago that this invasion was coming. After we took count of our soldiers and our defenses, we realized that, trapped behind Akkad's walls, we could not withstand such a vast army as now faces us."

Eskkar told them about the three-pronged invasion forces now marching into the Land Between the Rivers. "Hathor, with our cavalry, has joined together with Isin and Sumer, to break the siege of Sumer. The Elamite horsemen coming through the Jkarian Pass, will be turned back by Engineer Alcinor and his artisans. However here, we must face the brunt of the Elamites. We are greatly outnumbered, but the narrow width of the Pass ensures that we cannot be flanked, and that the enemy cannot overrun us by sheer numbers."

He let his eyes roam the ranks, and saw no signs of anything more than the usual nervousness that preceded every battle. "Our enemy is unprepared for this fight, while we have trained for nothing else. From Akkad, Lady Trella continues to send us what we need to fight. The Elamites are many, but they have only a few days supply of food and water. Nor will they be able to resupply from their own storehouses. By now, Sargon and a large force of Alur Meriki and Ur Nammu warriors have crossed the northern mountains and fallen upon the Elamite villages and supply lines."

That brought some murmurs from the assembled host. Many had wondered why Sargon was not at his father's side. Others wondered why not even a small force of Ur Nammu warriors had come to fight beside them, as they had done in the war against Sumer.

Eskkar held up his hand to quiet the men. "That means the enemy will fight here only with what they brought, and with each day that we hold them off, they will grow weaker and weaker. Though we Akkadians chose to fight here, we do not fight alone. The cities of Sumer, Isin, and the others in the Land Between the Rivers stand with us, even as we stand with them."

Another cheer broke out, and Eskkar waited a few moments. "So it only remains for us to break the Elamites' will. When they first came into this Pass, they expected us to tremble in fear at the sight of them and their numbers. They thought they could brush us aside without effort. Instead, we killed many and drove them back. Now it is they who know fear. They ran from our arrows and spears, and today they will dread every step they take toward our lines."

He gestured down the slope. "Look at their dead, lying in their path. They will trod on their own kind, and know what fate awaits them. When we break their attack here, when they see that they cannot pass, they will be forced to return to their own lands, desperate for food and water. It will be many years, if ever, before they dare to challenge Akkad's soldiers and the Land Between the Rivers!"

"Akkad! Akkad! Akkad!" The soldiers gave voice to their pride, and this time the shouts continued. Eskkar held up his hand, and at last they grew quiet. "We've won the first battle. But today, each of you must fight not only for yourselves and the man standing beside you, but for all your comrades here. Remember your families back home. If we fail here, your families and friends in Akkad will suffer slavery and death. You must fight with as much strength as if we stood atop the city's walls. You will show these invaders the might of the soldiers of Akkad."

Eskkar drew his sword and raised it high. "And today, I will fight beside you, and the Elamites will break themselves on our shield wall." Eskkar took another deep breath, and then, in his most powerful command voice, bellowed out the challenge. "We will not let the Elamites pass!"

Knowing their King would fight beside them brought a roar of assent that echoed off the cliff walls. The spearmen joined in, striking their thick weapons against their shields, until the noise turned into a savage drumming that elevated the men's shouts to a new crescendo that seemed like it would never cease. The din, amplified by the cliff walls, rolled down the Pass.

Eskkar glanced over his shoulder. He saw the Elamites staring up at the Akkadians, uneasy about this challenge, wondering what it meant, and more than a little nervous about what was to come. "Akkadians! Remember only this – kill the man in front of you! No one, not I, not Akkad, not your companions, will ask more than that!"

Another roar went up. Eskkar turned A-tuku's head and rode up and down the line. "Akkad! Akkad!" He shouted the war cry again and again, and the soldiers repeated the name, louder and louder, until it appeared the very walls of the Pass had joined in the refrain. The sound echoed from the cliffs with such force that it seemed that they would collapse in on them.

Satisfied, Eskkar rode back through the formation. Dismounting, he ordered A-tuku taken to the rear, along with his cloak and long sword. That weapon would be of little use in close combat. The Elamites, now shouting their own war cries, had finally started to move. Esskar pulled his leather-lined bronze helmet over his head, and laced the straps under his chin.

The heavy metal protected most of his forehead, while two long strips of bronze covered his temples, and reached nearly to the bottom of his ears. Belting his shorter sword around his waist, he accepted his shield from Pekka, and moved behind the ranks of the infantry at the center of the line.

It would be the most dangerous position within the formation, the place where the battle line would be most likely to sag, and Esskar wanted the men beside him to be aware of his presence. The Elamites would have to kill Akkad's king if they wanted to break Esskar's spearmen.

All this had been planned earlier with his commanders. Mitrac commanded the archers, and once again he would launch the arrow storm the moment the Elamites drew within range. His bowmen needed no further orders on how to pick their targets, or when to shoot.

Alexar had the left flank, anchored by the rocks and with the slingers above him. Drakis commanded the right flank, with the high cliff walls at his side. Both he and Alexar had support from the picked bowmen on Franar's platforms.

Muta would hold some of his cavalry in reserve, but the rest, with their shorter bows, would fight dismounted, to augment Mitrac's archers at closer range. Muta would also send the reserves into position as needed. Shappa, too, had already received his orders – hold the rocky flank and make certain no Elamites worked their way through the boulders.

Esskar turned his attention to the invaders, on the move at last. Like a flowing river of men, they advanced through the Pass, crossing the low point and then beginning the gradual rise that led, six hundred paces ahead, to the ranks of the Akkadians. Despite their first repulse, the Elamites looked confident enough. They knew they had the advantage in numbers.

The forces of Akkad took up their positions. No shouts of bravado any longer. As they had trained, they readied themselves in silence, the better to hear the orders of their commanders. That very silence, Esskar knew, would unsettle the enemy. He had learned that in the lands of the Elamites, both sides would shout their challenges before the fighting began, each hoping to frighten their opponent.

The invaders started up the slope, the first rank holding their shields to the front, while those behind raised shields overhead to protect against the descending arrows. The Akkadian infantry, too, waited patiently. By now less than four hundred paces separated the two armies.

Eskkar glanced at Mitrac, standing behind his bowmen, bow in his left hand with an arrow already fitted to the string, while his right hand blocked the sun's rays from his eyes. If he saw Eskkar's glance, Mitrac ignored it. When he deemed the enemy was within range, Mitrac would give the command to unleash the arrow storm.

The Elamites increased their pace, gathering momentum and preparing to come to grips with the Akkadians. Then Eskkar heard the enemy battle horn echo up the slope, and with a shout, the mass of Elamites started moving faster and faster.

Nonetheless, Mitrac's clear voice carried up and down the line. "Remember, shaft to the string, string to the ear, and arrow to the mark."

That adage had been part of the men's training for more than ten years. It reminded the archers to make sure they fit the shaft properly to the bowstring, and then fully draw the weapon, so that the arrow would be launched with the maximum force. Eskkar heard many of the bowmen repeating the saying, as if to take strength from their commander's words.

"Draw!" Mitrac's command lifted every bow, the sharp bronze arrow tip pointed halfway to the sky.

Eskkar saw the first rank of Elamites had reached one of the marker stones. Mitrac's lead bowmen had identified three boulders that marked the distances for the archers. The farthest one stood two hundred and fifty paces away. A long shot, but not impossible, given the Akkadians' stronger bows and their advantage of holding the higher ground.

"Loose!"

With a whistling sound, the first flight of arrows rose up into the air. Before most of the shafts had reached their highest point, another sixteen hundred missiles sped toward the Elamites. By the time the first arrows arrived, a third flight had leapt from the bowstrings.

The first wave, launched at extreme range, did little. Eskkar saw just a hundred or so shafts reach the Elamites, and most of those impaled themselves on the enemy's shields. But a few short moments later, the second wave arrived, only a little more ragged than the first. The extra paces the enemy had advanced made a difference, and Eskkar guessed more than a thousand arrows of the second volley had rained down upon the advancing ranks.

As before, many struck the shield wall. But this time a few shafts slipped between or underneath the wooden protection, or struck the third and fourth ranks of the enemy soldiers. The advance slowed a trifle, though it continued on. Even so, the closer the Elamites came, the greater the force that each striking arrow would impart. By now the fall of arrows on the Elamites was continuous, as the more efficient bowmen worked their weapons as quickly as possible.

The enemy, racing up the slope as fast as they could run, slowed as gaps appeared in the front ranks and those immediately behind them. Akkadian arrows continued to fall, striking harder now as the range decreased. At two hundred paces, the Elamite archers, several ranks deep just behind the shield wall, began shooting their own shafts.

But the distance remained yet too great for their smaller bows, and the Elamite bowmen had to expose themselves to use their weapons.

Nevertheless, the Elamites grimly charged on, determined to close with their enemy. At a hundred and fifty paces, the Akkadian cavalry, more than a thousand men fighting on foot, began to arch their own, smaller shafts, up into the sky. With their arrows added into Mitrac's volleys, nearly twenty-five hundred bowmen loosed death on the invaders, a steady stream of missiles that tore into any exposed flesh and added to the toll of dead and wounded.

The Elamite archers in their now ragged formation, trying to aim their shafts on the run, could barely reach the Akkadians. Already the enemy front rank had been torn apart, the shield bearers either dead, wounded, or falling back, leaving the massed archers without protection. Arrows plunged into the throng of men, some enemy soldiers struck two and three times.

The bodies of the dead from the first battle now hampered their advance and threatened to disrupt their formation. New casualties added to the problem, slowing their progress and opening up wider gaps in the Elamite front line.

Arrows continued to fly. Eskkar had no idea of how many shafts Mitrac's archers had launched. Eskkar gazed at his bowmen, saw their thick arms and powerful shoulders working without ceasing, their tall bodies supported by sturdy legs.

Lesser men would have begun to tire, but these Akkadian bowmen had practiced their craft for many long days. They still had plenty of strength to pull each shaft to the ear before releasing, as Mitrac demanded.

In a normal battle, the archers would have emptied their quivers by now, turning themselves into simple swordsmen, with little leather armor to protect them. But replacement shafts continued to arrive, as supply men dashed between the lines, carrying fresh quivers to the grunting archers.

Despite their losses, the Elamites pressed on. Their archers had finally drawn within effective range, and loosed their arrows. Most of the shafts imbedded themselves in the spearmen's shields, but within moments, the enemy arrows extended their reach into the Akkadian bowmen. The Elamite leaders, sensing that their men could close the gap, encouraged the men forward, shouting at them to rush in and kill the Akkadians.

The Elamite advance, slowed somewhat by Mitrac's arrow storm, burst into a run as they began their final charge. However their once-even lines and formations had deteriorated into a ragged mass of infantry, some still carrying shields, but most just waving swords. Now the attackers were less than forty paces away, screaming their war cries.

Eskkar, peering over the top of his shield, noticed them breathing hard, weakened by their rapid advance up the slope. For a few moments, Mitrac's archers continued to pour shafts into the crowd of men coming toward them. But at about twenty five paces, the Akkadians could no longer safely target the enemy front ranks. The bows rose up, and again targets were selected from the rear ranks.

The shouting Elamites, relieved to avoid Akkad's arrows at last, raised their swords and hurled themselves toward the Akkadian shield wall. But before they had closed to within ten paces, Alexar shouted another order, the drum boomed out, and the first two ranks of Akkadian infantry burst into a run, as they charged the oncoming Elamites.

The first line held their spears low, the back part of the shaft gripped tight between the inner arm and chest. The second rank carried their spears in the usual position, the long weapon held level above the shoulder, ready to thrust forward at any target that presented itself.

The Akkadians needed only a step or two to add momentum to their attack, and their long spears ripped into the onrushing Elamites. Sharp spear points burst through shields and bodies, the weapons sometimes passing through a man's belly and into the flesh of a soldier in the second rank.

Caught by surprise at the unexpected counterattack, the invaders hesitated. It didn't matter. The long spears were again thrust forward, impaling the attackers. Even when an infantry man lost his spear, ripped from his grasp by a dying enemy, the Akkadian simply lowered his shoulder behind his shield and drove forward, drawing his sword and wielding it as efficiently as a spear, striking upward with short, savage thrusts. For a few moments, the Akkadians continued the killing.

Nevertheless, the overwhelming numbers of the Elamites halted the charging line of the Akkadians. But before the enemy could overwhelm them, Alexar's drum beat out again, this time with a different rhythm.

The first two ranks of Akkadian spearmen fell back with a rush. They darted and twisted through the third and fourth ranks, who moved forward to take their place. Two more ranks of fresh spears again greeted the invaders. The Akkadians aimed for their enemy's face and upper body, and the screams of the wounded now rose up, as flesh was torn from bone.

Another wave of enemy soldiers went down, the dead bodies often wrenching the spears from the Akkadians' hands.

The savage counterattacks slowed the Elamite advance for a few moments. Then, pushed by the steadily advancing rear ranks, the sheer weight of enemy soldiers shoved the Akkadian spearmen back. All the same, in those few moments the first two ranks of Alexar's infantry had reformed their line, many of the men snatching up new spears from those stocks carried into the Pass by the supply men. Now the third and fourth ranks of Akkadians fell back, dodging between their companions. Then with a crash that echoed off the cliff walls, the two armies came together.

Akkad's spearmen, even faced with such overwhelming numbers, still managed to take a step or two forward before the collision, using the force of their bodies to drive home their long weapons. But after that, the first rank of spearmen had no opportunity to use their spears.

Instead they snatched swords from their scabbards, and flung themselves against their shields, pushing desperately with their feet, trying to keep their footing even as they thrust their blades into the legs, bellies, faces, and shoulders of their attackers.

The deafening din increased, as section by section, the entire Akkadian battle line stretched across the Pass stood against the surging Elamites. For a few moments, the Akkadians, tucked behind their shield wall, had the advantage. The second and third ranks could still use their spears, driving them into the screaming faces of the Elamites. But then, slowly, inexorably, the spearmen were pushed backwards by the greater numbers of their attackers.

Many of the dead Elamites remained upright, unable to fall to the ground while the two armies pressed against each other. Nothing could be heard over screams of the dying and wounded, the roars of men fighting with all their strength, and the clash of arms.

Despite the onslaught, the Akkadians held their formation. But although the Elamites had not trained for such a close-fought encounter, the sheer mass of the attackers made Alexar's infantry take that first step backward.

Eskkar realized the danger. Another pace or two to the rear, and the line would be overwhelmed. Drawing his sword, he rushed to the center of the line, already pushed out of shape. "Chandra, Pekka, Myandro, to me!"

Some Akkadian bowmen, with no good targets at such close range, dropped their weapons, drew their swords, and joined the fray. Many of them flung themselves against the spearmen's backs and pushed with all their strength, everyone straining to halt the enemy's advance.

Most of Mitrac's men, however, kept their bows in hand. Each time the Akkadian line sagged rearward, opening the slightest gap between the two forces, Mitrac's bowmen shot shaft after shaft into the disordered ranks. Meanwhile Muta's archers, from their slightly elevated position, kept shooting at the Elamite rear ranks, trying to slow the assault.

A spearman, struck by two men at the same time, collapsed at Eskkar's feet. Using his shield and bulk, Eskkar hurled himself into the gap, thrusting his sword into a man's face so hard that the enemy's attempt to block the sword failed. Then Eskkar used the pommel on a second Elamite pressed up against his shield. With help from Pekka and Chandra and the other Hawk Clan guards pushing with all their strength, they thrust the Akkadian line back into position.

Mitrac and his most skilled bowmen still plied their weapons, stepping close to the battle line to shoot precisely aimed arrows from distances as short as a pace or two, into the heads of enemy soldiers. One Akkadian shaft grazed Eskkar's helmet before finding its mark.

The battle raged on, everyone shouting and screaming, hacking and grunting, men cursing as they struggled, the sound of sword on shield, or blade on blade making a din that now overcame even the screams of the wounded and dying.

Only the brute strength of Akkad's infantry prevented the Elamites from breaking the line. Pushing with their shields and thrusting with their swords, they piled up the Elamite dead in heaps. The Akkadian spearmen stepped on the corpses and wounded as they wielded their weapons. The line wavered and bent, but it did not break.

Eskkar, as battle-crazed as only a barbarian from the steppes could be, roared his family's war cry as he fought in the front line. One enemy sword thrust was blunted by his breastplate, and a second by the gauntlet on his right arm. But Eskkar turned aside the enemy's strokes, using his shield even as he jabbed with his sword.

While he might no longer have the strength of his youth, Eskkar's height and bulk gave him an advantage. The long years of self-discipline and daily training ensured that he yet possessed plenty of power in his sword arm.

The assault, still in doubt, continued. The longer the fighting raged, the harder the Elamites fought, taking strength from their numbers. Eskkar sensed it, and increased his efforts to drive back the center. But the enemy held their line, and Eskkar felt himself driven back a step. He redoubled his efforts, killing two men in as many strokes, but even that success required another step to the rear.

Then suddenly, some of the pressure against his shield abated. To his surprise, the Elamites slowed their advance. Nevertheless, the outcome remained uncertain. Eskkar saw the enemy soldiers glancing to their right, toward the boulders. Through the din, he heard a new sound – the young and higher pitched voices of Shappa's men. From the heights of the cliff on the Akkadian left flank, slingers and bowmen were hurling their stones or loosing their shafts into the crowded group beneath them.

Eskkar fought on, until those opposing him took a few steps back. Then a group of Muta's fresh reserves surged into the front rank, interposing themselves between the enemy and their King. Their courage and ferocity allowed Eskkar to disengage from the battle line and assess the situation.

Holding his shield to his eyes, he scanned the field of battle from side to side. The left cliff wall and boulders seemed alive with slingers, all of them screaming and launching their missiles into the mass of Elamites below.

Breathing hard, it took a moment before Eskkar grasped the situation. The slingers must have driven back the Elamite soldiers attempting to force their way through the boulders, and now they had turned their weapons against those enemy soldiers assaulting Eskkar's left flank. He saw that the Elamite attack on his left had faltered, and the enemy was moving backward, unused to this type of assault from above.

That meant the center needed to stand firm no matter what. "Hold the line!" Eskkar shouted. "Hold the center!"

He glanced to his right, where the battle line had also sagged rearward. The enemy had drawn even with the fighting platform, leaving it almost exposed. But Drakis, commanding on the right side, now hurled his reserves into the line. Muta, too, surged the rest of his archers forward into the center and the right flank. Another blast of arrows, launched directly into the screaming faces of the enemy, halted the surge and drove them back.

In those few moments, the Akkadian spearmen in the center regrouped their line into its normal deadly formation. Some had snatched up fresh spears, and now they rushed forward, thrusting with their weapons and using their shields, driving back the Elamites on the Akkadian left flank.

Alexar had also managed to regroup his spearmen. Despite the heat of battle, he ordered a counterattack, and his men surged forward against the retreating Elamites. But Alexar quickly saw a better opportunity and halted his men's advance. Instead he bellowed the order that turned them toward the still desperate struggle in the center. With a deep roar, two ranks of Akkadian infantry struck the center of the Elamites.

Eskkar quickly took in the change in tactics. He glanced to his right, and saw Drakis shouting and pushing his men back into

position. The right flank was going to hold. Only the danger to the
center still threatened to break the line. Eskkar raised his sword. "To
me!" His words boomed over his men. Calling out the names of his
guards, he moved back into the line, strengthening the center.

Again Eskkar found himself in the forefront, with men attacking
him from three sides. But an arrow from Mitrac's great war bow
penetrated one man's eye, snapping the man's head back. Eskkar
blocked one thrust with his shield and another with his sword. Then
a Hawk Clan guard thrust a long spear into the belly of the Elamite
on Eskkar's right. Whirling his heavy blade around, Eskkar struck
the forearm of the man pinned against his shield, sending the enemy
soldier to his knees with a nearly severed arm.

A small volley of arrows from Mitrac's archers helped to halt the
Elamites, already reeling from Alexar's charge. The enemy began to
give ground, moving backward. Those who still had shields ducked
behind them, while others just retreated as quickly as they could.

Those few arrows were more than the Elamites could bear. They
had fought bravely enough. But with most of their shields gone, they
didn't have the discipline to smash through the bristling wall of
Akkadian spears. Nor did they have sufficient archers to disrupt their
enemies.

The now ragged advance stopped, and no amount of orders could
drive the Elamites forward again. Too many of their fighters had
ducked behind their own men. They knew it was certain death to
stay in the front ranks.

In twos and threes, they turned and slipped back through the mass
of men who still had not engaged the Akkadians. However small that
first retreat, it quickly spread through the remaining ranks of the
Elamites. The entire forward movement collapsed, as more and more
of the leading elements abandoned the attack and fled, their panic
spreading to those behind them.

Now Mitrac's archers, snatching up their bows once again,
finished the ruin of the assault. They targeted anyone who held his
ground. Individual Elamite commanders and subcommanders, many
still urging their men to resume the fight, died under the onslaught of
arrows, some men struck by four and five shafts.

Once started, no effort by the enemy leaders, those few who
survived, could hold them back. All the Elamites began to retreat,
desperate to get away from the deadly spears, not to mention the

never-ending arrows and stones that seemed to find every gap in their shields or armor.

The enemy, unwilling to face Akkad's reforming shield wall, kept moving backward. Another wave of arrows struck at them, and turned the retreat into a rout. The Elamites broke, lost what little discipline remained, and ran for the rear, ignoring the exhortations of their commanders.

The ground, covered with Elamite dead and wounded, hindered their retreat as much as it had held up their advance. Arrows struck unprotected backs, knocking many of the fleeing men to their knees. The slaughter continued until the Akkadian arrows could no longer reach the disorganized Elamites.

The second Elamite attack had failed.

All the same, the arrow storm that followed the Elamites back down the slope was far less than it had been at the beginning of the attack. Many of the Akkadian archers had dropped their bows to draw swords. Other bowmen had been killed, and some were just too exhausted to fight. Before a man could count to thirty, the Elamites were scrambling out of range.

Eskkar watched the enemy soldiers, once down the slope and out of range, slump to the earth in exhaustion, despair visible in their movements even at that distance. He realized his own arm was shaking, and looked down to find a line of blood dripping from his shoulder. Something, an arrow or a sword, had nicked the upper part of his right arm.

"Bring a bandage for the King," Chandra called out.

Eskkar glanced at his bodyguard, and saw Chandra swaying on his feet, a bloody gash on his left arm. "Where's Pekka?"

Chandra shook his head. "He went down with an arrow in his mouth."

Eskkar grimaced, too tired even to swear at Pekka's demise. A good man who had served his Lord faithfully for many years.

Hamati, one of the lead bowmen, moved to Eskkar's side. "Let me clean your sword, My Lord."

Numbly, Eskkar let Hamati take the weapon from his grasp. Someone handed him a water skin, and Eskkar drank deeply, then splashed water on his face. By then he'd caught his breath.

Alexar and Drakis moved up and down the ranks, steadying their men, and shouting out words of praise for the bravest. Their subcommanders ordered their men, in groups of ten and twenty, back behind the lines to refresh themselves from the water skins.

That water, carried by brute strength up into the Pass from the spring thirty miles distant, now proved its value. The thirsty Akkadians gulped down as much as they could hold, then returned to their positions, permitting another detachment to follow their example.

By the time the sweating men had quenched their thirst, and resupplied themselves with new spears or more arrows, most had recovered their determination. In spite of their losses, the Akkadians had once again driven back the enemy.

Nevertheless, everywhere Eskkar gazed, he saw exhausted men. The archers and spearmen, their arms numb with fatigue, dropped to the ground and tried to catch their breath. The close-in fighting had continued far too long, and hundreds of Akkadians were down, dead or wounded. The Elamites had nearly broken through.

Eskkar watched as men fell to their knees. Others leaned on their swords or spears for support. Those most tired or injured lay prostrate, too weak even to lift their heads. Some of the Akkadian dead lay in mounds two or three high. Alexar's infantry had been forced to tread on the dead and wounded from both sides in order to come to grips with their enemy. Looking down the slope, Eskkar saw even higher piles of enemy dead.

"Get the commanders." Eskkar needed to take a deep breath before he could shout the order. "Clear the battlefield of our dead."

The fight might have ended for now, but much remained before anyone could dare relax. The Elamites could renew the assault at any moment.

However Modran's soldiers had received a brutal mauling, and were in no mood for a second attack. After a careful study of the discouraged Elamites, many still gasping for breath on their knees, Eskkar realized that the fighting had indeed ended for the day. The second battle of the Dellen Pass was over, and his Akkadians still held the Pass.

31

From his perch high on the cliff wall, Shappa had enjoyed a clear view of the approaching Elamites and the defending Akkadians. In the battle of Isin, he'd fought on the level plain, and in the confusion of every battlefield, seen only the massed troops of the enemy horsemen opposing him. Today, however, the incredible sight of the invaders moving up the slope held his attention, until the first flight from Mitrac's archers snapped into the sky.

Never before had Shappa commanded so many men, not even at the Battle of Isin. Once again, the King was relying on Shappa's force of boys and young men to hold back a much larger enemy force. Nevertheless, the piles of boulders and jumble of ledges gave his lightly armed force an advantage.

The enemy, taller and stronger, armed with sword or spear, and burdened by shield or armor would have to clamber over and around those rocks if they wished to come to grips with their foes. And with only one hand free, the danger of slipping and falling would beset the attackers.

Shappa's slingers and bowmen, partially protected by the cliffs, would unleash a storm of stones and arrows at any Elamites attempting to move through the rubble at the base of the cliff. Nor could the attackers simply hold their shields to the front as they crawled over and around the boulders.

Shappa had men stationed at every level, some clinging to their high perches near the top of the cliffs. Projectiles would strike the Elamites from above as well as from the front. And launched from the heights, they would hit home with even more force.

He and his fighters had heard the King's speech. Most of Shappa's men had families and kin in Akkad, and every one of Eskkar's words had struck a chord in their hearts. More important, the slingers trusted King Eskkar. If he declared that the enemy must be fought here and now to protect the city, then here they would fight, to the last man if necessary, to hold back the Elamites.

Shappa turned his gaze back toward the enemy, and studied them as they advanced through the arrow storm. Soon he could pick out his own foes, a block of men carrying shields and bows and heading his way, their faces turned not toward the battle line, but toward the cliff face.

While the enemy would hurl the brunt of his forces at Eskkar's spearmen, Shappa saw that at least two thousand men would attempt to flank the Akkadian line by scrambling through the jumble of rocks and spires where Shappa had placed his men.

When the Elamites reached the start of the boulders, they turned to their right and into the rocks. They intended to force their way through the obstacles and attack Eskkar's rear. While the main thrust of the enemy would fall upon the lines of spearmen, enough enemy fighters to turn the tide of the battle were crawling through the rocks and spires, determined to brush aside Shappa's force of six hundred lightly armed men.

All the same, Shappa and his men were ready. Two hundred were armed with the small bows, smaller even than those carried by the Akkadian cavalry. At long range, the shafts would strike with little force, but close up and in these rocks, at distances of twenty or thirty paces, the arrows would be effective enough.

And for Eskkar's purposes, a wound would be just as good as kill. An injured enemy wouldn't be likely to continue advancing over and around boulders, carrying a shield and his weapons. Fortunately, the supply porters had delivered plenty of the small arrows Shappa's bowmen required.

The rest of Shappa's men carried their slings, two lengths of plaited leather attached to a pouch. And while his slingers might lack the brute strength of Mitrac's archers, Shappa knew his men could whirl the sling and hurl a stone or bronze bullet hard enough to take down a man.

In addition, all his men carried their long, slightly curved knives. These blades, made from the finest bronze and sharpened to a keen edge, were intended to slash an opponent. They could hamstring a charging horse or man with equal ease. Against an enemy armed with shield and sword, if it came to that, Shappa's men would have to rely on their speed and agility, striking quickly and darting away.

Like the rest of Eskkar's army, Shappa's slingers had plenty of water and projectiles for their weapons. They had chosen their places with care, and those on the heights could fight without exposing much of their body. His second in command, Markesh, led the two hundred and fifty men who would meet the Elamites on the ground. Shappa commanded the remaining three hundred and fifty, who would strike from the cliff wall.

The clash of arms filled the Pass with the sounds of battle, as the Elamites finally reached Eskkar's lines. But Shappa only had time for a brief glance in that direction. His own enemy was upon him. He could see them, twisting and climbing their way through the ruins of broken cliff wall and boulders.

"Markesh!" Shappa cupped to hand to his mouth, to make sure his words carried to the men below. "They're coming!"

Markesh lifted his head, and waved acknowledgement.

Shappa saw the men below preparing themselves for the onslaught. His own men needed no warning. Heads peering from behind their protective rocks and boulders, they could see the Elamites for themselves. The slingers now waited for Shappa's command.

He dropped a bronze ball into his sling's pouch, then took one more look at his men. They were ready enough. Shappa moved to the side of the boulder that sheltered him, and flung the bullet toward the enemy.

"Now! Target the bowmen. Kill them all!" Shappa's voice broke at the last word, but his men understood well enough.

A hail of stones from above and arrows struck the Elamites scrambling toward Eskkar's flank. Many missed their mark, the missiles clattering or shattering against the boulders. When the bullets impacted a hard surface dead on, a puff of dust marked the spot.

A competent slinger could launch ten or twelve stones in the time a man could count to sixty, and much faster than most men could work a bow. Those men using slings exposed little of themselves as they worked their weapons, while the bowmen had to stand more in the open to aim and loose their shafts.

The savagery of the attack caught the Elamites by surprise. Their swords were useless until they could close with their enemy. Most raised their shields to protect themselves from the deluge of missiles. Shappa heard the Elamite soldiers shouting for their archers to kill the slingers and stop the barrage.

But the enemy bowmen, while more potent with their weapons, found it difficult to use them on the uneven ground, or even from behind the shelter of the boulders. Any Elamite who dared to show himself drew the attention of every slinger and archer above them.

While the slingers clinging to their perches kept the enemy bowmen from loosing their shafts at those on the rocks walls, the Akkadians at the base of the cliff prevented any of their foes from advancing. Leaning out from behind a boulder to loose a shaft, or stepping into the open for the briefest moment to hurl a stone, the devastating projectiles of Shappa's men halted the Elamite advance.

Shappa heard little of the brutal fighting the Akkadian spearmen engaged in. He concentrated his attention on the cramped battlefield below him. When he could, he shouted orders to his men, telling them again and again to target anyone who appeared to give orders, or those brave enough to lead the way through the rocks.

Most of the time, however, Shappa couldn't make himself heard above the battle din. Arrows soon broke against the rocks all around him. The Elamites, too, had picked out the man giving orders and tried to bring Shappa down.

But his men, well trained and quick as cats on their feet, needed little direction. Anyone who moved was targeted, the stones raining down from the slingers even faster than those of Shappa's archers.

Though a flung stone usually needed to strike an opponent's head to be immediately fatal, a hit to any part of the body brought plenty of pain, and slowed the soldier's movement. And a bullet shattering a shin or elbow, cracking a rib, or reaching a man's groin, put an enemy out of the fight almost as well as a head shot.

The enemy wounded added to the confusion. Instead of remaining in place, many of them tried to retreat, which only slowed the Elamites still struggling forward. Even so, no matter how fast Shappa's men rained death down on their enemies, the sheer number of Elamite bowmen finally came into play.

Shappa saw his own companions toppling from the cliffs, to fall twenty or thirty paces to the jumbled rocks below. Nevertheless, those enemy soldiers who worked their bows or lifted their shields left themselves exposed to Markesh's men. Arrows struck the bellies and thighs of the Elamite soldiers. For a time, they continued to fight, exchanging shafts with Shappa's men, but that, too, stopped.

At last, the advance halted. The enemy foot soldiers huddled behind any shelter they could find, any boulder large enough to protect themselves, until they could scramble away from the deadly cliffs. Hunched over, they fled back over the obstacles that had slowed them down and left them vulnerable to the rain of death from above. Their dead and wounded lay scattered behind them, many hanging face down from the boulders.

At first Shappa's men cheered at the enemy retreat, but then Shappa heard the sound of the battle raging below, as Eskkar's spearmen were locked in deadly embrace with the flood of advancing Elamites. For a moment, Shappa stared open mouthed at the sight. Men struggled face to face, killing and thrusting, screaming and shouting. He saw Alexar's infantry line, the Akkadian left flank, start to sag, and realized with horror that the Elamites would soon break the thin line of Akkadian spearmen.

"Markesh! Markesh! Target the enemy! We have to slow their attack!"

His subcommander glanced up, a grin on his face. Shappa gestured to the main battle line. It took Markesh only a moment to grasp the situation. Shappa turned to his slingers and started shouting orders, but they had already seen what needed to be done.

They raced nimbly over the rocks until they reached positions where they could attack the Elamite main force. Soon stones and projectiles hurled through the air, aimed high, and targeting the enemy soldiers just behind the front line. The rain of bronze bullets and small arrows, coming from the rocks, caught the Elamites by surprise.

Even at a distance, the missiles carried death and injury. With so many men jammed shoulder to shoulder, nearly every stone or shaft struck some part of an enemy's body.

The Elamites tried to lift their shields, but found them pressed tight against the back of the soldiers in front of them. Some managed to wrench their shields loose and raise them up, but they provided little protection.

In moments, thousands of bronze bullets from Shappa's nearly six hundred fighters had been hurled into the mass of Elamites. The unexpected attack from above unnerved the enemy. They slowed their advance and tried to step back, away from the hail of death.

Shappa, dropping stones into his pouch and hurling them with all his strength, saw the attack weaken on Eskkar's left flank. The slight reprieve enabled the Akkadians on the battle line to recover. With a shout, Alexar's spearmen, reinforced by the archers and Muta's men, drove the Elamites backward.

Once the movement to the rear began, the entire line was affected. Elamites in the center glanced to their right, and saw their comrades retreating. The enemy soldiers in the front ranks couldn't see just how precarious the Akkadian position had become. Even those who had fought their way nearly through Alexar's men started to retreat, fearful that the stones would soon rain down upon them.

Now the middle ranks of Elamites, despite being out of range and untouched by the slingers, also started to move to the rear. With the pressure of Eskkar's left flank eased, the Akkadian bowmen plied their weapons, aiming into the center of the invaders.

The attack faltered, and in the space of a few moments, thoughts of retreat swept over the Elamite front line. And once they started moving back down the slope, nothing could stop the frightened men, not the commands of their leaders or even the large number of Elamites still uninvolved in the fight.

Shappa and his men kept hurling stones for as long as they could, until the enemy moved out of range. Exhausted, Shappa slumped to the ground, breathing hard. His right arm, despite its powerful muscles, trembled. The sound of his men cheering lifted his head. The enemy was in retreat, and once again, Shappa and his force of slingers had done their part.

Midafternoon came before Eskkar could sit down with his commanders. The battle gods had spared all of his senior men from death, though several had taken wounds. By the time they assembled to take stock, the Akkadian battle line had been cleared of its dead, the wounded moved to the rear, and fresh stocks of arrows and spears distributed to the men.

The slingers had scrambled all over the battlefield, recovering their precious bronze bullets and smooth stones. Their efforts to support the left flank had nearly consumed their supply of projectiles.

"How many spearmen did we lose?" Eskkar directed the question at Alexar.

"Close to a thousand dead, or wounded and unable to fight." Alexar had a thick bandage wrapped around his right thigh, and blood spatter covered his tunic.

Eskkar turned to Mitrac. "How many?"

"Seven hundred and sixty," Mitrac said. He too, had blood on his head. An arrow had brushed his ear, ripping through the fleshy part, and a red tendril still dripped down onto his tunic. "Muta lost another hundred and sixty."

"Shappa?"

"One hundred and twenty dead or wounded, Captain," Shappa said. "Most of those died when we moved out onto the ledges to turn our weapons on the main force of Elamites. We were exposed to the Elamite bowmen."

The number of dead slingers would have been much higher, if Mitrac's archers had not decimated their Elamite counterparts. "Your men turned the tide, Shappa," Eskkar said. "I think the Elamites were about to overrun us."

Eskkar turned to the scribe seated on the ground just behind him. "How many dead is that?"

"Two thousand, one hundred, My Lord."

Eskkar forced his mind to consider the toll. Almost a third of his army was dead or unable to fight. A devastating number, and there would be more fighting. "And the enemy losses?"

"Our men are still counting and collecting weapons, My Lord," Zerla said, "but it seems that we killed at least six thousand." The senior clerk had to clear his voice. "We wounded who knows how many more."

The number of wounded in a battle usually equaled the number killed, Eskkar knew. "How many men do the Elamites have left?"

The scribe glanced down at his slate. "At least three thousand dead or wounded in the first assault, and another eight or nine thousand today . . . the enemy likely has at least eighteen thousand men able to fight."

The Elamites had endured a second bloody defeat, but they had nearly broken through. Only the quick thinking of Shappa and his men's bravery had turned the tide today. When the Elamites returned, they would have archers ready to sweep the ledges, and probably an even larger force of men determined to push their way through the rocks.

No one spoke. The numbers told their own story. They all knew Modran still had more than enough men to break through the Akkadians' defenses. With so many dead or wounded, the remaining Akkadians would not be able to withstand another frontal attack.

"We need to delay them," Eskkar said, "weaken them before their next assault." He turned to Shappa. "Take two hundred of your men and harass the enemy tonight. Just fling stones at them from the darkness, anything to keep them off guard and disturb their sleep. We need to delay the next onslaught. Every day we can hold them makes them weaker. They're already short of food and water, and if they don't receive new supplies, soon they'll be too weak to fight."

Alexar's men had found several wounded Elamites unable to flee. A quick interrogation had confirmed the lack of food, and even more important, water.

"If they get resupplied . . . and now they have less mouths to feed . . ." Alexar let the words trail off.

"We'll have to assume Sargon can cut their supply line," Eskkar said. "That may take a few more days. Resupplied or not, we have to hold them. Whatever water they had will be gone by tonight. I don't think they can mount more than one final attack, not after taking such losses."

After a battle, a choking thirst fell upon every fighter. Even Eskkar's men had nearly emptied the vast number of water skins to quench their thirst. Nevertheless, water skins continued to arrive, carried by Trella's porters from the spring at the mouth of the Pass.

"Let's hope they don't come again tomorrow," Drakis said. "We could use another day of rest."

"That's what Shappa's night raid is for, to convince them to wait another day." Eskkar looked at each of his commanders. Their faces were grim, but he saw no signs of men ready to give up. They understood that they could never make it back to Akkad without leaving the infantry and slingers behind, and no one would suggest that cowardly action.

Eskkar knew he needed something bold and unexpected if Akkad were to defeat the Elamites. His men could not withstand another such attack. The two battles had given him some ideas, but he still lacked the missing piece, the part of the plan that would offer the best opportunity for victory. "Is there anything else we can do?"

"Let's send the prisoner back with a message to all the Elamites," Alexar said.

They still had the captured horseman Eskkar had questioned when he first arrived at the Pass.

"What message?"

Alexar laughed, a grim sound with little mirth. "We tell them truth, that Akkad cannot be defeated, that King Eskkar has never lost a battle, and that our most powerful gods have promised us victory."

Everyone chuckled at the idea.

"No, I mean it," Alexar insisted. "We march him down the slope, with twenty or thirty of Mitrac's archers behind him. They stay back, just out of range, and send him close enough to be heard, and make sure he repeats the message. That way, everyone in the front ranks will hear his words."

"Will anyone believe him?" Drakis didn't sound convinced.

"Most of the time, men believe what they want to believe," Eskkar said. "Many of Modran's soldiers are hungry and exhausted. They've seen their companions struck down. By now they have doubts about this campaign and their leaders. Yes, only some will believe the words, but all will remember them when they next march into battle."

"And if he doesn't deliver the message properly, we riddle him with arrows," Mitrac finished.

"Do it," Eskkar said, "send him back just before sundown." It might not count for much, but it couldn't hurt. "Any other suggestions?"

No one spoke. Eskkar grimaced, but before he could offer his own suggestions, Muta spoke.

"I have an idea." Muta hadn't lost many men in the fight, and hadn't said much during the discussion. He had emerged unscathed from today's fighting.

Enslaved by the nomads who lived in the western desert, Muta had received his freedom with Akkad's help and risen to be second in command of all the Akkadian cavalry. "By now, the Elamite soldiers and commanders are convinced they can overwhelm us. They'll attack based on what they saw today. Suppose we give them something different from what they expect?"

Eskkar and the others leaned closer, everyone eager to hear some new battle plan. "Tell us, Muta, what else can we do?"

Muta took a deep breath. "They won't be expecting a cavalry attack. Charging downhill, we could break their line."

"Charging over the enemy dead and into their front line, I think you'd lose most of your men," Alexar countered. "You might disrupt them for a time, but you can't attack such a mass of men on horseback."

"If the Elamites break our line, we'll lose most of our men away, trying to cover the retreat."

Eskkar rocked back on his heels, no longer listening to his commanders' words. Muta had provided the missing initiative for which Eskkar had sought. Now the parts fell into place in rapid succession.

He looked up, and saw everyone staring at him. Eskkar smiled. "Muta has given me an idea. I think there is a way after all for our cavalry to break the Elamites. Or at least part of them."

Speaking carefully, Eskkar sketched out his bold, even desperate, plan. One by one, his commanders added their ideas, suggesting improvements, until every head nodded in agreement.

Eskkar turned to Shappa. "Once again, you and your men will have to buy us the time we need."

Drakis laughed. "It will be like Isin. Slingers and boys too small to swing a sword or lift a spear will decide the battle."

Shappa ignored the rough compliment. "We can do it, Captain. We'll hold the line as long as you need."

"Then let's get moving," Eskkar said. "We've all got plenty to do before dawn."

32

Midafternoon arrived before Lord Modran, teeth clenched and a grim look on his face, finally met with all his commanders. Less than half of them had survived, and Modran's soldiers still licked their wounds. Two battles in four days, and nothing to show for it, except thousands killed and even more wounded.

The dead bodies festered everywhere, and the unceasing cries of the wounded grated on Modran's ears, though the sounds grew steadily weaker, as thirst and loss of blood took their toll. He ordered his commanders not to waste any food or water on anyone who couldn't fight.

Meanwhile, flocks of carrion birds, attracted by the smell of blood and decomposing flesh, circled their way raucously through the air, their mocking cries seemingly directed at Lord Modran.

After the retreat, the discouraged soldiers had moved to the rear, pushing and shoving, cursing at their leaders. Modran's soldiers had scattered all over the Pass, and now many were unable to find, let alone regroup, into their proper units.

And when they did locate their companions, the troops involved in the fighting swore that they would not face the Akkadians in the front ranks again. After this attack, every Elamite soldier knew how slim the odds were of surviving in the first battle line, even in a victory.

Modran heard the bitter words, but didn't bother to berate his men. He knew about soldiers' anger after a retreat, and today's debacle stood far above a mere movement to the rear. His soldiers understood, perhaps better than their commanders, that lives had been wasted.

Thousands of men dead, and after all that blood, the Akkadians still blocked the Pass. Today's rough count of the dead and badly wounded had reached over seven thousand. After eliminating the numbers of the siege men, porters, livery men, and other non-fighters, Modran had just over seventeen thousand men able to fight.

Nevertheless, by the time General Martiya had taken the count of the dead and wounded and collected his subcommanders, Lord Modran had regained control of his anger at today's disaster. Now his surviving unit commanders stood together, shoulder to shoulder, each blaming in a loud voice someone else, mostly the dead commanders, for the failure to breach the line.

Martiya, too, had given vent to his own frustration. "We were breaking them. Their center was ready to collapse. But a few boys with slings drove back our men from beneath the cliff, and we lost our chance."

One of the subcommanders, his right hand shattered by a slinger's stone, voiced his thoughts. "Those were not boys, and they threw so many stones at us that . . ."

"Stones, arrows, spears," Modran shouted, "no one retreats until the order is given." He glared at the soldier until he lowered his eyes, no doubt wishing his commanding general had taken a stone to the head.

"We should have attacked again," Martiya said. "The Akkadians were ready to break. Another assault would have overwhelmed them. Instead we're likely to waste the rest of the day collecting the men and moving them back into position."

"There's still time," Modran said. "We will wait until dark, then move our men up, and launch a night attack. In the darkness their bowmen won't be able to pick and choose their targets. We should get close enough to rush them." He turned to Martiya. "Can we do it?"

"Mmm, a night attack, it's not a bad idea." Martiya rubbed the scratch on his face. "They won't be expecting an assault after dark. We could form a column, and instead of trying to hit the entire line at once, we strike at a single point of their position, say their right flank. That would keep our men away from the slingers, who need the height of the cliffs to be any threat. By the time the Akkadians shifted enough men over to stop us, we could break through and overrun them by sheer numbers. Once behind the line, we can slaughter them all."

Modran hadn't considered attacking at a single point, but the idea sounded workable. A column of a hundred men abreast, with fifty men lined up behind each soldier in the front rank, would be unstoppable at night. Even the Akkadians couldn't kill so many fast enough. It would be easier to organize and move the soldiers in a column, rather than trying to keep a line the width of the Pass intact and moving forward in unison.

"We could feint attacks at their center and left flank," Modran said, thinking out loud. "By the time they realized we were concentrating on their right flank, the bulk of our forces would be on top of them."

"Who would lead the attack?" Martiya's question wasn't an idle one. Whatever contingent spearheaded the assault would take heavy causalities even if it broke Eskkar's line.

Modran wanted to send the remnants of General Jedidia's men to the front again, but he didn't trust them. Any setback, no matter how small, would have them running once more to the rear. "We'll have to use the Immortals. I don't trust any of the others."

The number of Immortals under Lord Modran's command numbered exactly two thousand men. Whenever one of them fell in battle, he was replaced by another handpicked fighter from the city of Anshan. Proven in many battles, they considered themselves the best of the Elamite army, and rightly so.

No enemy had ever withstood their attack. The Immortals were proud fighters, and their pride would not let them suffer a defeat. Personally loyal to King Shirudukh, for this campaign he had assigned them to Lord Modran.

Modran's private guards were selected from the best of the Immortals. So far, the entire force had been held in reserve. Modran hadn't been willing to see them decimated by Akkad's archers, especially so far from Akkad's walls. This situation, however, called for desperate measures.

"We can count on the Immortals to continue the assault, no matter what," Martiya agreed. "With them leading the way, the others will follow."

"Then it's settled." Modran took a deep breath, and stared up the Pass. Nearly a mile away, he could make out the Akkadians. A line of men still stood across the Pass, waiting. His own soldiers, slumped to the ground, showed despair and defeat with every movement.

"As soon as it's too dark for the Akkadians to see, we'll move the Immortals up. We'll have five thousand men behind them. Use the rest of the cowards to convince the Akkadians we're attacking them head-on once again."

Martiya nodded. "If we start our preparations as soon as darkness falls, we should be ready by midnight, or a little later. Have you received word from Zanbil? Are more supplies on the way?"

Modran had not heard from the first messengers he'd dispatched to Zanbil, and their failure to return added to his rage. He'd ordered one of them to report back at once, as soon as they delivered his message. That man should have returned two days ago. Zanbil had plenty of supplies by now, with more arriving each day from the south. Modran needed those supplies, needed them now. He'd made sure that his messengers understood the urgency of his demands.

The second group of messengers, twenty in number, also should have reached Zanbil by noon today. That meant that large quantities of supplies must already be on their way. Nevertheless, he could not wait much longer. Already his men were eating the dead horses, and with no firewood for cooking, gagging on the raw meat.

Even if the food arrived late, Modran knew it would help restore his men's confidence and strength. More important, the hundreds of water skins he'd demanded would keep his army fighting. Once they broke Eskkar's ranks, all the Akkadian food and water supplies would be theirs.

"No, I've heard nothing from Zanbil," Lord Modran said. "The first messengers and supplies should have returned by now."

"Well, it doesn't matter," Martiya said. "We've got to attack soon. Otherwise our soldiers will be too weak from hunger and dry from thirst to fight well. We have to go tonight."

Modran nodded, his jaw clenched. It had come to that. With his vast army, he now had only this one chance to beat the Akkadians. "Make sure the men know what's at stake. If they want to quench their thirst, they have to break Eskkar's line. He's got plenty of food and water."

"Yes, damn him." Martiya spat on the ground. "He's still getting supplies from Akkad. By the gods, how did he ever manage to accomplish that?" Martiya smacked his fist into his palm. "Food and arrows, and water, too, most of it carried by farmers and tradesmen."

That no longer mattered either, Modran knew. "For tonight's attack, make sure every man knows his battle position. Tell them to get some rest, but make sure there are no delays forming up and preparing for the assault."

"There won't be," Martiya said. "Still, I'd feel better if I knew more supplies were coming."

Their situation had indeed turned desperate. But Modran had more serious stakes at risk. If he failed to defeat Eskkar's men, King Shirudukh would almost certainly have Modran's head on a spear. All Shirudukh would need to hear was that thirty thousand soldiers, including a force of Immortals, could not brush aside less than ten thousand. Trivial details about the narrow confines of the Pass, or lack of food and water, would not mitigate the King's wrath.

No, Modran had no intention of returning to Elam with that message. Even if the King let him live, Modran would be forced to beg for his life at Chaiyanar and Jedidia's feet, removed from his command, his wealth confiscated, his men dispersed. Modran would watch while Chaiyanar and Jedidia reaped the rewards of the invasion. By now Sumer would be ready to fall, and Jedidia was no doubt wreaking havoc in the empty lands north of Akkad. If he met no resistance, he, too, might decide to ride for Akkad.

Those thoughts stiffened Modran's determination. He'd overwhelm Eskkar's lines if he had to sacrifice every man in his army to do it.

"Break Eskkar's line, Martiya," Modran said. "Break their line, and we'll be at Akkad's gates in five days."

"We will." Without waiting to be dismissed, Martiya spun on his heel and walked away, his fists clenched in anger.

Modran ignored the slight from his second in command. Instead he turned his gaze on the rest of his sullen commanders. "You know what's at stake, and what you need to do. Any man that falters will be put to the sword. The Immortals will lead the way to victory."

One by one, heads nodded in approval. The Akkadians, forced to defend the entire width of the Dellen Pass, no longer had enough men to resist a concentrated attack on their right flank. They, too, must have taken heavy losses in today's battle. Thoughts of victory took root in every Elamite commander. The darkness of night, and the strength of the Immortals, would break the Akkadians' position.

As soon as it grew too dark to see, Shappa ordered his slingers to move out. Once again, Markesh led the way through the darkness, crawling on his hands and knees for the first hundred paces. Two hundred and sixty slingers followed behind him.

None of them carried bows. Even in the dimmest moonlight, a bow's silhouette was too distinct, too noticeable. For tonight's attack, slings were the preferred weapon. Nearly silent, they could be used from a crouching position.

Each slinger carried twenty-five bronze bullets. Markesh hadn't wanted any extra weight of projectiles to slow down his men. Without the extra missiles, they could move easier and faster through the darkness.

The Elamites, as they had done each night, established a strong perimeter across the width of the Pass, to give plenty of warning should the Akkadians attempt a night attack. But the line of enemy sentries stood only a hundred paces in front of their main force. Obviously, the Elamites had discounted the idea that the numerically inferior Akkadians might try to attack a much larger force, even at night.

So far, neither side had tried to use the darkness of night for an assault. Moving heavily armed men across a broken field littered with dead carcasses everywhere sounded foolhardy. The noise from any such attempt would be easily heard.

Nor did soldiers like the idea of fighting at night. Everyone knew that after dark demons rose from their secret pits to wander the earth, eager to snatch men's souls from their bodies and carry them to the bowels of the earth. Dying at night or lying wounded in battle left the victim's body and spirit even more likely to be taken.

The Akkadian slingers, however, had trained so often at night that such fears had no effect on Shappa's men. After years of training, not a single slinger had fallen victim to a demon, and Markesh doubted tonight's raid would be any different. After all, the demons had feasted on the dead and wounded Elamites for many days.

Markesh traveled slowly. He would have liked to stay on his hands and knees, but the distance to the enemy camp was too far for that, so he and his force moved at a crouch. He stopped often to rest and listen for any sounds from the Elamites. But he heard nothing out of the ordinary, just the usual noise from the enemy camp, a background of talk and men stumbling about in the darkness.

There were very few campfires, of course, not since the first night after the two armies had faced each other. What little wood remained, probably from broken shields, went to the fires of the Elamite leaders. He could see the glow from those much farther back behind the Elamite front line.

By the time Markesh had traveled to within two hundred paces of the enemy sentries, the moon had risen high into the night sky. No challenge had greeted them, and every time he looked toward the Elamite camp, he saw nothing out of the ordinary.

Now he stood nearly upright, and studied the enemy camp. Nothing had changed, nothing moved . . . something had changed. The handful of remote campfires, tiny beacons of light, now shifted and flickered. For long moments, they even disappeared.

Puzzled, Markesh stared at the distant fires, while his impatient men bunched up behind him. The campfires couldn't be seen from Eskkar's battle line, except as a vague glow on the rocks. But here, closer to the enemy, Markesh could make out the unusual flames as they flickered from red to dark.

"What is it?" Eletti, his second in command, whispered the words in Markesh's ear. "Why are we stopping?"

Suddenly Markesh understood the odd flickering. Men, large numbers of men, were passing in front of the low flames. And large formations of Elamites moving about in the darkness meant only one thing – the Elamites were readying a night attack.

Markesh gripped Eletti's shoulder. "Get back to our lines as quick as you can. Find Eskkar first, and tell him I think the Elamites are preparing for a night attack. Go!"

"But what . . ."

"Just go, and don't stop for anything. Run!" He pushed Eletti toward the rear, then turned to his men, dim shadows crouching on the ground. "Spread out and start moving. We need to get rid of those sentries and launch our attack the instant we're in position!"

The Elamite sentries, one hundred men, saw nothing in the shadowy land between the two forces. They kept their eyes up the slope, where the Akkadian battle line remained dark and silent.

Many of the guards swung their gaze toward their own camp, watching the shifting mass of soldiers. None paid any attention to the ground close to their own lines.

Rumors had swept the camp of a night raid even before the leaders of fifty and twenty received their orders from Modran's subcommanders. Those stories had gained strength when the men glimpsed the Immortals moving about. By now even the sentries could see the haughty Immortals and other detachments move into position.

The first stone struck one of the sentries full in the chest, knocking the breath from his body and breaking two ribs. The injured man gasped at the sharp pain, but softly, and only the guard to his right turned toward the noise. The movement saved his life, as a second stone glanced off the side of his head. Falling to his knees, he called out, giving warning before another missile knocked the breath from his body.

A third man cried out, while a fourth sentry, struck in the head, died instantly. Before the rest of the sentries realized what was happening, more than six hundred missiles had been hurled at their line. Men dropped, hit by the unseen projectiles. Others shouted from the pain or broke into curses.

Some yet unscathed, watched in disbelief as their companions fell. Then they turned and raced back toward the main body, voicing the alarm as they ran. In moments, half the sentries were dead or down, and the rest fleeing to the rear.

Markesh ordered his men forward. Crouched over, he led the way, counting his strides as he went. When he reached fifty, he dropped to the ground. The enemy camp was less than seventy paces ahead. Markesh dropped a stone into the sling's pouch, and hurled it toward the Elamite camp.

On either side of their leader, the other slingers moved into a rough line and followed Markesh's example. A swarm of bronze bullets flew through the night.

No orders were given, and none were needed. The men knew what to do – spread confusion within the enemy's camp.

General Martiya, still moving his force of Immortals to the front, heard the exclamations and shouts of his men. Soldiers cried out that they were being attacked, that the Akkadians were assaulting the line. Everywhere men fumbled for their weapons and shields. The bowmen strung their bows and readied their shafts, but no one had a target. If men were moving out beyond the sentry line, Martiya couldn't see or hear them.

"Form up!" Martiya's bellow brought the first semblance of order to his men. "Hold the line!"

Arrows flew out into the darkness, most aimed at nothing. Martiya reached the front ranks as the men lined up, ready to meet an attack. He saw one man drop to the ground, and even in the dim moonlight Martiya glimpsed the bronze bullet that struck the man's head. Only then did he understand that a force of those cursed slingers was out there, causing confusion in the Elamite vanguard, and not a full-fledged attack by Eskkar's soldiers.

Meanwhile, the rain of bronze projectiles continued, striking men at random, many of the missiles landing twenty or thirty paces to Martiya's rear. Then, just as suddenly as it began, the missiles ceased coming. By that time the Elamites were launching arrows into the night, shooting at shadows that seemed to flit from one place to another.

But Markesh and his men were already gone, still crouched over and scrambling back toward the safety of the Akkadian battle line. Behind them, they left a camp in confusion, full of dead and wounded. His two hundred and sixty men had flung over six thousand bullets at the Elamites, more than enough to wreak havoc on the enemy camp for a time.

The moon revealed that midnight had passed before General Martiya regained control of his men. Without even waiting for Modran's permission, he had canceled the order for the Immortals to launch their attack. The slingers' raid, like the sting of a thousand bees, had shaken the entire camp. Any chance of launching a surprise attack on the Akkadians had vanished.

Modran, his face red with fury, screamed at Martiya. "How dare you cancel the order to attack! The men were in position. They would have . . ."

"They would have been cut to shreds. Every Akkadian would have been on his feet and in position for an attack. The Immortals would have been slaughtered."

Modran, speechless for the first time in his life, glared at his commander. "But we were almost ready."

"If the slingers were close enough to fling their stones, they were close enough to see the Immortals forming up on one side of the Pass. They probably sent word even before they began their attack."

"Is there any way to try again?" Modran's voice now held an almost pleading tone. "There's still plenty of time before dawn."

Martiya had soldiered for too many years, and knew better than to argue with an enraged superior. But now was not the time for polite acquiescence. "The Akkadian attack accomplished little. It killed just over a hundred men, though many more were injured, My Lord. But it succeeded in accomplishing what Eskkar must have intended. It rattled the men's nerves. If we had started to move out into the darkness, even a single stone from a slinger would have panicked the men. And since the traitor delivered his message, some of the men are convinced the gods themselves oppose us. They're muttering that we should turn back, return to Elam."

Modran ground his teeth in frustration. The Akkadians had forced a captured Elamite cavalryman to shout a message loud enough to be heard by most of the front ranks. By the time anyone thought to put an arrow into him, the poisonous words had taken hold. Now many remembered and repeated the stories about Eskkar, that he'd never lost a battle, and that the gods protected him and his city.

"We can try again tomorrow night," Modran said. We can have our men out in advance. We can . . ."

"By tomorrow night, we won't have a drop of water in the camp, My Lord. Unless some supplies arrive from Zanbil, we'll be too weak to launch another assault."

The mention of Zanbil renewed Lord Modran's rage. The first pack train bringing fresh water and food was already two days late. Tomorrow, however, should bring a large number of supplies.

"The supplies will be here tomorrow," Modran insisted, "or by the gods, I'll put every man in Zanbil to the torture.

"If we wait for them, and they don't arrive, by sundown we'll be too weak to fight. That means we have to attack at dawn, and go with everything we have. Damn the losses. If only a hundred men survive to stand over Eskkar's corpse, that will be enough."

"The night attack would have succeeded," Modran said.

"Yes, I think it would," Martiya said. "But the chance for any more night attacks from either army is gone now."

"You know what's at stake, Martiya? You understand what failure means?"

"Shirudukh will probably have both our heads. Better to lose the entire army than return without destroying the Akkadians."

Modran swore in frustration. Eskkar had confounded them once again, probably without even knowing what he'd done. "We'll use some of the Immortals to drive the rest of the rabble forward. Our men are more afraid of them than they are of the Akkadians."

"One last assault," Martiya agreed. "If we lose, we'll be on our knees begging King Shirudukh for our lives. If we live through the fight."

After Eletti had carried back the first warning, Eskkar and his commanders had formed up the men and readied themselves for an immediate attack. But as soon as Markesh returned, Eskkar and his commanders, along with Shappa, heard the full story from Markesh, including everything he'd seen about the confusion in the Elamite camp.

Alexar and Drakis shifted extra men to the right flank and warned everyone to stay alert.

Meanwhile, fifty of Shappa's men were once again out in no man's land, acting as sentries. When the Elamites decided to come, Eskkar's men would have plenty of warning.

"I should have realized the Elamites would try to avoid the cliffs and Shappa's slingers in their next attack," Eskkar said. "They were probably planning to drive a wedge through our lines, and then take us from the rear."

He turned to Shappa. "Without Markesh's raid, they probably would have caught us by surprise. We might have been overwhelmed. That makes twice you've saved the battle, Shappa, and you, too, Markesh."

Everyone congratulated the two slingers, slapping them on the back. By now the whole camp knew what had happened, and stood ready for the next attack.

"They probably won't come tonight," Alexar said. "But we'll have to keep the men at their post."

Eskkar agreed. "It will be long and sleepless night for our men, and probably a hard fight in the morning."

"And then it will be over," Drakis said.

"Yes," Eskkar said. "One way or another, it will be over."

33

Six hundred miles to the southwest . . .

On the same day that Eskkar and Lord Modran's armies faced each other in the Dellen Pass for the second time, Hathor and King Naxos of Isin sat on their horses and surveyed the Elamite cavalry moving toward them. Midday had come and gone, as the Akkadian leaders watched the Elamite horse fighters, close to seven thousand strong.

"They ride well," Hathor commented.

"Plenty of open plains east of the Zagros Mountains," Naxos said. "I'm sure they've learned how to ride down helpless villagers."

A wide stream, one of the many branches of the Tigris, separated the two forces. By now the enemy knew better than to try and force their away across a stream before they had their full strength prepared for the effort. For three days, the Akkadians had led the pursuing Elamites all over the lands to the northwest of Sumer, keeping just out of their reach.

Yesterday, however, Hathor had turned the troop toward the east again, as if returning to the countryside well north of Sumer. In the afternoon, the hard-riding Elamite vanguard had caught up with the rear guard of the Akkadians. That led to a brisk skirmish that accomplished nothing, except for fifty or so dead on either side. The encounter provided a grim warning to both armies – the final battle, whenever it occurred, would likely prove a deadly affair.

As the chase progressed, the Akkadians continued to move eastward. Farther northeast lay Akkad. No doubt the Elamites assumed the Akkadians rode toward the safety of Akkad's walls. But such was not Hathor's plan.

Both sides had grown weary, galloping more than thirty miles each day, always at the alert for a counterattack or ambush. Those worries added to the stress on both armies. Regardless, Naxos and Hathor had one big advantage that, hopefully, the Elamites knew nothing about.

Twice, well after darkness had fallen, the Akkadians had met up with Yavtar's fighting boats. Upon leaving Sumer after the surprise attack, Hathor's messengers had raced across the land and made contact with one of Yavtar's boat captains. Once alerted to the location of the cavalry, Yavtar's crews began the first of their own and very dangerous missions.

The day following the capture of the Horse Depot, eight boats had found the Akkadians after dark, delivering grain, food, and extra arrows to the cavalry. Two nights later, another group of seven boats had delivered much the same cargo before pushing off and vanishing into the mist that hovered over the black water.

Now, after three and a half days of hard riding, the Akkadians and Elamites studied each other across the stream.

"They'll cross soon enough." Naxos shaded his eyes with his hand as he stared at the Elamites. "They're feeling more confident every day, watching us run from them."

"We won't be running much longer." Hathor had developed this part of the plan himself. "It's nearly time to set the trap."

Naxos snorted. "Let's hope they take the bait. We'll be fighting for our lives if this plan you and Eskkar cooked up goes wrong."

Hathor couldn't hide his grin. After the successful trip through the foothills, followed by the attack on Sumer, Naxos had grudgingly conceded that Eskkar knew something about both warfare and tactics. Nevertheless, Naxos always found something to grumble about.

"Nothing in battle is certain, Naxos. But Eskkar's idea has worked for him before, and there's no reason to think it won't work again. Unless you have a better plan to defeat seven thousand Elamites without losing half of our men?"

"No, not yet." Naxos's cheerful tone took the sting out of the words. "For now, we play our part, running from these Elamite dogs as if we're afraid to face them. I still don't like it."

Nevertheless, Naxos gave the order, and the Akkadian cavalry, close to five thousand riders, moved out, once again heading east.

Hathor glanced at the midday sun, high in the cloudless sky. The hottest part of the afternoon still awaited the sweating men and horses. For the first time in three days, Hathor ordered the men to ride at a slightly slower pace. The Elamite cavalry, after they finished crossing the stream, would be less than half a day's ride behind their Akkadian foes.

The Elamites had gradually closed the gap between the two forces, thanks to their fresher horses. Hathor's mounts had been carrying the weight of their riders for more than a month. The Elamite cavalry leader, Simaski – reputed to be yet one more of King Shirudukh's cousins – would be expecting to catch up with the Akkadians well before sundown tomorrow.

For this part of the plan, Hathor had taken charge, as Naxos agreed that the Akkadians had trained more often for this type of attack. The speed of the march, the direction they traveled, even the rest periods had to be calculated precisely. Hathor wanted to reach a certain campground just before dusk, and he wanted the Elamites, too, to make camp at another particular location.

By now the enemy had enough renegade guides in their service to provide all the information Simaski needed about the countryside between Sumer and Akkad. Hathor counted on those guides to suggest the best place for the Elamites to make their own camp tonight. The choice should be an easy one, with the presence of a small stream that promised plenty of water for the thirsty and tired enemy horsemen and their mounts.

The sun had already touched the horizon when Hathor's force reached the camping place he had chosen nearly a year ago, along the banks of another, wider branch of the Tigris. The water presented a more difficult crossing, and one that the Akkadians would not want to risk in the growing darkness.

The weary men dismounted, then tended to their animals, making sure they drank plenty of water. The last of the grain was distributed, and the horses enjoyed the unusual bounty to go along with the thick grass that grew beside the riverbank. The men, too, ate well, finishing up the last of the supplies delivered only last night by Yavtar's boatmen.

With the enemy so close behind, Hathor posted a strong guard around his camp, just in case the Elamite scouts, who were keeping the Akkadians in sight, were tempted to raid the Akkadian encampment. Tonight of all nights, that must not happen.

Spread out along the riverbank, Hathor's men unrolled their blankets and dropped to the earth, to get as much sleep as possible.

For Hathor and Naxos, however, there would be little rest tonight. Just after dark, Hathor sent out a scouting party of his own, under the command of a veteran soldier named Asina, with special orders.

Twenty men had left the camp, pacing their horses in the dim light of the half moon. Asina and his men were to ride one mile back toward the Elamite scouts, dismount, leave their horses behind, and proceed on foot. If the enemy outriders remained true to their habit, they would have camped for the night about three miles away.

But before they bedded down, they would dispatch one or two riders to return to the main force and report on the Akkadian position. At least that was what the Elamites had done for the last three nights.

Hathor wanted all those scouts killed, down to the last man. Asina, one of Hathor's best men, had orders to ensure no one escaped, and that no message of warning was sent back to the main Elamite camp.

Simaski's camp, if the Elamite commander had stopped where Hathor expected, would be about ten miles behind their scouts. Hathor's plan called for a long night of traveling on foot. Each man would lead his horse and carry nothing but his weapons and a small skin of water, most of that intended for the horse.

Hathor and Naxos gathered their commanders and explained the plan. None of the leaders expressed surprise. They had trained often enough for a night march, and expected that one would happen sooner or later. The horsemen, after a few groans at the thought of the long walk in the dark followed by a sharp fight, prepared themselves and their mounts, then went to sleep.

Well before midnight, Hathor gave the order that set the cavalry in motion. The weary soldiers woke, rubbed the sleep from their eyes, and collected their weapons and horses. The night march began.

The Akkadians traversed the mostly level terrain, sprinkled liberally with tall grass, at a good pace. The landscape allowed the cavalry to spread out over a wide front. Hathor's Akkadian horsemen led the way, since they had trained for many months riding and walking after dark.

For all the men, the walk was a hard one. Each man had to remain alert and careful of his footing. No one wanted to risk a horse stumbling into some hole in the ground.

Three miles to the west, Hathor met up with Asina and his scouts.

"There were eight men, Lord Hathor. We killed them all. Only one of our men was slain."

"You're sure none got away?"

Even in the darkness, Hathor saw Asina's flashing teeth.

"I counted the horses before we rushed them. Only eight horses. None of them escaped as well."

Hathor grunted in relief. "Good. Send those horses to the rear. I don't want any of them trotting back to the Elamite camp ahead of us and alerting the enemy. Then rejoin your men, get your horses, and scout on ahead. We've still a long way to go."

Hathor caught up with Naxos, walking with some of the men from Isin, and gave him the news.

"I hate this walking. My feet already hurt."

Hathor laughed softly. "No horse fighter likes walking, which is why the Elamites won't be expecting us to double back. They believe we wouldn't dare to ride in the darkness."

"Will we get there in time?"

Hathor glanced up at the moon. Thin clouds crossed the tiny orb, dimming the already feeble light. "Yes, we should be there well before dawn. And we'll have the sun at our backs."

"You say Eskkar came up with this idea? Something from his past?"

"That's what he said. He convinced me it could be done. We started training, and once the horses got used to traveling after dark, it worked out pretty well. We lost a horse here and there, but that was a small price to pay to move a cavalry force ten to fifteen miles at night."

In the last month before the ride south through the mountains, Naxos, too, had trained his men in the same technique, walking and guiding a horse at night. But the men from Isin did not have as much experience, and so Naxos agreed to let the Akkadians lead the way.

The landscape they were crossing made the journey easier. The level ground and soft earth sprouted only the occasional clump of sand grass. Hathor had trained his men on far more difficult ground.

Nevertheless, Hathor heard some of his men complaining as they walked. They hadn't gotten enough sleep to fully refresh themselves. By the time they reached the Elamite camp, they would be even more weary. Still, Hathor had no doubt that they'd be able to fight. Months of hard training had inured the men to such hardships.

The steady strides of men and horses ate up the distance. As they walked, Hathor kept track of the moon's descent, but the army's progress kept pace.

The darkness of night had not yet started to fade when Hathor for the second time made contact with his scout, waiting patiently along the line of the march. Once again, Asina's teeth gleamed in the darkness.

"The enemy is less than a mile ahead, Lord Hathor," Asina said. "They're on the far side of the stream, with only a few guards posted. We should be able to close within a quarter of a mile before they hear us. The stream's water makes a good bit of noise, and it should help mask our approach."

"Well done, Asina," Hathor said. "Stay with me, so you can guide our men directly to the enemy's position."

"Should we give the men some rest?" Naxos had remained close, to hear any reports as soon as they came in.

Hathor took another glance at the stars above. "No, I don't think so. It will take too long to stop the men, and then get them going again. Better to just keep moving. But we'll pass the word to the men to slow down a bit. And remind them to keep quiet."

Hathor considered the last stretch of the long night's march the most dangerous. They had to get close enough without being seen, or more likely, heard. If the Elamites heard them coming, they would react fast enough, finding their horses and preparing their weapons. Hathor needed to catch them before they could mount up and ready themselves for battle.

The long line of men, still stretching over a front a quarter mile wide, continued its slow progress. Hathor jumped at every clink of sword and every grunt or soft whinny the horses made, expecting the alarm to sound. But the enemy cavalry remained unaware of Hathor's approach, and the distance slowly closed.

"There!" Asina clutched Hathor's arm. "You can see the stream."

It took a moment before Hathor glimpsed the thin ribbon of water, glistening faintly in the dim moonlight. Behind it, he saw a darker mass of men who covered the ground.

"Keep moving," Hathor hissed. "And keep those horses quiet!"

For the first time, Hathor wished he'd brought some slingers with him. They might have been able to slip up on the sentries, and kill a few of them.

Suddenly Hathor could make out the herd of horses, held in rope corrals behind the sleeping men. The Elamites had placed their mounts as far away from the stream as they could, so that the water wouldn't be fouled by the animals. The stream itself would appear to provide a barrier in the event an enemy tried to raid their horses.

Glancing up at the sky, Hathor saw that in the east, the deep blackness of the night had softened into grayness. Already some of the Elamites would be waking from their slumber.

By now only three or four hundred paces separated the Akkadians from the stream, and yet no alarm had sounded. He again glanced behind him, and saw the first faint shade of pink appearing at the horizon. The carefully contrived plan of maneuver and countermarch had brought the Akkadians to the precise place they wanted, and they had arrived just before dawn.

A shout from the Elamite camp floated out over the stream, but Hathor no longer cared. He swung up onto his mount, and his bellow carried to the far ends of the Akkadian line. Tired, weary, and footsore, his men had finished the march with only a few moments to spare. Now all they had to do was fight and win. Otherwise they were going to be slaughtered.

"Mount up! Attack! Attack!"

In moments the ground thundered under the horses' hooves. Leading the way were the six hundred Akkadian horsemen who could use a bow from the back of a galloping horse. The first ragged volley of arrows flew into the air, aimed at the frantic crowd of half-awake men scrambling to their feet.

But the second volley, and by far the most important, flew not at the Elamite soldiers, but arched up into the sky, to rain down upon the horse herds that were just beyond the men.

The densely packed horses, already skittish from the shouts and the hoof beats of the Akkadians' charging animals, panicked as the shafts dropped down from the sky, wounding hundreds of beasts. They broke away from the charging front line of Hathor's riders, tearing asunder the flimsy rope corrals. Once started, the stampede quickly spread to the rest of the Elamite mounts.

By then the first of the Akkadians were splashing across the stream. Hathor and his riders knew the water flowed little more than ankle high, barely enough to slow their galloping horses. With their war cries bellowing over the camp, Hathor's cavalry tore into the disorganized Elamites.

Caught unprepared, unable to reach their horses, the Elamite cavalry, tough enough when mounted, was no match for the charging Akkadians. Once in among the enemy, Hathor's men used their swords to slash or dismember the panic-stricken Elamites, hacking at everything that moved while shouting Akkad and Isin's war cries.

The rising sun, now providing more than enough light to distinguish friend from foe, sent its first rays over a savage fight that quickly turned into a slaughter. Swinging their bloody swords again and again, the Akkadians rode their way through the camp. Many of the enemy were struck down from behind, or tumbled to the earth by Hathor's warhorses. Others crashed to the earth from the slicing blows that opened the flesh to the bone or knocked a fleeing man to the ground.

Hathor ranged along the widening front, directing his fighters, many of whom still had their bows, to turn their weapons on any knot of men trying to resist. The arrows flew into the unarmored men, most of whom had barely managed to find their swords, let alone their leather jerkins.

Naxos, roaring like a demon from the pits, led a contingent of Isin riders that charged right through the enemy ranks and into the open space where the Elamite horses had been corralled. Isin's King turned around, and struck again. This time he and his men attacked the thickest bulk of the enemy, and cut them to pieces.

Though the Akkadians were outnumbered at the start of the attack, the dismounted Elamites could do little. Only on their right flank, bypassed by the Akkadians, did enough enemy soldiers manage to find their weapons. Even so, most ran for their horses, desperate to mount up, either to fight or flee.

The sun climbed higher above the horizon, and still the killing continued, as blood-crazed Akkadians unleashed their rage upon their enemy. Naxos had his warhorse killed under him, but one of his personal guards managed to find another for the King. Naxos continued his attacks, challenging any group of Elamites that caught his eye.

At last Hathor realized his men had overwhelmed the Elamites, and now they searched for any enemy left alive. Shouting with all his breath, he managed to collect a few hundred riders to his side. Asina added another fifty or so, and Hathor ordered him to take command of the men and start rounding up the scattered horses.

When Asina galloped out of the camp, Hathor continued assembling his men. Now the groans of the wounded and dying men sounded over the blood-soaked campsite. The screams and cries of the injured horses, some driven mad from the pain, amplified the noise.

When Hathor finally glanced at the sky, he saw the bright blue sky of a new day. Waving his sword high, he called out for his commanders. One by one they gathered to his side, some still shouting in their excitement, others angry at being recalled from the slaughter. The battle, if such it could be called, had ended.

Across the grasslands, small bands of Akkadians still pursued their enemy, cutting them down as they ran. At last even these satisfied their blood lust and returned to the camp, horse and rider equally exhausted. Naxos, his killing rage finally subsided, joined Hathor at what remained of the center of the camp.

Isin's King clapped Hathor on his shoulder. "What a fight! We killed them all. Killed them all! And I got Simaski!"

"By Ra, that is good news!" Hathor meant every word. "Are you sure it was him?"

"Yes, Simaski was trying to rally his men, but one of my soldiers hamstrung his horse and the crazed beast threw its rider. Before Simaski could find another mount, we were on him. I put my sword right into his back!"

"Well done, Naxos! That should keep the Elamites from regrouping."

"We killed all of them," Naxos repeated, unable to control his excitement.

Hathor grinned and clapped him on the shoulder. "Not all of them, but enough. Now we must take stock."

For the rest of the morning, the men counted the dead and dying, finishing off those Elamites still alive. Horses, too, were rounded up and driven back toward the camp, but this time to a site five hundred paces from the killing ground.

Just before noon Hathor and Naxos sat facing each other on stools that must have belonged to the Elamite Simaski. After washing off most of the blood splatter in the stream, the two leaders received the reports of the commanders, who had taken count of the battle. Almost forty-two hundred Elamites dead, and the rest, a good number of them wounded, had scattered in every direction. Many had tossed aside their swords and weapons to run all the faster.

"I can't believe how many we killed," Naxos said, "against such a small number of our own men lost."

"I saw the same thing happen in Egypt, and even at the Battle of the Stream, where Eskkar broke the Alur Meriki. A hard and unexpected strike, and panic overtakes your enemy. Look how many Elamite sandals we found. They never had time to lace them on."

"And swords and horses, too," Naxos said.

The number of captured horses reached almost three thousand, with another few hundred dead animals littering the battlefield. Less than four hundred Akkadians had lost their lives or taken wounds.

As the last of the tally was added up, Hathor turned to Naxos. "You have won a great victory, King Naxos. The Elamites who survive, even if they manage to find a horse, are broken men."

"Tomorrow we'll start hunting them down," Naxos declared.

"If I may suggest, King Naxos, that may be left to one of your commanders. You and I, and at least four thousand riders, have a more important target to strike. Sumer awaits us. If we can get there before Chaiyanar learns of his cavalry's defeat, we can strike another heavy blow to his army."

Naxos took in a deep breath. "I suppose that's what Eskkar would do."

Hathor shook his head. "It's what you would do, too, once the battle rage left your blood. And after today, you need not compare yourself to Eskkar. As your friend, and his, too, I say no man ever fought harder or killed more men by his own hand than King Naxos of Isin."

"It has been many years, Hathor of Egypt, since I have called any man my friend. But you have helped me win this victory, and the glory is as much yours as mine."

"We've ridden side-by-side for many days," Hathor said, "and fought together. Even if we were defeated, I would still call you 'friend.'"

For a moment, Naxos seemed at a loss for words. "I suppose you'll want to ride to Sumer at once."

"The men and horses need some rest. Tell each of the men to pick an extra mount from those we captured. But by midafternoon, we ride for Sumer."

Grand Commander Chaiyanar surveyed the walls of Sumer from beneath the shade of his awning, which kept the late morning sun away from his chair. The city still resisted his efforts, but since the raid by the Akkadian cavalry, he'd driven his men ruthlessly. His subcommanders and foremen, a length of rope in their hands, strode among the men sweating at their tasks, administering the lash on anyone not working to his utmost.

Each day, the line of trenches drew closer to the walls. Chaiyanar's men, protected from arrows by tables, planks, logs, fresh hides, even piles of sand, anything that would stop an arrow, moved ever nearer.

Yesterday he'd launched his first all out assault, flinging three thousand men, backed by a thousand archers, against the northeast section of Sumer. For a few moments Chaiyanar thought his men would carry the city. A handful of brave soldiers actually surmounted the wall, but the defenders had somehow rallied and hurled back the attackers.

The Elamites wasted over a thousand men killed or wounded in the attempt, but the Sumerians had suffered heavily as well. Even so, never had Chaiyanar lost so many men before in a single assault, and a failed one at that.

Chaiyanar ignored the casualties. He remained determined to overwhelm the defenders as soon as possible, no matter what the cost. Once inside the city, his men could hold it against any remaining Akkadian forces. Ships from Elam could resupply him, until the last of Eskkar's fighters died under Lord Modran's attacks.

Each day he received reports from his cavalry, busy pursuing the Akkadian horsemen as they fled to the north. His cavalry commander, Simaski, had maintained close contact with the enemy horsemen, by now at least two days ride away from Sumer.

Today Chaiyanar didn't care whether his own men caught up with Eskkar's cavalry or not. All that mattered was keeping the Akkadian cavalry away from Sumer long enough for the Elamites to breech the walls and storm the city. Once Chaiyanar's men were within the walls, the Akkadian horsemen would be no threat.

The last report Chaiyanar received had been two nights ago, and Simaski declared that he expected to come to grips with the Akkadians the next day. No messengers had arrived yesterday, but that might mean a battle had been fought. Today's news, he felt certain, would describe that encounter.

He had no doubt about his horsemen. Tough fighters, they would match up with Eskkar's cavalry man for man. The two thousand man advantage the Elamites possessed would guarantee a brutal battle. No matter who won, the Akkadian horsemen would be eliminated as a fighting force and a threat to the siege of Sumer.

By the end of today, the cavalry battle between Simaski and the Akkadians would be of no importance. Once Chaiyanar captured the city, his men would man the defenses. Already his diggers and soldiers had moved the trenches to within a hundred and fifty paces of the wall. At midafternoon, Chaiyanar intended to launch two fresh attacks, one again at the northeastern section of the wall and Sumer's main gate, and the other at the south side.

The completed trenches ensured that his men had only a short distance to cover to reach the base of the city's walls. During the assault, his bowmen would sweep most of the defenders from their position. This time Chaiyanar expected to overcome any resistance.

Once in control of the city, he would kill every soldier, every able bodied man left alive. No matter how many of his men died in the attempt, he intended to capture Sumer today, before night fell. His commanders had already learned the price they would pay for any failure – they would be executed.

He sipped from his wine cup, as he watched his men's progress. Yes, today would be the day.

From Sumer's wall, Jarud and King Gemama observed the same progress. They kept their expressions under control, not wanting to send any discouraging signals to their men. But both knew another attack appeared imminent.

Yesterday's onslaught had nearly taken the city. Almost five hundred irreplaceable defenders, archers and fighting men, had died holding off the Elamites. Many leaders of ten and twenty had died as well. Neither the King nor his Captain of the Guard felt certain they could hold off another assault.

"When will they come?" King Gemama's voice held more than a trace of resignation.

"No later than midafternoon." Jarud's flat voice showed no emotion, even though his favorite nephew, Jaruman, had taken an arrow in the eye during yesterday's fighting. Having no son of his own, Jarud had raised the boy when his brother died, treating Jaruman as if he were his own son. "The Elamites will try to get as close as they can before they rush us. But they'll want enough daylight remaining to finish off any resistance."

"We can move all of our men to this section," Gemama said. "We should be able to drive them back."

"Today they'll attack in at least two key places, perhaps three," Jarud said. "We'll move men around, but we may not have enough soldiers to stop two or three attacks at the same time. Chaiyanar's commanders will be probing other spots as well. If they see any sections unguarded, they'll attack those points, too."

"What can we do?" The King sounded resigned.

"We fight. Better to die fighting than be slaughtered like cattle, or turned into slaves. Besides we're . . ."

"Gemama! Aren't you going to welcome me to your city?"

Jarud and Gemama turned to see Yavtar on the rampart, striding toward them, a big grin on his face.

Astonished at Yavtar's presence, Gemama forgot his dignity and threw his arms around his old friend. "Yavtar! How did you get here? Did you . . ."

"My boat just docked. Your men were kind enough to open the river gate for me. I was nearby, and thought I'd pay you a visit." Yavtar nodded to Jarud. "I'm glad to see you're both alive."

"Perhaps not for long, Master Trader," Jarud said, though he, too, had a smile on his face. Stories about Yavtar appearing here and vanishing there abounded. Many thought the wily boat master had sold his spirit to the river demons, who transported him wherever he wished in the dead of night. All the same, Eskkar's Master of Boats, never went anywhere by chance. "The Elamites are readying another assault."

"Well, you'll have to hold them off a little longer," Yavtar said. "I didn't risk coming here in daylight just so I could pick up a sword. And I don't intend to be taken prisoner."

"You should leave as soon as you can, Yavtar," Gemama said. "You may not get another chance."

Yavtar chuckled. "Too late, my friend. By now my boat has already unloaded its supplies and departed for the north."

"Then you're trapped here with us," Gemama said, a sigh of sadness escaping his lips.

The Akkadian trader glanced out over the wall. "I see that Chaiyanar is readying his men for another attack. That's good."

"Good? Are you mad? We barely drove them back yesterday." Gemama's high pitched voice broke at the end.

"So what news do you bring, Master Trader?" Unlike Sumer's King, Jarud's voice held no emotion.

"Well, it seems Chaiyanar hasn't yet learned that his cavalry has suffered a great defeat two days ago. Those of Simaski's forces who survived are scattered to the northwest. Meanwhile, Hathor and Naxos are on their way here."

"What's happened?" Jarud grasped Yavtar's shoulder. "Is the Elamite cavalry destroyed?"

Yavtar shrugged. "Hard to say for sure, but definitely dispersed and defeated, according to Hathor. Apparently he and Naxos surprised the Elamites, caught them still asleep at sunrise the day before yesterday. Naxos claims they slaughtered more than half the enemy, captured most of their horses, and broke the rest."

"Are you certain they're coming here?" Gemama couldn't keep the excitement from his voice. "Can they get here in time?"

"Well, that's what the bloodthirsty Naxos said last night. He said they would be riding at dawn, and should be here sometime after midday. He and Hathor wanted you to be well prepared. So I took ship just before midnight. We sailed throughout the night, and now I'm here to watch the battle. Hopefully Hathor's cavalry will arrive in time."

Near Sumer, the wide span of the Tigris meant that boats could move without interference from troops on shore. A fast-moving boat driven by ten or twelve strong rowers could navigate the river by day or night with equal ease.

During daylight hours the vessels stayed in the center of the channel, safely away from the reach of the Elamites. That ability let them far outrange cavalry, which needed to stop and rest the horses.

Jarud gripped the grinning Yavtar by his arms. "By the gods, that's what we needed to hear!" He turned to Gemama. "I'll spread the word to our men. Knowing that help is on the way will make them fight harder. We'll hold out until Hathor arrives. Meanwhile, I think we'll prepare a few surprises for the Elamites."

"Before you rush off, I've brought you some reinforcements." Yavtar turned and gestured to a man standing a few paces away. He wore a bow slung across his back and a fat quiver of arrows hung from his hip. "This is Sabatu. He's been trying to get here for the last few days, but his boat ran aground and he had to turn back. He's here to fight against Chaiyanar."

"King Gemama, Lord Jarud." Sabatu stepped forward and bowed low at the introduction.

"Sabatu knows how to command men," Yavtar offered, putting his hand on Sabatu's shoulder. "I promise you, he knows how to use that bow. If you need someone to help lead the fight, you can rely on him."

"Every man is doubly welcome." King Gemama's voice carried his appreciation.

"My nephew was killed yesterday," Jarud said. "He commanded twenty archers at the main point of attack. More than half his men died or took wounds. They could use someone to lead them who can use a bow."

"Then I place myself in your service, Lord Jarud." Sabatu nodded to Yavtar. "Again, my thanks to you for getting me here."

"Come with me, Sabatu. We've got work to do." Jarud dashed off, racing down the steps and calling for his subcommanders, Sabatu trailing behind.

"Yavtar, you've saved us all." Gemama took a deep breath. "I thought I'd be dead by nightfall. But what of Eskkar and Akkad? Do you have any news?"

"Not much. Two days ago I learned Engineer Alcinor managed to close the Jkarian Pass, so that should keep the Elamites out of the northern territories for a while longer. Other than that – by now Eskkar and Lord Modran are probably locked in battle in the Dellen Pass."

Both men knew that if Akkad fell, sooner or later, Sumer and Isin would be taken as well.

Yavtar again glanced over the wall, taking his time to study the enemy's positions. "Not many guards to the north, and less than a thousand cavalry riding patrol, I'd guess. Most of those well south of Sumer and the rest dispersed." He shook his head. "You think Chaiyanar would have learned his lesson. It's his Elamites who are about to be caught between your walls and Hathor's cavalry."

"I pray to the gods that Hathor's men aren't held up," Gemama declared.

"I thought you didn't believe in the gods."

"Today, Yavtar, today I believe in all of them, even the most foolish. I've sworn an oath to sacrifice an entire goat to each and every one."

"I didn't think you had a whole herd of goats in the city."

"I'll buy twenty from the first goat herder who comes back to Sumer." He took a deep breath and let it out. "May we all live through the rest of the day."

"If we do," Yavtar said, "I'll sacrifice a goat, too. Only one, though."

34

Inside the City of Sumer . . .

Sabatu had participated in two sieges in his lifetime, and in both instances the armies of Elam had overwhelmed the hapless defenders in less than ten days. He recalled the confusion behind the walls during those assaults, but that was as nothing compared to the noise and turmoil he now experienced within Sumer's walls. Fearful men and women wandered around, crowding the lanes. Children dashed about, babies cried, and the occasional dog barked, all adding to the tension in the air.

Following his new commander, Sabatu trailed behind Jarud, the Captain of Sumer's Guard and the man in charge of the city's defenses. Jarud ignored the chaos, barreling his way through the throngs, shouting orders as he went. Sabatu, trying to keep pace, had nearly tumbled down the steep steps that led from the battlement to the ground, and then almost lost Jarud in the crowd. By the time they reached the main gate, Jarud had collected two subcommanders, who jogged alongside. Sabatu found himself breathing hard.

The commander of the gate, his left arm in a sling, stood on a small platform before Sumer's main entrance. Two young boys, perhaps ten or eleven seasons, stood beside him. Both had red strips of cloth wound around an arm – official messengers.

"Bila!" Jarud shouted even before he reached the injured man's side, "all of you! We just received word that Hathor and Naxos have defeated Chaiyanar's cavalry and are on their way to Sumer. They'll be here before sundown. We'll have to hold off the Elamites when they attack until the Akkadians arrive. Then we'll break the siege and finish off Chaiyanar!"

The cloud of gloom that hung over the men's faces vanished at the news. Bila, the commander of the main gate's defense, appeared stunned. "Are you sure, Captain Jarud? How did you find out?"

"Yavtar brought a boat in. This man," Jarud jabbed his finger at Sabatu, "arrived with him. Tell them what message Yavtar carried."

"It's true," Sabatu said. "The Elamite cavalry under Simaski was defeated and scattered two mornings ago, about ninety miles to the northwest. Lord Hathor and King Naxos – he killed Simaski himself – are on their way here. Yavtar and I met up with them last night. They . . ."

"That's enough, Sabatu." Jarud had no interest in hearing the details. "You can tell them the rest later. Bila, you'll have to hold the gate until Naxos and Hathor arrive no matter what. And I want your men prepared for a sortie. If we move fast enough, we may be able to catch Chaiyanar between our forces."

Jarud spun on his heel and started off, then realized he'd forgotten Sabatu. "Bila, put Sabatu in charge of Jaruman's men." Then he was gone, vanishing into the swarm of people hanging about. A few started to cheer at the news.

"All right, get our men ready," Bila ordered, speaking to the two subcommanders Jarud had brought with him. "Sabatu, come with me. I'll give you your men and show you where to stand. I hope you can use that bow."

Bila's expression as he took in Sabatu's hands revealed his doubts. But following orders, Bila led Sabatu up the steps beside the main gate, to the left side of the parapet. "Here's your new commander." Bila turned and rushed back down the steps.

Sabatu found himself facing eleven men, all of them slumped against the parapet. A few had wounds wrapped with dirty bandages spotted with blood. They looked weary, and they stared at their new commander with indifferent eyes. Sabatu took a deep breath. He recognized all the signs of lax discipline. Well, he'd dealt with that before.

"On your feet, all of you."

No one moved. One man shrugged. "We'll get up when the Elamites come."

Sabatu smiled. There wasn't much room atop the parapet, but he took a single step closer. At the same time he whipped the bow from his back, and using plenty of muscle, rammed it into the man's stomach.

A regular bow might have snapped from such a thrust, but the hard wood and extra width of Sabatu's weapon withstood the stroke easily.

The man, taken by surprise, gasped in pain.

"Get him up. Now!" He swept the bow through the air with a humming sound. "When I give you an order, you'll obey it, or I'll put a shaft into the next man that doesn't."

To emphasize that he meant what he said, Sabatu jerked an arrow from his quiver. With speed that would have impressed any of Akkad's master bowmen, he nocked the arrow and launched it, seemingly without aiming.

The missile traveled less than ten paces, and buried itself into the wood of a pole that held one of Sumer's standards.

With a rush, the startled men climbed to their feet, two of them dragging upright the one who'd felt Sabatu's bow in his belly.

"First, I'll tell you the good news." Sabatu told them of Yavtar's meeting with the Akkadians, and that their cavalry were on the way even now. The men shook off their lethargy in an instant. Cheers erupted, to join with those already arising from the mass of people below the gate, as they, too, received the news and spread the word.

"Now for the bad," Sabatu said, after he'd given them a few moments. "Chaiyanar and his men are coming, and they're coming with everything they've got. It's our job to make sure they don't take this gate, and a lot of us are probably going to die holding them off. But if they get over the walls, every man they don't want as a slave will be slaughtered. Those allowed to live," he lifted both his hands, to show them where his thumbs had been broken, "will never hold a weapon again."

It took a moment for his words to sink in, that Sabatu had faced Elamite torture and survived, and that he'd somehow managed to become a commander and a master bowman. His arrow, still protruding from the pole, attested to his words.

"But there's more," Sabatu went on, striding up and down before his new charges. "As soon as the Akkadians get here, Captain of the Guard Jarud wants Bila and his men to open the gate, and attack Chaiyanar's soldiers. Jarud wants to take them from the rear. More important, you men are going to see to it that I'm the first man through this gate. I've got something to settle with Grand Commander Chaiyanar, and I don't want to miss the chance to greet him. If any of you want to follow me, I'll make sure you receive five silver coins. And if . . ."

"Make it ten, and I'll follow you anywhere."

Sabatu grinned at the speaker, a short, swarthy man with the long, ropy arms that made for a good bowman. "What's your name?"

"My name is Hurin of Uruk, Commander." He picked up his bow. "And I can shoot as good as you. Want to see?"

"Later, perhaps, Hurin from Uruk." Sabatu couldn't keep the smile from his face. "All right, it's ten silver coins, even if I have to borrow them. Now shut up and listen. It's better if you know everything."

When Sabatu finished, smiles covered most of their faces. Every one of them had lost friends and kin during the siege. More than a few wanted a chance to revenge themselves on the hated Elamites. If there were some coins to be earned in the process, so much the better.

"Good! Now let's make sure we're ready for them when they come."

35

Grand Commander Chaiyanar, after stepping onto the back of one of his kneeling clerks, mounted his warhorse. A bronze breastplate covered his chest, and a red-plumed helmet of the same material protected his head. A short sword forged by the master sword-makers of the Indus hung from his waist.

A glance at the sky brought a frown to his face – the sun had already marked the midpoint of the afternoon. All the same, the well-planned assault on Sumer was about to begin, and Chaiyanar knew that many decisions would need to be made during the attack. He would direct the final charge himself, the one that would swamp the defenders and sweep them from the northern wall and main gate.

The first foray, however, would come on the eastern wall, another weak point that his men had identified. Two thousand soldiers, backed by eight hundred archers, would attack there. The Elamite trenches had snaked their way close to that wall, too, and it was very possible Sumer's defenses might be breached there as well.

Meanwhile, a second and smaller Elamite force would launch another thrust at the southernmost section of Sumer's defenses. A thousand men and two hundred bowmen would try to overwhelm the southern wall, or at least draw off as many of the defenders as possible.

Once those attacks had begun, Chaiyanar would fling the remainder, and by far the largest portion, of his assault forces at the north wall and Sumer's main entrance. Under his direct command three thousand men, backed by fifteen hundred bowmen and all the support troops, would attack a strip of wall barely a hundred paces wide. Chaiyanar felt certain his men could overcome the defenses there.

The western side of the city, that closest to the Tigris, would be ignored. The narrow land gap between the river and the walls made it too difficult to marshal enough men to try an attack.

His remaining cavalry, less than a thousand men, still ringed the city. Earlier this morning, Chaiyanar had dispatched most of them, over five hundred, to guard the southern approach. He wanted plenty of warning in case the Akkadians once again tried to sneak up on his army from that direction.

The Elamite horsemen also had orders to make sure no one got out of the city by land or river. The Sumerians had at least twenty boats nestled along the docks, and Chaiyanar wanted to make sure no rich merchants or any of the city's leaders made their escape that way.

He had learned of the destruction of the supply cove only yesterday. The loss of the beachhead and the disruption of supplies from Sushan hit Chaiyanar hard. He'd never expected to find an enemy behind him, nor to have his link with Elam cut. But that no longer mattered now. Once he had Sumer under his grip, the supplies could come up river direct to the city's docks.

Chaiyanar's men had already received their orders – no matter what resistance they encountered, the northern wall and main gate must be taken. After Sumer was captured, if any of its people resisted, they would be put to the sword. By sundown, he expected to ride through Sumer's open gates, while the city's few surviving inhabitants knelt in the dust with their heads bowed.

The usual difficulties of preparing men for battle had already delayed his attack, but plenty of daylight still remained. He issued the final orders that would commence the offensives on the southern and eastern walls.

That accomplished, Chaiyanar sat on his horse and waited. He studied his men, crammed shoulder to shoulder in the many trenches. They would launch the offensive. The rest of his soldiers stood just out of arrow range. Ladders, shields, ropes, carts, everything needed was at hand, and his three thousand soldiers appeared ready enough.

They would be supported by fifteen hundred archers, who would follow behind the rush to the walls, and try to keep the defenders pinned down and unable to use their weapons.

Yesterday's foray had nearly succeeded, and today even greater numbers of Elamites would hurl themselves at Sumer's ramparts.

Chaiyanar had committed all his troops to this onslaught. Nothing would be held back. Even the siege workers would add their weight to the attack, carrying extra arrows and ladders, and a few water skins. Only the remnants of his cavalry would not partake in the storming.

At last Grand Commander Chaiyanar heard the drumbeats that signaled the southern and eastern wall attacks had commenced. From where he sat on his horse, Chaiyanar now heard the shouts of his men, even if he couldn't see them. They would have risen up from the trenches and rushed toward the bulwarks. The din of battle grew louder, as the city's defenders added their clamor. Chaiyanar shifted his gaze to the strategic north wall and main gate, and the Sumerians facing his men.

He saw many of their heads turned toward the other walls. They knew that an assault there had already begun, and now they would worry that they might be attacked from within their city. That fear would work to his advantage. It also meant the time had come.

Chaiyanar gave the order, and his own battle drum began to sound. With a roar that echoed off Sumer's wall, his men leapt from the trenches and earthworks that sheltered them. Ignoring the arrow storm that greeted them, they raced as fast as they could run across the open space toward the city's wall. Many went down, struck by Sumerian arrows. Nevertheless, a wave of men, shouting their war cries, quickly reached the base of Sumer's north wall.

Arrows continued to fly from the wall, hundreds of them. Chaiyanar watched as many of his men were killed, but the dead and wounded men were ignored, even trampled underfoot. In moments, the last of the open space before the north wall had filled with the Elamites.

The losses scarcely slowed the assault. Ladders were rammed against the sides of the city's wall. Chaiyanar's fifteen hundred bowmen had also moved forward. Now they stood exposed as they targeted any defenders who showed themselves, either to shoot at his soldiers or to try and dislodge the ladders.

Stones were hurled blindly over the rampart and took their toll. But the first wave of Elamite attackers flung themselves onto the ladders and started climbing. Chaiyanar moved his horse closer, staying just out of range and urging his men to the attack.

A shout from behind finally caught Chaiyanar's attention. He turned to see three horsemen galloping at a dead run toward him, waving their arms and bellowing something incomprehensible. But even before the men pulled their lathered horses to a halt beside Chaiyanar, he had lifted his gaze over their heads, toward the low hills less than a half mile away.

A large force of cavalry, hundreds and hundreds, was riding smoothly down the slope. As soon as the riders reached the level ground, they put their mounts to the gallop, waving their bows and swords in the air. For an instant, Chaiyanar thought Commander Simaski and his men had returned.

"They're Akkadians! Thousands of them!" The first scout to reach Chaiyanar's side gasped out the words, even as he gestured to the men now galloping toward them. "They broke through our line, and they . . ."

By now the thunder of the charging horses' hooves echoed over the flat land that surrounded Sumer. For a moment, Chaiyanar stared open-mouthed at this dreadful apparition, a seemingly endless wave of horses flowing down the hill like a river. Akkadian cavalry! Here! Impossible!

"Recall the men," he screamed. "Sound the retreat! Sound the retreat!"

The terrified drummer standing beside his leader obeyed, and immediately the rhythmic drumbeat sounded. But the din of battle added to that of the charging Akkadian horses, and masked the drum sound. The brutal fighting at the north wall still occupied all of the Elamites' attention, and most never heard the drum, or if they did, understood its message. Savage fighting erupted along the top of the wall, as many of the Elamites tried to force their way over the top.

However Chaiyanar knew that no longer mattered. There wasn't enough time to get his soldiers into the city and take control. "Get the men back here," Chaiyanar bellowed, furious that no one heeded his order. "We have to drive them off!"

By now the Akkadian cavalry had closed to within a few hundred paces. At last the Elamite commanders directing the assault heard the pounding hoof beats as well. One by one, they, too, turned to stare in stunned surprise at the approaching horsemen.

A single glance told the Elamite soldiers that their attack was doomed. The wall could not be carried before the enemy cavalry arrived. The war cries of four thousand riders added to the onslaught, and their swords glinted in the sunlight.

The first flight of Akkadian arrows flew into the air, launched by the riders at the front of the charge. In moments hundred of shafts struck the rear of the Elamite attackers. Chaiyanar's personal guard and staff numbered twenty men, and four of them went down with shafts protruding from their bodies. The next wave of arrows, aimed higher, struck at the ranks of the Elamite bowmen, most of them still facing the north wall and main gate, and shooting their weapons.

Chaiyanar kicked his horse into motion. He had to get away from these Akkadian horsemen. His soldiers attacking the northern wall were doomed. Pinned against the wall, his men would be shot to pieces. Already he saw Sumer's bowmen daring to lean over the wall, aiming arrows at the frantic Elamites now scrambling down the ladders even faster than they'd climbed up only moments before.

Without having to worry about counter fire, the Sumerian archers atop the wall killed their enemies as fast as they could work their bows.

The Elamite bowmen tried to turn about to drive off these unexpected attackers, but by then the Akkadians had drawn far too close. Flung lances devastated the Elamites, knocking men to their knees. Then the cavalry smashed into the panicked archers, tearing their ranks to shreds and hacking at anything that moved.

The warhorses added to the killing, hammering aside anyone in their path and trampling underfoot those who went down. Some of the riders, still shooting their bows, continued right through the disorganized ranks of Elamite bowmen. The horsemen now wielded their swords on the rear ranks of the Elamites.

Chaiyanar ignored the turmoil. Abandoning his staff, he raced his horse as close to Sumer's wall as he dared, weaving the powerful beast around both friend and foe. If he could reach his soldiers assaulting the eastern wall, he might be able to regroup them and establish a defense. Or they might even had surmounted the wall. He swept around the corner, and could see his men still fighting. But they looked no closer to success than Chaiyanar's northern attack.

By now his soldiers, too, had heard the hoof beats of the horses and realized what the sound portended. The Sumerians added their voices to the din, rejoicing in the arrival of the Akkadians. Chaiyanar glimpsed his men fleeing from the southern wall, and knew that the attack there had also faltered.

Chaiyanar glanced up at the Sumerians. The eastern wall appeared packed with soldiers, and hundreds, perhaps thousands of people. The defenders, crammed atop the parapet, fought like wild men, hurling the ladders down, striking with axes, swords, and spears. Most were not even soldiers, but they had resisted the trained attackers nonetheless.

Chaiyanar reached his men, galloping into their midst, but despite his frantic shouts and waving arms, he could not restore order to his wild-eyed soldiers. All organization had given way to chaos, and the first instinct of every Elamite soldier was to flee. Everyone remembered the slaughter that resulted from the Akkadian cavalry attack of five days ago. Those few Elamites who heard their commander's words ignored them.

Close on Chaiyanar's heels came another wave of Akkadians, no doubt those not needed at the north wall killing ground. Not so many this time, but enough to ride behind the Elamite line, and keep them penned into the area between the horsemen and Sumer's eastern wall.

With a screech that rose over the din of battle, Chaiyanar saw Sumer's main gate swing open. Instantly a wave of soldiers poured through the widening gap, spears, bows, and swords in their hands. In moments hundreds of screaming Sumerian fighters had raced out of the city and charged into the still regrouping Elamites.

One look told Chaiyanar that the battle was lost. Even though his men still outnumbered their foes, the sudden appearance of the Akkadian cavalry had wreaked havoc upon his men. Fear swept through his disorganized soldiers. Even if they wanted to fight, soldiers, archers, siege workers, and support men were crammed together and unable to form a battle line.

With the charging Akkadian horsemen now augmented by soldiers from within Sumer and supported by archers from its walls, the tide of defeat washed over the panicked Elamites.

Arrows flew through the air. Every Sumerian or Akkadian that could pull a bowstring launched as many shafts as he could. Chaiyanar realized his own escape was cut off. He saw only one chance. If he could overwhelm the Sumerians who had sortied forth from the city, he might be able to get his men inside the main gate.

Drawing his sword for the first time, Chaiyanar waved it over his head. "Follow me, into the city. The gate is open! Into the city!" He wheeled his horse around to face the open gate.

But before Chaiyanar's words could reach enough of his men, an arrow struck his horse's chest, digging deep into the left shoulder. With an almost human scream, the animal reared up, eyes wide with pain and lashed out with its front hooves. Then the beast crashed back down with a jolt that loosened Chaiyanar's grip. The wounded animal kicked out with its hind legs, and that motion pitched Chaiyanar forward over the horse's shoulder. He tumbled to the earth, his head striking a discarded shield with enough force to knock him senseless.

When Chaiyanar regained consciousness, the din of battle had ceased. Instead of thundering hooves and the boastful war cries of his men, he heard only the usual aftermath of battle – the wretched pleas and moans of the wounded, and the laughter of the victors. He pushed himself to a sitting position, and tried to take stock of what had happened.

His eyes wouldn't focus and the ground beneath his legs was tinged with red. Blood had congealed over his left eye, and he rubbed that away with the back of his hand. Then he perceived all too clearly the battle ground, covered with heaps of the dead and dying. A second look revealed only Sumerians walking among the corpses, finishing off the injured, and already busy looting their bodies of anything of value. Chaiyanar's own sword had vanished, and his breastplate, its laces cut, rested on the ground a few paces away.

"He's coming around," a voice said.

Chaiyanar glanced behind him, and saw two archers standing there regarding him. One had a wide smile on his face, and his bow was slung across his back. The other held a bow in his left hand, but no arrow rested on the bowstring. He wore a sword on his hip, but the weapon hung in its scabbard. That, more than anything else, convinced Chaiyanar the battle had indeed ended.

"You don't remember me, do you, Grand Commander Chaiyanar of Sushan?"

Chaiyanar turned again and stared at the soldier holding the bow. The man's voice sounded familiar. Then Chaiyanar's eyes went wide with horror. The bowman had spoken in the language of Elam, with the accent of the nobility. Comprehension came with a rush, as Chaiyanar's mind put the face and voice together.

"Sabatu!"

"Yes, Sabatu. I'm glad you remembered my name, Grand Commander Chaiyanar. It was my arrow that brought down your horse. I could have killed you then, but I wanted you alive, so that you could look into my eyes as I took your life from you."

"Sabatu, wait. Tell them who I am. We can return to Sushan together. I'll give you anything you want, gold, a new command, anything!"

"You would ignore the royal order of King Shirudukh?" Sabatu's words mocked Chaiyanar for daring to suggest such an action. "You would presume to disobey the one who sentenced me to death, and the one whose orders you carried out so efficiently. My wife, my children, tortured and murdered one by one in front of me, while you took your ease in the comforts of your palace."

"Please, Sabatu, please . . ."

With a growl, Sabatu took a step forward and lashed out with his foot. The sandal caught Chaiyanar flat on the face, the force of the blow breaking his nose. His head snapped back, and blood gushed from his nostrils.

"Hurin, tie his hands behind him," Sabatu ordered. "Make sure they're as tight as you can make them. He won't be needing them any longer."

Hurin, laughing all the while, cut the sandal laces from a dead Elamite, and used them to fasten Chaiyanar's hands. By the time he recovered from Sabatu's kick, pain lanced through Chaiyanar's wrists, as the leather stretched and pulled tight.

"King Eskkar of Akkad promised me your life, Grand Commander. You wanted to ride into Sumer as a conqueror, but you'll walk through the gates like a slave, at the end of a rope. You'll die slowly, a little each day, and I will spend every moment with you. I swear by all the gods in Elam and Sumer that, day or night, I'll not leave your side. Not for a moment. I'll make sure you suffer more than any man who has ever died by your order in Sushan's marketplace."

"Sabatu, please!" Chaiyanar managed to get to his knees. "Shirudukh will give you gold, all the gold you desire, if you set me free."

With a movement almost too quick to follow, Sabatu snatched an arrow from his quiver, nocked it to the bowstring, and drew back the shaft. The bronze tip, almost touching Chaiyanar's face, pointed toward Chaiyanar's left eye. "Look at my hands, you dog. 'Break his thumbs,' you said. Now my hands are weak, and I don't know how much longer I can hold back my arrow."

"By the gods, mercy, Sabatu! Please don't kill me."

With a snarl of rage, Sabatu shifted his aim and released the bowstring. The bronze tip sliced through Chaiyanar's left ear.

The former High Commander of Sushan screamed, as much in fright as pain.

Taking his time, Sabatu selected another shaft from his quiver.

"You're not going to kill him before I get my ten silver coins, are you?"

"Oh, no, he won't die that fast." Sabatu let the bow go slack. "Hurin, there's a ring with a ruby stone on his finger. You can have that for a start."

Chaiyanar cried out, as Hurin twisted the Elamite's fingers. "Can't get it loose."

Sabatu leaned forward, his face only a hand's breadth from Chaiyanar's. "Use my knife. It's very sharp. Cut it free." He drew the blade, Daro's gift, from its scabbard, and dropped it beside the squirming prisoner.

"Ah, no need, I've got it!" Hurin stood and held the ring up to the sun. "This is worth more than ten coins."

"You'll earn the rest by helping me torture Grand Commander Chaiyanar."

"No! You must not torture . . ."

"Is this Chaiyanar?" Another man strode over to join Sabatu. An older man, his tunic was splattered with blood. A grim expression covered his face.

"Yes, and he's my prisoner, Captain Jarud," Sabatu said.

"Grand Commander Chaiyanar, I'm glad to see you're still alive." Jarud laughed, a chilling sound that seemed out of place on the bloody battlefield. "My name is Jarud, and I am the Captain of the

Guard for the City of Sumer." Anger and hatred now showed in his clenched jaw and narrowed eyes.

Chaiyanar shivered as much at Jarud's dour countenance as at his words. But Chaiyanar saw the possibility of avoiding Sabatu's torture. "I am Chaiyanar, Commander of the Elamite Army. My cousin is the King of Elam, and he will pay a rich ransom for my safe return."

"Oh, yes, I'm sure he would. And I'm sure King Gemama would be interested in speaking with you, and welcoming you into our City. But yesterday, my nephew Jaruman, died defending Sumer's gate. One of your archers killed him. He was a good man, like a son to me, and I will mourn his loss for many days."

Taking his time, Jarud slid his sword, still stained with blood, from its scabbard. "I swore as I held Jaruman in my arms and watched him die, that I would kill many Elamites to avenge his death."

"King Shirudukh will pay three hundred gold coins, no, five hundred, for my safe return." The words gushed from Chaiyanar's mouth, even as the blood from his broken nose dripped down his chin. He tried to stand, but Hurin pushed him back onto his knees.

"You came into our land, killed our people, and tried to sack my City." Jarud took a step closer and stared down at the frightened and cringing leader of the Elamites. "Each day from the wall I watched you, sitting under your awning, taking your ease while your men prepared to kill thousands of Sumerians who had done you no injury. But I will avenge my nephew. That will require that I kill one more Elamite. Just one. And after I kill you, I'll have your head nailed to Sumer's gate and your body cut into pieces and fed to the dogs, so that your spirit is cursed forever in the afterlife. May the demons there burn your body in the pits for all time."

Chaiyanar lurched forward, his face lifted imploringly. His mouth agape, he gazed up in horror as Jarud raised his sword.

"No!" Sabatu stepped between the prisoner and Jarud. "King Eskkar promised me that I could have Chaiyanar. He killed every member of my family. For that, I swear to you that he will die a slow, very slow and painful death. You can come and watch each day, and hear his screams of pain."

Jarud glared at Sabatu. "He will die right here, with my sword in his belly, while I watch him bleed to death."

"Hold on, hold on! What are you two doing?"

King Gemama, accompanied by Yavtar, had wended his way through the bodies to reach Jarud's side. "I'm glad you captured Chaiyanar alive. This filth must repay the gold that Sumer has wasted fighting. Crops have been lost, houses burned, tradesmen killed . . . his ransom will repay much of that expense. We must keep him alive."

"I think King Eskkar would like to speak to Chaiyanar," Yavtar added. "He should be sent to Akkad. After he spends a few days with Annok-sur and her pain givers, the Grand Commander will reveal everything that we want to know. Then Eskkar can ransom him or give him back to you so you can torture him to death."

"Yes! Yes! I'm worth a great ransom," Chaiyanar pleaded. "Do not let these men kill me."

With a snarl, Sabatu fit another arrow to his bow. "He is my prisoner. My arrow brought him down, and his body belongs to me."

Jarud hefted his sword. "No, he dies now. He's as cunning as a fox. He'll find a way to get himself ransomed."

"Wait! Hold your sword, Jarud." King Gemama stepped in front of the captive. "Put down your bow, Sabatu. I may have a way to satisfy everyone, if my good friend Yavtar will agree. He does owe me a favor or two, as I recall."

Yavtar lifted his hands and let them drop. "He's not my prisoner. Do whatever you like with the scum."

"Good, good," Gemama said. "Now let me see this man." He turned and peered down into Chaiyanar's bloody face for a long moment. "This dog is not Grand Commander Chaiyanar," Gemama declared. He glanced around. A dead Elamite lay a few paces away.

Gemama stepped over to the corpse, and pointed down at the body · with his finger. "That is Grand Commander Chaiyanar. He was killed during the attack, so there can be no ransom."

Sumer's King returned to stand in front of the prisoner. "For daring to impersonate Chaiyanar, I order this common soldier to be tortured to death by Sabatu. When the prisoner is ready to die, Captain Jarud can run his sword through his belly. That way all will be satisfied. Sabatu? Jarud? Is that not right?"

"Oh, damn the gods!" Jarud lowered his sword and spat on the ground. "I suppose it will have to do. But Sabatu must swear to let me deliver the final blow, and Chaiyanar must know it is I who sends him into the fire pits."

Gemama faced Sabatu. "Will you agree to this? You can torture him as long as you like."

Sabatu's eyes went from Gemama to Jarud. He took a deep breath, then nodded his head. "I will keep him alive for Captain Jarud. I swear it on my honor."

Chaiyanar, his eyes wide with fear, gaped in silent terror as the men talked about his coming torture and death. "You must not do this. I am Grand Commander Chaiyanar and I . . ."

Yavtar, who happened to be closest to the prisoner, kicked him in the side of the head. "This filthy soldier, to save his own life, still claims to be the Elamite commander. He should not be allowed to speak to anyone."

"Well, I can take care of that," Jarud declared. He returned his bloody sword to its scabbard without bothering to clean it, and then drew a slim knife from its sheath. "Who wants to hold his head?"

Even though Chaiyanar's hands were bound, it took all four of them to hold him fast while Jarud cut off his tongue. When Jarud finished, he held up Chaiyanar's bloody tongue, so that everyone could admire it, and then spat again, this time in Chaiyanar's face.

"Time to get back to work," Jarud said. "We've got to clean up this mess, and Hathor and Naxos will need food and supplies, before they can start hunting down the remaining invaders. I won't feel satisfied until every last Elamite is dead or driven into the sea."

Chaiyanar, blood still dripping down his chin, stared at his captors in horror.

"Come with me, Grand Commander." Sabatu grabbed the dazed Chaiyanar and jerked him to his feet. "I will lead you into the City of Sumer, and you can receive the reward you deserve. I promise you that your first night in Sumer will be one you will remember. But not for long."

Later that evening, Yavtar and Gemama sat together on the terrace of the Palace. Yavtar had dined with his old friend. The servants had all disappeared, out in the lanes celebrating the destruction of the Elamites, so there was no one to cook a proper feast. Even so, King Gemama had plenty of fine wine yet stored in his cellar, and two pitchers of his best rested on the low table between the men.

The people of Sumer, jubilant that the siege had been lifted, would get little sleep tonight. Already three boats had arrived, two from the north, and one from Lagash. As word spread that the siege had broken, food and supplies would once again flow into the city.

"How do you think King Eskkar is doing?" For Gemama, it was no idle question. If Akkad fell, Sumer would soon be facing another, perhaps even more intense siege.

"Well, he's getting all the supplies and weapons he needs," Yavtar said. "My boats have hauled little else for the last three months."

"Even so, Eskkar will be outnumbered."

Yavtar waved his wine cup in the air. "He'll find a way to even the odds. You know, I fought with him many years ago, when he recaptured Akkad from Korthac and his Egyptians. I transported Eskkar and his men down the Tigris to Akkad. I gave into a foolish impulse and volunteered to fight beside Eskkar and his men. But even then, I knew the man wouldn't be stopped. He was greatly outnumbered and locked outside the city's walls. Yet he got in and slew the Egyptians. Killed all of them. Except Hathor, thank the gods."

"Men say King Eskkar has the luck of the gods."

"You can believe that, if you must," Yavtar said. "But Eskkar has mastered every kind of warfare and way of fighting. Most of all, he knows how to win." He chuckled. "But I can tell you a secret, something else about Eskkar that few even in Akkad know."

"And what is that, old friend, that makes you laugh?"

"Eskkar, the King of Akkad, hates to waste gold. He's going to be really annoyed when he finds out about Chaiyanar."

"I thought you weren't going to tell him."

"Oh, not me. But Trella will find out, sooner or later. However, it's more than likely that King Shirudukh would not have paid a single gold coin. It's said he has no patience with those who fail him. But if there were a ransom, I can tell you what Eskkar would have done to Chaiyanar. He would have cut off both his hands before selling him back to Susa."

"Barbarians are a bloodthirsty lot." Gemama shivered. "Perhaps it is for the best, though. "We would have had to guard Chaiyanar's worthless life day and night while every man in Sumer demanded his death. All the same, my people would never have forgiven us if we turned him over to Akkad, let alone sent him back to Elam. At least this way Jarud will avenge his nephew and the ransom be damned."

"Yes, barbarians do like to wallow in blood." Yavtar filled his cup again, then lifted it high. "To King Eskkar of Akkad. May he destroy the Elamite Modran and save the Land Between the Rivers."

"If he does, I will sacrifice a goat to the goddess Inanna, may she . . ."

"Not another goat," Yavtar pleaded. "One more sacrifice offered up, and the last goat will vanish from the land."

36

The Elamite supply station at Zanbil . . .

The morning after the capture of the supply depot at Zanbil, Sargon awoke to find he had slept through the dawn, something he had not done in months. Groggy, he pushed himself to his feet, and discovered that the sun had already lifted clear of the horizon. He and Garal had spread their blankets in a quiet place next to one of the huts. To Sargon's surprise and despite the hard ground, he enjoyed a good night's rest for the first time since they started riding east.

The strain of riding for days on end, and not even knowing if they could reach Zanbil in time, had worn on Sargon's nerves. War, he'd come to realize, occupied a man's thoughts from dawn until dusk, and then plagued the night's rest.

This coming fight – he regarded the capture of the village yesterday as nothing of consequence – would be his first campaign. This time he bore a good share of the responsibility for the plan's success or failure. Unlike Garal and most of the warriors, Sargon had all the worries that went with any campaign – would they reach their goal, would they achieve their objective, would the Elamites fall upon them and destroy all of them.

Another concern – would he fight bravely or would he dishonor his name – troubled him as well. Thoughts of whether he might die in battle always lingered, as they did with every warrior, in the back of his mind.

Sargon had worked with his father and Chief Bekka to map out the route as well as the timing. Sargon's presence with the Alur Meriki was meant to ensure that the warriors played their role in the battle, and did not wander off on some senseless raid to loot and pillage. Though Sargon never mentioned it, Chief Bekka understood that

Sargon would decide when the Alur Meriki's oath to Eskkar had been fulfilled.

Part of the responsibility for stopping the entire Elamite invasion now rested on Sargon's shoulders. His concern also included the warriors themselves, already hundreds of miles from their homes, in a hostile land, with a large and formidable army of fighting men ready to fall upon them. Mistakes on his part might mean the deaths of hundreds, including many of his friends.

The easy capture of Zanbil had resolved little. To the north, General Jedidia and his six thousand horsemen might emerge from the Jkarian Pass any day, on route to Zanbil for supplies and another pathway to the Land Between the Rivers.

To the west, Lord Modran and his forces, should they fail to breach Eskkar's defense of the Dellen Pass, might turn about and fall upon the Alur Meriki. Farther to the south lay the large city of Sushan, which, if his mother's spies were correct, now housed the Elamite King and his own force of dangerous Immortals.

Nevertheless, now was not the time for such apprehensions. Sargon went down to the stream, to relieve himself and wash his face and hands. The warriors had occupied the village because the clean flowing stream was far too valuable to ignore. Later, after he ate a healthy meal from the Elamite supplies, he intended to take a swim and clean his clothes. But when he straightened up from his ablutions, he found Garal, always an early riser, striding toward him.

"Sargon! Come at once," Garal said. "Our men have captured some riders coming through the Pass."

He and Garal jogged across the village until they reached the place where Chief Bekka, Subutai, and the other clan leaders had gathered. Ten or twelve warriors, their horses tethered nearby, surrounded three prisoners kneeling on the ground. Sargon saw the fear on their faces, as they stared wide-eyed at the menacing barbarians encircling them.

Sargon moved closer to the Elamites, but waited until Bekka told Sargon to proceed. Then he turned to face the wretched men, now staring up at him.

"If you wish to live, if you wish to avoid being tortured, you will answer my questions, truthfully and without hesitation. Or you can choose silence, and the torture will begin."

They seemed surprised that any of the barbarians spoke their language, but they all hastened to assure Sargon of their cooperation. His mother had suggested that not many of the Elamites would be eager to die for their King.

Sargon ordered the men separated. Then he and Garal began the interrogation. This one lasted much longer than yesterday's, as these men had much more information to divulge. The men were questioned, and each man's answers compared to the other two. Well before midmorning, Sargon felt certain he had extracted the truth from them.

He and Garal joined the three clan chiefs still in Zanbil, Bekka, Subutai, and Suijan. Den'rack, Virani, and the others had departed to patrol the approaches to the village.

"What did you learn?" Chief Bekka's voice had a hard edge. No doubt he, too, worried about the Elamite forces that might easily surround him.

"The day before yesterday, Modran's army reached my father's battle line and tried to break through. Apparently the fighting lasted some time. The Elamites were repulsed, and with heavy losses. Modran is preparing to attack again. But in case his army is delayed, he sent these three messengers back to Zanbil, to demand more supplies be sent on ahead, especially food and water, and as fast as possible. Then the messengers were to continue on until they reached King Shirudukh at the city of Sushan. They would tell Shirudukh of Akkad's decision to fight the decisive battle inside the Dellen Pass. The riders took extra horses, and rode all day and into the night. Last night they halted about ten miles away, when it finally became too dark to ride."

"Two days ago?" Bekka rubbed his chin in surprise. "That means they covered more than seventy miles through the Pass in less than two days. I didn't think dirt eaters could ride that well."

Sargon decided that now was not the time to remind Bekka that, in the past, the warriors had frequently underestimated the capabilities of the villagers. "Modran demanded that the messengers travel as fast as they could, even if it meant killing the horses."

Bekka shrugged. "At least your father has survived the first encounter, and this Modran now realizes it may take some time to break through the Pass. It also means that Modran is not already on his way here."

"The prisoners didn't think Modran would attack again for another day or so," Sargon said. "If this is true, and my father can hold them off in a second battle, Modran will soon be desperate for the supplies he is already expecting. If we can occupy Zanbil for another two or three days, the Elamites may have to retreat."

"If Eskkar drives them off," Bekka said, "we may soon have nine thousand Elamite horsemen coming back through the Pass, looking for food and water. Yet if there is nothing here for them to eat, we should be able to out ride and out fight them easily enough."

If the Elamites were low on food and water, their cavalry would ride as hard as they could to reach this place. The rest of Modran's infantry fighters wouldn't be far behind, driven by the same need.

"All the same, his army is not likely to abandon their attack for some time. It will probably be another few days before we learn what happens . . ."

The sound of a galloping horse interrupted the conversation. In moments, a sweating warrior on a well-lathered horse pulled up before the Sarum.

"Chief Bekka, we spotted a supply train coming up the trail from the south. At least two hundred pack animals, and perhaps fifty or sixty guards, about half of them mounted. Chief Suijan and Chief Den'rack have moved their men out of sight, to let the dirt eaters approach this place."

Bekka glanced at Sargon.

"I suggest, Chief Bekka," Sargon said, "that we let them ride in. You might conceal some of your warriors in the huts, and we could bring out the women and prisoners. Seeing them standing about should help lure the Elamites into the village."

Bekka never hesitated. "Do it."

Sargon turned to Garal, and soon the two of them were giving orders, shifting men from place to place, and removing any signs of their warriors. In the center of the village, Sargon stood beside the eight women who had survived the raid. Many of them were scarcely able to walk, after the repeated rapes. Most were bruised as well, but Sargon knew that those signs wouldn't be visible until the supply column had fully entered Zanbil.

Sargon told the women what would happen to them if they tried to warn the approaching Elamites. Since they knew how many men

Sargon had at his call, they nodded dejectedly. They understood that only Sargon's presence had saved their lives yesterday.

He stood there as the long line of men and animals wended their way into the village. The leader had nearly reached the marketplace before he noticed something was amiss. Sargon shouted the order, then pushed the women back toward their hut.

Warriors burst from the nearby huts, bows in hand, shouting their war cries, and loosing shafts as fast as they could. The Elamite commander leading the column managed to grasp his sword, but two arrows struck him from his horse, his blade still half in its scabbard. Most of the warriors used their bows. Others pulled guards from their horses using their swords or impaled them with their lances. Many of the Elamites tried to flee, but now hundreds of warriors, previously out of sight to the east and north, galloped at full speed, to cut off any possibility of escape. In moments, a ring of mounted clan warriors encircled Zanbil.

The guards, caught by surprise, had little chance. By the time the last of Den'rack's warriors arrived, almost all of the Elamites were dead, and the rest died moments later. Garal ordered the men to secure the pack animals and collect the weapons.

Before long Sargon faced another four prisoners kneeling in the dirt, the only survivors of the supply column. By now, Sargon knew exactly what to say and what to demand. His third interrogation took little time, and soon he and Garal stood once again before Chief Bekka.

"The men guarding the supply column say that there is only one more caravan coming behind them. It should arrive here in two days. After that, Lord Modran's forces will be expected to live off Akkad's lands, or get supplies from Sumer. The supply caravans were to keep Modran's men fed until they were through the Dellen Pass and could establish the siege around Akkad. Once there, they were to forage for themselves."

"Can you be sure they are telling the truth?" Bekka seemed suspicious at how easily Sargon had obtained the information. "How will this second caravan be guarded?"

"Yes, I believe them," Sargon answered. "I promised that they would live, if they spoke the truth. All the guards were questioned separately, and their stories agreed. As for the next supply group, it will be guarded by about the same number of soldiers. Without a warning from Zanbil, they will ride in as carelessly as these men did."

"We will stay here and take the second caravan," Bekka said. "Then we will burn everything that we do not need. Since no more men or supplies are coming to Zanbil, we will be free to raid the countryside."

And that, Sargon knew, might lead to trouble. His father had asked the Alur Meriki to cut Modran's supply line, and by capturing the one remaining convoy, they would have accomplished that. Which meant the warriors had completed the task Eskkar had asked of them, as well as fulfilled their oath.

"If your fighters could stay a few days after that, Chief Bekka," Sargon said, "you might be able to attack any Elamites trying to leave the Pass."

"Eskkar said that once Modran's forces turned aside, Akkad would be safe. I will not put our warriors against the thousands of men Modran will have, even in defeat, without good purpose."

Sargon nodded. Bekka spoke the truth, and the Sarum of the Alur Meriki had done all that Eskkar had requested. Sargon forced a smile to his face. Bekka's decision was not carved in stone. Circumstances could yet change Chief Bekka's mind.

A little after midday, Sargon rode the mile and a half from Zanbil to the eastern mouth of the Dellen Pass. Garal and some of the others had gone there earlier. Sargon knew they were hoping to catch more messengers coming from Modran.

To Sargon's surprise, a large group of Ur Nammu warriors were there, led by Chinua and Fashod. Jennat, another of Sargon's companions, stood beside Chinua. Den'rack, a new clan chief of the Alur Meriki, was also there. Den'rack had a handful of his own warriors with him.

Sargon hadn't seen much of his friends in the last few days, as they had been tasked with riding patrol. After an exchange of greetings, he learned that no new messengers from Modran had made the journey. Sargon hadn't expected any more Elamites to come through so soon on the heels of the others, who arrived only this morning.

Sargon saw Garal sitting on a large boulder by himself, staring up into the Pass. Sargon left the others and strode over to sit beside his companion.

"So, what do you see, Garal?"

"I see nothing, Sargon."

"What did you expect to find here? A horde of Elamites running for their lives?"

Garal faced his friend, and for once Garal's cheerful countenance had disappeared. "I expected to see glory. I expected to fight a great battle, to prove to Chinua and Subutai that I am worthy to one day become a leader of our people. Instead, there will be no battles, no fighting. Bekka already has his bags of loot, and he will raid the countryside on his return to the western lands, gathering even more. Even Subutai thinks the same, that our task here is completed."

"Well, what else is there?" Sargon felt more than a little surprise at his friend's words. "Don't forget, General Jedidia's force may soon be upon us."

"I know. But I also know that I have almost twenty seasons. Long before that age, Chinua had fought in his great Battle of Isin against the Sumerians. He proved his worth to everyone, on that field of battle. What can I say that I have done on this campaign?"

"You've done your duty, and no warrior can do more. My father will . . ."

"Your father followed Chinua into the fight at Isin. Now it is time for me to lead the way into battle." Garal turned his face away, and once again stared up into the Pass.

"What battle? There is no . . ." Sargon saw the glint in Garal's eyes. "You mean you want to ride into the Pass? To do what? Attack Modran's army?"

Garal nodded. "Not attack his soldiers, but what will Modran have at the rear of his forces? Nothing but porters and laborers, even slaves brought along to work on the siege of Akkad. And horses. There will be thousands of horses at the rear."

"Their riders will be there, too, guarding them."

"Did you not say that cavalry would be useless in the Pass?" Garal stood and faced his friend. "Modran will need all his men, so he will dismount his fighters and send them to the front. A small force of brave men could raid Modran's rear guard, and capture hundreds of horses. We could drive them all the way back here, before we turn north and ride home."

Sargon opened his mouth, then closed it again. Garal had that determined look on his face that Sargon knew all too well. His friend meant to do it, to ride deep into the Pass, to try and accomplish some great deed to make his mark as a future leader of his people. A foolish idea, but Sargon had lived with the Ur Nammu long enough to understand the things that mattered to a warrior.

Nevertheless, the more Sargon thought about it, the more impressed he grew with Garal's wild plan. A large number of horses would almost certainly be at the rear, and lightly guarded. Even a small raid on Modran's army might convince him he had enemies at his back as well as to the front. It might even relieve some pressure on Eskkar and his men.

Even if Eskkar were defeated, the loss of so many valuable horses might seriously weaken Modran's ability to continue his march and lay siege to Akkad.

The more Sargon thought about the idea, the more appealing it sounded. It would certainly put fear into the hearts of the Elamites. Not to mention that such a plan had never even been considered by his father, or Subutai, or Bekka, for that matter.

Garal wanted to prove himself before his fellow warriors. Sargon, too, had something to prove. A successful attack, unplanned by his father, would finally take Sargon out of the shadow of the all powerful and cunning King of Akkad.

Jennat and Den'rack wandered over. Since the day Sargon had risked his life entering the Alur Meriki camp to plead for Chief Bekka's help in fighting the Carchemishi, Den'rack had stood by Sargon's side. In the last two years, the two had become friends as well.

"Garal, what do you see that makes you look so serious?" Den'rack's casual words broke the lengthening silence. "Are the Elamites coming?" But his lighthearted tone disappeared when Garal met his gaze.

"I want to ride against the Elamite rear." Garal's flat voice conveyed his serious intent. "I've grown weary of slaughtering helpless guards and pack handlers. It's time I fought against a real enemy. I think we could strike a heavy blow against the Elamites, and capture many horses."

Den'rack turned to Sargon. "Is he serious? To take men that deep into the Pass?"

"Yes, he's serious. So am I. All I've done so far on this campaign is question prisoners. I think we could take the war to Lord Modran, and help my father at the same time."

Before Den'rack could reply, Jennat stepped forward to stand beside Sargon. "I'll ride with you. I haven't been wounded in more ' than two years. It's time I added another scar to my body."

Everyone laughed. Jennat, too, had ridden with Sargon into the midst of the Alur Meriki. None of the Ur Nammu had expected to survive that encounter with their hereditary enemies.

Sargon straightened up. "Come. We need to speak with Chief Bekka and Subutai."

It didn't take long for Garal's bold plan to spread throughout the camp. He and Sargon first presented the idea to Chinua, then Subutai, who shook his head and insisted on calling a war council of all the chiefs. Soon Chiefs Bekka, Suijan, Den'rack, and Fashod joined Chinua and Subutai. When Bekka, Sarum of the Alur Meriki and leader of the expedition, took his place, the boisterous discussion that had continued since Garal's arrival ceased.

Bekka took in the large crowd that stood behind the circle of leaders. Nearly every warrior in Zanbil wanted to hear what was said. "So, Garal of the Ur Nammu, you want to ride at least seventy miles into the Pass, over rough country, and attack the rear guard of Modran's army of thirty thousand? Is that what you're proposing?"

"Yes, Chief Bekka." Garal explained what he and Sargon had discussed. Then he enumerated the value of the raid to King Eskkar, and the benefit to their clans if they captured a large number of horses.

Bekka grunted. "What do you say, Subutai?"

"Any force that rides that far into the Pass is likely never to emerge. Even a wounded snake can lash out at its attacker. To accomplish what Garal proposes, it would take at least a hundred warriors, probably more. The Ur Nammu cannot risk so many men for a raid that is likely to accomplish little."

Chief Suijan, second in command, spoke next. "Young warriors always want to ride to war, to fight for honor and glory. But this is foolish, and even if you succeed in capturing a few horses, by the time you return here, you may well have five thousand mounted dirt eaters close behind you."

Fashod offered a different, more compelling, objection. "If Eskkar's Engineer blocked the Jkarian Pass, then we will soon be facing General Jedidia. Even if he decides to return to Sushan, he must come through this place. We may need every warrior to ride against Jedidia."

Chief Unegen, Chief Chinua, and the other leaders said much the same thing. Too much risk for too little reward.

When the chiefs finished, Garal spoke. "It is true that a raid such as this is dangerous, and with great risk. But I would still like to strike at Modran's army. If a hundred men cannot be spared, perhaps a handful can yet accomplish much. There may be enough warriors who would be willing to ride beside me."

Den'rack, who had said nothing, now lifted his hand to draw Bekka's attention. "Garal is my friend, but I do not believe a few riders can inflict enough damage. Nor can the Ur Nammu risk one hundred horsemen. But perhaps fifty warriors each from the Alur Meriki and the Ur Nammu could ride together. I am certain that at least that many of our warriors would offer to join with me. We would be willing to ride with Garal and Sargon."

The mention of Sargon's name reminded Bekka that he had forgotten to ask Eskkar's son for his reasons for wanting to go. "What does Sargon say?"

"Chief Bekka, I believe we should take one hundred men into the Pass. We have plenty of horses now, enough for two mounts for every rider that goes. But my main reason to want to go is that it may help my father. If the Akkadian line is broken, and the battle lost, Akkad will fall. But perhaps even our sting might turn Lord Modran aside, or just give King Eskkar more time to defend his position. If I fail to do everything in my power to help Akkad's soldiers, how can I ever face them with honor? And we will not ride merely to capture horses. Remember what your stampede did to the Carchemishi. It broke their ranks and destroyed their will to fight. We might accomplish as much."

More than two years ago, Bekka had led his Alur Meriki warriors against the Carchemishi invaders who were about to destroy the Ur Nammu.

"I stand with Sargon," Den'rack said. "If you approve, Sarum, I will find fifty warriors willing to ride with me."

"Perhaps I was hasty," Chinua said. "It may be that such a raid is important enough to venture, even weighed against the risk. If Subutai permits, I, too, will ask for fifty volunteers from the Ur Nammu, to ride beside Den'rack and the Alur Meriki."

Bekka furrowed his brow. He did not want to lose even fifty men. But Sargon had spoken the truth. A small effort might be enough to halt or delay Modran's advance, and perhaps save the army of Akkad. That meant Bekka and the clans might yet be responsible for Eskkar's success.

While Bekka had grown friendly enough with the King of Akkad over the last few years, Eskkar's defeat of the Alur Meriki at the Battle of the Stream still rankled many of Bekka's warriors.

As Sarum of the Alur Meriki, Bekka had more than fulfilled Eskkar's demand for men, and he had already broken the Elamite supply line. If he did nothing more, honor would still be satisfied. Still, while a small part of Bekka's deepest and darkest thoughts wanted Eskkar to be destroyed, Akkad's King was, after all, an Alur Meriki warrior, one who had offered the hand of friendship to his old clan.

However Eskkar's defeat would see the Land Between the Rivers turned into another Elamite province. Sooner or later that would deny the northern regions to both the Alur Meriki and the Ur Nammu. With Eskkar and Akkad conquered, the Elamites would turn their vast army against the Alur Meriki, especially after this raid into their own territory. Even the possible loss of fifty warriors meant nothing compared against that.

Bekka lifted his gaze. The long silence had remained unbroken, and every clan chief could guess the conflict that had just taken place within Bekka's heart. Now every man waited for his decision.

"Den'rack, I will allow you to take fifty warriors with you. All must be volunteers, but I'm sure there are enough young warriors eager to make a name for themselves. If Chief Subutai is willing to risk another fifty men, then the raid against Modran can proceed."

"Once long ago," Subutai said, "Eskkar risked his life to help the Ur Nammu. Now I must make the same choice, to help him at his time of great need. Garal may ask for fifty volunteers."

"Fifty warriors requires a chief to lead them," Chinuà said. "I volunteer to go as well."

"No. You are needed here." Subutai's voice conveyed the force of his decision. "Garal can lead our men. This is his idea, and I see he burns for the chance to fight."

"I will place our men under Chief Den'rack's command," Garal said. "He will lead us with honor."

"No, that will not be allowed," Chief Bekka said. "If anything goes wrong, if many Ur Nammu warriors are killed, I want no blame to fall upon Den'rack and the Alur Meriki."

"I agree with Chief Bekka," Subutai said. "On so small a raid, the Ur Nammu and Alur Meriki must have a single leader. Sargon should lead the raid, with Den'rack and Garal as his war chieftains. That way, Sargon will bear the responsibility for leading the warriors."

"That is wise," Den'rack said. "I accept Sargon to lead the raid. He will command us honorably."

"I, too, agree," Chinua said. "His father fights for his life. Sargon will do what must be done."

"Sargon," Bekka said, "do you accept command of these warriors? The odds you will face will be daunting."

Every eye went to Sargon. Surprise still showed on his face at being asked to lead the warriors, a possibility he had never dreamed of. The situation had spun out of control with a few words. Even so, Sargon didn't hesitate. He'd never considered such a role, but he recovered fast enough.

"I accept command of these brave warriors. I will pray to the gods that I lead them with honor and to victory."

Bekka and Subutai exchanged glances. The decision was made. If the King's son died on a foolhardy raid, his blood would not be on their hands.

Sargon had just received his first command.

37

Sargon and his new commanders wasted not a moment. Modran might be sending men back into Elam at any time. Den'rack and Garal quickly chose their men, who then assembled the required weapons, food, and water. At the same time, warriors took their pick of the captured horses. Once again, Sargon would undertake a long and dangerous ride leading a spare mount.

Fifteen additional horses would carry extra supplies, mostly food and water. Some of the supplies would be hidden along the trail, to provide sustenance on the return to Zanbil. The pack horses would provide still more additional mounts should they be needed. The extra horses could be abandoned at the first sign of trouble.

Though the sun had already started its descent, the war party left Zanbil at a fast canter, one hundred men, two hundred and fifteen horses. Two scouts ranged about a mile ahead of the troop, to bring word of any Elamite cavalry or more messengers for Zanbil.

Changing horses twice, they rode until it grew too dark for safe travel. As soon as Sargon swung down from his horse, he asked Garal and Den'rack to join him. To Sargon's surprise, both Garal and Den'rack brought another warrior with them. Jennat accompanied Garal, and Yassur, the warrior who had spied on the Carchemishi camp two years ago, followed Den'rack.

Garal smiled at Sargon's look of surprise. "When the leader of a war party speaks with his commanders, it is the custom for each to bring one of his clan brothers with him."

"Yes, it is as Garal says," Den'rack agreed. "This way, no commander can claim to have forgotten or misunderstood orders."

Sargon shrugged. "What I want to say is that either you or Garal have more experience leading warriors than I. What formalities had to be observed in front of Chief Bekka and Subutai need no longer be followed. Now that we have left them behind, I would prefer that one of you take command of the warriors."

Den'rack chuckled. "Ah, but for us, it is even more important to follow what you call the formalities. You were given the command by Chief Bekka, so you must keep it."

"I agree," Garal said, "but we should all be guided by Den'rack. He is the oldest and the most experienced. All of our warriors will take confidence if we listen to his advice."

Sargon nodded at what his mother would call a polite fiction. But clearly Garal wanted to put aside any attempt by his men to take command. It would be Den'rack who offered 'suggestions.' Their serious expressions convinced him not to push the issue.

"Then I also agree," Sargon said. "But both of you must speak your minds. Den'rack, in the morning, you will set the pace. We should travel as fast as possible, but if we can strike a blow at the Elamites, we will need to have enough strength in our horses to fight or outrun any pursuers. Now, perhaps you could share your thoughts with us."

"We've already traveled about ten miles," Den'rack said. "If we cover thirty miles tomorrow, and again the next day, we should reach the rear guard of the Elamites just before sundown. That would give us time to scout their position before it grows too dark, and then we could launch a night attack, like the one Bekka led against the Carchemishi."

Since none of them knew exactly how the Elamites had positioned their troops, there wasn't much else in the way of planning they could do now. They did, however, talk about what they would do if they met any enemy horsemen returning to Zanbil.

When the small war council broke up, Sargon felt satisfied. He had no interest in glory, and was more than willing to give that and any credit to Den'rack and Garal. All Sargon wanted was the opportunity to strike a real blow at the Elamites. Any diversion or delay he and the warriors inflicted on the enemy would relieve pressure on Eskkar and the Akkadians.

Garal's idea for the raid, Sargon understood, matched what Eskkar would have done. Sargon's father never let an opportunity pass by to strike a blow against his enemies. Sargon now had the chance to follow that code.

Even so, for the first time since he had ridden out of the warrior staging camp seven days ago, sleep didn't come easily, and when it did, Sargon's gloomy dreams kept jerking him awake. He finally recognized the signs for what they were – the fears of a young, inexperienced commander leading older and likely wiser men into battle.

All the same, his commanders needed him to lead. Sargon belonged to neither the Ur Nammu or the Alur Meriki, and so both could follow him into battle without any loss of honor. He had one last thought before he settled into a deeper sleep. Ordering men to risk their lives by following his orders wasn't as easy as he expected it to be.

In the morning, well before the sun had cleared the high peaks of the Dellen Pass, Sargon and his men mounted and continued their rapid journey, moving as fast as the ups and downs of the trail permitted. The excited jabbering of young warriors, most of them eager for their first battle, soon disappeared under the pressure of the grueling ride. Not to mention that everyone had to struggle with a second horse and the extra supplies.

Noon came and went without event. But just before midafternoon, one of the scouts came racing back to their main troop.

"Sargon," the man shouted, "riders are approaching."

Sargon raised his hand and brought the column to a halt. "Did they see you?"

"No. But they can't be far behind."

"How many?"

"Not sure," the scout replied. "At least ten, maybe more."

Sargon knew the numbers made no difference. Their trail was too prominent and fresh. The Elamites would notice it before they had ridden a hundred paces. The warriors would have to fight, regardless of the odds. At the same time he wondered what had happened to the second scout, but there was no time even to ask the question.

Den'rack and Garal took charge. They placed all the men to the left side of the passage, where a few large boulders offered some concealment. The spare horses and pack animals were handed off to the youngest warriors, who cursed their misfortune, while the rest readied their weapons.

By then Sargon could hear the hoof beats echoing off the rocky walls. Garal and Den'rack moved their horses to either side of

Sargon's mount. Every man readied his weapons, and Sargon unslung his lance. The sound of hoofbeats grew louder, and then with a rush, a band of riders appeared, curling around a large boulder that marked the trail.

Den'rack gave a shout. In an instant more than eighty warriors surged forward, screaming their war cries. That sound, as much as the sudden appearance of so many barbarians, panicked the Elamite horses as well as their riders. Caught by surprise in the narrow confines of the Pass, the enemy riders dragged their horses to a halt as they tried to turn them around and flee. But the Elamites had no chance of escaping the ambush.

Leaning forward, Garal launched the first shaft, putting an arrow into the soldier leading the way. More missiles tore into the surprised mass of riders, their path forward now completely blocked by Sargon's warriors. Then the Elamites were too close for the warriors to work their bows.

Sargon, his mount driving forward as eagerly as the rest, leaned low beside his horse's neck, his lance clutched tight in his hand. An enemy soldier, a shaft sticking into his shoulder, still managed to draw his sword. Sargon thrust the sharp lance into the man's chest, knocking him off his horse and tearing Sargon's weapon from his hand.

He drew his sword, but by then fighting had ended. The Elamites had numbered less than twenty, and all were down, caught by surprise and overwhelmed by numbers. The second scout, brandishing his bow and shouting in triumph, appeared. He had hidden himself while the Elamites rode past, then killed the only enemy who managed to turn his horse about and try to escape back up the Pass.

"Stop the killing," Sargon called out. "Garal, see if any are still alive."

Garal flung himself from his horse and sword in hand, inspected the bodies. He gave a shout as he dragged a dazed and wounded man to his knees. The prisoner had an arrow protruding from the fleshy part of his chest close to his armpit. Blood had already soaked his tunic, and more continued to flow.

Either the shaft had unseated the rider, or more likely, his panicked horse had tossed him to the ground. The wounded man was the only survivor, and from the look of his injury, he wouldn't last much longer.

Sargon dismounted and approached the Elamite. "You're the only one left alive. If you want to live, you'll answer my questions."

Dazed, the man glanced up at the fearsome warriors, many with blood still on their swords, who surrounded him.

"Where were you going, and what message did you carry?" Sargon seized the man by his hair, drew his knife, and held it to the man's throat. "Answer me now, if you want to live. Or are you eager to die like your companions?"

The words came out in a rush. Just a common soldier, he knew little. The riders were bound for Zanbil, to speed up the delivery of additional supplies. Lord Modran had demanded more food and water, as well as shields and any planks in Zanbil. Apparently Modran had tried a second time to force the Akkadian lines in the Pass and suffered another defeat.

After the battle Lord Modran had become enraged, vowing to break the Akkadian army blocking his way, if he had to kill half his army to do it. Sargon asked a few more questions, but obtained nothing else of value. Exhausted by his wound, the prisoner's head sagged onto his chest.

Satisfied that he had learned all he could, Sargon thrust his knife into the dying man's heart. With a gasp more of surprise than pain, the man collapsed on his back, his eyes going wide for a moment before death took him.

Sargon took no pleasure in the killing. But as leader of the warriors, he had to show strength before them. No enemy, no matter how badly wounded, could be allowed to live and possibly cause harm to the warriors or their plans. Sargon could have ordered one of his men to kill the prisoner, but that would have shown weakness.

Ignoring the body at his feet, Sargon turned to his men. "My father's army still holds the Pass, and now has twice driven back the Elamites. Tomorrow we will strike their rear, and bring confusion to their ranks and fear into their hearts."

A cheer went up from the warriors. Not a man had been lost in this fight, so quick and ruthless the action. Buoyed by their victory, the warriors were now ready for anything.

"Warriors! It is time to ride hard," Sargon shouted. "Strip the bodies of everything useful, even their clothing, and bring up the extra horses. We may need them."

Another cheer went up. In moments, the naked bodies of the dead had been dragged behind some rocks, and looted of their weapons and valuables. The extra horses were collected, and once again Sargon led the way deeper into the Dellen Pass.

As they rode, Den'rack and Garal exchanged glances. Both men smiled. Sargon was indeed learning how to fight, and how to command.

38

B y midafternoon of the next day, Sargon's warriors were near exhaustion. Every man had pushed himself to the utmost. Even the horses looked spent, despite their frequent rests while their riders changed mounts. The last twenty miles of their ride had taken them over the hardest part of the Pass, and stretched both man and beast to their limits.

The ride gave Sargon a better appreciation of Modran's dead messengers, caught by surprise after the arduous ride. They, too, had covered the rough ground with remarkable speed. But now the slope of the trail tended to be mostly down, and Sargon knew they had drawn close to Modran's army.

"Sargon! A scout is returning." Den'rack, riding at Sargon's side, showed little effect from the punishing journey.

Sargon looked up to see a rider galloping toward them. Sargon halted the warriors, who bunched up around him, all eager to hear the news.

Pulling his horse to a stop, the man blurted out what he'd seen. The rear guard of Lord Modran's army lay just over a mile ahead.

This time Sargon had to see for himself. He halted the warriors and ordered them to stay where they were. Then, with only Den'rack, Garal, and the scout, Sargon rode the final mile through the Dellen Pass. When the four reached the second scout, Sargon swung down from his mount, and the leaders covered the last fifty paces on foot.

The scout pointed to a sloping boulder, and they scrambled up the slippery stone until they reached the top. Flat on their stomachs, they peered down the trail at the back end of Lord Modran's army.

A little over a quarter mile ahead, Sargon studied the rear guard of Modran's troops. Not really soldiers, of course. These were the siege workers, the diggers and sappers, the carpenters who would construct ladders and shields, butchers and cooks to feed everyone, and livery men to help with the pack animals.

At least a hundred tents, crammed into every part of the Pass, provided shelter. Only a thin ribbon of the trail, enough for two or three horses side by side, remained open in the center of the Pass.

"Where are the horses?" Garal sounded surprised. "Wouldn't they keep the horses at the rear?"

"They'll be up ahead," Sargon said. "The cavalry would want their mounts as close as possible, in case they needed them. There must be some just around that curve in the trail. These are only the laborers that Modran will use in the siege of Akkad. Most are unarmed."

"With so many tents," Den'rack said, "there may be two or three hundred men between us and the herds."

"Probably more," Sargon said. His experience with Akkad's soldiers and their support units gave him a better grasp of the Elamite's numbers. "But I don't see any fighting men, only a few guards. Modran isn't expecting any threats from his rear."

Sargon kept studying the enemy position. The men camped before him were clearly not fighters. No doubt most of them would panic at the first sight of a sword.

"When we ride into them, the noise will alert the guards up ahead who are protecting the horses," Garal said. "They'll be waiting for us."

Still thinking through the problem, Sargon didn't reply at first. "Perhaps. But there may be a way to make this work for us."

He sketched out his idea, one simple but daring enough to appeal to the warriors. Both Den'rack and Garal offered suggestions and improvements. Soon a workable plan emerged, risky, but one that would satisfy every warrior's craving for blood and honor.

"Then it's settled," Sargon said, hoping that his idea wouldn't get them all killed. "We'll have to prepare the warriors with care. Each one will have his task."

"They'll be ready," Den'rack said. "This will give everyone more fight than they imagined."

"Then as soon as night falls, we go." Sargon turned to Garal. "If this works, you'll have a better story to tell around the campfire than Chinua."

Garal chuckled. "As long as I'm alive to tell it."

The evening shadows arrived early in the mountainous terrain. The siege workers ended their day even before the shadows began to lengthen. They had little energy, receiving a smaller ration of food than the rest of Modran's fighters. Water was even scarcer, and many of them had little more than a mouthful since the morning.

The few guards posted were lax as well. Tasked with keeping anyone from trying to desert and head back through the Pass toward Zanbil, they kept their eyes on the trail to the west. But they turned quickly enough when they heard the sound of hoof beats echoing off the cliff walls.

Two riders appeared, pushing their horses hard up the slight incline. The leader of the guards, a heavyset man almost too old to fight, moved to the center of the trail, and raised his hand.

The two messengers, wearing the tunics and emblems of Modran's personal staff, pulled their lathered horses to a stop.

"What news from Zanbil do you bring?" The guard got right to the point. "Is food and water on the way?"

"Yes, and we've urgent news for Lord Modran," Sargon answered. "There's a company of horsemen right behind us carrying supplies and weapons. Clear this rabble from the trail."

The guard stared at Sargon for a moment. He didn't recognize the messengers, but that meant nothing. Modran's staff was large enough for two armies. He turned his eyes to the second man. "How far have you ridden?"

"From Zanbil and beyond," Garal snapped. "My commander ordered you to clear the way. The reinforcements, a hundred men and a hundred pack animals, are right behind us."

Both messengers spoke the main Elamite language. The guard didn't recognize their accent, but with so many men from different lands fighting in Modran's army, that was to be expected.

The sounds of horses approaching grew louder. Down the slope came the reinforcements, moving at an easy canter and riding in a column of twos, most of them leading extra pack horses.

"Let's ride," Sargon said. "Lord Modran is waiting for us."

The guard and his men shrank aside, and Sargon and Garal put their horses to a canter. With the main troop almost upon them, the guard ordered his men to clear a path. They knew none of Modran's cavalry would think twice about trampling some lazy laborer or overly officious guard.

Then the horses trotted past, guided by grim looking fighters. The leader of the guards gave them the briefest glance as they rode by his post. The next guard post, at the rear of the horse herds, would take the reinforcements through.

In moments the troop of riders had come and gone, disappearing up the trail, and the guard resumed his main duty, making sure no one deserted Lord Modran's army.

Sargon breathed a sigh of relief as they left the rear guard behind. Garal, riding at his side, laughed softly.

"Well, the first part of your plan worked. The rest of the warriors are coming through."

"It will not be as easy to get out as it was to get in," Sargon said. Still, he, too, smiled in the deepening darkness.

He and Garal had dressed in garments taken from the dead messengers. Just as important, they both spoke Elam's main dialect, and that more than anything disarmed the sentry's suspicions. The rest of Sargon's men had been told to keep their mouths shut, and just ride through at the same steady pace. A handful of warriors had also donned whatever usable clothing they'd taken from the dead.

All the warriors had removed their feathers and any signs that would mark them as men of the steppes. They had also left their lances, a favorite weapon of the steppes fighters, behind. Their short, curved bows, worn across their chests, attracted no attention.

If Sargon and Garal had been challenged, they would have abandoned their plan to reach the enemy horses. Instead, they would have attacked the rear guard, and done what damage they could.

But the deception – Sargon remembered his father telling him that all warfare is based on deception – had worked perfectly. Now the entire group of warriors had moved into the gap between the support troops and the first of the horse herds. That gap, less than a quarter mile long, soon ended.

Once again Sargon saw a handful of sentries watching them approach. But this time Sargon didn't halt. "Messages and supplies for Lord Modran," he shouted as he brushed past the guards.

"Clear the way, you fools," Garal shouted.

Nevertheless, Sargon slowed his horse to a trot. The horse herd, held in by ropes and separated on both sides of the trail, might be spooked by any large group of fast moving riders.

A hundred paces behind them, Den'rack matched Sargon's pace, and his men followed his lead. They kept their eyes straight ahead, as if their only interest lay in reaching their destination. They followed the trail as it twisted and turned its way through the Pass.

The place selected by the Elamites to hold the horses was mostly flat. Small guard details of two or three men were posted every three or four hundred paces. Their assignment was to make sure some drunken fool didn't stampede the horses, or possibly steal one in attempting to desert. Most of these sentries didn't even bother to look up as Sargon's warriors rode by in the gathering darkness. Each assumed that someone else had cleared the riders.

"By the gods, how many horses are there?" Garal spoke just loud enough to be heard by Sargon.

Sargon had been wondering the same thing. Many of the horses in the herd, lifting their heads to stare as the troop trotted past, showed more interest in their passing than did the guards. He kept counting, estimating the size of this herd.

Modran had entered the Pass with nine thousand cavalry. Likely he would keep a good sized force of horsemen near the front lines, in the event his Elamites could break Eskkar's position. The rest would be kept here, in the rear.

Moving with care, Sargon's force rode by the first horse herd, then the second and a third. The Elamites appeared to be keeping the herds about a quarter mile apart, which made sense with so many horses.

He tried to keep a rough count of the horses. Each herd numbered between three and four hundred horses, with ten or twenty guards for every group. If the herds grew too large, no one would be able to find a particular horse. After Sargon passed the fourth herd, they encountered a large campsite with at least two hundred men taking their ease.

By now no one even glanced at Sargon's men as they rode by. Everyone assumed that he was riding to the front of the camp and Modran's headquarters.

After passing two more herds, Sargon guessed he had ridden past more than two thousand horses. He raised his hand, and slowed the warriors to a gradual halt, easing to a stop just between the last herd and the one up ahead.

"I think we've come far enough, Garal," he said. "If we go any deeper into the Pass, we'll never get out alive."

"Yes, I think this is more than enough glory for anyone, at least for me."

"Let's hope we don't get more glory than we bargained for," Sargon said. "I don't want to be remembered as the fool who rode into the center of Modran's army and disappeared.

Den'rack and the others joined them.

"We've ridden far enough," Sargon said. "I'll take sixty warriors and stampede the herds ahead of us toward Modran's front line. Jennat will take forty warriors and stampede the herds we passed back down the trail."

Neither clan leader had wanted that assignment. Both Den'rack and Garal wanted the honor and danger that would arise from moving toward the soldiers. And so Den'rack had placed Jennat of the Ur Nammu, and Yassur of the Alur Meriki in charge of driving the smaller herd back down the Pass and toward Zanbil.

Sargon, too, refused to lead the rear movement. "Jennat, wait until we've stampeded the next herd, then start your attack. That may give us both a few extra moments of surprise." He turned to Garal and Den'rack. "Are you ready?" He didn't want to waste any more time debating the assignments. Some too alert guard might wonder why the riders stopped in the middle of the Pass, with nothing but horses in front and rear.

"Yes! Let's ride!" Garal's loud voice echoed off the walls, and the nearby Elamite horses lifted their heads.

Den'rack began the stampede. He kicked his horse forward, letting loose a war cry that startled every Elamite horse. His booming voice filled the Pass. "Ride, warriors, ride!"

Garal matched him stride for stride, leaving a cursing Sargon three lengths behind. Giving voice to their war cries, the sixty chosen warriors moved forward, spreading out as they did. Arrows were launched at the herd in front of them. In moments both sides of the Pass erupted to the thunder of hundreds of horses on the move, all heading west toward Modran's battle line, guided and urged on by Sargon's warriors.

The Elamite horses, many struck by arrows meant to wound, not kill, turned away from the shouting and war cries bearing down on them. The flimsy ropes holding them in snapped unnoticed. The horses, their fear intensified by the screams of the wounded animals and the scent of blood, raced through the Pass, heading west.

Even the hard and rocky ground of the Dellen Pass shook under the horses' hooves. The next herd, already spooked by the increasing sound, started stirring as well. The moment those animals saw the oncoming horses, they, too, stampeded away from the approaching and thoroughly frightened horses. Adding to the panic were the screaming war cries and sharp arrows of Sargon's warriors.

By the time Sargon reached the third holding place, at least a thousand horses galloped ahead of him through the Pass. And while in a normal stampede the animals might run a quarter mile before slowing down, the presence of the warriors driving them along with shouts and arrows, and even their swords, ensured that the herd did not stop.

Elamite guards, caught by surprise as much as their horses, were trampled underfoot or forced to run for their lives to the sides of the Pass. Those that made it clung to the rocks, weapons and tools forgotten. They watched helplessly as the horses, kept to a frenzy by the strange horsemen, raced past. Campfires, cooking utensils, sleeping blankets, even tents disappeared under the hooves of a thousand terrified horses.

Den'rack, leading the way and launching arrows as fast as any of his men, finally held up his hand. Sargon and the others slowed to a stop beside him.

"Time to go back," Den'rack shouted. "The horses will run for at least a mile now. We must turn around."

Some of the eager warriors wanted to continue riding, but Sargon, too, recognized the danger. The farther into the Pass they went, the more Elamites they would encounter, and the easier it would be for them to be trapped. He gave the order and the reluctant warriors turned their horses around.

This time Sargon led the way at a gallop. They needed to close up behind Jennat as fast as possible. His forty men had to drive well over two thousands horses, and keep them on the move so that they ran all the way back through the Elamite rear guard and down the Pass.

As Sargon's warriors raced eastward through the now empty portion of the Pass, the Elamites began to recover from their surprise. Shouts and curses, and even a few arrows were launched at the galloping riders. Sargon, glancing behind him, saw one warrior take an arrow in the throat and pitch from his horse. But then that section of the trail lay behind them, and they kept riding, urging their tired mounts to run as fast as possible.

At last Sargon glimpsed Jennat's warriors a quarter mile ahead. The much larger mass of horses had obviously required more work to stampede, and more urging to continue. But soon Sargon's riders added their voices to those of Jennat's men, and the massive herd, though slowed now to an easy gallop, kept moving.

They swept through what was left of the invaders' rear guard, and Sargon saw the flattened tents. More than a few bodies littered the ground, proof that some of the laborers had not managed to reach the safety of the cliff walls in time.

Then the last enemy camp lay behind them. The Elamites would pursue them, of course, but it would take them a long time to regain control of their horses, find their mounts, and regroup.

Den'rack, his quiver empty, slowed his horse and joined Sargon. "We're stampeded more horses than Chief Bekka did to the Carchemishi."

Sargon grinned. "Now you have your own story to tell."

Both men laughed, and they continued down the Pass. Neither man noticed that Garal wasn't with them.

Lord Modran stood outside his tent after meeting with his commanders, angry at the time wasted in coordinating the plans for the final assault. His commanders, so efficient in laying siege to walled villages and cities, and so resourceful at attacking opponents on open ground, seemed both confused and incompetent in the Dellen Pass. The large size of the Elamite army added to the chaos, consuming food and water at an alarming rate, and all the while accomplishing nothing.

Once again Modran cursed the King of Akkad. Eskkar's men maintained their ranks efficiently, and his supply line continued to deliver war materials to his men. The sight of the steadily arriving food, water, and weapons had sapped the morale of Modran's soldiers, as they contrasted their plight with those of their Akkadian enemies.

Earlier in the evening another disaster had befallen Modran's army. The Akkadian slingers had done far more than just disrupt his night attack. With a handful of stones flung through the darkness, they had exposed his plan of attack and unnerved his soldiers.

The insignificant raid had changed the order of battle from a night attack to a full assault at dawn. With it, the certainty of victory had vanished, too, and tomorrow promised another savage conflict. Modran's anger seethed at every delay.

Regrouping his men took far longer than he expected. Fueling his rage, none of Modran's supposedly fearless commanders, so loud and boastful when the march started from Zanbil, had offered to lead the attack. Finally Lord Modran and General Martiya had decided the marching order for the morning's battle.

Every one of his subcommanders knew tomorrow's fight would be brutal and bloody. They'd come close to breaking Eskkar's line in the last encounter, but this one promised to be even more vicious.

Although the Akkadians had suffered heavy losses of their own, the Elamite soldiers recognized the truth – Eskkar's soldiers were not going to flee in terror, not going to retreat, not going to give ground. They had shown their enemies that they were willing to die on their feet and fighting to the last to defend the Pass.

No such beliefs supported Modran's soldiers. They fought because their leaders ordered them to. Thoughts of quick conquests and easy lootings in the lush countryside of the Land Between the Rivers had vanished. Without that lure, and confined within the Dellen Pass, the old bitterness between the disparate groups that comprised the army returned.

No matter who won tomorrow's battle, thousands of Elamites were going to die. No soldier wanted to be one of those dead, in order to allow others to win the war.

Both Modran and Martiya recognized the signs. The men would have to be driven into combat. To support the morning attack, and make sure his men didn't waver, Modran's Immortals, two thousand men, were divided into two groups.

The largest, fifteen hundred strong, would attack in a column and try to break through Eskkar's right flank, much the same plan as the discarded night attack. The remaining five hundred would be spread out behind the rest of the assault force, ostensibly to act as the reserve, but with orders to kill any soldier who failed to press the attack or tried to retreat.

After receiving their orders, the gloomy subcommanders headed off to their own tents and their own preparations. Modran breathed a long sigh of relief. He expected to lose half his remaining men in the coming battle, possibly more. Such a thought, unthinkable only ten days ago, now meant little. He had to win. After squandering so many men, a furious King Shirudukh would strip him of his rank and wealth the moment the news reached Sushan that Akkad remained undefeated.

Suddenly Modran felt the ground beneath his feet tremble. At first he thought it was an earth shaker, a fearful prospect here inside the Dellen Pass, where cliffs could topple onto the trail and flatten hundreds of men in an instant. But the shaking went on, and he soon recognized the sound of hoofbeats. Before he had time to react, the soldiers outside his tent erupted into shouts. Horses were galloping through the camp, neighing and rolling their eyes.

One animal raced past Modran, and he saw an arrow protruding from its rump. No doubt some fool of a soldier had mistaken a horse for an Akkadian.

Some of his men tried to catch one or two of the horses, but most of the soldiers just scattered, eager to get out of the way of the half-crazed animals. Confusion swept through the camp. Men who had just turned in for the night, hoping to get a brief respite before the battle, shouted that they were under attack, that the steppes barbarians had stampeded the horses. Other voices blamed the men in the rear guard, or even some of Jedidia's troops, forced to join Modran's army and fight under his command.

Modran's tent lay a quarter of a mile behind the front of the Elamite line. His cavalry's horses, divided into ten herds, stretched nearly two miles from Modran's quarters, in the opposite direction. From the sheer number of horses, he realized that something had spooked several herds, causing the frightened beasts to race through the entire Elamite camp.

Many of the winded horses now trotted into the peaceful and empty space between the two armies. Whatever had happened at the army's rear to spook the animals, the stampede had finally slowed, then stopped.

The Elamite soldiers closest to the Akkadians had panicked as well, thinking their foes had launched a second night attack. A babble of voices rose into the night, with everyone speaking at once and each man knowing as little as his companions.

For the second time that night, Modran shouted for Martiya and for his other commanders. This time, it took even longer for them to reassemble. Modran, his face white with rage, ordered his leaders to get their men under control, and find out what had stampeded the horses.

Midnight had passed before a weary Martiya dismounted at Modran's tent. "It was a barbarian raid." Martiya shook his head. "I still can't believe it, but one of my men recognized their war cries, watched the way they rode. Somehow they got through the rear guard without being stopped, moved half way through the horse camps until they got to the middle of the herds, then stampeded our horses."

Modran felt his jaw drop. "Barbarians! Here? Why would they ride into the Pass, just to stampede our horses?"

"My Lord, they stampeded the horses in both directions." Martiya kept his voice calm and his words soothing. He knew Modran's patience had vanished. "Once they got the horses moving to the west, they turned around and raced back toward the east and Zanbil, driving a large herd ahead of them."

"How many horses . . . how many barbarians were there?"

"Not that many, maybe fifty or sixty," Martiya said. "But they drove off more than two thousand horses. And the rear guard is a shambles, full of injured and dead men trampled underfoot. Horses are wandering around and through every camp. Some of our supplies were destroyed as well, not to mention the hundreds of injured or dead horses."

Modran recalled how difficult it had been to find and pay for each and every one of those animals. Now many were gone, stolen by barbarians. The loss of the siege workers meant nothing, not now. "Can we get the stolen horses back?"

Martiya scratched his chin. "It's almost seventy miles to the mouth of the Pass, and I don't think even barbarians can control that many horses that far. Probably half will drop out and turn aside into the rocks. But at least ten or twelve hundred will be gone for good. My cavalry commander is getting his men organized and mounted. He can have three hundred men on their trail at daylight."

"The barbarians ride at night! Why can't your men do the same?"

"These barbarians have stolen almost two thousand horses, My Lord." Martiya kept his tone respectful, though he, too, wanted to vent his frustration. " If they lose a hundred of them riding in the dark, they won't even notice."

The more Modran thought about it, the less he liked it. By daybreak, the barbarians would have covered plenty of distance, at least ten or fifteen miles. Without leading extra horses themselves, Martiya's men were not going to catch the raiders, not tomorrow.

Modran made up his mind. "No. Let them go. But post a strong guard at our rear, in case they decide to launch another raid."

"That's not what worries me," Martiya said. "If the barbarians entered the Pass, that must mean Zanbil is gone, overrun, its supplies taken or destroyed. I don't think we'll be getting any help from there."

Speechless for a moment, Modran stared at his general. The impact of Martiya's words took a few moments to absorb. "Eskkar! Could he have done this? Turned the barbarians against us?"

"They say he was once one of them. He may have paid them to raid Zanbil and disrupt our supply line. It would explain why none of your messengers to Zanbil have returned."

"Then we've no food coming," Modran said. "We need those supplies now more than ever."

Martiya took a deep breath. "If we want to eat and drink anything tomorrow, we're going to have to take food from the Akkadians."

Modran found himself clutching at the hilt of his sword, still belted around his waist. "What should we do about tomorrow's attack?"

"Our soldiers are uneasy over the idea of barbarians behind them. They're worried we'll be attacked again. Many of them want to turn back."

"Damn the cowards!" Modran's bellow of rage echoed off the cliff. "A handful of men dead and some horses stolen by barbarian scum, and our men are frightened to death? Put a few of the weaklings to the sword. That should silence the rest. Tell the men the horses mean nothing, that we won't need them once we've crushed the Akkadians."

Modran's anger and frustration threatened to rise to the surface. He took a deep breath, and tried to regain control of his emotions. "Martiya, tell the men that there's no food in Zanbil. Tell them that as soon as we defeat these accursed Akkadians, every man will have his pay tripled for the rest of the war. That should put some courage in their backbones."

Martiya glanced up at the moon. More than half the night had passed. "Perhaps it might be better, My Lord, to wait another day before attacking Eskkar's lines? That would give the men time to get some rest and recover their will to fight."

"The longer we wait, the stronger Eskkar becomes. Even now, our men are beginning to doubt that we can win. Some are saying foreign gods protect the Akkadians, and that Eskkar has never been defeated, cannot be defeated. The more time our soldiers have to dwell on such thoughts, the weaker we become. We attack at first light as planned. And remind them that any man who falters will be killed on the spot. The Immortals will break Eskkar's battle line."

Martiya saw that Modran's mind was made up. "Yes, My Lord." Martiya turned and strode off into the night. But deep within his heart, doubt about tomorrow's battle had already taken hold.

Lord Modran got little sleep the rest of the night. He and Martiya found themselves forced to answer a host of questions. The stampede had disrupted not only the rhythm of the camp, but the very position of the men. The cavalry, most to be held in reserve for the final effort, still had not collected enough mounts for the three thousand man reserve. Every commander and even subcommanders sought guidance and clarification of the simplest orders.

When he did finally lie down, alone in his tent, Modran found he could do little more than toss and turn. Eskkar and his puny force had to be defeated, destroyed. Had to. Not since Modran's youth had he fought in a battle to the death. Tomorrow's fight had to be won, or Modran faced death as surely as if Eskkar shoved a sword into his stomach.

When Modran did slip into an uneasy sleep, dark dreams made him toss and turn. But soon enough, his servant woke him.

"It's time, My Lord. Dawn approaches."

Rubbing his eyes, Modran pushed himself to his feet. "I'll come." He laced on his sandals and armor, then belted the sword around his waist. Other than that, he'd laid down fully dressed.

A single torch burned outside his tent. Martiya, still rubbing the sleep from his eyes, approached the war table. Modran stood and watched as Martiya went through the final preparations. At last,

Martiya gave the order, and the commanders departed to join their
men.

By the time the first glimmer of gray weakened the black of night,
the Elamite army waited in their ranks, ready to attack. Modran
would pace his horse alongside his infantry, until he reached his
observation post just beyond range of the Akkadian long bows.
There he would take command of the cavalry reserves and wait for
the breakthrough. Martiya and his staff would lead the actual assault.

The eastern sky turned pink, outlining the mountains to the rear.
As soon as the first rays of dawn banished enough of the night for
his men to see their feet, Martiya gave the order. A drum began to
beat. The third Elamite attack had begun.

Earlier that night, Eskkar, Alexar, and the other commanders stood
at the center of their battle line, staring down the slope into the
darkness. All of them had heard the sound of horses on the move,
and the tumult from the Elamite position. At first Eskkar thought a
night attack by the Elamite cavalry was in progress.

The Akkadians, sleeping at their positions, roused themselves and
prepared to receive another assault. But instead of war cries
emanating from the enemy position, they heard only shouts of
confusion and the whinnying of horses.

Shappa's slingers, out in the empty space between the two hosts,
reported that riderless horses were wandering up the slope, picking
their way through the dead bodies that littered the ground. Eskkar
counted at least twenty of the curious animals, who trotted almost all
the way to the ranks of the Akkadians before they decided to turn
back down the slope.

"One of their horse herds must have stampeded," Alexar said.
"Must have run right through the camp."

"One herd wouldn't make that much noise," Muta said. "That
sounded like a lot of horses."

"Whatever it was, I don't think they're going to try again tonight,"
Eskkar said, thinking out loud. "They'll need time to recover their
mounts, and then position themselves once again for the attack."

"If there were more than one herd stampeding, then they may
postpone another assault," Drakis said.

Eskkar thought about that. A big stampede would normally require
a day or two to recover the horses. But here in the Pass, the beasts

had no place to scatter. Nor had they proved very useful. "No, I think they'll still come tomorrow. Modran hasn't any time to waste chasing after loose horses. He's running low on food and water, and by now Sargon and the warriors will have cut the Elamite supply line. Either Modran turns back, or he throws every man against us tomorrow."

"The warriors have had enough time to reach Zanbil," Alexar said. "Do you think Sargon had anything to do with the stampede?"

"On most days," Eskkar said, "I'd say only a fool would ride seventy miles into the Dellen Pass and challenge Modran's army. But some of Sargon's warrior friends are eager for glory. Remember Chinua leading the charge at the Battle of Isin? They might have decided to try and steal some horses."

"Well, whatever happened," Alexar said, "it's not likely to help us tomorrow."

That seemed true enough, Eskkar decided. "Tell the men to stand down, and get some more rest. Tomorrow promises to be a long day."

Garal had waited until Den'rack and Sargon gave the order to turn back. He, too, wheeled his horse about, but moved to the side, slowing his mount until the other warriors had put their horses to the gallop. As soon as the last of the Sargon's riders passed Garal by, he turned again and headed west once more, leaning low against the neck of his horse as he raced back up the Pass.

Racing through the darkness as fast as he could, Garal managed to catch up to the rear of the stampeding horses just as the Elamite guards and soldiers rushed into the gap, trying to stop the panicked animals. All the same, plenty of horses ran about in every direction, and the disorganized efforts of the Elamites kept the frightened mounts moving forward. The rush of the herd to the west continued, though most of the horses slowed their pace to a canter.

Clinging to his horse, Garal urged the animals onward. He kept in the middle of the trail. Whenever the horses near him began to slow down, he jabbed the point of his knife into the nearest flank. That resulted in the wounded animal neighing in pain and breaking into another gallop, which helped keep all of them moving.

The horses, now spread out over the width of the Pass, continued their movement to the west and through the main force of the enemy.

Fortunately for Garal, the ground now sloped downward, making it easier for the horses to keep on the move.

The galloping horses had kicked the occasional Elamite campfires into ashes. None of the milling soldiers thought to look closely at the running horses, nor did they expect to see one man hunched over, his silhouette barely visible in the darkness. One mile passed, and still no one had sounded an alarm. Even those who did notice him never imagined that an enemy would be so bold as to ride through their camp.

Another half mile passed under his horse's hooves, and Garal had not yet reached the leading edge of the Elamites. The number of horses still running had diminished, and he guessed that now only a few hundred continued their rush through the Pass. Regardless, the soldiers moving about fixed all their efforts on getting the mounts under control, and as far as Garal could tell, none of them had seen him as he slipped by.

At last Garal saw blackness ahead, the empty space that marked the end of the Elamite's position. Two small campfires still burned, and he picked out a line of enemy sentries. Nevertheless, most of them were still focused on the horses, while the rest kept their eyes to the front, in case the Akkadians should try to attack.

Urging on a handful of horses, Garal rode right between two guards. If they saw him, they failed to give the alarm, and no arrows hissed by his head or into his back.

Once in the open space, Garal sat upright on his horse. About twenty mounts still trotted along, turning aside now that they had reached an open space of relative calm. He guided his mount alongside a weary horse and grabbed its dangling halter. With two horses, he might survive should he lose his own.

Ahead, he glimpsed three more campfires, strung out in a line across the width of the Pass, that had to mark Eskkar's battle line. Now all Garal had to worry about was getting an arrow in his chest from one of the Akkadians.

He took one last glance over his shoulder, and decided that he'd ridden far enough from the Elamite front line. Taking a deep breath, he called out to the unseen sentries. "Akkadians! Akkadians! I bring a message from Sargon of Akkad!"

Slowing his tired horses to a walk, he repeated the words again and again. A shadow flitted across his path, but Garal didn't slow.

The Akkadians would have their own scouts out in the empty space between the lines. Now he had to hope one of these didn't put a shaft into him.

"I bring a message from Sargon of Akkad!" The line of campfires drew closer. Now he was less than a hundred and fifty paces away.

"Halt! Stay where you are!"

Garal pulled back on his halter, and raised both hands high in the air. "I am Garal of the Ur Nammu, and I carry a message to King Eskkar from his son, Sargon of Akkad."

Voices whispered in the night, but Garal couldn't make out the words. Then another figure rose up right before him, and a large hand grasped the halter rope. "Keep your hands away from your weapons."

Garal did as the man ordered. After a moment, his horse started forward again, this time responding to the tugging from the man leading it. Garal noticed movement behind him, and glimpsed another shadowy figure guiding the second horse. He knew that armed men watched his every move, ready to kill him.

Ahead, Garal saw a line of spearmen, the bronze tips of their upright weapons glinting even in the near darkness. A few of the spears lowered just enough to point at his chest. Then the line parted, and Garal and his extra horse passed through the ranks and into the Akkadian camp.

A brawny arm reached up and pulled Garal from his horse. Other hands seized his weapons, casting them onto the ground. A man on either side grasped his arms, and they half led, half dragged their prisoner away from the front line.

"Who are you?"

The man spoke even before Garal stopped moving. A soldier with a torch appeared, and waved it in front of Garal's face.

"I am Garal, of the Ur Nammu, son of Chinua. I come with a message from Sargon of Akkad, for King Eskkar."

"Bind his hands," a voice ordered.

The men holding him jerked his arms down and behind his back, but before they could fasten the rope, another voice ordered them to stop.

"I know this one," Drakis said, peering into Garal's face. "I've seen him in the Ur Nammu camp. Let him go."

Garal took in a deep breath and let it out with relief. Death had come closer to him in the last hundred paces of his journey than in his wild passage through the Elamites.

"I know you, too, Commander Drakis. I am glad to see you are still alive."

Drakis laughed. "Well, tomorrow might change that. But follow me. I'm sure the Captain will want to talk to you."

A moment passed before Garal realized that 'Captain' was another title for King Eskkar. With a most un-warrior like sigh of satisfaction, Garal followed Drakis and his men through the darkness.

"And you managed to slip through the entire Elamite army?" Eskkar still couldn't quite believe what the young warrior had accomplished, even after hearing the story for the second time.

Garal, with food and water in front of him, nodded. "Yes, My Lord. But the Elamites will attack soon. The messengers we captured revealed that Modran has run low on both food and water."

Eskkar glanced up at the night sky, full of stars. "We think they will come today, with the dawn. Modran cannot retreat without at least making one more effort to break our lines."

Garal opened his mouth, then closed it again. No sense in asking whether King Eskkar thought he could repel the assault. There was only one answer to that question. "We have weakened his cavalry, and driven off many of his horses."

"The loss of a few horses will not change Modran's plans," Eskkar said. "But you have done far more damage than you think. Your ride through their lines will have many of his men looking over their shoulders in tomorrow's fight. And the stampede will have robbed them of much of their sleep this night. Before they can advance, they will have to round up those loose animals. The men who face us tomorrow will be tired from lack of sleep, and weakened by the doubt you have placed in their minds. That is worth much more than the horses they lost. The news you bring of Sargon and Subutai is most welcome. You and the warriors have struck a heavy blow against Lord Modran."

Garal nodded, but Eskkar saw the disappointment on the young warrior's face. "You have done a brave deed, Garal, braver than anything any warrior has ever done. More important, you have given us the will to fight. Now we know for certain that Modran's supplies are exhausted, and that he will soon have to retreat. That knowledge will put bronze into the muscles of our spearmen and archers tomorrow."

"My Lord, when you fought against the Sumerians at Isin, my father Chinua rode at your side and led the charge. If you would permit, I would like to fight by your side this day."

"I would welcome the sword of a man as brave as yourself. But be aware, that the arrows will fly thick where I stand."

"I will take my chance, as will your other soldiers."

"Then you will have it. But it may be, Garal, that you can help far more by taking another task. Let me tell you what we've planned."

When Garal learned about tomorrow's battle plan, he nodded. "Yes, that will be as dangerous. I'm sure I can do more good with your horsemen than fighting at your side."

Eskkar turned to Muta and Drakis. "Make sure Garal has a good supply of arrows and as much leather armor as he can carry. He's going to need it."

39

G eneral Martiya took his position alongside the Immortals, on their flank, about ten men behind their front line. He had taken command of Modran's best troops, to make sure they punched through the Akkadians no matter what. Drawn up in a tightly-packed, solid column one hundred men wide and fifteen men deep, they would provide the hammer stroke against Eskkar's right flank.

Each Immortal wore a leather helmet wrapped in a bright red cloth, and each fighter carried a sturdy shield that would stop most shafts from penetrating. The front three rows carried spears in addition to the sword each man wore at his waist. Today the spears served another function – to make sure the soldiers in front kept moving forward.

Positioned just ahead of the Immortals, another three thousand troops had massed. Their sloppy formations and nervous glances were all that could be expected from troops who knew they were being sent to the slaughter. Their purpose was to absorb the Akkadian arrows, shielding the Immortals until they'd drawn close enough to launch their charge. The Elamite front ranks knew the Immortals had orders to impale any man that faltered or tried to retreat.

Behind the Immortal column, Martiya saw almost thirty-six hundred cavalry poised to attack. Many of his horse fighters had fought dismounted and died in the second battle. With so many horses stolen or killed, less than half of the once vaunted Elamite cavalry remained.

Lord Modran had taken direct command of that force, and he would ensure that they were hurled into the battle at the right moment. The rest of the Elamite cavalry would fight on foot today, attacking the Akkadian center.

That would hold Eskkar's troops in place, and prevent reinforcements being shifted to Eskkar's right flank. Once Martiya and the Immortals had opened the tiniest gap in the Akkadian flank, Modran would drive his cavalry through the opening and into Eskkar's rear. Then the slaying would begin.

Martiya knew Modran burned to take his revenge for the humiliation of the last five days. Both men dreaded what punishments King Shirudukh would inflict upon them after yet one more defeat. The sneers and contempt from General Jedidia and Grand Commander Chaiyanar would be almost as bad. The upcoming fight would be brutal, but if Martiya could lead even a handful of soldiers up to Akkad's gates, Modran and he could claim a victory.

Eskkar, too, watched as the darkness gave way to gray, and soon the first rays of the sun sent gold and pink light into the sky, outlining the high peaks of the Dellen Pass. In moments, Eskkar saw the enemy positions, as dawn rose over the mountains.

Today he sat astride A-tuku, a sign to all his men that nothing would be held back. He'd chosen A-tuku to carry him into the battle, despite the risk to the animal. If Eskkar were killed during the fighting, he didn't want A-tuku to fall into enemy hands, a humiliating trophy that the Elamites would flaunt throughout the land. Better that they should both die in combat.

Mounted, Eskkar could see all the way down the slope. For once, the Elamites stood in formation, ready to advance. By the time the attack began in earnest, the Akkadians would have the sun in their eyes.

As he stared at his enemies, a drum sounded from somewhere within their ranks, and Modran's soldiers took that first step forward. Eskkar knew the Elamites were battle-weary and that they suffered from shortages of food and water. Would they fight harder because of that lack, or would they give way when the brutal fighting began?

In the Alur Meriki Clan, Eskkar knew older warriors sometimes led the way into battle, risking their lives in the front ranks to preserve the lives of the younger, more vigorous fighters. In such situations, the older men often fought harder, before their strength or resolve gave way to fatigue or doubt. In that way, the old gave their utmost to help the Clan, and if the gods decreed, died with honor.

Eskkar recognized that Modran had positioned a large force of men in front of the Immortals, to shield them as much as possible. That force, its lack of enthusiasm recognizable even from a distance, would be sacrificed to protect the precious Immortals.

Eskkar had managed to snatch a few moments of sleep during the night, not enough to refresh him, and he felt the tiredness in his bones. Approaching his fiftieth season, he'd grown far too old for a tough campaign such as this, let alone fighting in the front lines. Battle should be left to the young, those quick with a sword, insensible to fatigue, and strong enough to ride and fight all day.

But today, Eskkar felt the urge to strike his enemies with his own hands, the same eagerness that his men had displayed when they learned how this last battle would be fought.

His guards approached, and handed Eskkar his helmet and shield. Brown stain, applied last night, covered the bronze helmet and breastplate. The dark coloring would help him blend in with the leather armor of his men. His commanders had not wanted Eskkar to be the target of every Elamite bowman. Leather gauntlets protected both forearms. Despite his annoyance, he wore a stiff collar around his neck, to protect his throat from arrows.

Eskkar fastened the helmet on his head and accepted his bronze shield. He carried the long sword over his shoulder, but also wore his shorter blade belted to his left hip. Last, his bodyguards handed him a slim lance, its tip sharpened to an extra keen point.

Raising his hand to shade his eyes from the sun, Eskkar stared down the slope at the advancing Elamites. Today they had no boastful shouts, no loud war cries designed to frighten his men. They knew such efforts would be wasted, and it would be better to save their breath for the final run and savage fight.

It would indeed be a hard fight. No matter what happened today, whether Eskkar lived or died, whether the Akkadians won or lost this battle, he intended to deal such a deadly blow to the Elamites that any siege of Akkad would be severely blunted, if not turned back.

Eskkar shook the gloomy thoughts away. The strength of his arm, honed by months and years of training, still served him well enough. He might be weary, but he doubted Lord Modran, even though nearly twenty years younger, had gotten any more sleep. Both leaders would contend today less rested than any of their followers.

All the same, Eskkar knew he only needed to keep up his strength for a little longer. The enemy would be tired enough, too.

The long night had proven grim for the Elamites. First their planned assault using the Immortals had collapsed in the confusion brought about by the sting of Akkad's slingers. Before Modran's forces had fully recovered from that, the horse stampede had further disrupted the formations.

By that raid, even the lowest and slow-witted of the Elamite soldiers realized that their leaders had lied to them, that no new supplies or reinforcements would be coming through the Pass. Now the day of the final battle had come, forcing Lord Modran to attack in daylight.

The Akkadians had made their own preparations, and they, too, had slept little. Eskkar glanced from one side of the Pass to the other. Everything looked much the same as in the previous battles. At least, he hoped it still appeared that way to Modran's commanders. Eskkar wanted them to believe his Akkadians would fight today's battle the same way as the first two assaults.

The longer Eskkar studied Modran's advancing formations, the more convinced Eskkar became that an attack by the Elamites last night would have succeeded. He could just make out the vaunted Immortals moving into position, behind a frontal mass of barely organized infantry. Modran obviously no longer cared about preserving his elite fighting force. Even in a victory today, they would sustain heavy losses. The Elamite commander had grown desperate indeed.

Eskkar felt certain that some of that same desperation had also seeped into the enemy commanders and even individual soldiers. The forebodings that had swept through Modran's men last night would still linger in their hearts this morning. That, and their lack of food and water, gave the Akkadians yet another advantage.

The outcome of the battle might well rest on just how anxious and fearful the Elamite soldiers had become. He glanced around at his own men. They, too, seemed subdued. They knew what approached, and word had spread about the Elamite Immortals, and their fighting abilities.

"Here they come." Drakis's cheerful voice broke into Eskkar's grim thoughts. "And just like Markesh reported, the Immortals are bunched together against our right flank."

Alexar galloped up to join them. "Muta's men are ready, Captain. As are my spearmen and Mitrac." He lowered his voice. "By Ishtar's honey pot, I hope this works."

Eskkar and Drakis both laughed at the crude joke, the sound making hundreds of heads turn toward their leader. "We'll know soon enough," Eskkar said.

The worries and qualms that had nagged Eskkar's thoughts during the night had vanished. The sight of your adversary often accomplished that. Only confidence remained. Whether his plan succeeded or failed, at least he would have taken the initiative. Waiting patiently for the Elamites to attack, and then suffering under their assaults was not the kind of fighting he preferred. That impatience was no doubt ingrained in the blood of every steppes warrior.

"That we will," agreed Alexar. "At least we have our own Immortal, Drakis, to match against those of our enemy."

Drakis would be commanding the right flank, where the brunt of the Elamite attack would fall. Even so, his combativeness and determination would spread to his troops, and they would fight hard and follow wherever he led.

"Then to your posts," Eskkar said. He turned his horse and cantered across the Pass, until he could see Shappa and his subcommanders. "Are you ready?" Eskkar's bellow easily reached up into the rocks where Shappa waited.

"Yes, Captain."

Eskkar grunted in approval. The final orders had been given. Today there would be no speeches to his men, nor any further orders to his commanders. They knew their tasks, what needed to be done, and how high the stakes. Every man seemed ready.

He trotted the horse back to the center of the line, settling beside Mitrac. The Master Archer stood by his ranks of bowmen, just as he had done in each of the previous attacks. Only today, most of the sacks containing the extra shafts had vanished. Instead, every archer had a second quiver belted on his hip.

"Once again I need your arrows, Mitrac," Eskkar said.

Of all of Akkad's soldiers, only Mitrac had followed Eskkar into every battle, starting even before the first Alur Meriki siege of Akkad, then known as the village of Orak. Mitrac and his deadly archers had played a key role in the campaigns at Sumer and Isin, and many others. He would do so again today against the Elamites.

"We're ready, Captain," Mitrac said. He waved his bow toward ten men who stood behind him. "My archers will find their marks, and every leader of ten knows what to do. Many of the enemy commanders have already been killed."

That, too, would likely be a factor today. While many Akkadian leaders of ten and twenty had died, the number was insignificant compared to the losses of their counterparts among the Elamites.

Eskkar took one last look at his reserves behind him, where a handful of mounted Akkadian cavalry stood waiting, positioned much the same as the previous two battles. He glimpsed Garal riding at Muta's side. The Ur Nammu warrior, feathers once again dangling from his bow, also had a lance slung across his back.

The rest of the horsemen had been moved farther up the slope, presumably to protect the Akkadian horses from the enemy's arrows. Only a small portion of the herd was visible before the trail twisted out of sight.

The drums of the Elamites changed their tempo, and Eskkar glanced down the slope. The enemy continued its advance, its soldiers trudging slowly up the Pass, the men shifting into their attack positions. For a long moment Eskkar stared at the oncoming invaders, studying the advance until he felt sure of their intent.

"It's as we expected, Mitrac," Eskkar said. "Good hunting to you, and may your arrows find their marks. And to you, Alexar."

Alexar nodded and trotted off down the ranks of spearmen, moving toward the far end of the left flank. Where once the Akkadian infantry had stood four deep, now only two ranks remained, except for the very center of the line, where another forty men formed a third rank.

Mitrac's bowmen had also lost many archers, and while they still maintained four ranks in depth, the spacing between each man had widened.

Modran's army, despite its two defeats, yet filled the Pass from side to side, a solid block of men. The Elamites remained quiet, knowing what awaited them. Even so, their masters would drive them forward with threats and the flat of their swords. Once they closed with Eskkar's men, the sheer weight of numbers would be in the Elamites' favor.

Everyone in the first four or five ranks carried some type of shield. Modran must have collected anything that could stop an arrow and given them to the front ranks for this final assault.

Watching his foes advance, Eskkar swore under his breath. He needed one more victory to make the Elamites cut and run. Even if his men just managed to hold them off, it would mean the end of the invasion. Eskkar needed something to make them hesitate, something to break their spirit and convince them that they couldn't win.

Win or lose, this fight was going to be close, and plenty of Akkadians were going to die. The loss of so many of his valuable spearmen and archers was bad enough, but to fail to defeat the enemy would make their deaths in vain.

Alexar cantered back toward the center, and waved at Drakis, who waved his spear in return. Alexar swung down from his horse beside Eskkar. "Our men are ready, Captain, at least as ready as they'll ever be. But it looks like it's going to be close. Good hunting." He handed his horse's halter to one of his men and strode calmly back toward his position in the center of the left flank.

Eskkar knew Alexar preferred to fight on foot, beside his men.

Then Mitrac's drum sounded and the time for orders and doubts had passed. The Elamites had moved within range.

"Loose!" Mitrac launched the first flight of arrows into the sky.

The third battle of the Dellen Pass had begun.

From his higher position up the slope, Eskkar could see almost the entire Elamite army, and he saw the weight of Modran's cavalry, grouped closer toward Eskkar's right flank. He guessed Modran had less than four thousand mounted fighters remaining, and the effectiveness of that force might be the key to victory or defeat today.

Nevertheless, almost eighteen thousand Elamites, a mix of infantry and archers, filled the width of the Pass. All of them urged on by their commanders, and determined to finish off the Akkadians once and for all.

But first the Elamites needed to come to grips with their enemy. Once again, more than fifteen hundred of Mitrac's archers continued to pour arrows into the advancing troops, slowing their approach. Another three hundred bowmen, Muta's dismounted cavalry, faced the approaching Immortals. Now they, too, began launching their arrows. The screening Elamite infantry lacked a sufficient number of shields, and the Akkadian arrows ripped into their ranks.

However despite taking heavy losses, the enemy commanders drove their men onward.

Eskkar, keeping his shield between himself and the enemy, trotted his horse behind the bowmen. He ignored the occasional shaft that overshot the Akkadian ranks. The Elamites, those who survived the arrow storm, were almost within charging distance. In another fifty paces, they would fling themselves forward.

The time had come. Eskkar raised his sword, and waved it back and forth. Two drummers, awaiting that signal, pounded out a quick beat, a special sound meant to alert every Akkadian in the Pass. That sound was repeated by one of Muta's men at the top of the slope. Almost at once, Eskkar felt the ground rumble. From higher up the Pass, a herd of horses galloped into view, running toward the Akkadian position.

More than a thousand riderless horses, urged on by the swords and shouts of another six hundred mounted Akkadian horsemen, burst around the curve in the Pass and thundered down the slope. The terrified horses stampeded down the Pass, driven to a full gallop by the swords and arrows of Muta's riders.

As soon as the animals appeared, the Akkadian infantry and archers abandoned their positions on the left and center, and raced toward the right flank, opening a wide gap in what had been the center and left flank of the battle line.

The Akkadian soldiers from the left flank, running for their lives across the width of the Pass, barely had time to reach the right flank. Brandishing their spears and bows, they created a wall of weapons and shouting men that kept the stampeding horses in the center and left side of the Pass. Still racing at a full gallop, the panicked Akkadian horses poured through the suddenly empty gap in what had been only moments before two-thirds of the Akkadian position.

The Elamites, about to launch their own charge, looked up to see a stampede of wild-eyed horses bearing down on them, with mounted Akkadian cavalry waving their swords and urging the riderless beasts on from behind.

The onrushing horses, fearful of the line of spears and bows brandished by Eskkar's shouting men, charged past the Akkadians and into the open space. Out of control, they jumped over the dead bodies littering their way. Although many of the beasts went down, the mass of crazed animals, driven by the loud battle cries of Muta's men, tore into the approaching Elamites.

The front ranks of enemy soldiers disappeared under the horses' hooves, trampled to death. Many of the Elamite soldiers panicked, as the animals continued to force their way through the advancing enemy, and even their great number of soldiers could not halt them.

The center of the Elamite assault collapsed. Men scrambled to get out of the path of the charging animals. The forward progress of the assault vanished. At the back of the Akkadian horses now appeared a line of slingers. Shappa and his four hundred men, hidden in the rocks just behind the abandoned front line, had raced into the wide gap where the Akkadian left flank and center had been only moments ago.

The slingers formed a rough line, and then they, too, moved forward, following the horses. Their task was to prevent the Elamites from regrouping and launching an attack at Muta's rear.

Running hard and using their stones, they kept the stampede moving, striking animals and inflicting pain that caused the panicky beasts to continue surging down the slope. Even those Elamites who managed to keep their feet and avoid the maddened animals had no chance to use either their swords or their bows.

For a brief moment, all of Eskkar's soldiers, with the exception of Muta's horsemen and the slingers, were packed together on the right flank.

Then a column of Akkadian archers, standing just behind the wall of spears, charged fifty paces down the slope, before halting and aiming their weapons toward their right. They poured arrow after arrow into the front rank of the few surviving Elamites who had screened the Immortals. Shooting at close range, sometimes less than ten or twelve paces, they inflicted such horrendous losses that those soldiers abandoned their position and fled toward the rear, despite the efforts of Modran's commanders and the Immortals to keep them in place.

The last of the three thousand infantry leading the Immortal attack vanished, either dead or running to the rear. Now the shafts of Mitrac's bowmen poured into the front and side ranks of the Immortals with a fury that devastated the battle-hardened and elite

Elamites. Each of Mitrac's archers, supplied with two quivers of arrows, had at least sixty shafts to launch.

The Immortals on Eskkar's right flank suddenly found themselves opposed on two sides, their front and right flank, by the entire weight of Akkadian infantry and archers. Almost two thousand bowmen launched shaft after shaft at the Immortals. Their advance slowed, but somehow they kept moving forward.

Brave men who had never known defeat, they continued advancing, the men in the rear replacing those in front who were struck down. Despite horrific losses, the Immortals struggled on, until they were within thirty paces of Drakis and his front line of spearmen.

But before Immortals could launch their final charge, Drakis bellowed an order and his drummers sounded their own call to action. More than twelve hundred spearmen burst into a run, screaming their war cries and leveling their spears as they rushed across the last bit of open ground that separated the two armies.

With a shock that echoed off the cliff walls, the Akkadian infantry tore into the tattered front ranks of the Immortals. Their long spears were driven forward on the run with all the strength in each man's arm, and even the Immortals' sturdy shields could not deflect them.

The entire front rank of the Elamites went down, most without striking a blow. A moment later, the second met the same fate, entangled by the dead in front of them, and driven backward or into the ground by the Akkadian spears that reached over their companions or between gaps in the line.

Meanwhile the last of the stampeding horses had charged their way past the disorganized mass of Modran's infantry that had advanced toward Eskkar's left flank and center. Now Muta turned his six hundred remaining cavalry away from the path of the stampeding horses, and swung them to his right.

Akkad's cavalry crashed into the right rear of the Immortals. Driving their horses ever forward, they flung their lances into the tightly packed enemy. Then they slashed and cut at anything that moved, their targets always easy to spot by the red headscarf.

No matter how fierce the Immortals might be, mounted riders always possessed the advantage against sword-wielding infantry, especially men bunched together in a thick column. That dense formation, formidable in a forward assault, proved much weaker when attacked on its flank.

Behind the Akkadian spearmen, Mitrac's bowmen and Muta's dismounted archers ran forward. They launched arrows at any target they could find, aiming for faces, legs, even sword arms.

What remained of the center of the Elamite advance, demoralized by the stampede and now the incessant hail of stones from Shappa's slingers, turned and ran. First the wild horses, followed by the charging horsemen, and finally the agile slingers proved too much for the already tired and thirsty enemy soldiers. Without any strong leaders to keep them moving forward, their flight to the rear soon turned into a rout.

The entire force of slingers now formed a thin line that stretched across the Pass. Eskkar had gambled that Modran would not waste any more of his troops trying to force their way through the boulders. That left the slingers free to abandon the cliff and rocks, and take a stand out in the open. The stones of Shappa's men now kept the horses moving down the slope, and prevented the Elamites from mounting an effective attack.

Nevertheless, the battle remained in doubt. Muta's attack had caught the Immortals by surprise, and now the elite Elamites desperately tried to regroup and face the danger that threatened them from front and flank. The din of the battle filled the Pass. Even the lone war cry of Garal of the Alur Meriki floated over the air, as Muta's cavalry recklessly pushed the attack.

Eskkar's horsemen, scarcely used in the first two battles, now took advantage of their opportunity. In their frenzy to strike at the Elamites, they inflicted heavy losses on the Immortals, disrupting their formation and weakening their resolve.

Less than a hundred paces from the attacking Akkadian horsemen, Lord Modran's cavalry struggled to push their way through the crowd of their own retreating soldiers. If they could charge into Mitrac's bowmen and attack Muta's horse fighters, they would relieve the pressure on the Immortals.

Ignoring the confusion in the center of the Pass, Drakis's infantry, after their first wild charge, continued moving forward. A relentless wall of spears, borne by shouting fighters, had stopped the vaunted Immortals from advancing, and began forcing them back.

General Martiya tried to rally the Immortals and the other troops still uncommitted to the battle. Waving his sword, he turned to face Modran's commanders and signaled to those fresh troops in his rear. Martiya realized the critical point of the battle had arrived. If the Elamite cavalry could be brought into play, they could run down the Akkadian bowmen. Without the archers, the spearmen would not be strong enough to break the Immortals.

But Martiya's efforts to order his reserves forward attracted the keen eyes of others. Mitrac saw the enemy commander waving his sword but looking to the rear. Halting his steps, Mitrac launched three arrows at the Elamite general, by now less than sixty paces away.

The first missed, but the second slammed into Martiya's left shoulder, spun him around, and knocked him down. The third arrow flashed into the side of one of the Immortals, and he, too, dropped to his knees.

Lord Modran, at the head of the cavalry reserve, watched Martiya disappear from sight, probably trampled by his own soldiers. Modran cursed the filthy Akkadian bowmen, who targeted anyone who looked like a commander. Even so, the battlefield was opening up. His own cowardly men, in their flight to the rear, had momentarily blocked his cavalry from advancing.

But now a gap appeared. Despite his infantry losses, Modran could drive his horsemen into the disintegrating center. In moments his cavalry could be behind Eskkar's line of infantry.

Raising his voice, Modran waved his sword over his head. The time to counterattack had come.

Suddenly a fresh hail of stones, flung by Eskkar's slingers, slammed into the closest of Modran's cavalry. One horse, struck in the forehead, went mad with pain, biting and kicking at anything within reach. Modran saw that the slingers, after helping rout the Elamite infantry, had now turned their attention to Modran's cavalry. They shifted their line and hurled stone after stone high in the air, targeting his horsemen. The hail of bronze bullets unnerved his men and their horses even more than a flight of arrows.

Nevertheless, many rallied to Modran's side. Ignoring the stones, the riders urged their horses forward, trampling on some of their own infantry in the process.

Garal had not followed Muta and his horsemen in their attack on the Immortals. Instead he kept his horse just behind Mitrac's archers. Garal had his own orders, to target the Elamite leaders. Voicing his war cry again and again, Garal continued loosing shafts at every enemy commander he could find. Now he observed the movement of men and horses beside Modran's standard.

So far in the brief encounter, the Ur Nammu Master Archer had already emptied one quiver. Guiding his horse with his knees, he loosed five arrows at Modran's commanders. The shafts struck two guards and one of the horses. A gap opened in the screen of men protecting Lord Modran. But before Garal could loose a shaft at Lord Modran, his horse stumbled and went down, tumbling the Ur Nammu warrior to the ground.

But Hamati, one of Mitrac's skilled bowmen, still led the remnants of those assigned to kill enemy leaders, and now he reached the same spot where Garal had fallen. Hamati had run farther down the slope than any of the archers, following after the horses. He had already killed two commanders himself, and his bowmen had accounted for another handful. Only four of his men remained, however. But then Hamati saw who Garal had been targeting – the flashing sword of yet another Elamite leader, and the enemy cavalry getting ready to launch their attack.

"There, behind the Immortals," Hamati shouted, pointing with his bow at the man with the sword. "Take him!"

Without another word, the five of them drew their bows and launched a small flight of arrows at the cluster of mounted commanders, now just over eighty paces away. A long shot for most bowmen, but not for these Akkadian marksmen. Three shafts missed, but one struck the horse in the neck, and another lodged in the rider's upper arm. The dying horse reared up in its frantic agony, pitching Lord Modran to the side.

Hamati's men, still not sure if they'd finished off their target, shot another flight into the massed cavalry nearby, the missiles striking down a few more mounted men. Glancing around, Hamati could see no other enemy leaders worth targeting.

"Just kill them all," he shouted, his voice rising above the din. He snapped a shaft to the bowstring and loosed another missile. "Akkad! Akkad!"

Another steppes war cry echoed between the cliffs and over the battle ground. Eskkar had reverted to the war cry of his youth. Urging A-tuku forward, Eskkar led his bodyguards and twenty of Muta's cavalry into the center of the enemy, this blow also aimed at the rear of the Immortals. He'd seen Modran's standard, and Eskkar hurled his small force directly at the enemy leader. If he could kill the Elamite general, the enemy attack would collapse.

But first Eskkar had to get past part of the Immortals. Many of them had started to fall back, unnerved by the savagery of the Akkadian counterattack. They still fought tenaciously even as they retreated. He charged into the disorganized throng of the enemy, hacking left and right with the long sword. He'd killed three men before the crush of bodies slowed his horse almost to a standstill.

A-tuku trampled another soldier before Eskkar, knowing that a rider on a slow moving horse made for an easy target, flung himself down. Dropping his long sword, he snatched the shorter blade from its scabbard. Grasping his shield, he lunged forward, thrusting and stabbing at the crowded mass of Immortals.

A spear slipped past Eskkar's shield and struck him in the chest, but the bronze breastplate deflected the killing blow. Knocking the shaft aside with his shield, Eskkar thrust twice at the Immortal wielding it. The second stroke caught the man in the mouth and ripped through the back of his neck, sending the choking man to the earth.

Then two Immortals hurled themselves at Eskkar. They recognized the armor of an Akkadian commander. Jerking away from one stroke, Eskkar used his shield to deflect the second man's thrust, then struck with his sword at the first man. The three continued to engage, each one stumbling over the dead and wounded, trying to strike and kill.

Enraged at the thought of Modran getting away, Eskkar reverted to his ancestry. Another Alur Meriki war cry burst from his lips, and he swung his sword with all his strength. One Immortal went down, and the second now faced the full fury of Eskkar's sword arm. Trying to take a step back, the second Immortal slipped on the bloody ground. Before he could recover, Eskkar drove his sword through the man's throat.

Behind Eskkar, Chandra, Myandro, and others from the Hawk Clan widened the gaps their Captain created. Fighting like wild men, they pushed past Eskkar and through the last of the Immortals. The bellowing war cries of the Akkadians now carried the sounds of victory.

The Elamite cavalry, after watching Lord Modran knocked from his horse and General Martiya wounded, were taken aback by the ferocious charge of the bloodthirsty Akkadians. They saw the Elamite center in ruins, the Immortals being slaughtered, and most of their leaders down. Many had already turned aside.

Too many arrows and stones had struck at the horsemen. Most realized that death awaited them if they continued the fight, even if they managed to sway the outcome of the battle. With frantic shouts to those behind, they turned their horses around and kicked them into motion.

Three of Modran's surviving guards, stopping only long enough to snatch up the stunned and wounded Lord Modran, followed the cavalry. Kicking their horses to the gallop, they scattered their own men and thus sealed the fate of the engagement. They rode hunched over, hoping an arrow didn't take them in the back.

Eskkar cursed in his rage, his path now blocked by the fleeing Immortals. He'd fought his way within twenty paces of Modran, but the enemy commander, surrounded by a handful of his men, had managed to get away.

All the same, Eskkar knew that once the Elamite cavalry started rearward, they had lost the battle. Even though they still outnumbered their attackers, the disorganized and panicked enemy turned, almost as one man, and fled, stepping on their own wounded in their panic to get to the rear. Many had seen General Martiya and Lord Modran go down, and decided the time had arrived to save themselves as best they could.

Only the Immortals remained. More than half of them had already died, but the rest, now trapped with their backs against the cliff, refused to surrender. Ranks of Akkadian archers poured shaft after shaft into what remained of the Elamite position, often from distances as close as four or five paces, while Alexar and Drakis kept driving the Akkadian spearmen against them, keeping them at bay and pinned against the cliff.

Their shields gone, and the rest of the army fleeing, the Immortals abandoned any thoughts of holding their ground. With a rush, they tried to retreat, but hundreds of arrows continued to tear into their ranks.

Drakis finally halted his exhausted infantry, and let Mitrac's bowmen finish off the Immortals. By the time the archers had emptied the remainder of their second quiver, less than a hundred Immortals remained alive. These had dropped their weapons and fell to their knees, begging for mercy.

Eskkar, leaning on his sword and breathing hard, watched the last of the fighting end. The Elamites fled down the slope, tossing swords and shields aside to run all the faster. As the battle fury left him, Eskkar found he could scarcely stand.

Though he had not fought as long as most of his men, the incredible effort he expended had nearly proved too much for him. The battlefield appeared blurry to his eyes, and his heart pounded in his chest, no matter how much air he drew into his lungs.

For a moment, Eskkar thought he would collapse to the earth, exhausted. But he managed to stay on his feet, though he lurched from side to side. The long years had finally caught up with him. He knew he'd grown too old for this kind of fighting and killing.

Stumbling over the battlefield, he found A-tuku wandering around, a bloody gash on his right flank. His favorite horse had survived the battle as well. Using the last of his strength, Eskkar swung himself onto the horse's back, paused to catch his breath once again, then rode back up into the Pass.

The only force that remained at the near original battle line was Shappa's slingers, who had bravely filled the gap until the tide of battle had swung completely in Akkad's favor. Once Eskkar arrived at what originally had been the center of the Akkadian position, he turned A-tuku around and let his eyes sweep the battleground.

Everywhere he looked, he saw the dead and dying. Others, too, had fought themselves to exhaustion, and many dropped to their knees while they tried to catch their breath. The overpowering smell of blood and human waste made it hard to breathe, and filled the Dellen Pass from wall to wall. Cries of the wounded, many begging for water, now echoed off the walls.

That sound, he knew, would gradually diminish as men died, and the victors finished off the vanquished. Nonetheless it was time for the Akkadians to tend to their own injured.

The third battle of the Dellen Pass had ended. And this time, the enemy had broken, caught by surprise by the unexpected horse stampede, then ripped apart by the savage countercharge of Alexar and Drakis's spearmen. The fearless slingers had held the center long enough. Finally the deadly arrows of Mitrac's bowmen had finished off the last few still fighting.

Eskkar watched the enemy survivors, running as hard as they could, until the last of them disappeared around the curve in the Pass. He cared nothing for them. They would run until they collapsed. When they recovered, they would run again, terrified of the Akkadian pursuit.

But Eskkar had no intention of chasing after them. Without food, many more Elamite soldiers would die before they reached Zanbil, and he doubted the survivors would find much succor there. Better to let them go. He didn't intend to waste even a single life of his soldiers in pursuit.

Someone shouted his name, and Eskkar saw Drakis waving his sword at him. For once after a battle, Drakis didn't look ready to die from his wounds. Aside from a few scratches, he had managed to avoid any serious injury. Behind him walked four spearmen, cursing their bad luck at not being allowed to go looting. They carried a wounded Elamite by his arms and legs.

The men carelessly dropped the injured man at Eskkar's feet, as he gazed down from his horse. Blood had seeped the length of the Elamite's left arm and across the front of his tunic. An Akkadian shaft had ripped completely through the fleshy part of his shoulder. Aside from the loss of blood, the wound didn't appear that serious, and the man might actually survive.

"Who's this?" Eskkar's voice sounded harsh in his ears. One glance at the wounded man's garments and Eskkar knew his men had captured one of the senior Elamite commanders. "What's your name?"

Martiya might not understand the language, but he recognized the King of Akkad. "General Martiya."

Eskkar understood the Elamite word for 'general.' He knew that Modran's second in command was named Martiya.

"Chandra! Guard this prisoner and bind his wound. If he lives, we'll take him back to Akkad. He might prove useful."

"Yes, Captain," Chandra said. His own hands and face were covered with blood, none of it his own. "I'm sure Annok-sur will be eager to talk to him."

Eskkar laughed, the hoarse sound releasing the stress that had built up over the last five days and nights. The stomach-twisting stench of death hung in the air, but to Eskkar, it smelled as sweet as honey. You had to be alive to savor it. He had survived another battle, and with luck, turned back the Elamite invasion of the Land Between the Rivers.

He stared down at General Martiya, who shivered in apprehension at the grim look. "By the time Annok-sur finishes with him, General Martiya will wish he died in the battle."

The sun had climbed nearly to its peak before Eskkar, wearing a fresh tunic and with the blood washed from his body, met with his commanders. Exhausted, dirty, splattered with blood, every one had taken at least one minor wound. Nevertheless, every face held a wide smile, and Eskkar knew at once that his men had suffered few casualties.

Eskkar, too, found himself smiling. "How many dead?"

"The clerks just finished the count," Alexar said. "Less than six hundred dead or wounded. We got off easy, Captain. The stampede worked. After all that happened to the Elamites last night, Muta's horses rattled Modran's men and took the fight out of them."

Despite the low number of today's dead, Eskkar knew he had lost nearly half the men he'd led into the Dellen Pass only six days ago, a staggering number for a city the size of Akkad. But a victory of this magnitude softened the blow. And soldiers could be replaced. After this triumph, many restless boys and men would flock to his standard once again.

"With Lord Modran's army destroyed," Eskkar said, "and General Jedidia's cavalry turned back, it's time for us to return to Akkad. Muta, you will stay here with your cavalry and half the infantry for ten days, until we're sure all the Elamites are gone. I don't want any one of them trying to desert into our lands or becoming bandits. I'll take a hundred horsemen with me, and start for home right away. Alexar, have every man that can march on the move at dawn tomorrow. They'll be needed in Akkad."

Groans greeted his orders, but the commanders understood the war hadn't yet ended. The fight for Sumer might have gone badly, and every Akkadian soldier might be crucial in the defense of their own city's walls.

"But before I leave," Eskkar said, "I want to send a message to King Shirudukh."

He called first for Garal, who had also survived the brutal charge into the enemy's ranks. "I want you to translate for me, Garal."

Eskkar swung onto A-tuku's back, and rode over to where the remnants of the Immortals sat on the ground, their backs against the cliff wall.

A line of fifty spearmen guarded them, backed by fifty bowmen. These were, after all, dangerous and desperate men. For a long moment Eskkar studied them.

Nearly one hundred and thirty dejected and defeated men returned his gaze. Except for those who had managed to flee, these were all that remained of Elam's once invincible Immortals. Now they waited to learn how they would die, and how much torture they would have to endure before death released them from the pain. Or when the endless drudgery of slavery began.

"I am Eskkar of Akkad." He made sure his voice reached all of them. Garal repeated Eskkar's words, with the same force. "You came to this land intending to conquer those who had done you no harm. For that the penalty is death."

Their eyes showed little emotion. They knew all too well what happened to captured soldiers.

"But you fought bravely until the last," Eskkar went on, "and kept your honor. For that, I will pay tribute to the powerful gods of the Land Between the Rivers. I give you back your lives. You may return to the lands of Elam. But each of you will leave behind the thumb of your right hand. That will make sure you remember to carry a message from me to the people of Elam and to King Shirudukh. Tell them never again dare to invade our lands, or the wrath of Ishtar and Marduk will descend upon them all. And if any of you should ever forget or disobey, I will call upon the gods to destroy you. I will unleash my soldiers on the people of Elam until your land is empty of life, the crops burned, and its herds slaughtered and left to rot in the sun. Tell them that, before they think of war again."

Looks of disbelief greeted his words. Expecting death, they had been granted life. Losing their thumb meant they would fight no more, but better that than death.

Eskkar turned to Myandro, the leader of the alert guards. "Cut off their thumbs. They will leave naked, and with no weapons. Escort them to the bottom of the slope and send them on their way. Kill any that try to return or pick up a weapon."

"Yes, My Lord," Myandro said.

Eskkar wheeled A-tuku around and took one last look at the battlefield. It was time to take care of Grand Commander Chaiyanar.

40

The eastern mouth of the Jkarian Pass . . .

Five days after the cliff came down in the Jkarian Pass, General Jedidia gave the order to turn about and head for the lands of Elam. Despite every available man searching, Jedidia had not discovered any way to get around the obstacle the filthy Akkadians had heaped in his way. While his men exhausted themselves in a futile hunt for another path, he had another thousand men trying to move enough rocks and boulders so as to force a way through the debris.

Those men labored in the heat of the day until their hands bled, and there were more than a few crushed toes and broken ankles. His men had scrambled over the barrier, but for the horses, the Pass remained closed. In the end, what Jedidia's Master Builder declared the first day remained true – General Jedidia did not have enough time, supplies, or proper tools to force a passage through the rubble-choked Jkarian Pass.

With a snarl, he gave the order to turn his exhausted men around and start the bitter journey back to their own lands. By then his men were already on half rations. At least they had located a tiny spring deep within the mountain. That provided just enough water to refill the skins, and keep the horses alive and moving.

The ignominious retreat galled on General Jedidia's stomach with every rearward step of his horse. Of necessity, he'd sent messengers to King Shirudukh the day after the cliff toppled, informing him of the debacle. Jedidia didn't dare show up in Zanbil without warning the King of what had happened.

Of course, other, more dismal messages would soon have to be sent. Now that he had abandoned his mission through the Jkarian Pass, Jedidia would have to dispatch more messengers with the bad news. However that particular embarrassment could be postponed until he reached Zanbil. Once there, Jedidia would halt his men, then wait for resupply before proceeding through the Dellen Pass.

He knew what to expect when King Shirudukh heard about the disaster. Jedidia would be ordered to place himself under Lord Modran's command.

That would mean an enduring humiliation for Jedidia. Worse, Jedidia would lose his opportunity to loot the Land Between the Rivers. No, Modran would carefully assign Jedidia to patrol only those places that had already been picked clean.

At the same time, if there were any fighting to be done, Jedidia knew it would be his own men sent to the front lines, to lead the attack and bear the brunt of any casualties. By the time Akkad fell and the other cities were subdued, Jedidia would be lucky to be alive and with half his command intact.

Despite the gloomy future awaiting him, Jedidia kept his troop moving at a brisk pace. Hunger gnawed at the bellies of both his men and their mounts. He needed food, and the horses needed grass to graze upon. Both would be available once back in Elam's northern lands.

On the third day after their departure, his cavalry exited the Jkarian Pass, and with a dismal sigh of relief, turned south. The grasslands provided the horses with a chance to assuage their hunger.

Jedidia's soldiers had much less luck finding food. For the sake of his men, Jedidia knew he should have left the accursed Pass days sooner. But he dared not face King Shirudukh without proclaiming to have done his utmost. If that meant a few hundred of his men died from hunger or injury, so be it.

A day after they left the mouth of the Jkarian Pass, the last of the rations was gone. Soon real hunger would sweep over his men. Only a few cattle and chickens stolen from the occasional farmstead kept starvation at bay. Fortunately, Jedidia's cavalry would reach Zanbil in less than two days, so his fighters would be spared the necessity to eat some horses.

A shout broke into Jedidia's unhappy thoughts. He glanced up to see one of his forward scouts galloping toward his commanders. Jedidia, riding beside Zathras, his second in command, didn't bother to halt the weary column. The scout reached Jedidia with a rush, and let his horse fall in place beside his leaders.

"General Jedidia, we found tracks about two miles ahead. Hundreds of horses crossed our trail. We followed the tracks for almost half a mile, until they rode closer to the foothills."

"You must be blind." Zathras glared at the scout. "There aren't a hundred horses left in these lands."

General Jedidia agreed. Every horse that could bear a rider had been pressed into King Shirudukh's service months ago.

The scout shook head. "My Lord, I know what I saw. The tracks came down from the foothills. The upper trail there is blocked for a half mile or so. But as soon as the riders got past that obstacle, they returned to the upper trail."

When Jedidia's men exited the Pass, they had faced a choice of routes. They could follow what the scout called the upper trail, which hugged the foothills most of the way south. Or they could continue down to the lower plains, where the grass grew more plentiful, and the landscape made for an easier ride.

Short of food and grass, he and Zathras agreed that the lower trail was their best route. But the upper trail, if one had a good horse and were in a hurry, was the shorter path.

"You're sure there were tracks from a hundred horses?"

The scout shook his head. "General, the earth was churned to mud in some places. That takes hundreds of horses, many hundreds. The tracks are fresh, only a few days old."

Zathras refused to believe his ears. "Only Lord Modran has any sizeable cavalry in these lands, and he took them all with him into the Dellen Pass. Why would he ride this far north before turning around?"

"How far ahead is this place?" Jedidia didn't like what he was hearing, but one way or another, he'd find out soon enough.

"About two miles, General," the scout said. "You can't miss the signs."

Jedidia turned to Zathras. "Have our men pick up the pace. I want to see this for myself."

With Zathras at his side, Jedidia moved to the head of the column. He wanted to examine the ground himself, before his men trampled all over it.

When they reached the spot, Jedidia halted his horse and stared at the earth. The scout hadn't lied. Jedidia found himself agreeing with the man – not long ago, several hundred horses had trodden the soft grass into a green and brown mush. He saw where the tracks came down from the upper trail. A rockslide had obliterated a quarter mile stretch of the upper trail. Any riders using that trail would have had to descend here.

Looking south and about three or four hundred paces ahead, Jedidia observed where the trampled ground slanted back toward the upper trail. So the unknown horsemen had returned to the upper trail as soon as they bypassed the obstruction. That meant the riders were traveling fast and not worried about the stamina of their horses.

The more Jedidia studied the ground, the more worried he became. Every cavalry force in the Elamite Empire, whether friend or foe, rode in columns of twos or fours. Even the cursed Akkadians followed the same procedure. The only people who rode in an untidy mass, in as broad a front as they could manage, were the barbarians of the steppes.

But where had they come from? Jedidia knew the Alur Meriki had departed Elam's lands more than two years ago, unable or unwilling to face a confrontation with Modran's cavalry. By now the barbarian clan should be far away, beyond even the Land Between the Rivers. Why would a few hundred return to Elam's territory and risk another confrontation?

More important, these riders hadn't come through the Jkarian Pass, which meant they must have traveled through the foothills far to the north. Nor had they turned east, to raid the closest farms and small villages that dotted the landscape of Elam's northern lands. Instead they had hugged the foothills, and if they kept moving south, the first large village in their path was Zanbil.

Jedidia swore an oath that startled his horse, as well as Zathras. "It's the Alur Meriki. They've come down from the north, and they're riding toward Zanbil and the Dellen Pass."

Zathras mouth gaped. "Why would they go there? It's a long ride to Zanbil."

"I'm not sure, but I'll wager that Eskkar of Akkad has something to do with it. He must have paid them to raid our lands, disrupt our supply lines . . ."

But Jedidia had never planned on being resupplied. The only force with a supply line was Modran's. If Modran failed to make his way through the Dellen Pass, and his supply depot was destroyed, he, too, might have to turn back.

The more Jedidia considered the possibility, the more he believed it. After all, Eskkar had somehow closed the Jkarian Pass, so why not the Dellen Pass as well? Where else would the barbarians go?

"Zathras, halt the column and summon the commanders. We need to make sure they're ready for a fight. Then we're going to ride as hard as we can for Zanbil, even if we have to kill every horse to get there!"

Just after midmorning two days later, General Jedidia sat on his horse atop the same small hill where the Alur Meriki had halted. He had the same good view of Zanbil, just over a mile away. The Alur Meriki warriors had seen him coming, of course. Their scouts had tracked his progress for over a day, and yesterday had even ambushed one of Jedidia's scouting parties, killing fourteen of the twenty men.

Jedidia brushed off the deaths without a thought. By his rough count, the Alur Meriki had about twelve or fourteen hundred men, perhaps less, certainly no match for his much larger force. All the same, the Alur Meriki seemed indifferent to his approach. They showed no signs of either retreating or attacking.

The barbarians had abandoned Zanbil when Jedidia's force drew near. They moved their fighters closer to the mouth of the Dellen Pass and about half a mile north of the opening. A good sized hill that backed onto the upper trail gave them a commanding position, as well as an excellent view of the surroundings. If Jedidia decided to attack, his fighters would be charging up the slope and into the teeth of a barbarian arrow storm.

"If we have to climb that hill," Zathras said, studying the ground, "we'll lose half the men. It will have to be an all-out charge, one single attack, and no turning back until they're overwhelmed."

Jedidia considered his options. He could keep confronting the barbarians with most of his force, while smaller contingents of his men went one by one to the stream at Zanbil for water. So water would not be a factor.

His main problem was food. Jedidia's men hadn't eaten much in the last four days, and they'd ridden hard. The lack of food manifested itself in the slack jaws and empty gazes of his men. If he were going to challenge the barbarians, it would have to be now, before his men lost more of their strength and the will to fight what was sure to be a desperate battle.

"We could move all our men to Zanbil," Jedidia said, "to get at the water. We're going to need that stream no matter what. And there might be food there."

Zathras snorted. "The barbarians have been here for what, four or five days? The cattle pen is empty. What they haven't eaten has probably been dumped into the stream or burned. Besides, if we do that, the barbarians will escape to the north, if that's their intention."

Jedidia glanced toward Zanbil. Three thin plumes of gray smoke still drifted into the air. Zathras was right. The Alur Meriki had received plenty of warning of his approach. They wouldn't have left anything useful in the village. Nonetheless, after Jedidia's failure in the Jkarian Pass, even a victory over these barbarians might soften the blow that was sure to come from King Shirudukh.

A ragged shout from the barbarians echoed off the mountains. A small band of riders, less than twenty, had emerged from the mouth of the Pass. Running their horses flat out, they turned off the trail to Zanbil, and instead followed the crest line to rejoin their companions.

"Do you think there are any more of them coming out of the Pass?"

Jedidia kept his gaze on the Alur Meriki. The newcomers had raced to the center of the barbarian position, and now were in an animated discussion with what must be their leaders.

Suddenly a huge cheer went up from their ranks, starting at the center and extending to the wings. Warriors waved bows, lances, and swords in the air. The undulating battle cry of the barbarians floated over the empty land between the two forces. The barbaric celebration continued for a long time, the noise grating on his nerves even at this distance.

Zathras swore at the sound. "What are they celebrating?"

Jedidia could guess the answer to that question. The riders had come from the Pass, riding at top speed. No doubt they brought a report of some victory over Lord Modran's men. And if Modran's army had suffered a defeat, or even been driven back, then Jedidia's situation had changed.

What a few days ago might have seemed a major disaster to King Shirudukh's invasion plans now might pale in comparison to Lord

Modran's failure. Jedidia's mind raced, as he considered the implications.

The silence dragged on, but Zathras knew better than to interrupt his commander's thoughts.

"Get the men moving," Jedidia ordered at last.

"Are we going to attack?"

"No, we're moving our men to Zanbil. We'll make camp there until we learn what has happened to Modran's army. If the news is what I think it is, Modran is in trouble."

"What about the barbarians?"

"If they come off the hill to attack us in Zanbil, we'll cut them down. Otherwise they can burn farms and villages from one end of Elam to the other for all I care. We're going to need every single one of our men. With luck, we'll soon be riding for Sushan."

"Then we're giving up on joining with Modran's army and riding toward Akkad?"

"Oh, yes." Jedidia laughed, a grim sound with little mirth. "Modran got the army and the target he wanted. If he couldn't handle it, that's his problem. I have a much better, and closer, goal. Now, let's ride for Zanbil, before those barbarians change their minds and decide to attack us here. Now start the men moving!"

Two days later, one of Jedidia's scouts found his commander sitting under an awning attached to one of the two remaining huts still standing in Zanbil. The man reported that a small troop of horsemen, riding slowly, was coming through the Pass. Jedidia summoned Zathras, and they again went over the plan they had put together the day before.

"Make sure they're the men we selected," Jedidia ordered. He and Zathras had picked the forty men themselves. They chose only tough, hardened men who would fight anyone for a few extra coins, and who would follow orders without question.

"What if Lord Modran is not with these men?"

"Then we'll see what they have to say. But if there's been a defeat, I know the man well enough. Modran will be the first one out of the Pass," Jedidia said. "He'll want to get back to Sushan and the King's ear before anyone else, to sweeten his side of the tale. And Zathras, take down my standard. I want my being here to be a little surprise for Modran."

Jedidia's men always set his standard, a long red and black streamer, into the ground wherever their General set up his command.

Jedidia went into the hut, the largest one in Zanbil, that he had taken for his use. He belted on his sword, and made sure his sandals were tightly laced. Then he ordered his warhorse brought up.

When he stepped outside, he saw that the horsemen had come into view from the mouth of the Pass. Jedidia counted them as they came down the trail. By the time the last had left the opening, their leader was halfway to Zanbil. Less than sixty men rode behind him, slowly pacing their horses.

Jedidia recognized the subtle signs of defeated men. No victorious soldiers, no matter how weary, rode with their heads down and shoulders slumped. Clearly, these men had fought and lost a battle somewhere inside the Dellen Pass.

Jedidia personal guards numbered twenty. He ordered half of them into his hut, and scattered the other ten near the stream, only a few paces away. The second hut concealed another twenty picked men armed with bows. He spent a few quick moments with his commanders, making sure they understood what to do.

When Jedidia felt certain they were ready, he glanced once again toward the approaching horsemen. One look was enough to recognize Lord Modran's tall figure leading the way.

"Stay alert, and ready your weapons." Jedidia checked his sword as well, making sure it slid easily in its scabbard.

He left the hidden bowmen, swung up onto his horse, and waited. The palm of his right hand felt moist, and he rubbed it against his tunic. The years of humiliation, of putting up with Modran, were coming to an end. Now Jedidia would gamble his life and his fortune for the ultimate prize.

"You! What are you doing here?" Modran's bellow rang out the moment he recognized Jedidia, though he was still almost seventy paces away.

Jedidia had no intention of entering into a shouting match. He waited until Modran drew close enough for Jedidia to see the vein throbbing on the man's forehead, and the bloodstained bandage on his right arm.

"Welcome, Lord Modran." He kept his voice affable. "Did your battle in the Pass go well?"

Jedidia already knew the answer to that question. Before the Alur Meriki departed, they left one of their Elamite prisoners, minus his thumbs, to carry a message.

And so Jedidia learned that Modran's forces had been stopped by Eskkar's soldiers in the Pass, and that the barbarians even had the gall to raid Modran's rear guard and steal hundreds of horses. They had also found time to loot his supply tents, inflicting yet one more hard blow against Modran's men.

"That demon Eskkar, curse his name, and his bowmen blocked the Pass. We fought for five days, but couldn't break through." He scowled at Jedidia. "Why are you here? You should be riding to Akkad, damn you to the pits. You should have been behind Eskkar, cutting his supply line, and attacking his rear! Without him being resupplied, I would have destroyed him!"

Jedidia lifted his hands and let them drop. "An earthquake blocked the Jkarian Pass, so we had to turn back."

"Where are your men?" Modran moved closer and practically screamed the words in Jedidia's face.

"Most of them are riding patrols. A horde of barbarians attacked Zanbil, and they're still nearby. But don't worry, you'll be safe here."

In his anger, Modran had pushed his horse almost alongside Jedidia's. "You will place yourself under my command," Modran cried, spittle flying from his mouth. "You and your men will obey my . . ."

Jedidia jerked his sword from its scabbard, even as he kicked his horse forward, bringing him even closer, close enough to run the sharp blade, driven with all of Jedidia's strength, through Modran's chest. His eyes went wide in surprise at the unexpected and swift thrust, and Modran never even got his hand on his sword.

Before Modran fell to the ground, Jedidia bellowed out for his men. A drum began to beat, but already Jedidia's personal guards rushed from the hut to protect him, their blades drawn or arrows nocked to the bowstrings.

Modran's guards, picked from the ranks of the Immortals, sat on their horses, stunned by the swift and unexpected killing. Their leader drew his sword, but immediately two arrows struck him down. Before the rest could decide what to do, the sound of five

hundred horsemen galloping toward the village center drew the eyes
of the Immortals and halted every movement.

Zathras, alerted by the drum, led his men from the east toward the
center of the village. From across the fields to the south, another five
hundred men heard the signal and rode toward Zanbil. Other units
appeared as well. In moments, Jedidia's entire force, nearly six
thousand men, raced toward the village.

Some of Modran's loyal guards drew their swords and moved
toward Jedidia. But he lowered his bloody sword and raised his
empty left hand. "Modran was a traitor to King Shirudukh, who
sentenced him to death. By order of the King, if you do not lay down
your arms, my men will kill all of you as traitors."

The chilling threat stopped Modran's men, some still with their
swords half-drawn. They could see the thousands of horsemen
charging toward them. While the remnants of Modran's defeated
army might outnumber Jedidia's force, that army, if the ragged mass
of hungry stragglers could even be called such, still stretched many
miles throughout the Dellen Pass. With General Martiya dead or
captured, and now Lord Modran fallen, his soldiers lacked any
senior leaders to tell them what to do.

A subcommander of Modran's personal guard grasped the
situation fast enough. Modran, who still twitched in the dirt at the
feet of Jedidia's horse, was already a dead man. Better to obey
General Jedidia's orders then fight another hopeless battle.

Besides, the survivors of Modran's army had enough of fighting.
King Eskkar's army had savaged the Elamites, including the
Immortals, and hurled back the invasion. One last glance at the grim
soldiers standing beside Jedidia, weapons at the ready, was more
than enough.

"We yield to the order of the King," the man shouted. "Everyone,
put away your weapons."

"A wise decision," Jedidia said, as the Immortals took their hands
off their swords. "What is your name?"

"My name is Jirsa, General Jedidia."

"Jirsa, you are promoted to commander of these men, and you will
place yourself under Commander Zathras's orders. You and your
troop will be well rewarded soon enough."

By then Zathras had raced his horse into the center of the village. One glance at Modran's now motionless body told him all he needed to know. "What are your orders, General Jedidia?"

"Prepare our riders. I intend to ride to Sushan at once, with five thousand men. You will stay behind, and as more of Modran's scum crawl out of the Pass, get them under your authority. As soon as you have them all, march toward Sushan as fast as you can."

Jedidia swept his gaze over his soldiers, all of them waiting to hear his plan.

"Men! We're going to Sushan, and stamp out the traitors responsible for Lord Modran's defeat by the Akkadians! And after we've finished, every one of you will receive five gold coins!"

A cheer went up from his men at the prospect of some easy wealth. But no one felt more satisfaction than Jedidia. One of his enemies lay dead at his feet. Now the time had arrived for another to join him.

41

The King's Compound in Akkad . . .

Twenty-two days after the victory at the Dellen Pass, Eskkar and Trella entered the private garden at the rear of their house. The early autumn shadows had brought a hint of coolness to the evening, and Trella wore a brown shawl over her shoulders to ward off the chill. Their sons and daughter were already seated when Eskkar and Trella turned the corner and joined the others.

As Eskkar escorted Trella to her chair, he had time for a glance at the garden. Red and yellow tulips in pots still bloomed, and four candles burned, set on the limbs of the two trees. Two long streamers of cloth, one white and one yellow, threaded and retraced their way through the branches, a festive decoration for the very few invited to tonight's gathering. The heady scent of jasmine, flowers and leaves crushed to bring out the pleasing tang, hung in the still air.

For one of the very rare times, no friends, commanders, guests, or loyal followers joined the family members. Tonight the family of Eskkar and Trella dined alone.

The servants had set the table for the private dinner. Sargon and his wife Tashanella were already seated. Zakita and Melkorak, Eskkar's daughter and youngest son, waited until their parents took their places across from Sargon and Tashanella.

Outside the Compound, the sounds of celebration from the city's jubilant crowds could still be heard, and Eskkar knew the noise would continue well into the evening. The three days of celebration for the end of the Elamite War had begun today, although most in Akkad had been rejoicing since the first word of Eskkar's victory at the Dellen Pass had arrived.

Eskkar carried that news back himself, galloping ahead of Alexar and the soldiers. Riding through the gates, he found Akkad's inhabitants, broad smiles on their faces, already cheering another victory.

Yavtar had raced upriver from Sumer to bring word of the breaking of the siege and a stunning victory by Hathor and King Naxos over the Elamites. Hathor and Naxos declared their intention to remain in the south for a time, hunting down the last survivors of Grand Commander Chaiyanar's once mighty army.

For Eskkar, the news brought indescribable relief. The years of meticulous planning and secret preparation had brought Akkad its greatest victory. The invasion had ended, and Akkad and all the cities of the Land Between the Rivers had escaped the brutal fate King Shirudukh had decreed for them. Instead of a quick victory, the King of Elam had lost two armies.

A body count of the enemy dead in the Dellen Pass revealed that just over thirteen thousand of Modran's army survived the final battle. Many of those would have died of their wounds before reaching safety. The once-vaunted might of Elam had dashed itself to death against the shields of Akkad's spearmen.

His luck had held yet again, Eskkar decided. He'd more than half expected to die in the Dellen Pass. And he had made a decision when he returned, though he told only Trella. He would not take up weapons again, either in this war, or any future conflicts.

The time had come for him to hang up his sword, or rather, to pass it on to another, and that's what he intended to do. Tonight. From now on, Sargon would lead the soldiers and fighting men of Akkad.

The day after Sargon's return to Zanbil from the raid on Lord Modran's horses, Sargon and a small troop of warriors had departed Elam. Some of the warriors roamed the countryside, ravaging the northern lands of the Elamites.

But Chief Bekka and most of his men had lingered near the mouth of the Dellen Pass, and two days after General Jedidia departed south, the Alur Meriki and Ur Nammu had fallen on the survivors of Lord Modran's army at Zanbil. Despite being outnumbered, they slaughtered thousands of weak and hungry Elamite soldiers. With that, the final battle of the war, the steppes warriors effectively destroyed the rest of Modran's army as a fighting force.

Afterward, the warriors sent back to the northern lands many of their riders escorting over two thousand horses, in three different herds. That staggering number that would ensure the Alur Meriki remained a potent force for many years. The Ur Nammu had also received a generous share of the captured herds, more than enough for their warriors.

After completing the arduous journey across the mountains, Sargon rejoiced to find a smiling Garal, thought to be dead in the Dellen Pass. After resting for a single day at the camp of the Alur Meriki, Sargon rode south and joined his wife.

Staying with her family and the Ur Nammu, Tashanella waited for her husband's return. Sargon rested at the main Ur Nammu camp for several days before husband and wife set out for Akkad.

Sargon and Tashanella had arrived in the city only yesterday. Wanting to travel as fast as possible, they left their young daughter in the care of Tashanella's mother.

Today Sargon and Tashanella, escorted by Hawk Clan guards, had walked the streets and lanes of the city. Everywhere they went, large crowds appeared, cheering the King's son. Everyone in Akkad knew the daring role Sargon had played during the conflict.

The inhabitants had always considered him to be one of their own since he was a child, the city's first born Akkadian. His past indiscretions had long since been forgotten. The serious young man who nodded and smiled at the crowd had replaced the callow youth.

Holding his wife's hand, Sargon had guided her through the tumultuous crowds. Her eyes wide with excitement, Tashanella, arrayed in the finest garments Trella could buy, had received almost as many cheers as her husband.

Much of that, of course, resulted from the careful preparations of Annok-sur and the women in her employ, but few in the cheering crowds noticed that. By her marriage to Sargon, Tashanella had become an Akkadian, and the city's inhabitants accepted her as one of their own. The Ur Nammu and Alur Meriki had also shared in the glory, and so Tashanella accepted the cheers in their name.

The resulting praise for the heir to the City of Akkad had been almost as great as that given to Eskkar, exactly as Trella desired. The day before Eskkar's return, when Yavtar's messengers brought the first news of victory at Sumer, the people of Akkad had held one day of festivity. Though that outpouring paled in comparison to the one honoring Eskkar when he returned to the city with the news of the defeat of Elam's main army of invasion.

Today's jubilant celebration portended something else besides another victory over Akkad's enemies. In a way, it sealed the unwritten contract between Eskkar and Trella, and the people of Akkad. His parents had anointed Sargon as their heir for all to see, and the entire city had also acclaimed and accepted their future ruler. Eskkar and Trella's line would endure, and Sargon was the living proof.

Sargon and Tashanella, still flushed with the day's excitement, had returned to the Compound only moments before. Now they could relax and enjoy the intimate family dinner.

Taking up the wine pitcher, Eskkar poured some into everyone's cup, letting each of them add as much or as little water as they preferred. Then he lifted his own cup high. "Tonight our family holds its own celebration. Tonight I want to give thanks to Sargon for the role he played in our victory. If he had not broken Lord Modran's supply line, none of us might be here."

Everyone else raised their cups and offered their own words of praise to Sargon.

"But there is much that still remains to be done," Eskkar went on, "and the most important work of all lies ahead. Starting tomorrow, we must plan for the future of our family, and our children yet to be born. Each of us here tonight, and our friends, must create the future that we desire – or else others will do it for us. That is why we must all work together, to ensure that everyone here, and your children and their children's children, all have a part in the Empire of Akkad that is to come."

He turned to Trella, who smiled approval, then lifted her cup and offered her own toast. "Eskkar and Sargon have enabled us to win a great victory, a victory so complete that it will be many, many years before Elam or any other land dares offer a challenge to Akkad. Father and son risked their lives not for glory or power, but to protect all of us here at this table. Nor should we ever let ourselves forget what debt we owe to so many of our friends. Yavtar, Alexar, Muta, Drakis, Hathor, Daro, Draelin, Shappa, and all the others who labored and risked their own lives to protect ours. Even King Naxos of Isin and King Gemama of Sumer have contributed to our victory and our salvation, as did Chief Bekka and Chief Subutai. Without all these leaders working together, Akkad might have fallen. That is a lesson all of us must remember. I expect that we will see even greater cooperation between our cities in the future."

"That is why everyone in this family needs to work together," Eskkar placed his hand over his wife's, "to protect and care for each other. If we do not care for each other, who will? One thing Trella and I have learned, is that a single man cannot lead or rule so many by himself. He needs his family, friends, and loyal supporters. They are the ones who will help us hold what we have against the many enemies who would take it from us."

"And there will be others," Trella said, "enemies from within and from without. If we as a family do not stand together against them, then sooner or later, we will be destroyed or replaced, and our rule will have ended. If we do not care for one another, then whatever we may accomplish will count for nothing."

She turned to Melkorak and Zakita. "You are both old enough now to play a role in the governing of the city. Sargon will rule in Akkad one day, after Eskkar and I are gone, and he will need your help, even as you will need his. The ties between brothers and sister are strong, and you must lean on each other's strength. Remember that, when others try to step between you, or attempt to manipulate you to their own ends."

"When I was a boy growing up in the Alur Meriki," Eskkar said, "every man and woman knew the most important loyalty was to their family. The family first, then kin, then clan. Sometimes the family needs more than we want to give. Sometimes the way will be hard, but honor demands much from each of us. In the north, Sargon risked his life many times to safeguard his wife, Tashanella, and his friends and companions. Then he risked it again by riding to Elam to help protect his mother and father, and his sister and brother. Honor, family honor, should always be your guide in the days and years ahead."

Eskkar let his gaze rest for a moment on each person at the table. They were, after all, the only people that he truly loved.

"Now I think it is time to enjoy not only our food," Eskkar said, "but the company each of us gives to the others. May all of you live long lives and achieve great tasks, and keep our family's honor high."

"Yes, now we can eat," Trella said. She summoned the servants, waiting nearby. Soon food covered the table, and the meal began.

"Father, what news comes from Elam?" Tashanella, her hand still resting on Sargon's arm, asked the question. She knew a messenger had arrived at the Compound just before the repast began.

"Ah, we have just learned that the Elamites have a new ruler," Eskkar said. "It seems that King Shirudukh was betrayed and murdered in his own palace by General Jedidia, who then seized the throne. Before that, he also managed to slay Lord Modran. With so many deaths in their leaders' ranks, there will likely be revolts in many of their cities, and long years of fighting amongst themselves. Trella believes the Elamite Empire may not even survive. Meanwhile, your mother and I are working on a suitable gift for the new ruler, one that we think will keep Elam occupied for the future."

"Yes, we are nearly ready to send a very special message to General Jedidia," Trella said, "but one that I think the new king will not be happy to receive."

The talk turned to lighter subjects, as everyone relaxed and enjoyed the first family reunion since the war began.

"Father, I'm curious about one thing," Sargon said. "Who was the man who first brought the warning of the coming war with Elam? Shouldn't he receive some praise as well?"

Eskkar drummed his fingers on the table, then glanced at Trella. "The stranger who came in the night . . . Trella and I have sworn never to divulge his name, unless some new danger threatens our family in the future. Perhaps someday we will reveal his name. But for now, that must be one mystery that remains unsolved."

"Yes, that is for the best," Trella agreed. "But we will repay him for his warning. If he still lives, I have an idea about how best to do that. I believe he will find it a most interesting and pleasant surprise."

Soon everyone was busy with their meal. Eskkar, however, left his food untouched for a few moments. His gaze rested first on Sargon, then Zakita, and Melkorak. His sons and daughter. The ones who would carry his blood down through the ages yet to come, the ones who would make certain his name would always be remembered.

Trella had spoken the truth. There would be many more challenges in the future. But for the first time, Eskkar knew that he would not need to face them by himself. His family and his loyal friends would shoulder much of the burden. Eskkar's remaining years would be devoted not to war, but to peace. It was past time, he decided, to study the stars and learn what he could from the wise men, as the old shepherd had advised Eskkar many years before.

He remembered Trella's words, whispered in his ear long ago, when she had challenged him to become someone greater than himself. From that day, he had worked hard to build the city that she wanted, and now others, his heirs, would someday turn that into a mighty empire. For the first time since that first day, Eskkar felt worthy of the extraordinary woman who sat at his side.

"Is something wrong with the food, Husband?"

"No, Wife." He smiled, then clasped her hand in both of his and held it tight. "Everything is as it should be."

42

The Elamite Palace at Sushan . . .

J ust awakened from a deep sleep, King Jedidia stepped onto his palace balcony. One look, and his teeth clenched in a seething rage. Oblivious to the cold night breeze on his naked body, Jedidia watched the harbor of Sushan burn.

Tall pillars of flame along the water's edge lit the night, and sent long red shimmers reflecting off the black water. Even from a quarter mile away, Jedidia heard the crackle of the fires above the shouts of the frantic boatmen struggling to save their vessels.

Not that the harbor itself was actually burning. But twenty or thirty of Sushan's boats, crowded together along the docks and shoreline, blazed furiously. Several nearby storage depots were also in flames, fed by the cargoes stored under their awnings and covered porticos.

Along the length of the docks, plumes of gray smoke rushed upward, one streamer twisting across the face of the full moon. That glance told him midnight had long passed, and that dawn approached.

Fully awake now, Jedidia counted seven Akkadian ships responsible for the ongoing destruction. They glided at will through the black water, oars flashing in the firelight. Every deck appeared crowded with archers launching apparently endless flights of fire arrows at any target they could find.

New blazes sprang up wherever an oil-soaked shaft struck home in the dry hulls of Sushan's ships. A few of Jedidia's soldiers shot back, but the unorganized response of Sushan's hastily turned out guard had no effect on the attacking vessels.

Brave men attempting to douse the flames died, too, as other shafts sought out anyone who dared approach the conflagrations.

They died in vain, Jedidia knew. By now, nothing could quench these fires. Months of hot weather had dried everything above the water line into tinder.

The leader of King Jedidia's personal guard, standing discreetly behind his sovereign, broke the silence. "My Lord, they slipped ashore and killed the guards at the watch station. Others landed by the docks, and used torches to set fire to the storage places and supply depots."

King Jedidia ignored the commander who, only moments ago, had awakened him from his comfortable bed with the grim news of the surprise raid. Of course the cursed Akkadians had killed the no doubt sleeping guards stationed at the mouth of the harbor, supposedly to prevent such an attack. If any of them remained alive in the morning, he would have their heads chopped off.

As he stared, Jedidia saw the ships maneuvering away from the shore, heading out into the river for their return voyage south. The raid had ended. By noon the Akkadian dogs who had recently harried Elam's supply route to the west during the war would have traveled the thirty-plus miles back to the mouth of the Karum River and disappeared into the Great Sea. They would have accomplished their mission unscathed, while leaving behind only devastation and destruction.

What ships the Akkadians had failed to sink or capture during the Sumer campaign now lay burning in Sushan's harbor.

The flames continued to roar as the last Akkadian vessel vanished into the darkness. Except for a few boats fortunate enough to be plying their trade up river, the remains of Sushan's merchant fleet would soon settle onto the harbor bottom.

As a result, the city would endure shortages of food and supplies for months, perhaps years. For the second time in as many months, Akkadians had struck a heavy and personal blow to Jedidia's authority, and as before, he could do nothing about it.

He turned away from the balcony. The unhappy commander and three of Jedidia's personal guards faced him, their faces pale as they awaited his instructions.

"Find out the extent of the damage," Jedidia ordered. "Talk to the trading masters, and bring them to the Palace at midmorning." The commander stood there, obviously expecting more instructions. But aside from mouthing empty threats or curses at the Akkadians, Jedidia had nothing else to say. "Get out. All of you."

He returned his gaze toward the water. The wind shifted, and within moments he inhaled the stench of burning wood and cordage. Another discomfort Jedidia would have to endure, courtesy of the thrice-damned King of Akkad.

Only thirty-six days ago, as soon as he slew Lord Modran, Jedidia had returned to Sushan in haste. He brought with him five thousand mounted fighters, the only effective fighting force within hundreds of miles. Riding all day and long into the night, Jedidia outran any news of his presence as well as his setback in the Jkarian Pass, and Modran's defeat and death.

With a handful of soldiers, Jedidia used his rank to gain entry to the city's main gate, and hold it open until the rest of his horsemen arrived. Once inside the serene city of Sushan, he took every advantage of his numbers.

Catching King Shirudukh and his soldiers by surprise, Jedidia's soldiers stormed the Palace, overwhelmed the King's personal guard of two hundred Immortals, and slaughtered all of them.

Captured alive, Shirudukh did not survive his men for long. After denouncing Shirudukh as a traitor and the one responsible for the defeat of Elam's armies, Jedidia ordered every member of his family and inner circle put to death. Jedidia had then shoved his sword into the King's belly, and stood over him, watching with satisfaction as Shirudukh slowly and painfully bled to death.

The rest of King Shirudukh's Immortals, eight hundred men, had camped outside Sushan, about a mile from the city. By the time they learned what had happened, the former King's head decorated a pike just outside the Palace's gate.

The only remaining Immortals within three hundred miles were stationed in Elam's capital city of Anshan. Shirudukh, with his armies marching into the Land Between the Rivers, had worried more about Anshan's security than any threat to himself at Sushan.

Jedidia sent word to the commander of the Immortals outside Sushan's gates, informing him of the destruction of Modran's Immortals in the Dellen Pass, and warning the commander that Jedidia's forces were ready to destroy them as well. The Immortals were ordered to swear oaths of fealty to Jedidia at once. Cut off from the city and with no hope of reinforcements, the commander prostrated himself and accepted Jedidia as the new King of Elam.

In a single day of bloodshed and torture, Jedidia had seized control of Sushan and its remaining soldiers. The new King of Elam, at least in name, now faced a new challenge – keeping his empire together.

In a fashion, Jedidia owed his newly-acquired crown to Eskkar. If the barbarian hadn't defeated Lord Modran in the Dellen Pass, Jedidia would not be King of the Elamite Empire.

But tonight the crafty Akkadian fighting ships had slipped unnoticed into Elam's waters and attacked Sushan itself, reminding his subjects that the war had not yet ended. They were wrong, of course. The war was in truth over. Jedidia had no intention of wasting more men or gold on a futile pursuit of a western empire. He would need every soldier and every gold coin just to maintain control of what remained of the Elamite Kingdom.

That challenge had occupied Jedidia's every moment since he placed the crown on his head. Soon enough, subjugated cities throughout the realm would be tempted to seize the opportunity caused by the destruction of much of the Elamite army. They would look for any excuse to revolt against his newly assumed authority. The ships burning in Sushan's harbor would add fuel to the fires of rebellion.

"Master, you must be cold." The slave girl who had shared his bed during the night slipped a soft blanket over his shoulders, holding it there until he reached up and clasped the covering.

"Come inside, My Lord. It will be dawn soon, and you should dress."

A few moments passed before the girl's words penetrated Jedidia's rage. For the first time, he noticed the chill in the air that his anger had kept at bay. With a deep breath, Jedidia turned away from the fiery spectacle and stepped back into his bed chamber.

Two scented oil lamps now burned, and he smiled at the naked girl standing before him. A former plaything of Shirudukh, she had worked very hard to satisfy Jedidia's every desire for the last few nights.

"Thank you." He reached out, took her by the arms, and let the blanket slip from his shoulders to the floor. Leaning forward, he kissed the warm lips, as he let his hands caress the soft throat. With a murmur of anticipation, she pressed her body against his.

Jedidia inhaled the jasmine scent of the girl's perfume, then slowly he tightened his grip, giving her a hint of what was to come. Her eyes went wide, but before she could protest, he snapped her neck with a savage twist.

For a moment he stared into her eyes, filled with more surprise than pain. He flung the dying body to the rush-covered floor. The slave was only the first to feel his rage. The lax harbor guards, the sentries along the river sleeping at their posts, anyone who had failed in their duty would soon join her.

Too many people had seen him humiliated by these Akkadians. He would not have this latest story whispered throughout the palace. His new subjects would soon learn the penalty for failure.

"Guards! Clean up this mess."

King Jedidia's midmorning meeting with the city's foremost merchants, traders, and boat owners began with a grim omen. As those summoned entered the Palace from the courtyard, they filed past a pile of seven bloody heads stacked just outside the entrance. These had formerly belonged to those commanders who had failed in their duties last night. Another twenty or so soldiers who fled their posts had already met their deaths in the marketplace.

The severed heads sent a somber and subtle warning to those attending the morning meeting – do not be too critical of the King.

Jedidia stood in front of his throne, arms crossed over his chest, and his fighting sword belted around his waist. Six guards lined the walls, three on either side, and their hard eyes promised a quick response to anyone who aroused the wrath of the King this day.

Off to one side, the four remaining members of former King Shirudukh's council of advisors also waited. They, too, had been summoned to the Palace, and now they huddled shoulder to shoulder at a narrow table along the Council Room's wall, facing the King.

The advisors had originally numbered six, but a few days after taking power, Jedidia had sentenced two of them to death by torture for their insults to him in the past. Then he confiscated all their goods, using their wealth to reward his favorite commanders and most loyal soldiers. Now the surviving advisors dared not raise their eyes to their new Lord.

Filling the space directly in front of King Jedidia stood eleven subdued merchants and wealthy traders, those who had suffered the

most serious losses from last night's raid. Despite their
apprehension, their voices soon rose in bitter protests, as they listed
their damages – fourteen river boats sunk or destroyed, including six
of the larger, sea-going vessels.

Only three of those had actually sunk. The rest had burned to the
water line, and would never set sail again. The Akkadian pirates had
also put to the torch nine barges and a handful of smaller craft. One
of the larger transports might possibly be saved.

Several of the grieving ship owners dared to raise their voices.
They demanded gold to pay for their losses, and protection from
future raids, as if Jedidia could, at a moment's notice, conjure up
fighting vessels and crews to equal those of the Akkadians. He let
the complaints go on for a time, until he could stand their jabbering
no longer.

"Silence! There will be no compensation! In war, men die, and
ships and cargoes are lost. Blame the dog Shirudukh, who led the
Empire into this war, then failed to win it. Deal with it as best you
can."

Jedidia did promise that more soldiers would guard the docks day
and night, as if that futile gesture meant anything. With nothing left
worth burning in Sushan, the Akkadians wouldn't be back for
months, if they bothered to return at all. By now the enemy boats
had resumed their patrols at the mouth of the river, the entrance to
the Great Sea. Their presence on that station had already prevented
any ships from entering Sushan's harbor from the southern waters
for almost thirty days, and ensured that none would be arriving in the
foreseeable future.

For a city that depended greatly on trade and supplies from the
Great Sea, that lack of commerce would cause suffering and
shortages for as long as the enemy ships remained off the mouth of
the river. Each day brought bitter complaints from the buyers and
sellers in the marketplace. A new word had sprung up to describe the
fleet of Akkadian ships menacing the city – blockade.

When the merchants' complaints silenced, Jedidia ordered all of
them out, leaving only the four men who had previously advised
King Shirudukh. By Jedidia's command, they now performed the
same service to their new ruler. Whether they could come up with
something useful remained to be seen. The advisors had said nothing
while the boat owners vented their frustration, though they, too, as

men of wealth, had suffered grievous losses from the Akkadian attack.

But before the doors to Jedidia's Council Room could close behind the last departing trader, another commander entered. The man halted ten paces from Jedidia, bowed low, and waited to be recognized.

"Yes, what is it now?" Jedidia couldn't keep the anger from his voice.

"My Lord, a man came to the Palace gates not long ago. He requested an immediate audience, and claimed he speaks for the Akkadians."

King Jedidia glanced at his advisors, but they appeared just as surprised. He wondered what fool would dare to enter his presence after last night's raid. "Bring the man in."

The commander left the chamber for a few moments. He returned half-dragging a prisoner by the shoulder. The man's hands were bound before him, and a large bruise discolored his left cheek. His once white tunic, covered with dirt and grass stains, attested to his rough treatment.

The oldest of the advisors, a wealthy merchant named Shesh-kala, chuckled at the sight, and Jedidia saw smiles on the faces of the other three. Obviously they recognized the captive.

"Who are you?" Jedidia's voice cut through the chamber, and his angry visage ended the grins.

"One of your most loyal subjects, My Lord." The man bowed. "My name is Kedor of Sushan. I'm a trader. I've lived here for almost forty years, when I'm not aboard my boat."

"You claim to speak for the Akkadian scum who burned our ships?"

"No, My King." Kedor bowed again. "Your soldiers, in their haste, misunderstood my words. I told them I bore a message from the King of Akkad, to be given only to King Jedidia of Sushan and ruler of the Elamite Empire."

Jedidia glanced toward his advisors, but no one met his eyes. The prisoner . . . Kedor? . . . waited patiently.

"How did you come by this message from the Akkadians?"

"My King, I was taken prisoner by the Akkadians at the beginning of the war, at the supply cove, just south of Sumer. The enemy swept down on the beach, killed everyone, and captured all the boats and supplies."

Jedidia had heard all about that surprise attack, and how the cunning Akkadians had emerged undetected from the impassable foothills to fall upon the landing site. After that, the destruction of Grand Commander Chaiyanar and his invading army had inevitably followed. At least the Sumerians had rid Jedidia of one problem – Chaiyanar's death solidified Jedidia's grip on the Elamite kingship. "And yet you survived?"

"Yes, My Lord. I'd taken refuge underneath some sacks of cargo on my boat. By the time I was discovered, the killing had stopped, and the bulk of the Akkadian horsemen had moved on, to attack our soldiers besieging Sumer. The Akkadians left a few hundred men to sail the boats. Their leader, a man named Daro, is one of King Eskkar's senior commanders. He took charge of the vessels, and has been using them to capture and sink our ships ever since. Daro is the man who led the raid last night that burned our ships. He set me ashore, just before his ships departed, to deliver the message."

"And why are you so favored by our enemies?" Jedidia's snarling words would have intimidated anyone. "Perhaps I should have your tongue removed for daring to speak for them."

Kedor ignored the threat. "After the Akkadians discovered I owned several boats, Daro held me aboard his ship for ransom. When word arrived of Eskkar's victories over our forces at Sumer and the Dellen Pass, Commander Daro also received new orders. He decided instead to use me to carry the message from King Eskkar to My Lord."

"Of course you decided to cooperate with the pirates?"

"My Lord, when you're surrounded by dead bodies, and a grinning soldier puts a knife to your throat, you do what you're told." Kedor shook his head. "Besides, I had nothing of value to tell them. Their plans had been made months before. They knew about the landing cove, they knew there would be boats there, and they intended to capture those boats, and use them to cut the supply line from Sumer. Everything proved easier than they expected, and Commander Daro soon expanded his raids all the way to Sushan's coast. They sank, by my count, at least thirteen boats, and captured another nine. With all their cargoes. They put every boat captain and seaman to death."

Jedidia knew all about that, too. The loss of those experienced sailors and their knowledge of the Great Sea was devastating. With effective training, soldiers could be quickly replaced, but it took years for a man to learn a sailor's skills. Even if Jedidia ordered the immediate construction of new ships, he would have no crews to sail them.

"My Lord, is there any reason to keep my hands tied?" Kedor raised his bound hands. "I am loyal to my King."

"I'll decide that," Jedidia said. "What is the message?"

Dropping his hands in resignation, Kedor glanced at the advisors.

Jedidia understood the look, but decided to ignore it. Whatever the message, the advisors would learn of it sooner or later. "Get on with it."

Kedor took a breath, straightened up, and paused for a moment to clear his thoughts. Then he began his recitation.

"Greetings from Eskkar of Akkad, and greetings from all the cities of the Land Between the Rivers, to King Jedidia of Susa and Elam. It was unfortunate that you were prevented from passing through the Jkarian Pass, and that I did not get a chance to face you in battle. However, my son, Sargon of Akkad, did oppose you outside the Dellen Pass. You were wise to avoid battle with him and the horsemen of the steppes, as they would have surely slain you and all your men."

Jedidia ground his teeth at the boastful lie. He had outnumbered the barbarians almost five to one, and without doubt could have destroyed them. But even then the prize of Elam's kingship beckoned, and he had no intention of wasting more than half his valuable soldiers killing ignorant barbarians.

Kedor saw the look on the King's face, hesitated, and then continued his delivery.

"I, Eskkar of Akkad, intended to come to Elam and kill the dog Shirudukh and his minion Modran by my own hand. But since you, Great King Jedidia, have saved me the journey, for which I give thanks, I offer to you this one, and only one, chance to end the war between Elam and the Land Between the Rivers."

This time Kedor paused to take a full breath.

"The cities of Akkad, Isin, Sumer, Uruk, and Lagash were put to much trouble and expense by the dog Shirudukh. That expense must be repaid. The sum of twenty thousand gold coins, each coin the equal to one of Akkad's own gold coins, or the equivalent in gold or silver ingots, is to be paid within twenty days. My ships that attacked your harbor will return on that date to collect payment.

"If payment is not received at that time, I, Eskkar of Akkad, will lead the soldiers of the Land Between the Rivers into the lands of Elam. I, Eskkar of Akkad, will unleash the warriors of the steppes on your northern territories. I, Eskkar of Akkad, will have my ships burn your harbors and sink your ships. I, Eskkar of Akkad, will destroy every city that resists me, yet I will spare and reward every city that joins with me to hunt down King Jedidia of Elam. My soldiers in their just anger will not stop until the head of King Jedidia rests at my feet. This I, Eskkar of Akkad, swear to you and all the gods, and most especially to the wise Goddess Ishtar and the great God Marduk, who will always defend and protect the Land Between the Rivers. I, Eskkar of Akkad, also declare that if any soldiers from the land of Elam ever dare to set foot on our lands again, I will bring war and destruction upon you, until all your cities are destroyed. There is no more to be said."

Silence filled the Council Room. None of the advisors dared to meet the King's eyes. After a moment, Kedor spoke again, this time in his normal voice.

"My Lord, I was given a gold coin by Commander Daro, as a sample of what was required. However, one of your guards took it from me. You may want to get it back. Daro also insisted I was to be returned with the ransom, alive and unharmed. If I am not, the amount of gold demanded is to be increased by an additional one thousand coins. If you accept the terms, a signal fire is to burn all through the night tomorrow, at the mouth of the Karum River."

Kedor paused, as if unsure whether he should speak again. "My Lord, I was also told to inform you that this message would be delivered to the other cities of Elam, so that all would know the devastation that awaits them should they ever wage war again on the Land Between the Rivers."

"Get out." Jedidia found his left hand had tightened on the hilt of his sword. He wanted nothing more than to hack Kedor's body to pieces. "Get him out of here."

The wide-eyed commander hustled Kedor from the chamber. The heavy door swung closed with a thud, leaving Jedidia and his six guards alone with the four members of his Council of Advisors.

Jedidia faced them. "Well, you heard Eskkar's demands. What do you suggest?"

No one spoke. He saw the trembling of their hands, and not one of them met his gaze.

"Fools, all of you! Do you think I will let that ignorant barbarian and his slut of a wife tell me what to do? Let them demand payment from my empire?"

Jedidia flung his words, along with a mouthful of spittle, at his council. He took two strides to stand in front of the most cunning of them, and the least trustworthy. "You, Aram-Kitchu, what do you say? Were you not once one of those filthy Sumerians?"

Aram-Kitchu bowed so low that his black beard touched the table.

"My King, I don't know what to say. I was born in Sumeria, it's true, but that land was conquered by the Akkadians, and I bear only hatred toward them. I've lived in Sushan for almost twenty years, and my loyalties are only to you, My King, and to Elam."

Again Aram-Kitchu bowed his head, as if to reinforce his loyalty. "As to the barbarian Eskkar, I can only say what I've heard, what everyone has heard who has dealings with Akkad. That King Eskkar is a man of his word. That he has never broken a promise or a trust, even to the lowest of his soldiers or the least of his people."

With a snarl of rage, Jedidia jerked his sword from its scabbard, and pressed the point against Aram-Kitchu's stomach. "You dare to threaten me with Eskkar's name? You are the one whose spies failed to warn us of the secret alliances between Isin and Sumer and Akkad. Your spies again failed to warn me about the Jkarian Pass, or that Eskkar would fight at the Dellen Pass. You are a traitor to Elam. I should put you to the torture before I add your head to the pile outside."

Aram-Kitchu stared at the sword, but shook his head. "My life is yours to take, my King. But not once did my spies fail to bring good information. Even so, King Shirudukh relied on many sources besides myself. Nor did he heed my warnings about Akkad. I advised him several times that the Akkadians were not to be taken lightly."

Jedidia hesitated. This Sumerian traitor had spoken the truth about that. The fool Shirudukh had laughed at the Akkadians, as if the mere sound of his name would frighten them into surrendering. Nevertheless, Jedidia still wanted to drive the sword into Aram-

Kitchu's belly, if only to hear the man's screams as Jedidia twisted the blade into his guts.

"Then what do you suggest that I do, Aram-Kitchu?' He pushed the blade harder against the man's tunic, and a spot of red appeared beneath the blade's tip.

Aram-Kitchu raised his eyes for the first time, and met Jedidia's gaze. "My King, I cannot help you if I am dead. But you must decide how to deal with the Akkadians. If you want to face the Akkadians in battle, I'm sure you can destroy any army they send against us. Your soldiers still out number them many times over."

With a horrifying scream, Jedidia raised his sword up and swung it down with all his might. But the blade smashed into the table, not Aram-Kitchu's head, and clove right through the finely carved surface in a burst of splinters. The other advisors recoiled at the blow, raising their hands in fear and shrinking away from the King's wrath.

The commander of Jedidia's guards outside the chamber heard the commotion and pushed open the door. He took a brief look, to assure himself that the King remained safe, and ducked back outside.

"Damn you, Esskar of Akkad! Damn . . ." Jedidia choked on the words, his tongue unable to match his fury. The big vein in his forehead bulged and throbbed as if it would burst.

Of course he dared not raise another army to fight the Akkadians. The soldiers who managed to survive the invasion had limped home beaten men. That attitude had already spread throughout the Empire and the rest of Elam's soldiers.

By now even the lowliest and most distant of his soldiers had heard about the unstoppable Esskar of Akkad – the cunning King who had never lost a battle, the King who cannot be beaten no matter how greatly outnumbered, the King who slaughters his enemies by the thousands, and, most of all, the King who had never failed to make good on his word.

The first time an Akkadian soldier set foot on Elam's soil, the Empire would erupt in revolt. Jedidia would be lucky if a handful of cities remained loyal. He'd never sleep again, without wondering if he would wake up with his head still on his shoulders. Any one of his men would gladly carry such a trophy to Esskar for the inevitably large reward that would be offered.

Jedidia felt wetness on his chin, and wiped it hard with the back of his left hand. A smear of red marked his fingers. The taste of blood confirmed that he'd bitten his tongue.

If he couldn't fight, what were his options? Jedidia felt a sinking feeling in his chest, the same one that had washed over him in the Jkarian Pass.

He glared at the four men cringing before him. "Well, what do you suggest, damn you? You are supposed to be my wise and exalted advisors. Give me your advice."

No one answered. "What would you do, Aram-Kitchu?"

The wealthy merchant kept his head low. "My King, since I lack your courage, I would pay the sum demanded. Eskkar is probably not eager to go to war, but he needs an excuse to refrain. If he receives the gold, the barbarian will no doubt keep most of it for himself, but he will use the rest to assuage his allies and soldiers, and satisfy their desires for conquest. With so much wealth in his hand, he will not bother to invade. He would already have more gold than he could get in any invasion, and without the cost in men and supplies. In a few years, five at most, you can recover most of the gold from your own people."

Jedidia knew that last statement was another lie. It would take at least eight or more years to recover such a huge sum. He would have to squeeze every coin out of every man in the Empire. Still Aram-Kitchu spoke the truth about one thing – in time the gold would be recovered. Life would be difficult, but at least Jedidia would keep his throne.

With an oath, he again swung his sword at what remained of the table, making the advisors shrink back in fright a second time. The smell of urine wafted in the air. At least one of the advisors had pissed himself.

"Raise the gold! I don't care what you do or how you do it, but raise the twenty thousand coins. Squeeze it out of every city, every village, every farmer, shopkeeper, merchant, priest, temple, every whore and beggar in the Empire. Sell anyone who can't pay into slavery, and put those who refuse to pay to the sword. My soldiers will give you whatever help you need. If you can't raise the amount needed, I'll confiscate everything of value you own, before I hang each one of you and every member of your family upside down in the marketplace."

No one uttered a word. Death might be the punishment for the slightest objection.

Jedidia glanced at one of his guards. "Send the traitor Kedor back to his new friends, and tell him that Elam will pay the gold." Sword still clutched in hand, Jedidia strode out of the room, followed by his guards, and leaving behind the stunned and shaken advisors.

The four men glanced around the empty chamber, as if to reassure themselves that they were alone and still alive. "By the gods, this will beggar all of us." The words came in a whisper from Sheshkala, who tugged at his white beard with a hand that still trembled.

"Yes, it will," Aram-Kitchu agreed. He glanced down at his tunic.

A small circle of blood had seeped through the garment, where the King's blade had pierced the skin. Aram-Kitchu had come that close to dying. Now for the privilege of staying alive, he'd have to give up most of his fortune, and spend the next few years groveling on his knees and working himself back into the new King's favor. Even so, Aram-Kitchu would dread the King's every summons, wondering when Jedidia would finally choose to put him to the torture before taking his head.

The King of Akkad's message had been cunning indeed. The sum demanded was just enough to bring the Empire, already facing disaster from the enormous cost of the war, to the brink of ruin, but not so large as to be impossible. Yes, Aram-Kitchu detected the shrewdness of Lady Trella's presence in the message. Eskkar could never have calculated the precise sum needed to beggar the Kingdom of Elam, or composed such a bold demand.

And then another idea took root deep in Aram-Kitchu's thoughts. Perhaps Lady Trella had presented him with the opportunity to get rid of King Jedidia, and take the kingship for himself. With enough gold to buy men and influence, such boldness might succeed in the troubling times soon to come.

But gold, of course, would soon be in short supply, as every trader, merchant, and even the lowest farmer hastened to bury his valuables beneath the dirt of his fields.

Then suddenly Aram-Kitchu, once known as Bracca the Sumerian thief, knew exactly where he could obtain such a large sum of gold, probably as much as he needed. It shouldn't be too difficult for Lady Trella to funnel some of Jedidia's gold back into Bracca's hands.

She and Eskkar would understand the advantages of having
Bracca rule the Elamite Empire. With enough wealth, Bracca could
buy the soldiers, mercenaries, and supporters needed to put himself
on the throne. Jedidia was, after all, a common fighting man, with no
friends or family to sustain him. Soon his unpopular policies would
bring hatred down on his name.

Once again, Bracca felt glad he had warned his old traveling
companion, Eskkar, about the coming invasion. Though Bracca had
done so because of their strong bond of friendship, that good deed
might now save his own life.

Bracca rose, and one by one, the others stood and headed for the
door. As the youngest, Bracca trailed the others out of the chamber,
but his thoughts remained elsewhere. He decided that with a
plentiful supply of gold, some help from his new friends in Akkad,
and a little luck, he, Bracca, would be the next king of Elam.

It would require time, perhaps half a year, but it could be done. He
might even take back his true name once again. King Bracca of Elam
and the Indus sounded much more imposing than King Aram-Kitchu,
and much more impressive than King Eskkar of Akkad.

(Readers: if you have not yet read *Battle for Empire,* the fifth novel in the Eskkar Saga, you may want to visit my website, www.sambarone.com and click on the Battle for Empire tab, to read the prologue)

Epilogue

The Palace at Akkad, 3109 BC (26 years after the war with Elam) . . .

Trella studied her grandson, Escander, reclining on the couch near the window. Outside, the birds had settled into the trees and started their twilight songs to welcome the end of another pleasant day. Dusk settled over the Palace grounds, and those who dwelt within its walls waited for the servant's call that would announce the evening's meal.

Tonight, however, Queen Mother Trella and Escander would again dine in her private quarters. In fact, Trella and her grandson had taken all their meals in her chambers for the last three days. The matters they discussed were far too important to risk anyone overhearing, and neither wanted to waste even a moment when so much of importance remained unsaid.

But at last the long story that had taken Trella deep into the past had ended.

To anyone watching, Escander appeared to have fallen asleep. Yet Trella knew her grandson had heard every word, memorized every important name, and grasped the sometimes difficult concepts that she'd related. He was the one person in the Palace that she could engage as an equal. But like every excellent teacher, Trella always knew when to let her pupil gather his thoughts and reflect upon what he'd learned.

"Tell my son everything," King Sargon had ordered. And so for three days, Trella and Escander started with their morning meal at her table, and continued on until dusk. Now, at the end of the third day, Trella had revealed the last of the secrets, some from as far back as thirty years.

Of those still alive, only a few recalled those days. Nevertheless, Trella had done much more than simply tell her grandson what had occurred long ago. Trella had explained the steps that led to every major decision, and showed how a ruler must think and consider, how to weigh the consequences of each choice, and evaluate every possibility.

A daunting task, but Escander had received much training as he grew to manhood, as had many of his brothers. Trella had insisted that the boy learn to memorize long passages, as well as dates and numbers. By the time Escander reached his twelfth season, he could count as well as any clerk. He had also impressed both his teachers and his grandmother with his nearly perfect memory.

Nevertheless, until now, neither King Sargon nor Trella had revealed to Escander, or to any of his siblings, the most important secret of all – the way of a ruler.

Even after all these years, Trella's memory for dates, names, and places remained as sharp as in her youth. She had filled each part of the long story with so much detail that the history of Escander's father and grandfather came alive, almost as real as if Escander had played a part in the doing and the saying.

"You must tell me everything, all your thoughts, all your plans, everything, Eskkar." Almost forty-five years ago, Trella had pleaded with her new master for the information she needed to help him. Not just the important facts, but all his feelings, emotions, worries, even fears. In time, her husband had learned to trust her instincts, and so he divulged to her every detail and thought he could remember, no matter how small or seemingly inconsequential.

"How else can I help you, Master, if you leave out all the little details?"

And now, Escander, the grandson Eskkar had never seen, benefitted from his grandfather's wisdom and knowledge. Trella's precise memory and keen mind served her well once more. All the thoughts and emotions of her husband Eskkar and their firstborn son Sargon now lay revealed to the next ruler of Akkad.

The story had ended, but Escander remained deep in thought. Finally he sat up and broke the silence. "I understand now why my father couldn't tell me these things. To admit such thoughts would have been too painful for him."

"Sargon has endured more than his share of suffering in his life," Trella said. "But he has overcome his hardships and done much good for the Kingdom."

"You think he means that I will rule after him?"

"Oh, yes. For more than a year, we've both known that you were the best choice, even more so than your older brother. In a way, his death in the north made certain that Akkad is ruled by the true heir of Eskkar. But we dared not tell anyone, either by words or deeds, of that decision. Otherwise you would have been an even greater target from your more ambitious and ruthless brothers. And sisters."

"They will still seek to get me out of the way."

Trella smiled. "Perhaps. But the difficulties that attend such plots are too numerous to count, and while there have been many conspiracies in Akkad's history, none of them have succeeded. Also there is much that I can do, your father can do, to prevent any new ones from flourishing. Nevertheless, in time, you must also be firm in dealing with plots and intrigues."

"When that day comes, I will do what is needed."

The smile left her face at the quick response. "You will have to be ruthless and efficient. The power and strength of Akkad depends on having a strong and wise ruler. The people gave Eskkar the authority to rule over them, and they passed that onto Sargon. If one day some ambitious fool, hungry for power and gold, takes the throne, the Empire of Akkad will weaken and fail. Eskkar understood that power was merely a tool for securing the safety and stability of our city. Only when our people were safe could they be truly happy, and truly productive. And accept our rule over their lives."

"I thought that commanding the soldiers would be the most difficult part of being a ruler."

"No, Escander, it is far harder to lead a kingdom than an army. In that, I was able to help my husband, who also had to master that lesson. But leading soldiers is important, too. Always remember how Eskkar controlled his troops. He divided the power among his commanders, he moved leaders from one position to another, and he kept them loyal by rewarding and honoring them. He counted every member of the Hawk Clan as his brother, and even today, the Hawk Clan guards his family and his memory. Above all, Eskkar cared for the lives of his fighters, and avoided those leaders who sought glory and wealth at the expense of their men. Most of all, he promoted only those best qualified to lead, regardless of their wealth or station."

"It seems there is much more for me to learn."

"Escander, in the time that I have left, I can offer you no better gift than this – a chance to master all that I have learned over the course of many years. One of the first and most important lesson for you to grasp is the use of terror. As a kingdom and a city, we are generous and loyal to our friends. But anyone who seeks to disrupt our ways or attack our people must learn the penalty for such activities. Remember what your grandfather did to the city of Larsa. The destruction of that city and the scattering of its people helped keep the peace in the Land Between the Rivers for the next twenty years. Even today, that message is still understood – those who go to war against Akkad will pay a heavy price. Your father also knows these things. Under King Sargon's rule, the Empire has grown in size, and yet each expansion has required even more effort to govern."

"Like what Father did to the Carchemishi," Escander said. "When I heard what he had done, it seemed overly harsh, even brutal."

"Yes, your father and I spent most of a day discussing that raid, and what Akkad's response would be. But after our soldiers ravaged their city, the Carchemishi changed their ways. Now all the peoples in those distant lands understand the simple lesson we intended. If they do not bother us, we will not bother them. The careful use of terror may save many thousands of lives and prevent costly wars. Induce sufficient fear in your enemies, and you may not have to fight them in battle. But do not avoid war when it is necessary. The longer it is postponed, the greater advantage it will be to the other side.

Remember, too, the application of military force, if sufficiently sudden and violent, often paralyzes political will."

"When the time comes, I hope you will help me as you do my father," Escander said. "You know so much about our people, and how to bend them to your will."

"If I am still here, I will offer you advice. But only if you ask," Trella said. "It is no shame to ask for help, but the sign of a wise ruler. However, always remember to guard yourself against flattery. Let everyone know that you take no offence in hearing the truth, no matter how unpleasant. Eventually you will come to trust your own instincts. Until then, listen to your Aunt Zakita and Uncle Melkorak. She has much wisdom, and he has mastered the art of planning and fighting."

Escander smiled. "I've heard all of Uncle Melkorak's sayings." Escander altered his voice to imitate his uncle's. "Never attack without concentrating your forces, conduct every pursuit with audacity and lethality, appreciate the importance of an ambush, always plan a strategic deception . . ."

"Stop!" Trella laughed at the imitation. "Melkorak is a great general, as well as a master trainer and teacher. You would do well to follow his advice." She changed her tone. "Don't forget to rely on En-hedu, who knows much but speaks little. She took Annok-sur's place after her death. En-hedu's spies and agents keep close watch on Akkad and the other cities, and it is through her and from them that we quickly learn what dangers and unrest are among our people. The knowledge she brings you of our friends and enemies is invaluable. In times of prolonged peace, the collection of intelligence about potential enemies is even more important.

Escander took his time considering Trella's words. "When I leave for the northern lands, there will likely be turmoil within the Palace. My half brothers and sisters will . . ."

"Be even more troublesome than usual," Trella agreed. "But Sargon and I have already spoken of what has to be done. I think I can promise that the most troublesome of your half-brothers will die in a training accident, and his mother from food poisoning. Others will be banished to distant parts of the Empire, where they will have no authority and little influence. Even so, they will be closely watched. If they appear too eager for power, they will be taken care of. Nonetheless, when your time comes, you must ensure that they submit to your authority or pay the price."

Trella observed Escander's grim look. "Does it trouble you to think of your brothers dying by your own hand? Then remember the lesson that Sargon failed to learn. Keep your sons and daughters close to you. No man, not even a king, needs more than two wives. If you want more women, do as I did for Eskkar. Bring in young, empty-headed girls to satisfy your needs. After a few months enjoyment, send them away or even better, marry them off to your soldiers. If they bear children, ignore them, and soon everyone else will do the same. Your father kept far too many of his women in the Palace, and now you have to live under that threat. Do not let your appetites bring the same fear to your own children."

"That is one lesson I will heed, I swear it."

"Good. And heed this lesson as well. Sometimes a son or a daughter can be more dangerous to your House than an enemy army. It may happen that in such a case, even banishment may not be enough. Remember, you must place the safety and security of your entire family and the people of your Empire over the love and affection you might have for one who is a potential threat. You must rear children that reflect your own values, if you want our line to endure. That is, after all, the test that Sargon nearly failed."

"I hope that the Alur Meriki can help me as much as the Ur Nammu helped my father. It seems he learned much more from them than he expected."

"Yes, Escander, that is true. He learned love and loyalty and wisdom without realizing it. No ruler is truly wise who cannot discern the faults of men, or the evil that may lurk behind a smiling face or flattering words. Your grandfather had that gift, though it is given to few men."

"What if I cannot master these lessons?"

"Oh, you can. Of that I am sure. You will make mistakes along the way, we all do. You will lose some friends, and gain new ones. Change is a part of life, one you must embrace. Rule your people honestly and firmly, so that no shift in good or evil fortune obliges you to change your ways. Because if adversity forces you to change, then you will find it is too late to resort to severity. Any leniency you may use will be wasted, for your people will see that you are forced to it, and will give you no thanks."

"So many decisions, so many things to consider. I'm not sure if I'm strong or wise enough to lead our people."

"Not today, Escander, not even tomorrow. Such understanding takes time. But when you return from the north, you will be ready. Your father and I will give you all the help and support we can in the beginning. But soon enough you will be able to stand on your own. I once asked Eskkar what he thought was the most important trait for a leader. He said that a leader, or any man for that matter, must be willing to fight for what he truly believes in, even if a hundred men tell him he is wrong."

"What of your own safety, Grandmother? When I leave for the north, you, too, will be in danger."

"There are always threats to our House, Escander. But I have survived more than one attempt on my life. En-hedu and the Hawk Clan are most efficient. Remember, your enemies are not the only ones who can use conspiracy as a tool. Do not disdain using it yourself because others frown upon it. Don't forget that murder can also be a tool, even if simple-minded people deplore it. Use all these as instruments. They are merely devices, however devious, means, however ruthless. A strong ruler must not hesitate to be deceitful if it is to his advantage. But always be fair in your dealings. Men are either to be kindly treated, or utterly crushed, since they can revenge minor injuries, but not graver ones."

"At least the army is loyal," Escander said. "Uncle Melkorak sees to that."

"You were always his favorite, though he, too, has had to hide his feelings. In him, you are fortunate. Melkorak is a good commander, but knows he would be a poor ruler. He always followed Eskkar's advice to spend time with the soldiers. Because when you visit with your soldiers and hear their concerns, you will detect problems in their beginnings, when there is still time to apply remedies. But if you take your leisure far from those who support your rule, problems will grow and fester, and you may wake one day and find that the disease is past any cure."

"It seems that ruling will be much harder than I expected, Grandmother."

"Oh, yes. You must not only consider your present difficulties, which are often easy to resolve. Learn to think years ahead, if you would be a wise ruler. That way you may escape one mischief without falling into another. As Yavtar used to say, when the sea is calm, think about storms."

"I remember the old farmer," Escander said, a wide smile on his face. "He took me fishing on the river."

"You were seven years old, Escander. I remember how happy you were that day."

"I didn't realize that Yavtar played such an important part in all the wars, or even that he spent most of his life on the river. He was a very kind and gentle man."

Trella smiled. "He advised your father to put to death the soldiers at Nuzi who revolted. He said that it was important to quell any such disorders by a few public examples. Yavtar told your father that ruthlessly killing a handful of rebellious soldiers would, in the long run, be far more merciful than being lenient, which often results only in more rapine and bloodshed."

Escander sighed. "So at times I must be ruthless, even when I might want to be merciful."

"Every challenge you will face will be different. Prudence often consists in knowing how to distinguish degrees of disadvantage, and sometimes in accepting a lesser evil as good. Keep your subjects united and loyal, Escander. That way you will be far more merciful than a ruler who, through too much mercy, allows disorders to arise and ends up with many people suffering and dying."

"Dealing with people, listening to their complaints, trying to convince them what is best, these are not affairs that I will be good at."

Trella laughed again. "Eskkar hated those things also. But he learned, in time, that politics is the art of the possible. He said it most closely resembled a long, dreary, military campaign that in the end, neither side wins completely."

Now it was Escander's turn to laugh. "I think that I am growing more and more like my grandfather. At least he was courageous and daring."

"He was, indeed. And it is better to be impetuous than cautious. In that, fortune will favor you. She esteems the young because they are bold and fierce. Eskkar always preferred a daring course that promised a quick end to a conflict. Because he was willing to take such chances, to risk his life for what he believed in, he saved many lives and achieved a great many victories."

"No man will ever achieve such triumphs again," Escander said. "King Eskkar will be remembered forever for what he accomplished."

"I think my husband would smile to hear such words. He knew great military deeds are soon forgotten, and already most people scarcely remember his name. When I am gone, his memory will fade away into the mist."

"Perhaps I can help keep his memory alive."

"Statues, battle memorials, and feast days?" Trella shook her head. "Eskkar would be embarrassed by such things. If you would give him honor and hold his memory, serve your people well."

Escander stood and stretched. "So, now it is time for me to go north. I will try to return as soon as I can."

"The Alur Meriki will know when you are ready to return. Den'rack is a wise leader, and Garal's grandson will see to your training. Meanwhile, in a few months I will spread the rumor that you are not doing well, and that you will need to stay in the north much longer. That way you can appear in Akkad without warning, and take up the mantle of heir."

"It may be many years before I come to rule."

Trella sighed, and shook her head. "No, I do not think so. Your father's bones already ache more than they should, and there are many days when pain sweeps over him. It is likely that you will be King sooner than you expect, so waste no time. Learn how to fight, and how to lead, and return as quickly as possible. You must prepare yourself to become a strong leader. Time drives all things before it, and may bring with it evil as well as good. The faster you return and help guide our people, the better for all of us."

"What should I do now?"

"Go to your father, and tell him you are ready to depart. You need say nothing more. He is a proud man, and for him, the less said of these things the better."

Escander rose and stepped around the table. He wrapped his arms around Trella's shoulders, and kissed her cheek. "I can never thank you enough, Grandmother."

"Oh, we'll see about that when you return, and after you become King of Akkad. Be warned, I may have a bride waiting for you."

He laughed. "Whoever you choose, I'm sure she will be both loyal and keen-witted. But if you haven't yet picked her out, try to find one who is beautiful as well."

"I will make no promises about that. A woman can have courage and honor as well as any man, and those traits are far more important than a pretty face or lush figure. Now go to your father."

Trella watched the door close behind him. "For you, Escander, the great adventure of life can now begin." She stared at the door for a long moment, then turned her chair so she could once again look out the window. The sun had set, and already darkness hid the hilltop where Eskkar's body rested.

She sighed, weary after the long days with Escander. At least she had finally fulfilled Eskkar's last and most important wish – that the line of Eskkar and Trella never end. Escander would be king one day, and he would father many children. Those yet unborn that will arise from his loins would ensure that Eskkar's line endured, that their blood would never vanish from the earth. Even Sargon's numerous offspring, soon to be banished to the ends of the Empire, would help continue their blood.

Her efforts had by now spanned more than forty-five years in Akkad's service. Now each additional day of life would be a gift from the gods. She would continue to help Escander, of course, but already Trella felt certain he would rule wisely on his own. The heritage of Eskkar would be reborn in his grandson, and would continue on, growing stronger and spreading wider with each passing generation.

Eskkar had finally conquered his last and greatest enemy – time. She rose and went to the window. Leaning against the sill, her eyes returned to the hilltop where Eskkar was buried, the gravesite now almost invisible in the darkness. "Master, soon I will rejoin you. Then we will be together once again, and never more will anyone or anything part us."

Almost she could hear him reply, as if he still held her in his strong arms, the way he had done that first night long ago. "And girl, who is the master, and who is the slave?"

Trella laughed at the vivid memory, and this time her voice was the sound of young girl once again. When her time came to depart, she would go willingly, for she knew that not even death or the power of the gods could keep them apart in The Land Beyond the Veil.

The End

Author's Note

Over the years, a few readers challenged my portrayal of Eskkar and his battle skills. They write that such acumen and knowledge of warfare could not have existed five thousand years ago, and that people in those times were less intelligent. My belief is just the opposite – IQ's were the same then as now, only people had more time to devote to a particular skill, whether sword-making, fighting, or commanding armies and winning battles.

Nevertheless Genghis Khan and his Mongol Hordes conquered half the known world with tactics and weapons little changed from those Eskkar employed – tough, well-trained, and expert archers mounted on strong horses, carrying swords and lances.

The Great Khan's greatest general, of course, was Subotai the Valiant. Before he died at the age of seventy-three, he'd conquered thirty-two nations and won sixty-five major battles. Subotai never suffered a major defeat. His tactics and strategic vision destroyed the Persian Empire, and the vaunted knights of Europe at the Battle of Sajo River, leaving the rest of Europe essentially helpless. Subotai's army had reached the outskirts of Vienna when news of the Great Khan's death arrived. Obeying the summons to return home, Subotai turned around his army and went back to Mongolia. It is quite possible that if the Khan had lived a few more years, Subotai would have reached England's shores.

All these Mongol victories were achieved with simple tactics –
ambush, night attacks, surprise assaults, concentration of forces,
appearing where least expected, maneuvering over long distances,
rapid marches, masterful logistics, and awarding commands based
on experience and skill, not birth or wealth.

The strategies employed by the Mongols and Subotai are still
studied today in the war colleges of many nations, including the
former Soviet Union, United Kingdom, and the United States.

For those interested in learning more about these tactics and the
men who employed them, I recommend the non-fiction story of
Genghis Khan's Greatest General – Subotai the Valiant by Richard
A. Gabriel.

Sam Barone
Prescott AZ

Acknowledgement

My thanks, as always, go to my wife, Linda, for all her help in the editing and proofing of this book. Her keen eye caught every mistake, and her determined quest for clarity ensured that the text is as readable as I could make it. Linda also worked with artist Trevor Smith – www.trevorsmithart.com – while he designed and polished the covers and maps. It is no exaggeration to say that this book would not have been possible without her help.

More thanks are due to Bill Morgan, my friend since the first grade. He gave the book its final read and spotted the lingering typos, and, as usual, under the rush of getting the book completed and ready for publication.

Of course, our two cats Minga and Norton helped out. Norton often climbed onto my lap, forcing a break in the writing process, but restoring a sense of calm to the author.

About The Author

Born and raised in Queens, New York, Sam Barone graduated from Manhattan College with a BS degree. After a hitch in the Marine Corps, he entered the world of technology.

In 1999, after thirty years developing software in management, Sam retired from Western Union International, as VP of International Systems. He moved to Arizona, to take up his second career as a writer.

Seven years later, the author's first Eskkar story, *Dawn of Empire*, was published in the USA and UK. It has since been released worldwide. *Clash of Empires* is the sixth book in the series.

History and reading have always been two of Sam's favorite interests. He considers himself more of a storyteller than a writer. "I write stories that I would enjoy reading, and it's a true blessing that others have found these tales interesting, informative, and entertaining."

Sam and his wife Linda, and their two cats (Minga and Norton) enjoy life in beautiful Prescott Arizona.

Sam's books have been published in nine languages and he has over 200,000 readers. He receives correspondence from all over the world. Sam enjoys hearing from his readers, and invites them to visit www.sambarone.com